OUR

BEAUTIFUL

MESS

BK CLARK

OUR BEAUTIFUL MESS

BRADFORD PRESS

Published by Bradford Press
Raleigh, NC

Edited by Elle Fort
Cover art and design by Rena Violet
Interior design by Jordon Greene
B. K. Clark author photograph by Bob Clark

Printed in the United States of America

FIRST EDITION

Hardcover ISBN 979-8-9895253-0-0
Paperback ISBN 979-8-9895253-1-7
eBook ISBN 979-8-9895253-2-4

Library of Congress Control Number 2024903946

Fiction: Romance
Fiction: Suspense

To my one and only.
You were the first person to tell me I could do this.
Thank you for the wings

Great Drinks,
Questionable Conversations

WOMEN EXISTED FOR NO other reason than to be the end of man. Danny was sure of it.

A pint of pale ale clunked against the wooden bar in front of him. He didn't look up at the man who served it, only stared at the cascade of golden effervescence floating to the creamy head on top. Such a simple perfection. Predictable. Reliable. A scientific masterpiece he could always depend on. Unlike —

"Eight dollars."

Danny snapped up. "Eight? For domestic beer?"

"It's craft."

"By who, Jesus?"

"Do I need to call security?" The bartender leaned his entire mid-sized weight on the bar, clearly trying to flex his arms.

Danny only stared at the wine stain streaked up his white sleeve.

He pointed at it. "You should always use a bar towel."

"Eight. Dollars."

Danny sighed and peeled off his coat.

The bartender took a step back, staring at Danny's boulder-sized arms covered in swirling black ink. "What are you doing?"

He dug inside the inner pocket of his coat before laying it over an empty stool beside him, holding up his wallet. "What's it look like I'm doing?"

"It looks like you need to put your coat back on."

Danny lifted one brow.

He'd been told his bulldog-build and resting scowl face screamed "fight me," but anyone who knew him knew he never started a fight unless he had to. An overpriced beer wasn't a reason. All he wanted was a simple drink before leaving his week from hell behind.

He studied the scratched name tag dangling from the bartender's button-down shirt. "I don't want to put my coat on, Chris. It's hot in here."

Chris kept his eyes glued to Danny's hand as he slowly slipped out a ten-dollar bill, held it up, and tossed it on the bar. "Eight dollars is a rip-off, man."

Maybe he wouldn't start a fight over an overpriced drink, but that didn't mean Danny could resist pointing out the principle of the matter.

"This is an airport, *man*, of course it's a rip-off." Chris crumpled the bill and didn't offer him change.

Danny mulled over the worth of two dollars and decided to let him keep it. He even contemplated telling him that bartending was an art he should take pride in, but figured that lesson might be unwanted by an underpaid airport bartender. He picked up his glass and got lost in the first sip.

Quiet fell around him, and he glanced up with froth caked over his mustache. Swiping his mouth, he followed the gaze of all ten men at the bar over his rounded shoulder.

A pair of long, slender legs below a pinstripe pencil skirt stepped down the three stairs in stiletto heels to the pit of the bar — which unimaginatively was called The Pit.

Beautiful legs were all Danny saw before he snapped back around and glued his attention to the beauty that never disappointed. Ale. Ale was the only woman he needed now. Every muscle in his body seized when heels ticked closer and stopped beside him.

"What can I get for you?" Chris said.

Danny scoffed at his complete one-eighty. All politeness and excited voice. Though after glancing up, he noticed Chris covered his wine-stained arm with a towel.

"Red. Anything dry or from Italy, please." The woman's gentle tone was laced with a smile.

Danny shifted in his seat to keep from connecting a face to the voice. He didn't want to know if she was as nice to look at as she was to hear. He took another long sip.

"Excuse me, is this seat saved for someone?"

From the corner of his eye, he watched powder-pink nails patting his coat. The same nails attached to a finger that displayed a sizable, sparkling stone.

Figured.

His sip turned into two large gulps that he let run out and over the beard he stopped trimming a week ago. Brought up to believe women hated men who lacked manners, Danny decided at that moment to lose all of his and belched.

She didn't gasp or leave like he hoped. She chuckled — *chuckled*?

"I only need a place to sit and give my feet a break from these shoes. I love the look of them, but my toes and calves are killing me."

He huffed and kept drinking. No way he'd fall for her attempt to get him to give her model-like legs a second look. He was on to her.

Bartender Chris glared. "Move your coat."

"Pick another seat."

"Actually, this is the last one," she said, smile still in her voice.

Danny slowly scanned the bar, looking everywhere but where she hovered. It wasn't a lie. Sucking in a breath, he released it with obnoxious gusto, snatched the coat, and draped it over his thick legs.

She slid in next to him. "Thank you."

He pretended she wasn't there. Especially when the sweet, delicate scent of flowering citrus wafted toward him. He buried his nose in the smell of hops and malted barley, blocking her scent, and wondered if he'd look disgusting enough to make her leave if he shoved napkins up his nose.

Chris slid a more than proper portion of red wine across the bar and ducked his head to get her attention. "I know you must get this a lot, but are you Madelynn Johnson, by any chance?"

Danny rolled his eyes.

"Depends on who's asking."

Chris belted an obnoxious laugh, and Danny's brow shadowed his eyes. "It's a real honor."

Chris held out a paw. She placed a hand in his and Uninterested Danny made note that he should've let go three seconds ago.

"May I also extend my deepest sympathies." Chris plastered a perfectly timed pout and covered her hand with his other.

Danny groaned into his glass. The man tried way too hard to impress this woman and needed to grow a pair.

Madelynn made a small grunting noise, and Danny noticed her hand remained trapped while she tried to pull back. His upper lip ticked. Not that he felt the need to protect her from sloppy, unkempt bartenders. No. It was Chris, he told himself. Chris with his embarrassing display was why his skin pricked.

He flicked a finger hard across the man's knuckles. "Clearly the woman isn't interested."

Chris released her hand and stammered, "I-I'm sorry, Madelynn. I uh . . . " He rushed, red faced, to the tired businessman with a loosened tie at the other end of the bar, asking for cheap bourbon on the rocks.

She sighed. "Thank you. I didn't think I'd get my hand back."

Danny propped fingers on the side of his face, shading it from her, and gulped more ale. He hated gulping. All he wanted was to sip and savor, but his blood pressure hadn't eased like he'd hoped after Chris left. Instead, it increased with loud thumping inside his eardrums. He had to get out of there, but he couldn't bring himself to waste an eight-dollar pint.

Madelynn swirled a finger over the rim of her glass. "Are you headed for home or leaving it?"

His face twisted. It wasn't her fault the question stung. How could she know that he ran from the home he thought he'd never leave, for the home he thought he'd never return to.

He buried his face in his ale without answering.

"Ah. You just want to drink in peace." Her finger stopped circling. "I can relate to that. I normally wouldn't come into a crowded bar, but I really needed this glass of wine. Here, let me buy you another drink and get out of your hair." She held up a hand to get Chris's attention.

Danny sprang out and shoved her arm down. "No." He took a deep breath, careful not to look at her, and adjusted his expression to as pleasant as he could make it. "Thanks."

"You have a nice smile."

A shudder ran through him, and his lips curled against his teeth. "This is how it starts isn't it?"

"I beg your pardon?"

The ale rippled inside his glass, swishing and swaying until it sloshed out. He crumpled a pile of napkins and scrubbed the mess. "First it's, 'Nice smile.' Then it's, 'You're so handsome. Look at how strong you are. This is meant to be. We're soulmates. Let's get married. Oh, but did I forget to mention that I'm sleeping with every other man in our building complex because you can't make me happy?'"

His jaw snapped shut and he closed his eyes. He didn't mean to say so much.

"I didn't realize." A distinct quaver was in her voice, and she cleared it. "I didn't realize my compliment would upset you so much."

Danny slapped the bar and she jumped. "The ring on your left hand. Or do you think I'm so stupid as to not notice you're a married woman? I don't need you to buy me a beer or tell me I have a nice smile. I don't want you anywhere *near* me. Take your undeserving, cheatin' ass home to your husband and beg his forgiveness, Jezebel."

She stumbled out of the stool. "I-I . . . " Her hands clinked and clattered inside a black clutch and retrieved a twenty, laying it on the bar without another word.

Danny swallowed down the rising bile of regret with the last of his ale. All he'd wanted was one drink.

Her fading heel clicks stopped near the stairs, and she turned. "For what it's worth, I'm sorry your wife hurt you like that."

Danny whipped around and confirmed what her voice had already told him. She was beautiful—of course she was. Tall and slender with an hourglass shape and golden-brown waves bouncing off her back. She didn't stomp up the stairs like he expected, but with the grace of a ballerina, tread quietly up and out of The Pit.

"Get out," Chris boomed. "Get out before I throw you out. That was freakin' Madelynn Johnson."

Danny fumbled his wallet back into his pocket. He'd never heard of Madelynn Johnson, but he knew he'd never behaved so terribly in his life.

"And for your information, asshole, she isn't cheating. Every man in here, but you, knows that's not possible."

Danny's eyes swept the room, catching all the glares.

Chris leaned in. "That cheater, as you called her, is the same woman who just came from a memorial for her late husband."

Danny's lungs emptied out. "*Late* husband?"

"Yes, you idiot. He died a year ago, but they had some fancy dedication for him last weekend. Where have you been for the last seven days? Every news outlet has replayed the event because of who her husband was."

Seven days. The same seven days Danny's world shattered when he heard six, simple words out of his wife's mouth. *"You were never the only man."*

"You deaf too?" Chris's fist hit the bar. "Get out."

Danny snatched his coat and ran up the stairs to the overcrowded terminal. He craned his neck left and right while he bumped elbows and zig-zagged around suitcases. He had to fix this. Had to find her. If for no other reason than to gain some control over the spiraling chaos that had become his life in such a short time.

He didn't care if she accepted his apology or not. He made a vow that it all stopped here. That the words his wife used to tear him apart would never bleed on to someone else ever again.

2

Flying the Friendly Skies

NOTHING IRRITATED DANNY MORE than being late. He'd arrived early enough to be the first in line to board and therefore the first to settle into his seat. So, when he heard the final boarding call for his flight and still hadn't found Madelynn, he cursed and sprinted toward the gate. Not only did he upset a stranger and couldn't apologize, now he'd have to sit in a sweaty shirt for a long flight.

"I'm sorry, sir," a petite, blond ticket agent said from behind the counter. "But we're overbooked. If you'd like we can—"

"Are you kidding me?"

She went rigid.

"If you read this." He held up his ticket. "It clearly says I have a seat on this plane."

"Actually, there's no assigned seat on that ticket, and because you arrived just before takeoff, all available seats have been assigned." She plastered a fake smile on her face.

Danny was convinced he'd be cursed with beautiful women telling him what he couldn't have for the rest of his life.

"I can either book you on a later flight . . . " She pursed her gloss-covered lips and gave him a once over. "Or you can upgrade to first-class for a fee."

"A fee? Shouldn't I get upgraded for free since *you* overbooked?"

She blinked with the full control of someone who handled a lot of angry people. "If you'd like, I can book you on the next flight. It leaves at nine a.m. tomorrow."

He squeezed his hands and leaned in, lowering his voice. "I can't leave in the morning. I have to arrive in the morning. That's why I bought a ticket for this plane."

There wasn't an emergency he rushed back for, but a promise to a friend that he'd be there. And if there was one thing most important to him, it was keeping his promises.

"I'm sorry, sir. There's nothing more I can do about it."

He had a feeling there was a lot more she could do about it, but he blew his chance for a favor the moment he snapped.

She showed all her gleaming teeth. "Would you like the upgrade then, or no?"

His eye twitched as he slapped down his card.

"Enjoy your flight."

Danny twisted to fit through the door of the plane. Despite Miss Spiteful Ticket Agent, both he and his thick frame were grateful to see the roomy and cushioned first-class seats. Taking a few more steps in, his small excitement fell.

In the seat next to the one he'd have to sit was another woman. From what he could see, she was gorgeous, of course, because God hated him.

He tried not to stare, but what the hell? Dressed head to toe in black, his seat mate appeared to have stepped out of a 1920s' fashion catalog. A cloche hat, complete with a rosette on the side, dainty gloves, and buckled thick-heeled shoes, all accented the cape or cloak—he wasn't sure which—that swallowed the rest of her. Half her face was hidden behind wide, dark-lens sunglasses.

Who wears sunglasses on an airplane?

That thought went nowhere because his eyes snagged on her only visible feature. A wide and full rose-pink mouth with a cupid's bow on top.

Dammit. He took a deep breath and lifted the overhead compartment to rid himself of his coat. He'd have packed it if he'd packed anything at all. But packing was the last thing on his mind when he rushed off to the nearest hotel. Not that he wanted any of their stuff anyway.

The overhead bin was jammed, so he turned to the one behind him but found it stuffed to the brim.

"Can you sit down?" said a short, balding man from behind him. "Not all of us can afford first-class tickets, so I'd like to go mingle with the rest of the peasants back there. If you don't mind." He pointed over Danny's shoulder.

Why did people keep trying to pick a fight with him today? He squared up with a few choice words on the tip of his tongue, but a soft hand tugged his arm. The woman in black pointed to the space beneath the seat and whispered, "It should fit there."

Between peasant passengers and whispering women from the roaring '20s, Danny wondered if he'd died without knowing and got trapped in hell. He plopped in his seat, too tired to continue the stare down with Baldy, and proceeded to stuff his coat under the seat, one punch at a time.

"Thanks," he mumbled to the woman next to him.

Instead of answering, she nodded and retrieved a brown leather journal from inside her cape. Her black-gloved hand went back in and retrieved a teeth-marked pencil.

Realizing he owed her at least a few words for helping him, not to mention they were stuck together for the night, he decided to try conversation. "Don't like computers?"

She shook her head and turned away from him, continuing to scratch words on paper.

Sufficiently satisfied with his failed attempt to be nice, he decided to try to get some sleep.

"Champagne?"

A tall brunette with plump red lips bent over him offering a glass of sparkling liquid on a tray. She was the perfect picture of what most men imagined a female flight attendant would look like. Hair neatly pinned back under a cap with a curved figure accentuated by her button-down jacket and pristine skirt sitting just above the knee.

Danny decided in that moment that if a man ever needed to

find a beautiful woman, all he had to do was not want one. He blinked and shook his head.

"Yes, please," Whispering Time Traveler answered.

The flight attendant didn't flinch at her whispering. If anything, she acted as if the incident was a normal occurrence. Danny wondered how many weirdos she encountered on a regular basis when she smiled sweetly to the flapper beside him and said, "Let me know if there is anything more I can do to make your flight more comfortable. Otherwise, I'll be back when we're in the air with your dinner."

"Not for me." Danny yanked out the pillow from behind his head and smothered his face. He kept it there until she left, surprised when he started drifting off to sleep the moment the plane backed away from the gate. Maybe because he hadn't slept since Jessica dropped her bomb. Or maybe because he'd learned just how much he'd relied on the comfort of her body next to him to fall asleep.

He shifted in his seat. Deep sleep called to him, and he didn't fight it. He needed strength for what waited for him when he landed. What he didn't need was the nagging question in the back of his mind of why the scent of citrus flowers followed him into his dreams.

SOMEONE TAPPED HIS CHEEK.

"Hmm?"

"We're here," a woman said.

"Jess?" His head popped up from a comfortable shoulder, and he dropped the pillow he hugged.

"Only me, I'm afraid."

Danny blinked hard and rubbed his eyes before looking toward the voice. The 1920s woman filled his line of sight. Or at least the back of her head since she faced the window.

A sickening brick dropped in his stomach. She wasn't his wife, or soon-to-be ex-wife since the divorce was uncontested. No, a stranger sat beside him with no clue of the raw memories being repainted in his mind.

It had started with a smile. The smile Jessica had while she listed off all the men she'd been seeing behind his back.

With that fresh punch to the gut, Danny cursed under his breath and stared into the blank screen on the back of the seat in front of him. His phone pinged, and when he glanced down, a calendar notification reminded him to order a spa package for Jessica's upcoming birthday.

He pressed the "off" button so hard his phone case cracked.

The plane bumped as the wheels touched down and he released a breath, turning to stare beyond the cloche hat. His hometown in the distance passed by his line of sight in short bursts.

His chest tightened. When Jessica had begged him to elope and move away because the cold island winds and the isolation made her depressed, he thought he was making the same sacrifice his father had made. The sacrifice of leaving their family history and heritage behind for a warmer climate to ease his mother's joint pain.

Instead, Danny had abandoned everything and everyone a month ago with nothing to show for it.

A memory of how he'd woken flashed, bringing his attention back to the black hat beside him. "My God, did I sleep on you? Why didn't you knock me off?"

The woman shrugged.

"But I'm a stranger, and I know for a fact you paid good money for this seat. Which I'm sure didn't include drool."

She chuckled, and he froze. He knew that sound.

"I don't know that we're complete strangers." She turned and extended a gloveless hand, but all he saw were the powder-pink nails. "If it helps, we can exchange names with a handshake and call it even."

His head snapped up from her hands, and he finally caught sight of her entire face—and, oh God, her face—her slap-him-upside-his-stupid-head, gorgeous face. All sense and reason evaporated as Danny full-on, jaw unhinged, eyes bulging, gawped.

Even Sloppy Bartender Chris didn't hold a candle to his reaction.

He croaked, "Madelynn?"

She glanced around and quickly put her glasses back on. "Shh, I don't need a mob." She smiled and pushed her hand toward him again. "Call me Claire. Madelynn is the name reserved for strangers who've never drooled on me."

"I'm sorry. I'm an asshole."

Her smile faded, and she dropped her hand, folding it with the other on her lap. "You were hurt by someone. That doesn't mean you're an asshole."

She toyed with the ring on her finger, twisting it in a circle, and he wondered where her thoughts drifted.

Recovering, she tucked her journal inside her cloak. "Besides, honesty, even if it's misinformed, is best. I've always preferred a kick to the face than a stab in the back."

Never had he related to a statement more. "I never shook your hand, sorry." He offered it. "I'm also sorry for the kick to the face. That's not my normal way with nice strangers."

Really, really pretty strangers he kept himself from adding.

"Well, since I was both kicked and drooled on, perhaps that's enough of a payment to finally get your name?"

"I'm in a lot of debt."

She softly laughed and he smirked.

"Danny Larsson, ma'am." He fake-tipped a hat and released her hand before any more of her warmth threatened to soak into him. "Why were you whispering last night? Are you feeling sick?"

"Oh, um." She squeezed her fingers together. "I thought you might not be happy about being stuck next to me, so I'd hoped with my change of clothes and sudden laryngitis, you wouldn't recognize me."

"I almost missed this plane trying to find you."

She removed her sunglasses. "To find me?"

He studied the curious look in her eyes, brows pinched together. "My words were meant for someone else. They never should've been given to you."

When she merely nodded in response, his eyes swept from her vintage clothing to the restless fingers tangled together on her lap. Her sleeve bunched slightly, revealing a scar on her left wrist. Faded pink and slightly raised, told him it was more recent.

She pulled on her sleeve, and he blinked away, reminding himself that this beautiful, soft-spoken woman was the same one who sat next to him while he slapped insults at her. Why hadn't she yelled at him? Or at least given him a dirty look. Nothing about her made sense.

She gasped, snapping him out of his thoughts, and removed the journal from her cloak again.

"Everything okay?"

"Just have to write this down before it runs away from me."

"Runs—?"

She held up a finger, silencing him, and scratched swirling script across the paper. Pausing once to gnaw on the teeth-marked pencil, she went back to writing and finished with a long sigh.

"Do you mind if I ask what you're writing?"

"The end of my career," she said. At his blank stare, a wide smile spread across her face. "So, I was right. You don't know who I am."

He grimaced. "Sorry, no. I don't watch a lot of TV. Are you an actress or something?"

"Only in private." He blinked, and she laughed. "I'm a writer, or was, if my agent is right about my ruining things." She propped her forehead against the window and fogged it with her breath. "It's why I decided to go to Solsken. I needed someplace quiet to figure things out away from nosy cameras." She rested back against the seat, missing Danny's paling face.

"*Solsken*?" he said with the proper Swedish accent.

"Are you familiar with the Island of Sunshine?"

"You could say that." He rubbed his beard, suddenly wishing he'd trimmed it. "Though there isn't a whole lot of sunshine this time of year, you definitely won't find snooping cameras there. Except maybe from tourists with phones. But there are plenty of places to go if you want to avoid them."

"You seem to know a lot about it. Is that where you're headed?"

"Yeah." He scratched his chin. "It's my home."

Claire had no idea how hard those four words were to say. Solsken wasn't just his home. The Larssons helped settle the island over a century ago, and his guilt from needlessly walking away tore deeper.

"Brandon and I had planned to visit, but we didn't get a chance before . . . " She stopped and bit her lip. Remembering how uncomfortable she'd become when Chris offered condolences for her late husband, he refrained from giving any.

"Anyway, I'm here now." She toyed with her ring again and smiled, but Danny noticed it was a practiced smile. The kind of smile one uses when forced into the public eye no matter what went on in your private life. Not wanting to dig too deep into what quieted her, he scrambled to think of something else to talk about.

She let out a long sigh.

"You alright?" He winced. He hadn't meant to ask that, but an invisible weight drooped her small shoulders, and out of nowhere, he had the urge to make it leave.

"Have you ever had an epiphany?" She stared down at her wedding ring. "A moment where you realized you haven't seen things the way you should, but when you discovered it," her breath shuddered out, "it's too late?"

He swallowed hard. "Yes."

She slowly faced him. "Then I guess you'll understand why I can't answer your question." Light-brown eyes penetrated his and he told himself to look away, to not search the depths that lingered inside, but he found himself sinking deeper.

She broke the bond by facing the window again, and he internally kicked himself for stupidly staring at her.

"Tell me more about your home," she said.

"Well," he cleared his throat, "the residents are private but also a close community. They're loyal to each other and the island.

"We thrive from tourism, but all of us look forward to getting our island back in the winter when they leave. Other than that, life in Solsken stays pretty much the same. So, it should suit your need for quiet. Will you be staying at the Solsken Inn?"

The taxiing plane slowed, and she slipped on her gloves. "No, I'm not so great with crowded groups of people. I found a nice private cottage for rent."

They pulled up to the gate and Danny stiffened in his seat. Eight hours next to this woman and he only used five minutes of them to get to know her. He couldn't explain what he felt. Anxiety? Panic maybe. He only knew it gnawed at him. Like something important was slipping away.

Gripping the armrest between them, he blurted the first thing that came to him. "If you're ever in need of a friendly face, drop by and see me. Though, for a quiet place to write, you may want to show up in the earlier hours to avoid a crowd. Sometimes they can get a bit rowdy."

Her brow furrowed. "Thank you."

The moment their eyes locked, he regretted the offer. Being close to her was the last thing he needed. Bolting up, he yanked out his coat and made an awkward salute without eye contact.

"Enjoy your stay in Solsken, Claire." He charged forward to be the first off the plane.

"Goodbye, Daniel Larsson."

Even with the soft way she said his full name, he never looked back because he knew this was how it started. The smiles. The laughs. The attraction. All the little things that led to an attachment. And it's the attachment he couldn't allow again. Without attachment, there could be no painful detachment—and pain was precisely what he planned to avoid.

So, when he was halfway up the loading ramp and remembered he never told her where he could be found, he continued without going back.

Too much was at stake. The gaping wound of his heart, to be specific.

He didn't know how to heal what he didn't break, but he knew one thing—if he ever found a way—he'd never let it be broken again.

What's a Good
Argument Among Friends?

IT'D BEEN THE LONGEST running feud on all of Solsken that the McClellans, not the Larssons, were the first to settle here. Therefore whisky — yes, without the bloody "e" — as opposed to vodka, was the established town drink. With good ale, of course.

Most residents who weren't from either family, were smart enough *not* to have an opinion. But ask any Larsson and they'd say they were first to the island and that's why they got to name the place. Ask any McClellan and they'd tell you, if they had the choice between the town name or the town spirit, they would've chosen the spirit like any good Scotsman. Therefore, that was proof they were first.

Just to be clear, the McClellans have never forgiven the Swedes for naming the town after a burning ball of gas.

Sunshine aside, Ian McClellan continued this long-running argument with Danny when the whisky and ale flowed. Call it family pride. Call it fun to argue over something that couldn't be proved since the town hall fire destroyed the records over eighty years ago. Nevertheless, this was their way of carrying on their families' tradition of following a damn good fight, fueled by drinking and arm wrestling, followed by more drinking.

This was precisely what Ian planned to do with him to get his mind off things until he saw Danny shuffling up the hill toward him. His chin rested against his chest, hands shoved deep in his pockets.

The sight of him both squeezed the air out of Ian's lungs and boiled his insides. Not once did Danny lift his head as he made the long trek up, weaving between rocks and stones covered in fanning dried grass. With each heavy step, his thick frame sank lower, as if he had reason to be ashamed of what happened. As if what she did to him was his fault.

The entirety of Danny's communication with him over what happened consisted of three short texts: *Moved in to hotel . . . Coming home . . . I wasn't enough.*

The last text was all Ian needed to put the pieces together, and it's also what sent him spiraling into his old self — the self he was still recovering from.

Nearing the top of the hill, Danny still hadn't bothered to look up, and Ian glanced to the sky, whispering, "Give me strength," before shouting, "oi."

Danny lifted his head.

"You said you were arriving at eight."

He looked at his watch. "It's a little after seven."

"Exactly. I was just leaving to come get you."

"I never said I'd be flying in at eight, just that I'd be here by eight."

Ian crossed his arms, pretending to be pissed. He knew why Danny left out that detail. He wanted to delay any uncomfortable conversations for as long as possible — by walking the whole damn five miles from the airport.

Adjusting the small ponytail that held the top of his blond hair away from his shaved sides, Danny dropped his head again before stopping in front of him. He stood to the height of Ian's scruff-covered chin, with his hands still jammed into his pockets, kicking a few small rocks aside.

Ian let out a heavy sigh. This wasn't Danny. This wasn't the confident guy he'd knew most of his life. The same guy who always made eye contact with a firm handshake to anyone he met.

No, this was her. The woman who not only stole his dignity, but his confidence too.

Ian had news for him. He wasn't going to stand around and let Jessica keep her claws on him, making him a broken shell of himself. Besides, what were best friends for except to build you up and encourage you?

"Well," Ian said.

Danny slowly looked up.

"You look like shit."

The corner of Danny's mouth tipped up. "I missed you too, Ian."

He grinned. "How was your flight?"

"Besides having to pay for first-class because they overbooked?" He shrugged. "Okay."

"Pay? Nah, my cousin that works for an airline said they can do that for free when they mess up. Usually offer it."

Danny stared at him and rolled his tongue over his teeth.

Ian pinched his lips together. "Of course, they could leave out that detail if . . . say . . . the customer wasn't nice."

Danny pointed a finger at him, ready to go off, and Ian smiled, waiting. He huffed instead and edged past him. "What are the numbers?"

He should've seen this coming. The "let's talk work instead of feelings." Not that Ian expected him to gush about feelings. That wasn't his way with the deep stuff. Those things had to be chiseled out of him one small detail at a time.

They walked along the outer rim of a tall, stacked-stone wall with sharp, jagged points like little soldiers in formation on top, keeping kids from climbing over it. Danny scanned the dark wooden building towering inside the wall. A nearly hundred-year-old replica of an ancient Viking design with trusses that crisscrossed at the top point. A structure Danny's great-grandfather had built.

A sign with the name *Flygande Norseman* dangled above a heavy wooden door. Painted under the Swedish name was the English interpretation, "The Flying Northman."

Danny unlatched the neck-high, picketed gate that opened to a pebble path leading to the entrance. He frowned when it yawned with a loud creak. "I should oil that."

"Don't you dare," Ian said. "How will you hear when one of the kids sneaks in at night? It's a rite of passage for them, you know."

"They never succeed. I don't get why they keep trying to break in here."

"Are you kidding me? They love it." Ian followed him along the gravelly path, past Danny's mother's dormant kitchen gardens, up four flagstone steps to the solid wood entrance. "I mean, all you have to do is swing open this door with that old sword of yours and roar like the Viking you are," he said. "They run screaming and are greeted by friends with high-fives for their bravery. You can't deny them their first feeling of manhood, Danny."

Danny shook his head with a small smile.

"I'd be ready for a big one too." He wiggled his brow. "Last I heard, they upped the ante."

He didn't add that they did so because Danny left, and they thought it'd be an easy victory.

"I better make it worth their while then." Danny forced a full smile.

With me? He should've known better than that, but Ian let it slide when Danny's shoulders dropped and he dug out his set of keys. He pinched the key he needed between his thumb and forefinger and hovered it over the lock.

Ian gripped his shoulder.

He didn't turn and Ian didn't speak. They stood still and let the silent messages pass between them. The same way they'd done from day one. The day Danny stomped into kindergarten, declaring, "This place is for idiots," and Ian knew he'd found his best friend for life.

They'd never needed a lot of words between them, only the right ones. But there were no words to be said that could fix what dripped off Danny's hunched posture.

Finally turning, he gave Ian a short nod, letting him know his silent assurance was enough — for now.

The door groaned inward, and they both stepped through. Ian waited as Danny stopped inside and lifted his cyan-colored eyes, scanning over all the corners of his past.

Memories stared back at him between the exposed beams dangling Swedish flags and old family crests mounted with swords and axes on the wall. Aged wooden tables that he'd spent half his life maintaining dotted the main room, with upside-down chairs resting on top.

His scanning stopped on the words *Välkommen Familj*, carved on the wall over a polished oak bar his father and uncle had installed by hand that spanned the length of the back wall. Danny let out a deep sigh.

"Numbers," he said again, and Ian knew that was all the wallowing he'd allow himself.

Ian motioned to the office and Danny stepped through, wiping his thick-soled black boots on the fiber mat inside the door. A habit he'd picked up from his grandfather who used to say, *"What's outside this door, stays outside this door. What's in here is all business."* Ian smiled because Danny didn't even know he did it.

Danny rounded the massive oak desk in the center of the wood-paneled room and sat in the swiveling chair behind it. "This it?" He scanned the single piece of paper with reported sales lying in front of him and lifted gaping eyes. "Ian, am I going bankrupt before I even get back?"

"Okay, so maybe that was a bad coming home joke." Ian lifted five more folded sheets of paper out of his back pocket and tossed them to Danny. "Biscuits are in the drawer."

"Not hungry."

"But you're too skinny. Eat."

"What are you, Marco's *nonna*?" Danny looked down at himself and lifted a brow. "I've been called many things in my life, but never skinny."

Ian clanked a stiff wooden seat in front of the desk and plopped down with a pointing finger. "Do not speak that vile Italian's name in my presence."

Danny smirked, knowing exactly why Ian reacted. Marco De Luca's family owned the only Italian restaurant on the island, and though they'd not been there as long as the McClellans or Larssons, they were well established in the community.

Marco once tampered with a whisky vat at the McClellans' distillery and left a bottle of Chianti under it. A harmless prank. None of the new whisky was ruined, but when he tried to avoid getting caught, he ran through their whisky storeroom and kicked over an entire case of imported eighteen-year-old single malt.

Ian was still bitter.

"Go on, open the drawer and eat," he said. "You may not be normal-people skinny, but you're Danny skinny, and I don't like it."

Danny grumbled and rolled his eyes, but opened the drawer. Ian waited with a small smile hidden under his hand.

"Annie." Danny pulled out a plate of Scottish shortbread decorated in tartan ribbons with a large tag that read, "Welcome Home, Danny Boy." Her biscuit recipe was famous on the island. She baked and sold the flaky, buttery gold at the local café when she wasn't busy being the town's head nurse for the town's head doctor — who also happened to be her husband.

Danny rubbed the ribbon between his fingers and said quietly, "Does everyone know?"

"You know I don't spread gossip, but I didn't think you'd want me to keep it a secret that you were coming back. Otherwise, you'd be mobbed on your first day." Ian tilted his chair up on the back two legs and stretched his long legs on the desk. "Pretty sure George bellowed, 'God save the Queen,' though." He spotted a small smile on Danny's face and continued, "These island traitors always did prefer a Larsson running this place over a McClellan."

Danny's smile grew. "I think customers prefer bartenders who let them drink what they want without lessons on why whisky and ale are the only proper drinks."

Ian threw up his arms. "A Cosmopolitan is the devil's drink, Danny. And just the other day a woman asked for a Blue Hawaii. Can you imagine it?"

"We stock blue Curaçao for a reason."

"This isn't a damn Tiki bar."

Danny rocked back in his seat and crossed his arms. "You told her no?"

"No, I called Emelie over."

"You called Em, my cousin, our only server, behind the bar to make a drink you could do in your sleep?"

"It's the principle, *bràthair*."

He puffed a small laugh and Ian grinned. A laugh wasn't a big victory, but he'd take it.

Lifting the plastic wrap, Danny grabbed a biscuit. "Thanks for telling them for me. I didn't want to make a big announcement." He studied the biscuit in his fingers. "I'm not looking forward to all the questions tomorrow night, though."

"There won't be any questions."

He paused mid-bite. "You know where we live, right? Any news is big news."

"Well, these people love you, and you won't be alone with anyone who suddenly gets nosy. I'll make sure there aren't any questions."

"Aren't you supposed to head to seminary?"

Ian shrugged.

"You said you were going to live on campus once I got back. You're not still discerning, are you?"

"Maybe. Yes. No . . . I don't know." He ran a hand over his face and into his dark waves. He thought he'd finished discerning. Checked and rechecked his heart and it very clearly pulled him in the direction of the priesthood. But when he received Danny's texts and the old him resurfaced, he'd left holes in the storage room drywall. Since then, all the old doubts had resurfaced. How could he shepherd a flock when all he wanted to do was murder sheep like Jessica?

"If anyone is meant to be a priest, it's you. Don't drop out, Ian."

Ian met the bright eyes that read his doubts. "I just need a few more days here, that's all."

Danny's stare hardened, and he leaned back in his chair, recrossing his thick arms. "There's no need. Flygande isn't for sale anymore since I'm back, and I won't let you stay just because you think I'm so broken I can't stand on my own two feet. I'll adjust."

"I'm not staying because of that," Ian lied. He also declined to inform him that he'd never put Flygande up for sale. He couldn't bring himself to let it go into anyone's hands but a Larsson.

"I'll give you one more day." Danny held up a finger. "Then you're in your car and over the bridge, if I have to throw you there myself." He picked up the papers of sales records, thinking he'd settled the matter. But Ian would be coming back every weekend, using whatever excuse he could, for the foreseeable future.

Ian snatched a big piece of flaky goodness off the plate and watched Danny. The man was a genius with numbers. He could look at all the data and within minutes see where the sales were down and know why and how to fix it. It's how he turned Flygande Norseman from a just-getting-by business into a booming tourist destination. It's also why his father wanted him to take it over when he retired. Danny had always planned to—until Jessica.

Nope. Not thinking about her right now. Ian munched and groaned. "This is Auntie's best batch."

"You say that about every batch."

"And it's not a lie." He shoved half of it into his mouth and savored how it melted on his tongue. "So, besides living it up in first-class, anything else happen on your trip?"

Danny's head shot up. "What? Why?"

The rest of Ian's biscuit fell to the desk.

"I mean, it was fine." He shrugged, but it was too late.

"Nuh-uh." Ian picked up his crumpling biscuit and shook it at him. "Now you have to tell me."

"There's nothing to tell."

"Bullshit."

Danny intertwined his fingers on the desk, trying to act casual. "Future priest means you have to get rid of your potty mouth."

"Have you ever met an army chaplain?"

"You want to be a parish priest."

Ian licked all his fingers. "Stop changing the subject. How pretty was she?"

"What makes you think this has something to do with a woman?"

Ian slowly smiled. "Because you're avoiding the conversation."

"There was nothing and no one. Now, go . . . go stack glasses or something."

Ian grinned and let his chair bang forward on all fours. "I really missed your ability to order me around." He crumpled the biscuit wrap and threw it at him. "I never got the mail from yesterday. I'll be right back."

Ian's fingers were on the handle of the door when Danny quietly said, "Thank you. For everything."

Ian swallowed down the pang of emotion before turning and plastering a smirk. "You don't have to thank me, but you do have to tell me who turned your pale-as-ass face beet red a minute ago."

A biscuit smacked his head. "*Oi*. Not the precious biscuits, Danny." Ian snatched all the crumbs from his clothes, popping them into his mouth like a starved man, and Danny snickered. He swung open the door and spread his arm, wide. "Parting is such sweet sorrow that it shall be until tom—" Ian slammed the door before another blessed biscuit lost its life and whistled all the way outside.

His smile dropped when he opened the mailbox and pulled out a manila envelope. There wasn't a return address, but he saw her name, Jessica Wilson, scrawled in red ink.

Wilson, not Larsson. Ian was relieved to see it changed back, but wondered if she'd done so before she even told Danny it was over.

A clinking sound came from inside the package, and Ian's gut twisted. His gut was never wrong, and it told him whatever hid inside could tear apart what little Danny barely held together.

4

Whisky, For God's Sake, Whisky

DANNY STARED AT THE package and Ian stared at him, chewing on the inner lining of his cheek.

Danny didn't move. Speak. Hell, the only sign that he was even still breathing was that he remained staring at the damn package.

Ian understood quiet Danny. He understood angry Danny. But he had no idea what to do with still-as-the-dead Danny. He cleared his throat. "So, should I start a bonfire?"

Danny's head snapped up. "Huh?"

Ian hated to remind him of why they both stared at his desk, but pointed and said, "What are you going to do with it?"

"Nothing."

"Nothing? Like let it sit there and burn a hole? Or nothing, you're going to throw it away."

"Nothing, I'm busy." He shoved out of his seat.

A slow smile spread over Ian's face, following Danny to the door. "Of course you're busy. We're both busy. What are we busy doing?"

"Cleaning."

Ian ballooned his cheeks and blew out a puff of air. "Right. Cleaning."

Unlike some people who exercised to blow off steam, Danny cleaned. He'd once told Ian that when he was upset, his eyesight became hypersensitive. Specks of dirt appeared that would otherwise be invisible. And with what he just went through, Ian had no doubt this clean-fest would probably kill him.

Danny wiped his feet before stepping out of the office. Ian did the same, wiping stupid Jessica away through the bottom of his shoes. "Okay, Mr. Scrub, where do we start?"

Danny pointed up and Ian slowly followed his finger. "How many years has it been since those were washed?"

"The flags?" Ian said. "Aren't you afraid they'll fall apart if you wash them? They have to be what? Fifty years old? Also, isn't it wrong to wash—"

"Not the flags, the beams."

"Beams? Like those wooden poles holding the upstairs floor, covered in years' worth of great conversation and pipe smoke?"

"Dirt. They're covered in dirt. But you're right about the flags, they shouldn't be washed. They need a good airing, though. We'll hang them outside while we clean."

He can't be serious. Ian may even take opening Jessica's package over this. Danny walked back into the office.

"Thank God." He wasn't serious, but Ian decided to give him a minute before going in to make sure he wasn't alone when opening it. He checked his watch and nodded. It was time.

A metal plate bulldozed him. "What the—"

"Out of the way, Ian."

Ian stumbled back as the top of a ladder came through the doorway, followed by Danny with a long line of metal rungs trailing behind him. "What's that, like a hundred feet? Where did you find it?"

"Twenty, and it's kept in the shed out back."

Ah, the shed. The same shed he got to by going through the office, into the storeroom, and out the back door. Sneaky bastard. "But why do you have it now?"

Danny stopped and stared at him as if *he* was the crazy one. "To reach the beams," he said slowly.

Of course. Of course he was absolutely—why would he be anything else—serious. Ian resigned with a long sigh. "Toss me the flags."

"I HAVE TO ADMIT." Ian took a long drink from his pint and wiped his mouth with the back of his hand. "She shines, Danny Boy."

Not only were the beams scoured and the flags respectfully aired, but every table had been turned upside down to fix every wobble. The hanging crests and dull blades were polished, and even the floors got a more than usual thorough mopping. All the old, frayed rugs were hauled out and replaced with plush new ones.

Danny looked around him with a critical eye and pulled his own pint. He sipped and studied, adjusted the coasters, straightened the napkins, aligned the bottles of liquor so all the labels lined up. Ian knew all of this was a delay. On his time, not hers, would Danny open it.

Danny unfolded a bar towel and picked up a glass, rubbing out a small imperfection. "You knew Jess wasn't ever faithful to me, didn't you?"

And there it was. Danny only shared what he needed, when he needed, and all Ian had to do was be there for it. He didn't answer because Danny wasn't asking.

"That's what you were trying to tell me before I left, when you said to be careful." He glanced up, and this time, Ian nodded.

Yeah, he knew and wanted to tell him everything, but she'd already driven a wedge between them at that point. She knew damn well why Ian didn't like her, but twisted and spewed lies about his reason for it and confused Danny.

If Ian had tried to tell Danny what she'd done to him before they eloped, he'd have risked confirming those lies and lose the only friend who'd been his brother in everything but blood.

Now there was no point in telling him. Ian took a deep breath. "You were the only man she chose to marry, so I'd hoped that meant she would change."

"She said you hated her because you were jealous of the time she had with me, but I think she was the one who was jealous of you. I should've seen it." He slapped the towel on the bar. "I should have seen what she was doing."

"Danny, don't do this to yourself."

"What? Be honest? Admit that I was too whipped to notice what everyone else did?"

"You were in love. Probably the only man that has ever truly shown her what real love is. Don't make something that beautiful sound so weak."

The glass Danny cleaned clanked against the bar, and his nostrils flared. Ian didn't care if he broke every damn glass in this place. He wanted him angry. Angry enough to not let Jessica send him reeling every time she felt like mailing him an envelope.

With long breaths through his nose, Danny sucked the anger back in and threw down the towel. "Import, Ian. You pick." He rolled his shoulders and marched toward the office without looking back.

Ian didn't argue. If Danny asked for the hard-to-get-to-the-island scotch, he'd rush it to him.

"Hello, beautiful." Ian stroked the olive-green bottle with a tinted label. "I have an important job for you." This upcoming dreaded event needed the distraction of the ever-faithful, Lagavulin 16. He snatched it and wedged two glasses between his fingers.

When he entered the office, Danny stared down at the package. It was open, but nothing had been pulled out yet.

Good. Ian set the bottle down. Whisky first.

Without taking his eyes off the package, Danny yanked the wood-topped cork with his teeth and spit it out.

That settled it. This bottle would be emptied.

Ian set Danny's glass within arm's reach and watched him pour while continuing to stare at the package. With anyone else, he'd be nervous, but Danny was the kind of bartender that could feel a good pour. He stopped at a perfect two fingers and set the bottle down.

Ian poured one finger for himself. A single shot was all he needed until he knew Danny would be okay.

Danny brought the glass to his lips, sipped, rolled it around his tongue, and swallowed with a hiss. "Nice smoke to it."

"Just the right amount," Ian said.

"Good caramel aftertaste."

"My favorite part."

Danny sipped again, repeating his swish, swirl, and swallow until he finished every last drop. He set down the glass. Ian tilted the bottle over the rim, watching him.

"Right." Danny dove for the packet, dumping the contents in one go, and Ian fumbled the precious liquid to keep it from spilling.

Broken seashells, a cd marked, "road trip driving tunes for my wife," an engraved silver-framed wedding photo, and a broken bottle labeled "honeymoon sand," fell out with a round object covered in a piece of notebook paper. Danny ignored everything but the paper-wrapped object. Wiping off sand, he held it up between shaking fingers.

"What is it, *bràthair*?"

Danny didn't answer, blinking fast as the shaking in his fingers spread up his arm and through his body.

Ian swallowed. Either tears were going to spill or Danny was about to blow.

And Danny didn't cry.

He tore off the paper and a whooshing breath escaped Ian. A gold loop hung from a delicate chain with the Swedish three crowns in the middle, studded in jewels. The same necklace Danny's great-grandfather had given to his great-grandmother on their wedding day and Danny had given to Jessica.

She'd stuffed it in a piece of notebook paper when it should've been in a protective case.

Ian waited for him to yell. Speak. Move. Anything but sit there shaking. Danny's eyes darted to the paper, and he snatched it up, reading. His chair slammed into the wall as he shot up, grabbed the bottle, and marched out of the room.

Ian picked up the paper.

I'm returning this negative energy to you. These things steal

my happiness every time I see them.

Ian flipped the paper looking for more and found nothing but a heart that said, **Sending all my light to you.**

"You've got to be shitting me." He crumpled the paper. "These things he gave to show he loved you steal your happiness? More like make you feel guilty, you manipulating, lying little—"

"Ian."

He whipped around to see Danny standing in the doorway. "I . . ." Danny scuffed his boot against the threshold. "I haven't been upstairs to the apartment yet and—"

Ian rose without a word and went into the storage room, returning with a large black trash bag. "I already packed all her shit. Was going to use it for target practice, but didn't want to waste the bullets."

The side of Danny's mouth ticked, and when their eyes met, Ian knew the thanks was there even if he wasn't able to form the words.

"I'm thinking it's been too long since we cleaned out the attic," Ian said, opening the bag and swiping everything in but the necklace. "Head on up and I'll join you when I'm done taking out the trash."

"Don't forget the necklace."

"I'm not throwing away your great-grandmother's jewelry, Danny."

"Donate it then."

Ian removed a handkerchief from his pants, carefully wrapped it around the necklace, and tucked it into his shirt pocket. "Yeah, no," he whispered. "I'll be hanging on to this until you're ready." He dropped the bag in the outside trash bin with a crash. "Bye, you stupid b—"

He froze, lid shaking in his hand. He had to do better, somehow, if he ever had hopes of becoming a priest.

Taking a deep breath, he glanced up to the sky and mumbled, "She's yours, so I won't curse her anymore."

That's all he could give. Maybe it was enough. Or maybe he

wasn't cut out to be a priest after all. He slammed the bin closed.

Hours later, with the attic cleared and dusted, Ian and Danny sprawled on their backs over one of the new rugs leading to the front entrance of the tavern, admiring their handiwork. On the floor next to them, the empty Lagavulin bottle sat beside two nearly empty pint glasses.

Ian couldn't remember who'd decided this was the best place to lie, but he had a vague memory of one of them gushing about how soft it was, probably him, and that led to them deciding to sleep on it.

"I think I knew," Danny said, without looking at him.

"Hmm?" Ian rolled to his side. "Knew what?"

"In here." He tapped his chest. "There were signs and I ignored them. Thought I could do what no other man could. Love her enough to heal all her past shit, you know?" He spoke with surprising control, considering the amount of alcohol swimming in him. He grew quiet before adding, "But I'm not what she needs."

"No person is, Danny, and that's the problem." Ian pushed up to sitting, clutched his spinning head, and flopped back down to his side again. "Instead of getting help, she ignored her issues by doing what she did to you and filled the rest with those hippie remedies she concocts." The spinning room became too much, so he rolled onto his back. "She needs a miracle, and neither you or I operate that department."

"Somehow, everything you just said makes sense."

Ian snickered. "Aye, we McClellans are the most eloquent after whisky."

"I'll drink to that." Danny gulped down the last of his ale and held it up. "I win."

"Bastard. You tricked me with yer sob story."

He chuckled and Ian grunted, belly slithering to his glass to take the last gulp. "Fine. I'll be the one to open tomorrow." He plopped onto his back again and groaned. "Now what? When we sober, we scrub the cedar roof?"

Danny tucked his hands under his head and let out a long

breath. "Nah. I'm finished."

Those three words weren't about cleaning, and for the first time since everything happened, Ian felt a drop of hope for him.

Home Sweet Home

CLAIRE GAPED AT THE haunting apparition of a home in front of her, convinced she'd starred in the world's biggest hoax — and life was its director.

Her eyes slowly fell to the glossy brochure in her hand, boasting of a cozy, picturesque cottage. A pretty red-metal roof and matching front door with a white stucco exterior surrounded by a classic white picket fence. Functioning shutters framed each window with flower boxes underneath.

She dropped it to look at the real thing again.

The fence resembled more of a wooden graveyard of broken teeth posts, and the outside plastered walls were the embodiment of melancholy. Gray, not white, with cracks and whole chunks missing. The pretty red roof and front door were faded from glory to sickly pink, and the half-hung shutters creaked and moaned as the wind threatened to rip them from their hinges.

There were no flower boxes.

"Are you sure this is the right place?" she asked the cab driver.

"Yup."

If she were of the right mindset, a place like this might inspire an idea for a new creepy novel. That is what her agent begged her for anyway. She waited for the spark. The niggling in the back of her mind when her muse showed up. But as the wind whipped salty ocean air around her, there was nothing. Not in over a year had there been anything.

At least not for the book she was contracted to write.

She glanced down at the pristine picture again with a sigh. When Danny left her on the plane, she had no intention of taking him up on his offer of a visit. She'd come to Solsken, not for a retreat in the sense of relaxing, but the kind of retreat where you turn and run away from something you can't fix.

Problem was, she thought she'd have a cozy cottage to retreat to.

"What do you want to do?" the cab driver asked.

Do? She wanted to scream at the irony. She'd finally taken the leap and broken away to a place far enough from her life. A place where she could breathe and quiet the plaguing echoes of her past. Maybe even conjure the means to reinvent herself.

And this is what she got.

You're so incapable, Madelynn. She stiffened at the sudden memory. *I swear, if I ever die, you'd better die with me because you couldn't survive a day on your own.*

Her husband, Brandon, had said it as a joke, but how could she argue the truth of it? On her first attempt at doing something on her own, she'd failed. Three months of non-refundable rent should've been a clue that something was wrong with the rental. Instead, she'd gotten it on the whim of feelings a pretty picture invoked.

But no one knew the anxiety that coursed through her at Brandon's recent memorial service as she stood outside the new mental health facility named in his honor. Surrounded by empty offers of sympathy, the shallow regrets for her loss suffocated her. Listening to her father's speech praising Brandon's amazing accomplishments, she'd been so small. So utterly empty as he went on and on about the son of his dreams. The great loss of so much potential. The one who never disappointed him . . . unlike her.

Claire sighed, rubbing the chill out of her arms. "I'd hoped for a bit more." She smiled unevenly at the cab driver.

"I bet."

"It's kind of cute though, isn't it?" He scrunched his nose and she laughed. "If only I'd learned to wield a hammer instead of a pen."

He lost interest in the conversation and pulled out his phone.

She lowered her head and squeezed her fingers together. Frustrated that the certainty that drove her from West Coast to East Coast, that pushed her to become more than someone's disappointment or widow, had abandoned her the moment she faced a problem.

"Well?" the cab driver said, without lifting his head from the phone.

She squinted at the cottage. Maybe she could find what she needed elsewhere and endure being surrounded by people for a little while . . . "Isn't there a Solsken Inn? Perhaps—"

"Fully booked," he blurted, then shifted on his feet. Keeping his eyes glued to the phone, he added, "I, uh, just checked. So it's here or nothin'."

"Oh." Cold air blew across her cheeks, drawing her attention back to the cottage. She weighed her options—one option surprisingly heavier than the other. After a lifetime spent dreaming and yearning, she couldn't bring herself to let go of this chance so easily.

Perhaps this place wasn't as bad on the inside?

Drawing closer to the cottage, she tilted her head. There were details there. A carved wooden trim of faded flowers and curling vines. Hearts and folkish symbols chiseled into the broken shutters. Clearly, at one point, this place had been loved, and these small details oddly drew her to the neglected home. She wondered about its history. What stories lived inside this humble shack?

Humble shack. She suddenly remembered the disgruntled little man who snapped at Danny on the plane. What word did he use to describe people in economy class?

"Peasants." She smiled, and then it came. The familiar tingle in her fingertips from her muse waking up had her ripping out her journal. "Mister Peasant of Peasantry." She named him and scribbled his brief description—stopped, thought of how his balding head barely came to Danny's broad chest, yet he didn't back down—and smiled wider while continuing to write.

"Disgruntled factory worker rallies against the gods, demanding better working conditions." She laughed. "Peasant indeed. Welcome to my character club, Mister Peasant."

"Ma'am?" the driver said.

She held up a finger and sketched a brief drawing of a gnome-like creature, balding under a pointed hat. "Now, Mister Peasant, what story shall I place you in? Perhaps in one of Maddy's fairytales."

A throat cleared and she froze. She did all those awkward things — said all those weird words out loud — in front of the cab driver.

This moment was why she reserved her first name for the public and her middle name, her favorite name, for herself. When someone said Madelynn, she became Madelynn. The only name her mother used, and usually only to correct her, made it easy to associate it with proper behavior.

For the life of her, she couldn't explain why she'd spontaneously told Danny to call her Claire instead.

She straightened herself into flawless posture and focused on the years of etiquette training forced on her as an "unruly" child before facing the driver in perfect Madelynn form. "I'd like to look around more before deciding, if you don't mind."

He nodded and leaned against the car, his fingers tapping in rapid beats on his phone.

She stepped toward a rewarding view and scanned her surroundings. The cottage was nestled in an isolated area off a long, grassy lane that led to the edge of the island. Steep white pines and hemlocks mingled with grand maples and oaks, clinging to the last remnants of colorful leaves. As she approached, they waved their spindly fingers at her. Beckoning.

Stepping further toward the cliff's edge, she held her breath. More evergreens dotted rock-cliffs that broke off into crumbles of stone, rolling like marbles into the gray sea. The scent of spruce and balsam rose on a breeze and picked up loose strands of her hair, carrying them away.

At least the brochure hadn't lied about the view. On a clear day, perhaps she'd even be able to see the shoreline of their North American neighbor. A hawk flew up and soared in front of her, gliding in place on the wind. She smiled and closed her eyes, taking a deep breath. This. This was what she needed. The serenity she'd hoped to find.

The wind continued to whistle, and she remained still, soaking up the smells and sounds. She was so engrossed in the sensory experience, she almost missed the sound.

"Madelyy-ynn . . ." the wind whispered.

Her phone buzzed and she jumped, rolling her eyes at her overworking imagination. Of course the wind didn't say her name. She lifted her phone and held up a finger to the driver, asking him to continue waiting.

A notification reminded her to contact Greyson. She smiled at the profile picture of him still in diapers as she, an eighteen-year-old mother, held him. The time in his life when he still thought she held the world in the palm of her hands.

JUST LETTING YOU KNOW I ARRIVED SAFE AND SOUND, she texted. YOU SHOULD SEE THIS PLACE. THE VIEW IS BEAUTIFUL. She flexed and released her hand, debating if she should say the other thing on her mind, and took a deep breath. WOULD LOVE TO HAVE YOU COME VISIT AND SEE IT WITH ME. She bit her bottom lip and hit send, hoping against hope for an answer. Three dots appeared and she smiled.

PRETTY BUSY THIS SEMESTER.

Her smile dropped. That's all he had to say? "Don't pressure him, Claire," she whispered.

OF COURSE, she replied. STUDY HARD. I LOVE YOU.

He didn't answer, and disappointment curled its familiar fingers around her throat and squeezed. She closed her eyes and inhaled. He'd answered her. That was something, at least. Rolling her shoulders back, she stared with determined eyes at what should've been the cottage of her dreams.

"Well?" the driver asked.

"I'm staying."

His relieved smile didn't match his nonchalant words. "Suit yourself, but here." He held out a business card between two fingers and winked. "If you need anything, call me."

"That's very kind of you." She smiled and paid him, studying the card as he left. The name Kenneth Greene lined the top with his phone number and a motel address underneath. She flipped the card, looking for the name of a taxi company, but it was blank. A second job maybe? She shrugged and tucked it away.

Determination restored and her carry-on strapped over her shoulder, she took both suitcases, one in each hand, ready to see what could be done to fix this place. She stopped—lurched forward—stopped again and groaned.

"Maybe you should've had Kenneth carry your bags *into* the house, Claire," she said, unaware that she'd stepped back into her lonely childhood habit of talking to herself. The habit she'd hid when Brandon had made her awkwardly aware of it.

She strained some more before giving up and letting go of everything but the one case with her most precious possession of journals inside.

When she'd told Danny she didn't like computers, what she meant was she despised them. Paper begot stories, and anything else drew a blank. Her transcriptionist was well paid to take her scribbles and make them digital for her.

She clunk-dragged her case up the single step to the porch, which creaked and bowed under the baggage weight. She waited to see if it would give way and silently cheered when it held. "See that, Brandon? Not completely incapable."

Guilt stripped the humor as quick as it came. "I'm sorry," she whispered and hefted the case, unlocking the door with a sigh.

Everything was going to be just fine.

She shrieked and the case slipped from her hands, falling with a bang.

The food and supplies she'd had delivered from the mainland lay scattered all over the floor in shredded bits and broken chunks.

Scratched and ripped furniture cushions were strewn about with their puffy white guts mauled into snowy piles.

"What in the—"

A door slammed down the hall and she cupped a hand over a scream.

Moaning creaks from wind or something else shook the door. "Who's there?"

What if it was the animal that murdered her cushions?

Finding a broken leg piece from a busted chair, she clung to her fading determination and forced herself to creep toward the room. Her head tilted, listening. There were no footsteps or sounds of movement from inside.

"*Hey.*" She gave the door two solid thumps and jumped back just in case.

No response.

There had to be a perfectly logical explanation inside there. Still, her entire body trembled as she slowly reached toward the door. "I mean you no harm." She figured it didn't hurt to keep talking if there was an animal.

When her fingers touched the knob, the rattling stopped. "H-Hello?" Nothing came. Sighing, she mustered up a speck of bravery and pushed the door open.

In front of her, a flannel comforter lay torn across a double mattress with sheets tangled and covering a broken end table. A shattered lamp littered the carpet. She groaned and braced against the door frame. Not even a bed to sleep in?

The wind whipped inside the room, hissing and fluttering the torn blanket, and that's when she noticed the wide-open window. She marched over and took hold of the bottom window rail.

"Ma-adelynn . . ."

She yelled out, slamming the window shut and locked it. Or tried. The lock wouldn't fully engage. Her fingers vibrated as she tested the seal of the window and it blessedly stayed shut.

Stumbling back against the wall, she pressed a hand into her chest. "You need sleep, Claire. That's all. The wind didn't say your name."

Her stomach gurgled and growled. Maybe she was just hungry.

She hadn't eaten on the plane like she'd planned because she'd given Danny her shoulder. He'd fallen asleep so fast and so hard she couldn't keep watching his head bob with his eyebrows troubled and drawn. It was an exhaustion of mind and body she understood, so she positioned herself to catch him the next time he went down.

What she didn't expect was how different the man who slept on her was from the man she'd met at the bar. The hard, bitter lines etched into his face gave way to vulnerable softness as he nestled into her side like she was his favorite pillow.

She didn't have the heart to push him away. Even mid-flight, when he'd shifted and sank further into her. The tip of his nose brushed the side of her neck. It was so delicate. So unintentionally intimate, she didn't dare move for fear of waking and embarrassing him. He'd softly groaned, "why," in his sleep, and she'd squeezed her eyes closed. She may not know his life, but she knew what heartache sounded like.

Then he'd hummed. His fingertips had reached out, stroked up and down her arm. She'd gone still, heart thundering until he adjusted with an incoherent mumble and dropped his hand.

The entire time he'd talked to her after he woke, she couldn't stop replaying that moment and had to continuously break eye contact.

Claire shivered out of the memory. "Food. You're just hungry and need food."

Making her way to the ugly pink front door, she opened it to retrieve her snack-filled carry-on.

She froze. A large, hairy creature snarled ten feet away from her, gnawing on her snack bag. It had taken her so many hours at the airport to find the cab driver and get here that the sun had already dipped below the western horizon, making the animal difficult to identify. Was it a small bear? Or wolverine, maybe. Did wolverines live here?

The animal suddenly charged, and she screamed, stumbling inside. She slammed the door.

"I'll just drink tea." Her shaking hand rubbed over her chest. "Tea makes everything better."

When she entered the "L" shaped kitchenette, she stopped, hand still clasped over her chest. A golden tin lay crushed with beautiful, dried tea leaves littering the floor.

Full-on desperation took hold, and she ran to the bits, yelling, "It'll be okay. You're okay." She wasn't sure if she was assuring the tea or herself.

A horrible thought sprang to mind, and she paused. What if the creature was rabid? Could she drink tea after a rabid animal touched it? Her mind conjured a scenario where she not only died alone, but foaming at the mouth.

Defeat slumped her back against the front door. The ferocious sound of her precious food supply being mauled continued.

Needy, needy child. She stiffened when her mother's words cut through her spiraling thoughts. She'd been five the first time she heard them, bursting in on her mother's weekly luncheon after her pet snail died. She hadn't known snails were disgusting and not suitable pets for young ladies, and her unsightly emotional display was quickly shut away in her room.

She curled her arms around her knees, much like she'd done then, trying to comfort herself.

It felt like hours before the growling stopped, and she let another thirty minutes go by before deciding to look.

Slowly creaking the door open, she peeked out — checked and double checked — then darted to her other case. Gripping the handle in both hands, she looked left and right, praying the creature didn't return for her as its next meal.

She quickened her pace, scraping her last case into the house. Desperate for any kind of sanity, she unzipped the case and dug to the bottom, removing a felted blanket. She wrapped it around her shivering body, plugged the cord into the wall and switched the knob attached to it on high.

Her electric blanket wasn't enough, nor were the hot tears that soaked her cheeks. She couldn't stop shivering. Brandon was right.

"You can't do this," she said. Her teeth chattered.

Taking out Kenneth's card, she held it tight against her palm. In the morning, she would admit defeat and call him. Until then, she would remain on the hard floor, hugging her body.

Fitful dreams soon swallowed her, and visions of hairy monsters and creepy winds gave way to a fractured memory . . . *His weight pressed against her . . . The stench of his breath . . . Cold metal against her skin . . . Warm flesh scraping under her nails . . .*

"Madelynn."

She screamed and shot awake, blinking in the darkness. The electric blanket laid warm against her damp cheek, her eyes darting around the dark cottage. His voice had been so close this time. She was sure of it. Whimpering, she fumbled for her phone. Did it vibrate three times, and she missed it? She opened the J.M. Security notifications.

POI SECURED. Their cryptic message told her exactly what she needed.

"He's not here." She hugged the phone to her chest, rocking. "Just a dream." She rubbed the scar on her wrist and tugged the blanket tighter. But she couldn't self-soothe this time. The shaking wouldn't stop.

If you're ever in need of a friendly face, drop by and see me.

"I need a friendly face, Daniel." She smeared the back of her hand over her damp face and ran to the hall mirror. Fixing her hair and hat, she snatched her purse and a journal to make her excuse legitimate.

Snagging the broken furniture leg in case there were more wild beasts, she ran down the dry, grassy lane. The roar of the wind filled her ears, playing tricks with her overactive imagination. She paused, heaving deep breaths, listening. She shook out the crazy from her head. That couldn't have been echoing laughter she heard. Still, she ran harder.

Nearing the end of the lane, she collided with an elderly man with a leashed dog, and she dropped the furniture leg. "Excuse me," she panted hard, "do you know where I can find a Daniel Larsson?"

"Larsson, did you say? Yeah, I know him." He pointed to a dark, Viking-shaped building. "Right in there. You're in luck, too, he's just come home."

Thanking him, she left, unable to focus on what his whisper of "Mother" meant.

All she knew was this had to stop. She couldn't keep letting desperation suck her into maddening chaos. There had to be a way to ground herself. To find her calm.

If only it could happen as easily as it had on the plane when she'd looked into a pair of blue-green eyes.

6

Not Only Opportunities Knock

A THUMP SENT IAN bolting upright. "*Fire.*" He blinked around the dimly lit tavern and scraped a hand over his face.

"Muma ffee thawpp," Danny mumbled, face down into the rug.

Ian closed his eyes again and flopped back down. Flygande wasn't on fire, so they'd live.

The knocking came again, more demanding this time, and Ian's eyes popped open. What if the neighbor's place was on fire, and they were trying to wake them before it got there?

Why the only thing that kept coming to his mind was fire, he couldn't say. Maybe it was all the fire that went down his throat last night.

Another knock.

"Mummffthp," Danny mumbled again, and Ian grumbled in response, forcing himself up.

If there was a fire, one of them had to save the other. Since it seemed Ian could move slightly faster than Danny, and had lost the bet, the responsibility fell to his sore shoulders.

He rubbed a knot. Why did they think sleeping on the rug over a hard floor was a good idea? Oh yeah, bloody whisky.

Pound, pound.

"Alright. Give me a second." Ian shuffled forward in bare feet and gripped his thudding skull. He couldn't remember taking off his shoes or belt and he pondered that mystery when he stopped at the entry, blinking. "Why am I standing here?"

"H-Hello?" a gentle voice said from the other side, and he plunked his ear against the door. "I'm looking for a Daniel Larsson and was told I could find him here."

Ian jumped back and stared at the door. There was a woman out there. A woman who wasn't Danny's mam, calling him by his given name. That sobered him better than a bucket of ice and a shot of caffeine. He unlocked the door and swung it open to darkness, not seeing anyone. "Danny, did you hear that voice?"

Danny answered with a deep rumble from his nose.

Ian squinted to where a hint of light splayed across the horizon. It'd only been a few hours since they'd fallen asleep. He peered harder into the darkness, his entire body leaned forward and —

He yelled, stumbling back. A woman dressed in black from head to toe with an adorable cloche hat stepped out of the past and into his line of sight. Ian gawked. She even wore sunglasses. She couldn't be real.

"I'm sorry, did I wake you?" she asked.

He startled. Apparently, he wasn't having whisky hallucinations. "I . . ." He scratched the top of his head and blew out, rattling his lips. "I don't know . . . I mean, it's okay. Can I help you with something?"

"A Daniel Larsson informed me that I could come here early to write if I needed a quiet place and friendly face."

He rubbed his scruff. "Friendly face? Are you sure you mean Danny?"

"Quite sure."

"When did he tell you this?"

"On the airplane."

"Did you say plane?" The grogginess of his brain cleared and he slowly smiled. "You were with him on the plane."

"We flew in together. Um . . . " She tipped up on her toes peering over his shoulder. "Is he here? Perhaps he could tell you I'm not lying."

"Oh, I don't think you're lying, and yeah," he used his butt to push the heavy door wide open, "he's right there."

She gasped. "Is he okay?"

"Sure he is. Just sleeping."

"I didn't realize he had no home." She covered her mouth with a gloved hand.

Ian burst out a loud laugh, and Danny mumbled something about him shutting the hell up. He slapped a hand over his mouth and pointed up. "See those windows high above the door? He lives in the apartment there but was too tired to walk up the steep stairs last night."

He left out the whisky bit. He didn't want to scare away the one woman who made Danny try to hide the fact that they'd met—and now he knew why.

With another quick look, he ensured the delicate, feminine features were what his blurred vision had seen. Tall and gracefully lean, even though her cloak swallowed her. She was timeless and beautiful, not to mention adorable, dressed like a living Agatha Christie character. The best kind. The one you think did it, but they're too nice and pretty to convince you completely.

Ian took her in one last time. Yeah, he had no doubt Danny didn't mention her because he'd been extremely attracted to her. "Come on in," he said.

The wind gusted and she looked left, then right, her body tensing.

Ian leaned out of the door, looking with her. "That's just Solsken saying hello."

Still hesitating, her eyes darted behind her, feet shifting.

"Everything okay?"

"Oh. Yes." She shook off whatever bugged her and removed her glasses, squinting as she stepped into the dim light. Her eyes dropped and glued to the floor.

Ian followed her stare and grinned when he saw those eyes were stuck on Danny. At some point last night, he'd removed his shirt and stuffed it under his face as a pillow. Not that it was strange—the man was a walking furnace. No matter how cold, he never slept with a shirt on. But he, like Ian, had also removed his belt and now his pants sank low with the top of his ass peeking out.

A snort slipped out, and Ian slapped a hand over his mouth to hold it in.

As if on cue, Danny stretched and shifted, making the dragon tattoo trailing up both arms and across his broad back flex and ripple. Without knowing it, his best friend was putting himself on full display for this woman. Who, from what Ian could tell, became timidly awe-struck.

Danny shifted once more, and his pants inched even lower. As fun as this moment was, Ian figured he should probably do something before he traumatized their guest with a full-ass-out. "Oi, Danny."

He groaned into his shirt.

"There's someone . . . " Ian turned to her. "What did you say your name was?"

"I didn't, but Madelynn."

"Madelynn is here to see you. Why didn't you tell me you invited a beautiful woman over so I could be dressed properly?"

Danny's face shot up, streaked with lines from his crumpled shirt. His ponytail released scraggly, blond strands, and he blinked hard until his bloodshot eyes settled on her and went owl-shaped.

He croaked, "Claire?"

"No, Madelynn," Ian said.

"Claire," Danny repeated as his eyes traveled from her flushed cheeks, down to her toes, and slowly back up.

Thick hangover or not, he sobered when he realized where he was. "Shit." He looked down at himself, back up to her, back down at himself, back up to her. "Shit."

"I'm sorry to wake you." She glanced at her feet. "You said early, but not what time. I-I'm not fully settled in my cottage, so I wondered if your offer for a place to write still stands."

He blinked once, shoved up to a stand — grip holding his pants — and stumble-ran to the stairs behind the bar. The upstairs door boomed shut.

Ian couldn't breathe. Laughter shook him so hard, and his head fell back against the open door, wiping tears. "Bloody brilliant." He tried to rein it all back in. "Well, Madelynn or Claire, it's really nice to meet you. My name is—" His hand shot through empty space and the sound of running feet retreated up the path to the gate.

"Wait." He skip-hopped over pebbles. "Don't go."

"I-I made a mistake." She rattled the latch on the gate. "I'm sorry. Tell him I'm sorry."

Ian placed a hand on the top of the pickets and she and the gate stilled. "You don't have to go."

"Yes, I do. I didn't mean to upset him again."

"Again? What do you mean again?" She jiggled the gate, and he quickly changed his question. "You said he invited you here, right?"

She nodded and released the latch, clutching her small purse in both hands. "I guess it looks like I lied about that."

"Not one bit. If anything, you showing up and him running away proves that it's true."

Her brow knitted together. "I don't follow you . . . Mister?"

"McClellan, but call me Ian." He glanced over his shoulder and caught Danny's bedroom curtain dropping shut. He smiled. "Listen, you're new to Solsken right?"

"Yes. I'm on a retreat, so to speak."

"Let me give you a true Isle of Sunshine welcome then." He swung his long arm toward the door. "If you've not eaten breakfast yet, I'll whip up some *fika* for you."

"The Swedish word for coffee break?"

"I see you've done your homework."

"But I don't drink coffee. I drink tea."

"Really? So does . . . " Not wanting to scare her off again, he kept himself from saying Danny. But yeah, against his Scandinavian blood, Danny embraced his mam's English side and preferred tea. While Ian, the pure-blooded Scot, drank coffee.

No one ever said they made sense.

"Anyway," Ian continued. "What I meant to say is tea is also acceptable."

She hesitated and looked down at her pointed shoes neatly aligned together. "I don't want to be any trouble."

"No trouble. I manage this place and we're happy to have you. *Välkommen.*" He butchered the Swedish accent, motioning toward the door again.

She shuffled down the path with carefully placed steps and Ian followed, smiling wider when he spotted Danny's curtain dropping again. "Nothing happened on the plane, my ass."

"What was that?"

"Nothing." He led her into the main dining room, and she stared wide-eyed at the décor, soaking in every detail. She wasn't passing judgment, but with the way she stood, poised and meek in her pressed '20s garments, Ian was glad they'd had their cleaning fest.

She rubbed her thin arms.

"Are you cold?"

"A little."

"Here, sit by the fireplace and I'll get one going."

She remained fixed in place, standing where Danny had lain a moment ago, and cautiously looked over her shoulder to the door.

Her staring made Ian check the door too. "Are you sure you're alright?"

She quickly faced him again and forced a smile. "Yes, I just don't want you to go to any trouble."

"Not any trouble. This time of the year, the temperature drops quickly when the sun is down, and as you can see, the fireplace is already stacked with wood, ready to go. Come. Come." He motioned to a cushioned chair next to a round wooden table by a man-sized fireplace, and he kneeled to light the dry kindling.

The flame licked the logs, and Ian clapped dirt off his hands. "Make yourself at home. It'll only take me a few minutes." He casually walked toward the kitchen and glanced over his shoulder to see if she was watching him. She stared thoughtfully into the flame, so he sidestepped and darted upstairs to the apartment.

Opening the door, he collided with Bulldog Danny.

"Oh, hey." Ian pushed the corners of his mouth down, but they sprang back up.

Danny curled his arms over his chest.

"Madelynn seems nice."

"Claire."

"Yeah, you said that. Mind explaining to me why you call her something other than the name she gave me?"

"It's what she asked me to call her."

"I see." Ian nodded with a thoughtful frown. "So, when you said 'nothing—no one' happened on your flight, what you meant was *no one* is called Claire, but only by you, and you did *nothing*, like give her a special invitation to come here to write, correct?"

He didn't move.

"Why didn't you just tell me?"

Danny lifted a finger to speak but clamped his mouth closed again, stomping away from him.

"Come on, Danny. Clearly you liked her and that's okay."

He threw Ian's belt at him. "No, I didn't. That's why I didn't say anything because I knew you'd make a big deal of it."

Ian almost, *almost,* reminded him of his grab-and-go reaction to her. Because not only did he watch them out the window, but he'd also snuck down to get his stuff before they walked in, probably listening to them through the door. Which would also explain why he was standing at the top of the stairs when Ian arrived.

"You know, it's not a sin that you liked her."

"Not now, Ian." Danny ran a hand through his hair and felt the messy clumps. He cursed and tore out the band, smoothing it back, but his thick locks wouldn't be tamed. He rushed over to the kitchen sink and shoved his head under the faucet. Under the stream of water, Danny slowly turned his head.

"Yep." Ian grinned. "It happened."

Danny groaned and slapped the spigot off. Snatching a hand

towel, he rubbed it over his hair. "I do the dumbest shit around her."

"I thought your disappearing act was endearing."

Danny flipped him off and Ian snickered.

"Why did you get her to stay?" Danny asked.

"Because you invited her, and you wouldn't have done that if you didn't want to see her again."

"I don't need this right now."

"You don't need gorgeous women showing up at your door?"

Danny's eyes squeezed into slits, prompting another grin from his friend.

"Look," Ian said. "I'm not pushing you to jump into a relationship. All I'm asking is that you don't throw away the chance of maybe enjoying someone's company — other than mine, of course."

Danny side-scowled at him and successfully smoothed his hair into the band so that all the shaved sides were visible.

"Nice haircut, by the way." Ian was glad to see he'd returned to what he called the Viking cut. He'd had it long before that popular TV series came out, but Jess had convinced him to grow out the sides, which made him look more hippie, less him. Which also meant he shaved it right after they broke up. Thank the saints.

Danny threw the towel at him and huffed all the way to the bathroom, taking more frustrations out on scrubbing his teeth. Swinging open the door, he grumbled past his still smiling best friend into his bedroom. After more grumbling and clanking, he came out with a clean, white t-shirt, faded black jeans, and his black boots.

Having no more excuses to keep moving around, he propped his hands on his hips with a long sigh. "She's upset at me, isn't she. That's why she tried to leave?"

"No. I think that had more to do with you running away from her when you saw her."

"I wasn't running away from her, I just—"

"She's staying for *fika*," Ian said. "You should come."

"I know what you're doing."

Ian slapped a hand on his chest and stepped back, pretending to be shocked. "Doing? I'm not doing anything but having *fika* with an incredibly attractive woman and inviting you to join us."

"Future priest, remember?"

"Priest doesn't mean women aren't attractive to me. It means I've chosen to marry the Church instead of them. Which reminds me, I need you."

"No. Forget it. You invited her. You're on your own."

"I hate to point out the obvious, but *you* invited her. I'm just cleaning up the mess."

Danny's face twisted with everything he wanted to say, but didn't. He relented with a defeated sigh. "I don't understand why she's here, though. I didn't tell her where I lived, so I thought she'd see that as a retraction."

"Wait, are you retracting? And why are we saying things like retracting?"

"No." He pushed past him into the kitchen and busied himself, wiping water drops that splashed from the sink. "I mean, this is a public place where the public likes to hang out. So, who am I to stop her?"

"Of course." Ian nodded emphatically. "Bad for business. Lots of different people come here for lots of different reasons." He couldn't keep his obnoxious smile under control.

"I know I said to come early. But why the hell is she here this early?"

"Maybe when you come for *fika*, you can ask."

"Stop smiling, Ian." Danny pointed at him. "She's not here for me. *Fika* doesn't mean anything. Besides, she's still grieving for her late husband and only came here to—"

"To write and see a friendly face, yeah, I heard. Well, I'm heading down to slice some bread."

"Which you can do without me."

"But she wants tea."

"You can make tea."

"Not like you. Whatever that milky crap is that you drink."

"Royal Milk Tea." Danny glared. "And it's delicious."

"Wonderful. I'll tell her you're making it." He swung open the door.

"Ian," Danny whisper-yelled, but he was already halfway down the stairs. Ian laughed when a slew of hissed curses followed him.

Instead of waiting for Danny, Ian made the tea he absolutely didn't need help with and set up the *fika* tray. If, by some miracle, Danny listened and came down, he wasn't going to let him avoid seeing her by pretending to be too busy.

Coming out of the kitchen, Ian grinned. Danny hesitated at the bottom step, grimace on his face, the toe of his boot pointing down. Like if he touched down, he'd catch fire.

"Here." Ian shoved the tray into his chest.

"There's tea on here."

Ian gasped. "How'd that get there?"

"Ian."

"Oh, I forgot something in the kitchen."

"Sure you did."

Ian laughed and Danny grumbled, but to his surprise, Danny started making his way to the dining room. The fact that he didn't keep arguing with him proved Ian was right. Danny really wanted to see her again.

Ian waited a few moments before sneaking into the dining room to make sure he wasn't needed. But when he came around the corner, he froze.

Danny stood at an empty table, shoulders drooped, staring at a handwritten note laid out on top of some cash. The contents of the tray rattled in his shaking hands.

Ian hesitated. Should he go, stay?

Danny slammed down the tray. "You stupid bastard. Of course she didn't come here for you."

Ian ducked back around the corner when Danny tore out of the dining room and into his office.

He let out a long sigh and picked up the note.

Daniel,

I'm sorry I bothered you this morning. It won't happen again. I hope this money covers the fika and any trouble I've caused.

~ Claire

It was innocent enough, but with what Danny had just gone through, Ian cursed the timing of it.

Knowing his best friend, he would use this as an excuse to pull back even more. To keep everything locked away and never move on. Never heal.

Ian rubbed a hand on the back of his neck. How the hell was he going to fix this?

7

Sometimes Fate Doesn't Need a Hand, It Needs a Kick

"WHERE'S EM?" DANNY ASKED Ian as he pulled the last of the chairs off the tables and straightened them. "Place is going to open in fifteen minutes."

"She usually rolls in at about five 'til."

Danny set a chessboard on a two-top table and positioned all the pieces. "She knows better than that. Thirty minutes minimum."

"I tried telling her that." Ian opened the wooden covers on the dart boards and replaced the chalk pieces with full ones. "But I got tired of hearing the 'down with the patriarchy' speech."

"This patriarchy is paying her to be here early."

Ian held up both hands. "She's your cousin. Feel free to tell her that."

Danny smirked, knowing exactly how Emelie was. Their relationship went beyond just cousins. When her mother had had a stroke and he'd stepped in to help cover the responsibilities that fell on Emelie's young shoulders, they'd grown really close. She became the little sister he never had, and their favorite pastime was bickering over politics. Ian was convinced Danny only indulged in the arguments to watch her face go splotchy.

It didn't matter how much they argued, though. They dropped everything to do anything for the other. Like when Ian told Emelie why Danny was coming home, he thought he'd hear another speech about the oppression of women in the archaic institution of marriage. Instead, Ian had to physically hold her back from jumping on a plane to, "Drown that bitch in her own 'happy' medicine."

That's really when Ian stopped getting on her about being late.

Danny headed to the back kitchen to check the food stock with Kevin, their deep-fry guy, right before Emelie waltzed in. Earbuds plugged in, blowing bubblegum bubbles, her fingers flew over her phone keyboard. Without looking up, she asked, "He in?"

"Yeah, he's mad you're late."

She slowly grinned. "Good. I plan to keep him pissy to remind him how much I've missed him."

Ian checked over his shoulder to make sure Danny was still in the kitchen before striding over to her. Emelie felt his presence and unplugged her ears.

"I need your help today."

She popped her gum, waiting for him to tell her why.

"He scrubbed the beams last night." He pointed up and she followed his finger.

"Shit. That's bad."

"Exactly, and the one thing he's worried about is questions about what happened with Jessica."

The signature Larsson scowl crawled across her face. "Nobody's going to ask him questions about her. They're just happy he's home and so am I."

"All I'm saying is he's worried about it, and we need to keep the talk to a minimum."

She sighed and nodded. "He never answered my phone calls, you know."

"Mine either. Barely even got a text. But she sent back all the stuff he gave her last night, and my back hurts. I don't want to clean anymore."

"She sent it all *back*?" Ian shushed her with a hand over her mouth, and she took a deep breath. "Fine. I'll keep 'em quiet."

"You're an angel."

"A goddess." She pointed a long finger at him. "Not a fat baby with wings."

"Those are cherubs, and they could still probably kick your goddess ass." He grinned, and she smacked his arm. "Manager abuse."

She laughed, and he caught her sleeve when she thought the conversation was over.

"I also need a favor."

She snap-popped her gum again and raised both brows.

"Can you keep an ear out for any talk about a woman dressed like the Great Gatsby?"

"Ian," she said his name with a warning. "What are you up to?"

"Nothing. I just need to find her and clear something up about Danny, that's all."

"I know you're up to something." She ran her nails through her wavy blond hair and pulled it up into a high ponytail, securing a band. "You always have plans and most of the time they don't work."

"My plans work fine. It's the people that don't. Will you do it?"

"Is she pretty?"

He slowly smiled and she cackled, giving him a high-five. "I'm so in."

"In what?" Danny's voice whipped them around.

"Nothing," they said at the same time, making them look extremely guilty.

He arched a brow but didn't push. "You're late," he said to Emelie.

"Oh, so now it's not enough that we've spent centuries being chained to our kitchens birthing your babies that we have to be slave-driven at our independent workplaces?"

He crossed his arms. "You were a baby once. I think."

"Misogynistic Overlord."

"Fem-Nazi."

She snickered, and he smiled as she plowed into him. "God, I missed you."

He sighed and wrapped her in a full hug. "Missed you, kiddo."

"You okay?"

"Define okay."

"I got your back. You know that, right? We all do. The entire Larsson and McClellan clan. The whole town, Danny."

Taking a deep breath, he squeezed her, letting her know he'd heard, and let go. "Thirty minutes, *minimum*, and your ass better be here."

She propped both hands on her hips. "Or what? You're going to cut my benefits and unlawfully fire me? You know, that figures. You man-apes are all the same."

"That's man-ape that gives you great benefits to cut, thank you very much."

"Whatever." She waltzed to the kitchen with a wide smile.

"And lose the gum."

She flipped him off and Ian, who'd been silently watching it all unfold, grinned. Damn, it was nice to have things back the way they should be.

WORD HAD CERTAINLY SPREAD that Danny was home, and Flygande Norseman packed out earlier than usual. It'd only been a month since he left, but his return was excuse enough for them to declare a holiday.

Danny was in his element. The man literally thrived off a crowded bar. The fast pace and the constant drink orders being shot at him gave him a massive burst of energy, twirling bottles and pouring mixed drinks into garnished glasses like they were an extension of his hand.

Not Ian though. Making whisky was more his pace. Slow and laid back with the smell of fermented grain around him. No demanding customers. No orders being yelled at him. Just him and his quiet distilling vats alone together — making magic.

"Ian?" Emelie called.

"Look," he yelled. "I'm still filling your last order, you drink sadist."

"George and Merv need you."

"Need me? Did they lose a chess piece or —" He stopped when he noticed a young, barely over twenty-one, out-of-town man next to Emelie staring directly at her chest.

She also noticed. "Take a picture, it'll last longer. Or better yet, remember that I have eyes, too, and that's the only place you should be looking."

"You're the one that stuck them in my face, sweetheart." He winked and kept his eyes where they shouldn't be.

"Imma stick my fist in your face next."

The man huffed at her threat, downed the rest of his beer, and snapped a finger at Ian. "Another."

Ian bit his cheek until the metallic taste of blood hit his tongue. Slowly, he dragged himself away to where Emelie beckoned and leaned his ear across the bar.

"We need a code or something," she said.

"What do you mean?" He kept half an eye on Creep. "Code for what?"

"For . . . you know." She tipped her head to Danny.

"You heard something about the woman I mentioned?"

"See George and Merv." She twisted away with another glare at Boob Man.

"Hey, Danny," Ian called. "I gotta check the chessboard, something's up. Can you handle it alone for a minute?"

He nodded and handed over two stouts to a local.

"What about my drink?" Creep asked.

Ian squeezed the lip of the bar. "Nah, man. You're done."

"You can't cut me off. I just started." He slapped cash on the bar.

"Your money is no good here," Ian said in a low voice. "Now leave."

"Who the hell do you think you are?"

"He's the manager and I'm the owner." Danny stepped up beside him, crumpling the cash into his palm. Ian knew he hadn't seen what happened with Emelie, or he wouldn't be this calm. Danny could read a potential bar brawl, though, and always had Ian's back, like Ian had his. "Door's behind you." Danny threw the cash and it bounced off his head.

"You know what, *dick*? You've just earned yourself a bad review."

"Be sure you get the name right." Danny leaned in close, flexed arms doing all the warning. "That's D-A-N-N-Y L-A-R-S-S—don't forget both 'S's."

Creep scoffed, but arched back, waiting it out for a few brave moments. Danny jerked forward, and the guy stumble-fell off his seat. Gathering his money, he tore out, bumping a few people as he went.

Ian snickered. "Danny, my boy, that was beautiful."

"With his 'review' comment, I was damn close to engraving the bar with his face."

Normally, that'd be a lie. Ian was the one who had a history of pulling stunts like that. But if Danny had seen what just happened with Emelie, that scenario could have been a very real situation. All because of—

Ian shook that thought away and pulled two ales to take with him. "But then we'd have to stare down at that ugly face every day. Bad for morale, don't you think?"

Danny smiled, and Ian ducked under the bar's connector counter, heading toward George and Merv.

"I'm telling ya, I know what I saw," George said to Merv, an elderly man across from him who puffed smoke from a pipe jammed between his teeth.

Ian smiled, taking in the odd sight of them together. Merv, with his dark sepia complexion and head full of thick graying hair, towered over balding George's stout, pale-as-the-dead frame. Merv was all warmth and sunshine where George was all raging storms and black clouds. They were opposites in every way, and Ian often wondered how the two of them stayed such great friends for so many years.

"I was taking Duncan for a walk," George continued. "When my dear ol' mother, God rest her soul, came tearing down the lane dressed like the spittin' image of her picture, looking scared, but," he scratched his chin, "well, she asked for Larsson. Why would she ask for Danny and not me?"

Merv moved his knight in position to take George's king. "Maybe she got tired of your old man in the afterlife and wanted some young blood."

"Watch it, Merv."

He gave him a toothy grin. "Checkmate."

George cursed and double checked the pieces, unconvinced he'd been beaten.

Ian's mind snagged on Claire being frightened. Was that why she'd been nervous earlier? "Your mam's spirit came down from heaven to visit Solsken, George?" Ian asked.

George harrumphed and crossed his arms. "I know what I saw."

"Where was it?" Ian said.

"Out near the lane toward Sven's old place."

"Sven's place? She must've gotten herself lost." Ian hated how Sven's kids never bothered fixing up his home or keeping it when he died. He'd barely gotten cold in his grave before they'd sold it. They hadn't even given the locals a chance to bid on it. "Did she say anything else?" Ian asked.

George and Merv stared up at him. He'd forgotten they both thought Claire was the apparition of George's mam and not a real person. His question was odd at best. "I'm kidding. Ale?" He plopped their drinks down and removed their empty glasses.

"How'd you know?" George asked, staring at the ale. "We hadn't ordered new ones yet."

"Your mam told me."

Merv keeled over and slapped the table while George reset the chessboard, grumbling curses. Emelie caught Ian's attention and nodded toward the dartboard group. Apparently, nodding was their code now.

"Hey, everyone. Aunt Annie, Doc, Gene, *Marco*, good to see you all, but one," Ian said, and Marco smirked. "Do you need anything?"

"Emelie just took our orders." Annie eyed him. "You feeling okay?"

"Fine. Only checking on *some* of my favorites." Marco snickered at his dig. Ian knew he was being childish, but didn't care. "Also, I wanted to thank you for the delicious biscuits, Auntie dear." He smiled but could tell she didn't buy it. He'd always stayed behind the bar when it was busy.

"Then she ordered two cases of mac and cheese," Gene, the local grocer, said to Doc Clark. Both oblivious to the other conversation around them. "*Two* and she put an order in for the same amount next week. How can one thin woman eat that much pasta?"

"You having trouble with macaroni?" Ian asked him.

"Yeah, some tourist with a love of antique clothing and apparently children's food. She asked if I could make a delivery later to some lean-to shelter, not her home. I told her I didn't offer that service and she handed me an extra hundred." He shrugged. "Now I offer delivery service."

"By the way, not just for children," Ian said. "I love mac and cheese."

Gene looked him over. "Only proving my point."

"Oh, *burn*." Ian shook his head.

They all laughed and clinked their nearly empty glasses together. All but Marco watched him grow up, so he knew he'd always be the McClellan kid to them.

"Gene, let me ask you something. Did she seem scared to you?"

He pursed his lips, thinking. "No. Quite calm. She smiled a lot. Oh, and she bought the last of my Assam tea. I'll have to order more for Danny."

"He's got plenty for now." Ian was out of excuses to keep standing there when Emelie walked up with their drinks.

"Send a note," she whisper-yelled in his ear.

"A note?"

"Yes, from Danny." She winked. "I'm assuming he's off his

game tonight because he's thinking about her."

"He's off his game? I thought he was on."

"You mean I noticed and you didn't?" She snickered, and Ian faux glared.

He wasn't about to suggest Danny could be off his game because a little over a week ago, his wife laid out all the men she'd been with like a grocery list. That would defeat the purpose of keeping people from asking him questions.

"Can we have our drinks now?" Doc asked.

While they'd been talking, the group was reaching for their drinks and couldn't catch them because Emelie kept swinging the tray. She quickly handed them off.

Would a note work? Could it really be that easy? Ian cleared his throat, getting their attention. "Gene, can I add a note to the delivery you're taking to her?"

Gene sipped Ian's family's island whisky. "You know her?"

"Danny and I do, but she'd left before he . . . *we* got to ask her something." He tried to ignore the growing smile from his aunt. "So, do you mind taking a note with you?"

Gene sipped his drink with a shrug. "Don't see why not."

Ian pulled out his kitchen orders' notebook, and with a small smile and silent prayer this lie was for the best, he scratched out a message.

8

Hungry for Life and Snacks

THIS CERTAINLY COMPLICATED CLAIRE'S plan to avoid Danny. She reread the note for the hundredth time, pacing her still crumbling, but now clean, little home.

Claire, I'm sorry I left so quickly. I was embarrassed by how you saw me. Whenever you aren't busy, maybe stop in so I can show you how good fika is with tea.

~Danny

"I don't understand." She sighed, arms dropping to her sides. She'd seen how he looked at her. The horror in his expression.

Embarrassed? She shook her head.

The familiar sting of missing yet another social cue dug in its claws. When Danny invited her to come the first time, he was just being nice. He didn't actually want her there.

She wrapped her cloak around her shoulders and read the note again with another sigh. Growing up in a museum of a home with only private tutors, she'd been purposefully isolated. As the only child of *the* Gregory Cooke, she was too good to attend even the best private schools and social events that other children in her social circle had.

Birthed through surrogacy to preserve her mother's countless cosmetic surgeries, Claire understood she existed not because her parents wanted a daughter, but so she'd carry on a family name. A family business.

And as she'd sat by the fire in Danny's tavern, the warmth

gathering into her limbs again, she'd come to the conclusion that if she was going to do this, truly learn independence and stand on her own two feet, she'd have to do it without asking for help.

Pulling her cloak tighter, she glanced down at the dark living room fireplace. Every attempt she'd made to start a fire proved ineffective, and the truth of that sank colder into her bones than the temperature.

She was failing at independence.

Seabirds screeched and glided outside her window, getting her attention. Inside or out, she'd be cold, so she might as well try to harness a bit of peace with the view. She snatched her journal. Perhaps it would help her find clarity and forget about the note.

As she tucked herself between two boulders, pencil in her mouth, the wind picked up the journal's pages with wild flaps.

"Little hard to write in this weather." She pressed down the pages and lifted her eyes, soaking in the rocky cliffs and soaring birds. Try as she might, even the view couldn't help her focus.

Every thought kept steering back to the enigma of *him*.

Danny snapping at her . . . cuddling her in his sleep . . . inviting her to visit . . . running away from her when she did—and now the note.

None of it puzzled her more, though, than the moment on the plane when his eyes never wavered from hers while she spoke.

As if her every word mattered.

She inhaled a deep breath. Countless words and conversations in her life, yet no one had ever done that to her before. And no matter how hard she tried to silence it, his sincere act had shaken a thought loose.

That maybe a lifetime of being irrelevant to those around her wasn't actually her fault.

She massaged an ache between her eyes. Or maybe she just needed more sleep.

The nightmares were getting worse. The one from last night was so vivid she swore she even *smelled* him and woke in a sweat, screaming, "*Henderson*."

But only another phantom voice had whispered back, and she'd scolded herself—palms pressed to her ears, hiding under the covers—for letting her years of spooky-novel-writing imagination make her believe it was real.

She shuddered out of the memory. Picking up her phone, she ran a finger over Greyson's baby picture. Wanting the calm his voice gave her, she'd almost called him after the nightmare. But then she remembered that the reason for her nightmare was also the reason he didn't speak to her anymore.

It wasn't Greyson's fault, though. She hadn't told him everything.

Rubbing the chill in her arms, her frown deepened. On most days, she was okay with being alone, but not on days that started like today. No. She realized she'd never fully be okay with being alone. Even if it meant admitting her mother was right. She was needy.

"It's been a year," she whispered. "What's one more day?"

Tears threatened to spill, and she sniffed hard to hold them back. Danny's note shook in her hand as she stared down at it and made her final decision. She wouldn't be answering it. Not having the heart to throw it away, she neatly folded and tucked it inside her cloak.

Going back to her journal, she leafed through the pages. No matter how hard things got, her stories always brought the relief of an escape. A place where she could be free to release all the hidden parts of herself. Like desires, humor, passions, and fixable relationships.

But none of them freed her more than the story in her hands. A small sketch of a wild-haired little girl stared back at her. Shoes untied, one striped sock up, the other down. A determined smirk quirked her left cheek. Claire blinked hard at the image blurring in front of her.

"What do you think, Maddy?" she asked the drawing. "My agent says stories like yours don't interest kids these days."

Maddy shook her head. "Are you kidding? They'll love me."

Claire smiled. The image she sketched of the little girl crossing her arms and tapping her foot was so much like the character she envisioned. Feisty and adorable. "But he said no one will buy it."

"Fiddlesticks." Maddy harrumphed. "Does he have kids?"

"I don't think so."

"Then what does he know?"

"Quite a bit, I'm afraid." Claire continued to sketch Maddy with a scrunched face and messy ponytail sticking straight up in the air.

"You have to try."

"Yes, but you and I both know even if I did, I'd probably mess this up, and you'd never see the inside of a book anyway." She stopped at the sudden truth of her words and her pencil tip slid down the page.

As if knowing she was riding the ocean of doubts, her phone buzzed. An email notification from her agent appeared, asking if she was on track for him to view the outline of her next novel by the end of the month. **I hope you're focused on that and nothing else. Or do I need to remind you of your contract?** He placed a smiley after it, as if that would make his demand seem like a friendly reminder instead of a threat.

She looked back at Maddy, whose face was smudged from Claire's disobedient tears, and gasped. Words she didn't realize she wrote stared back at her.

You will mess this up.

The wind whipped a blistering chill that soaked the words into her bones. She shivered and pulled her cloak tighter.

You have to stop daydreaming and start living in the real world, Madelynn. Brandon had never called her Claire, even though she'd insisted upon it when they first got together. *If Allen says the book won't sell, the book won't sell.*

Claire stared at Maddy's smudged face, blinking drops from her eyes. Her agent knew what was best. Right?

"You're never going to finish me, are you?" Maddy said through the tears Claire penciled onto her cheeks.

"I think I have to stop daydreaming."

Maddy tucked her small hands into patched pockets and scuffed her Mary Jane's against sketched gravel. Claire didn't dare draw her with her face looking up. She couldn't bear to see her own broken dreams reflected in the little girl's eyes.

"I'm sorry, Maddy." She clenched her eyes closed and snapped the cover shut. Stumbling to a stand, and before she could question her decision, she threw the journal over the edge of the cliff.

Padding footsteps came running up behind her, and she twisted around right as a black, hairy creature lunged for her. She screamed and dropped to the ground. The beast sailed over her head and over the cliff. She screamed again when it disappeared.

It was him. The same creature who'd torn open her snacks had just leaped to his death in front of her.

A long, high-pitched whistle came from behind her and an elderly woman in a rain jacket with a hood pulled tight over her tawny, weathered face came over the peak of a rock-covered hill. Her long, coarse, gray hair dangled in a single braid that shifted over her shoulder as she looked left and right, stepping between rocks.

"Gunner?" she called. "Where ya at, boy?" She whistled again and Claire's heart dropped.

How was she going to tell this dear old woman that she just lost her pet? What if the news literally broke her heart, and she keeled over from it? Claire would be chased off the island for killing a beloved resident.

The woman spotted her and froze. A moment later she moved — no, ran — fast. This person, old enough to be her grandmother, rushed toward her at breakneck speed.

"I said, are you hurt?" She dropped down in front of Claire, who remained sprawled on the ground.

"I . . ."

"Speak up, child. I can't help you if you don't speak."

Claire brushed at the dried grass sticking to her cloak. "I'm fine, but I'm sorry. H-He's gone."

"What's that you said?" The woman bent her ear down. "Who's

gone?"

"The animal. It . . ." She pointed over the rock, unable to say it.

"Oh, Gunner? Did he knock you over?"

She shook her head and slowly sat up. Technically, he didn't touch her. "I'm really sorry. He's gone."

"That ornery ol' bastard ain't gone, he just doesn't remember his age." She stood and whistled again. "Gunner, get your ass back up here."

Claire was certain the woman had become so overwrought with grief she didn't hear her right. "But—"

Black appeared in the corner of her eye, and she yelled when the beast bounded over the edge and toppled her for real this time.

"Don't eat me." She buried her face in the grass, waiting for the tearing of her limbs. A cold, wet snout shoved in between her arms and face, and she screamed again.

"Come on, you old bat," the woman said. "Git off her. You scared her enough."

The animal began to whine in Claire's ear, and a thump hit the top of her head. Warm, sticky saliva drenched the side of her face.

He was . . . *licking* her?

Slowly looking up, she was greeted with a nudge of a wet nose to the side of her head. "But . . . "

"He didn't mean to scare ya," the woman said. "The old saying is true. You can't teach an old dog new tricks."

Claire wiped her wet cheek and glanced down at what had hit her head. Her journal lay on the ground in front of her. A little wet with some fresh canine teeth marks pressed into the leather, but other than that, unharmed.

"Maddy," she whispered, and a tear fell as she clutched the journal close.

She went still. She'd exposed all her needy emotions in front of a stranger, and now the teasing would start. Quickly poising herself, she prepared for it.

Gentle brown eyes met her instead and a pile of wrinkles appeared at the corner of her eyes as she smiled. "I'm Gertrude. Gerty for short. Solsken's official tour guide during the summer months. And as I'm sure you've guessed, this here is Gunner, a trained rescue dog. Both of us are the oldest of our kind on the island." She held out a hand to help her up. "You must be new here."

Claire stood on shaky legs. "Yes. I came a few days ago."

"I figured as much since you got lost. Most tourists don't wander up this way. Old Sven's place isn't exactly welcomin'."

"Oh, I'm not lost. I live here."

Gerty cocked her head, looking her over. "Did you fall hard?" She checked her forehead. "'Cause you just said you live here."

"I do live here." Claire pointed to the cottage. "I rented this place for three months."

"Three? Honey, I think you need your money back."

She winced. "Non-refundable, I'm afraid."

"Damn cheatin' city folk. Sven's kids never should have sold it to an out-of-towner," she said. "You can't possibly stay here."

Claire didn't know what came over her. Perhaps she did hit her head because instead of agreeing, she lifted her chin and said, "I can, and I will."

Gerty laughed. "Well, you got spirit, that's for sure. And spirit is what you need if you're goin' to stay that long in this place."

Claire went speechless. This woman didn't try to force her to leave or tell her she was incapable — but that she had what it took?

"I'm your neighbor." Gerty pointed over the small ridge of stone and grass. "Only neighbor, actually, so if you need anything, just holler. Oh, and don't let Gunner bully you into giving him snacks." She ruffled his matted coat. "He's a glutton for junk food."

That explained her devoured munchie bag. The dog sat panting happily up at her and Claire didn't have the heart to rat him out. Not after he'd risked his life to save Maddy.

A burst of air gusted around her, and Claire almost expected to hear her name again, but it merely blew. She swayed to catch her balance.

"Careful near these edges or the wind's liable to throw you over the cliff."

Claire stepped away and pulled her cloak tighter. "Does it get much colder here?"

"Bitter cold. My bones can hardly take it, but I think I'd die faster if I left."

Claire gazed at the cottage, empty of wafting smoke from the chimney. If it got much colder, she'd freeze to death long before learning to survive on her own. "Do you know anything about fireplaces?"

"Sure do. This one giving you trouble?"

"I tried to start a fire and the house filled with smoke."

"Sounds like the flue is closed. Let me help ya."

"Oh, I don't want to bother—"

"There's no shame in asking for help when you need it." Her steady gaze penetrated Claire's. "Solsken may be beautiful, but not a single one of us would survive here long without getting help from our neighbors now and again." She turned and marched straight into the house.

Claire looked down at Gunner, whose tongue hung to the side. "She's right. I want to do this alone, but the truth is, I have no idea what I'm doing."

He nudged her hand with his nose.

"Don't worry. I won't tell her you ate all my snacks, but can we call a truce? My snacks for saving Maddy?" She cautiously reached toward him, and he licked her hand. She laughed, taking that as a yes, and headed toward the house.

When she opened the door, a fire blazed, filling the home with a welcoming warmth. Gerty pointed to where the open and close was for the flue, showed her how to operate it, then took a moment to scan the place.

Claire felt a pang of embarrassment. She'd done what she could with everything inside. Swept, re-stuffed the cushions, and pinned the holes shut. Even taught herself how to hand wash her sheets and line dried them.

She'd been so proud of what she'd accomplished, but how insignificant it must look to Gerty.

"I hope to get it nicer." She squeezed her hands together.

"It looks much better than it did," Gerty said, and Claire let out a breath. "Sven built a solid home here. Roof's in need of repair, but should last one more winter." Gerty smiled, looking around again. "I told Gunner all this place needed was someone to love it."

He whined when he heard his name, and Gerty patted him. "I know, old boy. I'm sorry we don't get out here as much, but you know how I get in the colder months."

"Does he like it here?"

"It was his home. He was born from Sven's last litter and still sees this place as his."

Claire stopped herself from exclaiming how that explained why he used her home and food as his own and smiled when an idea hit her. A way to say thank you for her help. "If you'd like, I'd be happy to bring him here sometime."

"I wouldn't want you to go through any trouble."

"A wise woman once told me that one can't survive here without help from their neighbors."

Gerty laughed and pointed a wagging finger. "Making me eat my words."

She smiled. "When's a good time?"

"Well, I ain't got much goin' on, so just stop by anytime you feel like it."

"Thank you for the fire."

"Anytime. Though, what's left of that cord of wood won't last long. Just talk to Danny Larsson at Flygande. He'll set you up with regular deliveries."

"Daniel?" Heat crept up her neck. "I-I couldn't ask him."

"Of course you could. His cousin owns the local sawmill and lumber yard, and he buys all the scraps that don't go for building materials for his bar fireplace. He sells it at cost for those who don't have oil heat, like this place. He'll be happy to help."

"I'm sure he would, but . . . " She chewed on her bottom lip.

Gerty watched her for a long moment and slowly smiled. "Good-lookin' man, isn't he?"

Yes. Yes, he was. To her, one of the best-looking men she'd ever seen. Pure, unforced masculinity seeped off every inch of him, and as hard as she tried, she couldn't erase the image of his beautifully sculpted, tattooed body sprawled on the floor.

Gerty cleared her throat.

"I'm sorry, what?" She touched her heated cheeks. "Oh, I wouldn't know if he's good-looking. I mean, yes, he is, but I-I wasn't looking."

Gerty smiled wider. "You can't freeze to death just to avoid him."

Claire stuttered a few times and fell silent. That had been her exact plan when she'd been told how she needed to see him again. Even weighed the option of telling her that she had to avoid him if she was ever going to forget the image she'd just re-pictured in her mind.

"You know where I'm at if you need me." Gerty gently squeezed her arm.

Claire huffed as she waved goodbye. She was out of excuses. At least this visit with him wouldn't seem desperate and needy. Firewood could be a business transaction, nothing more, nothing less.

Wanting to see his heart-stopping, tropical ocean eyes looking at her again had absolutely nothing to do with it.

9

Let the Beatles Work Their Magic

SATURDAY MORNING ARRIVED AFTER another restless night for Danny. Being back in his own bed helped only enough to fall asleep. It did nothing to stop his body's unconscious need to reach out in the middle of the night to cup the curve of Jessica's hip the way he'd always done. When his hand fell through empty space and grasped a cold sheet, he jolted awake.

One month. She couldn't even give him one month of being faithful.

His anger sprang thick enough to chew, but this time not at her. At himself for his naïve belief that she'd change for him.

He sat with his legs over the side of the mattress, holding his head. With nothing to distract himself, the early mornings were always the hardest. Nights of fitful sleep, startling awake, remembering everything Jessica said and did . . . he was so tired of this damn cycle.

His stomach soured and he rubbed over it. If this didn't stop, he'd end up with an ulcer.

The soft orange glow of his digital clock caught his periphery, reminding him he'd set an alarm the night before. With a grumble, he reached out and flipped it off.

Six a.m.

He stared at the numbers. Was this some kind of sick joke? Almost every morning this week, he woke up before his alarm to see those same numbers.

Once—only once did Claire disrupt his life at this time a week ago, and he couldn't stop associating it with her.

He scrubbed a hand over his face. "Not today."

He wouldn't think about her today—except he already had. Or rather, the frustrating fact that several times this week he'd almost asked a local if they'd seen her or knew where she was staying. That's a nightmare scenario he didn't need right now. Him, recently divorced—the town gossips cooking up a non-existent love affair.

Outside, his gate creaked, and he sprang up, throwing back the curtains. The hint of morning barely colored the horizon, making it hard to see clearly, but he knew someone had come in. Was it her? The overhang below his window blocked his view of the door, so he shoved his legs into sweatpants and crawled inside a shirt.

Making a quick stop in the bathroom, he splashed water over his beastly hair, but didn't bother to tie it back.

The stairs complained under his heavy steps and tavern floorboards creaked in protest. He stopped just shy of the door and rubbed his forehead. What would he say if she were there? I'm glad you're here? Sorry I was so stupid last week? No. None of those would work because he absolutely wasn't hoping she stood on the other side.

He ran fingers through his hair and huffed a breath, settling on acting surprised. He unlocked and swung it open.

He didn't need to act.

A couple of barely teen boys screeched and ran, stumbling through the gate without falling.

Dammit. Not Claire, and he fell embarrassingly short of the goal of getting them to pee themselves. That Viking scare would go down in Solsken history as one of his weakest ones on record.

"And stay out," he yelled, but the damage was done. He'd have to work hard to keep his reputation intact. If he cared about that right now.

He shut the door and plunked his head against it. Maybe she'd already left Solsken. Actually, with his luck, he was sure of it.

It shouldn't bother him that a woman he hardly knew would only remember him as the hungover guy that slept half-naked on the floor of his tavern, then ran away from her. But it did.

Maybe if he hadn't introduced himself as a jerk and then slept on her for eight hours, he might not care so much.

Her shoulder. He had to stop remembering how well he slept on her shoulder.

As he simmered tea leaves for Royal Milk Tea and added the milk and sugar in a dazed stupor, he remembered something. Claire was famous. According to Chris, the bartender, so famous he should've known all about her.

He shouldn't. Should he? He sipped tea, staring at his phone on the kitchen table. Searching for her on the internet wouldn't necessarily make him a creep, would it? Not if he only did it to find a way to get a message to an agent or something, explaining the misunderstanding. Then maybe he could forget it—forget her—and move on with getting his crappy life back in order.

He snatched the phone before his brain fully woke and talked him out of it.

What started as a simple search, hours later, had him down yet another rabbit hole. There was no writer named Madelynn Johnson. Nor was there a Claire Johnson. There was, however a Madelynn Claire Cooke-Johnson, but no books written under that name.

"Well, shit." Cooke wasn't just any family name. No, of course not. Cooke had to be one of the wealthiest families in the US. Old money that dated back before even his family settled in Solsken.

Grumbling, he rubbed his brow and tried a different search. Written under a pen name of only her initials, he finally found her books. And he'd definitely heard of her. Not because he read any of them, but because someone he knew was literally obsessed with them. And he'd more than once made fun of them for it.

Gothic horror. Mild-mannered, quiet Claire wrote gruesome tales set in historical settings. He couldn't picture it.

Though more of a niche fan base in the US, to the rest of the world, especially the UK where most of her stories were based, she was practically worshipped. Image after image of cosplayers in strange, demented costumes of demons, ghouls, vampires, and werewolves doing live reenactments of her novels.

I'm writing the end of my career.

He thought about the answer she'd given him. If she was this successful, what could she possibly write that would end her career?

He closed the browser tab before he spent hours pointlessly searching for answers and was brought back to the main search page.

A picture of her popped up and he tilted his head. It wasn't a full image, just a thumbnail, but his eyes slid down the evening gown glued to her curves. Why the hell did she cover all of that in a bulky cloak?

He hovered a finger over the picture, debating if he should.

Most people had seen the picture, right? It's not like it was private. His finger pressed down before his good sense could stop it, and his phone filled with her.

His breath filtered out in short bursts. The cream-colored gown displayed strong hints of a long, lithe, dancer-shaped body underneath. Her hair, tied in a low side-twist, exposed the nape of a slender neck, and more than once, he zoomed in for a closer look. Especially at the back of the dress, draped low, showing smooth, touchable skin.

She was elegant and graceful and—he'd never admit it out loud—sexy as hell. That is, if he was looking. Which he wasn't. Nope.

Dammit. Yes, yes, he was.

A man stood at her side. Her husband, he figured. Tall and handsome in a pretty boy sort of way. He was clean-shaven and middle-aged. At least ten years her elder with dark, peppered hair and a lean, muscular physique.

Danny decided almost immediately that he didn't like him,

but couldn't come up with a good reason why. The man had died, after all. Why should he be bothered by him?

At first, he thought it was the cocky smile he wore while she held her face in a humble half-downturn. Or maybe it was the possessive way he gripped her side or the way the article said, **Dr. Brandon Johnson was seen out with his wife tonight for the premier**, like she was a nobody beside him. Not even worth naming.

Who the hell was this guy anyway?

After a little more digging, he found that Brandon hadn't come from much, but quickly rose to fame by his association with the Cooke family, making him sought out by the rich and famous.

"Well, isn't that convenient."

Without realizing, Danny started comparing himself to the man and quickly came to the conclusion they were nothing alike in appearance. Where Brandon was sleek and wore fine suits, Danny had his tattoos and beard, spending most of his days in jeans and a t-shirt.

His mood soured. If Claire had a type, Danny wasn't it.

"It doesn't matter anyway." He sighed but allowed himself one more close look at her face. Probably the last time he'd see it.

Her bright-red lips were held in her practiced smile, not her real one, and he wondered if that was because of her husband or the cameras.

Shutting off his phone, he sent it sliding across the dining table. This had to stop. He'd known her for only a week. What right did he have to judge her smiles?

Dragging a hand over his face, he eyed his living space. Between more grumbles and sips of tea, dust and dirt he hadn't seen before now clung to the bottom of a dust rag.

EMELIE STILL GAVE DANNY lip for the hell of it, but she never came late for work again. Especially when he explained that he needed her to help train a McClellan newbie.

Though the McClellan and Larsson rivalry was legendary on the island, Flygande Norseman had always been the unofficial Larsson-McClellan neutral zone.

Any McClellan that wanted to be in the whisky business was required to work at Flygande and learn about the customers they made whisky for. Every Larsson had to work there for one season during the busy summer months, regardless. This gave them a taste of hard work and a good lesson in their family history.

At thirty minutes to eleven, Danny opened the front door to retrieve the local paper, and a body toppled over his feet. A feminine body, hidden underneath a black cloak and hat, with wide sunglasses peering up at him upside down.

"Claire?"

"Good morning, Daniel." She lay across his boots. "Your note wasn't clear on what time I should come. But I figured it should be after sunrise this time." She smiled — her *real* smile.

"Note?" He peered around. "How long have you been out here?"

"Umm . . . " She patted herself down, looking for her phone, and he unknowingly stayed focused on the shape of her mouth wrong-side-up. Specifically, how her bottom lip was fuller than her top.

Emelie smacked his arm, jolting him. "Who's this and why is she lying at your feet?"

Apparently, the view of her mouth made his brain freeze because the dummy who'd lost his damn mind forgot to help her up. "Uh, this is Claire."

Claire waved and Danny clamped around her moving hand, swinging her up. She yelped and swayed to catch her balance.

"Sorry." He snatched her waist, steadying her as his pulse thundered inside his eardrums.

She was here, not gone. Right here in front of him, still smiling. She glanced down at his hands firmly glued to her sides, and his fingers sprang open and dropped.

"Claire?" Emelie gaped down over her. "Oh my gosh, it's so

nice to meet you."

Danny darted a cockeyed look at her. He'd never heard his cousin squeal like that before. "You know her?"

"You look cold." She ignored him and shoved him out of the way to drag Claire in. "I'm Emelie Larsson."

"Larsson?" Claire slowly removed her glasses. "As in, Daniel's wife?"

Danny went still, and Emelie barked a laugh. "Hell, no. Cousin."

"Oh, I see." Claire's smile returned as she followed Emelie into the dining room.

Daniel remained frozen, arguing with himself. He had to be wrong. There was no way it was anger that had flashed in Claire's eyes.

"I was beginning to think you weren't real." Emelie hooked her arm through Claire's and walked her to the lit fireplace.

"Not real? What do you mean?"

"Ian had . . ." She clamped her lips closed and plastered another smile. "Never mind, sit, sit." She motioned to a chair. "Danny and I will get you something warm to drink, maybe a full *fika*?"

Claire turned and looked only at him. "I'd like that."

It wasn't until she said those words that he released his first breath since seeing her.

"Come, hubby." Emelie grabbed him, still chuckling, as they made their way to the kitchen.

"The new McClellan kid, Finlay, or is it Fin? Anyway, he needs to learn the back kitchen." Danny pushed through the swinging kitchen door. "I caught him circling like a lost puppy."

"Finney?" She propped a hand on her hip. "Finney is who you're going to talk to me about?"

"Yes?" Danny said slowly.

"You're unbelievable. How do you know her?"

"Who, Claire?"

"Oh my God, you're going to pretend like a gorgeous woman wasn't lying on your feet a minute ago?"

"I didn't ask her to. She fell on them."

She quirked a brow. "Right, and that's why you couldn't stop staring at her."

"Staring? I wasn't staring."

"It's okay, you know." Emelie's voice softened as she touched his forearm. "You don't owe Jess anything."

He held up a warning finger. "Just like I told Ian, I'm not doing this with you, or-or with anybody."

"Doing what?"

"You playing dumb won't work either. There's nothing going on with me and Claire."

"Okay." She nodded. "Well, tell that to your face next time."

"What's wrong with my face?" He touched it.

She slowly smiled. "Nothing, except it was *very* happy to see her."

He turned his back and rolled his eyes. Was he that obvious? "It was surprise you saw not happiness." She snorted and he ignored her, pulling down two teapots. "Grab some *kanelbullar*, would you?" He pointed to the warming tray of fresh cinnamon rolls brought in from the local Swedish bakery.

Using metal tongs, she placed two on a plate. "So, you told her what Jess did to you?"

The pot clanked on the tray and he steadied it, taking a deep breath. "'Course not, why?"

He wasn't really lying. He never mentioned specifically that it was Jess that did those things to him.

"She seemed pretty pissed when she thought I was your wife."

"You misunderstood."

Damn, even Em saw it? His hands shook as he sliced *limpa* bread and cut a triangle of farmer's cheese from a wheel, placing a cheese-slicer to the side of it. He could feel her watching him, and it wasn't helping. "Hand me some *kladdkaka* and go make sure Fin isn't lost."

"Sure thing, hubby."

He remembered something and turned around. "Em?" She held the door half open, and he motioned for her to come back in. "Do you know anything about a note?"

"Uh . . . no." She rushed for the door again.

He stepped in front of her. "Did you send her a note?"

"'Course not."

"What did Ian tell you about her?"

"Nothing." She pushed to get past him and he blocked her way. She crossed her arms. "This is harassment."

"Sue me." He dipped his head. "What note was Claire talking about?"

"How should I know?" she said louder. So loud he was afraid Claire might hear.

He whispered, "You better not have done what I think you did."

"Me? I did nothing." She held up her right hand. "Scout's honor."

"You hate the scouts. You can't use their honor."

She grinned, ducked under his arm across the door, and slipped out.

He yanked out his phone and shot Ian a text. DID YOU SEND CLAIRE A NOTE?

SORRY, CAN'T TALK. BUSY. Danny could feel his grin through the phone, and it was confirmed when the next text popped up. YOU'RE WELCOME.

Danny cursed him under his breath and spent extra time preparing the tray for *fika*. Small plates and spoons with brightly colored Dala horse napkins. His family wasn't from the Dalarna province, but tourists loved the symbolic wooden horses.

He made sure everything was carefully placed. With the knowledge of some note and everything else wrong and embarrassing he'd done in front of Claire, he needed to show that he wasn't a complete moron.

The tray organized to his liking, he straightened his back and headed out to the main dining room. Before reaching the corner that led to the giant fireplace, he stopped to take a breath. His palms sweated and his eardrums slammed with his pulse. He couldn't remember ever being this nervous. Why was he so damn nervous?

Forcing himself forward, he came around the corner, half

expecting to see her chair empty. Instead, his eyes fell on her gentle, yet scrunched face bent over and focused on a journal. He kept watching as she stopped writing, sat up straight, and pressed the eraser end into her bottom lip—the full, plump lip he was staring at again.

The thundering in his ears grew louder, and he closed his eyes, ordering his heart rate to calm the hell down. Plastering a neutral face, he took the last steps toward her. "I wasn't sure if you liked Royal Milk Tea, so I made a pot of regular too."

She jumped with a squeak and clutched her chest. "I didn't see you coming."

"Sorry." He stood in place, awkward, teetering the tray.

"What was it you said?"

"Royal Milk Tea. I wasn't sure if you liked it."

"I've never heard of it."

He forced himself forward again. "It originated in Japan and was one of Lennon's favorites. My mom is a huge Beatles fan. So, she taught herself how to make it."

Claire blinked but didn't respond.

Heat crept up his neck and reddened his ears. She stared at him as if he sprouted an extra head.

"Uh . . . here." He plopped down the tray. "Eat and drink whatever you want." He spun on his heel, rubbing his forehead. How did he mess that up so badly?

"Daniel?"

He stopped but didn't turn back around.

"I'm not sure what any of what you said means, but would you like to join me? I need to ask you something."

His mind bypassed the needing to ask him something, and he peered over his shoulder. "Which part don't you understand?"

"Lennon? Beetles? Is your mom an entomologist?"

"You've never heard of the band, the Beatles?"

"Oh, they play music?"

He nodded slowly. "They did, yeah."

"That explains it." She smiled weakly. "I lived a bit sheltered and married young. Brandon didn't care much for music." Her fingers traced the outline of a Dala horse. "I also wasn't allowed anything other than classical with a bit of baroque growing up. If you'd mentioned Mozart, Beethoven, or even Handel, I would sound less stupid."

"You don't sound stupid. I was surprised that's all."

It hadn't occurred to Danny that he still faced away, looking at her from over his shoulder. But he was pretty sure this was a legit reason to put Brandon on his *really* don't like list. How do you not like music?

"Well, I'm ignorant at least," she said. "Texting and email are as much technology as I use. Like you don't watch television, I don't use computers or the internet. So, if they're famous, I still wouldn't know about them."

From everything he saw about her on the internet, he could understand why she'd never want to be on there.

Crap. He'd internet stalked her this morning.

"But," she continued, smoothing out the napkin, "I'd like to learn about the Beatles if you want to tell me." She motioned to the space across from her. "I can't drink and eat all of this myself, and I'd hate for it to go to waste."

A loud clang echoed, stealing her attention, and she watched Fin lifting a chair he'd dropped.

"Unless this is a bad time for you."

"It's not a bad time for him." Emelie appeared out of nowhere and twisted Danny around in the right direction, giving him a little shove. "I'll even get some Beatles playing over the speakers so you can hear them for yourself. Lennon was a *god*. Don't even get me started on McCartney." She fanned herself.

Unable to glare at Emelie for both eavesdropping and being obvious, Danny was out of excuses and made his way to the table. He moved a chair across from her and lowered down, looking anywhere but her face. He'd spent all morning creeping on her life and couldn't shake how awkward he felt about that. Like he'd intruded on her without her permission.

"Can you tell me what all these beautiful treats are?"

Swedish baked goods were something easy to talk about and he pointed to each one, naming them. The more he talked, the more she smiled, and he began to relax. The same kind of relaxed he'd been on the plane with her.

She oohed and aahed, and a bit of family pride swelled up in telling her about their origins and what made them delicious. Before he knew it, he smiled right along with her.

Dual English singing voices pierced the air with, "I Want to Hold Your Hand," and Danny's face blanched.

He was going to kill Emelie.

"Oh. This is catchy." Claire tapped her toe, missing Danny's reaction. "Would this be classified as rock and roll?"

"Can you excuse me for a moment?" He tore out of his chair.

Before he made it to the office where the stereo was located, Emelie switched it to "Paperback Writer" and came barreling out, grinning.

"Claire, it's your song."

He didn't have time to ask how she knew Claire was a writer and glared as she whooshed past him. At the sound of a squeal, he turned to see Emelie pulling Claire up by both hands. They started dancing what looked like the Mashed Potato, laughing.

The corner of Danny's mouth tugged.

Emelie never liked Jessica and that, like many other things, had been a topic of tension between them. With how close he and Em were, he hated that they didn't get along. Now he understood why. She'd seen straight through to who Jess really was, long before he did. His stomach coiled in a knot.

"Join us, Daniel." Claire squealed as Emelie spun her around.

"Nah, I'll just watch."

Emelie fake pouted and Claire said, "You're missing out."

He disagreed. Especially when she removed her cloak, and he finally caught an eyeful of Claire. Still in all black, his gaze trailed down over hip-hugging slacks to their flared bottoms, back up to a cropped sweater short enough to expose the tight lines of her stomach.

He didn't know which vintage year she was wearing, '60s or '70s. He only knew it looked good, really damn good, on her.

Shit. He half-turned and stared up at the beams. Ugly beams. He would think of ugly but clean beams and how sore he'd been from scrubbing them. Not Claire — her accentuated curves in tight pants and cropped shirt — no, not Claire.

Beams.

He rubbed his forehead and cursed under his breath. He should probably put something more exciting on the ceiling if this kept up. Or worse yet, if he didn't get this adolescent rebirth under control, his cousin might notice, and he'd never live it down.

"Oh, come on, you can still dance." Emelie's voice did the trick, and he rolled his shoulders before lowering his eyes. To his great disappointment, Claire seated herself and pulled the cloak over her shoulders, swallowing herself inside.

Damn. Damn. Damn.

"Are you leaving?" he asked.

"No, not yet." She sipped the Royal Milk Tea, and he waited for a reaction.

Nothing came. Maybe she hated the tea?

"What's going on?" he whispered to Emelie, who walked up to him, shaking her head. He hoped she had the secret woman code for whatever switched Claire's whole demeanor. She sat rigid in her seat, stirring the liquid in her cup.

"I think she thought she embarrassed you."

"What? No, it wasn't that, I was —" He stopped himself too late. A light sparked in her eyes and a slow smirk wormed up her cheek. He rolled his eyes. Dammit, she knew.

"Maybe you should tell her that then."

"I can't tell her *that.*"

She snickered. "No, definitely not *that,* but you better tell her something to keep her here. I like her."

He blinked. She already liked Claire and they'd just met. Maybe he wasn't irrational with how quickly he felt the same way.

Emelie elbowed him. "Go, now. Fix."

His recent track record proved he couldn't fix anything, but he rubbed the back of his neck and forced a deep breath before striding over to the table as gracefully as his thick legs allowed. "Are you enjoying yourself?"

"Yes, quite." She continued to stir her tea with a stiff posture, not making eye contact.

"Do you like it?" He pointed to her cup, desperate to figure out what had changed so quickly in her. She was a completely different person.

She forced her unreal smile. "I love it, thank you."

He gripped his frustration on the edge of the table and leaned forward. "And what are your thoughts on the Beatles?"

"I think they're . . ." She froze mid-stir, and her tea-colored eyes slowly traveled from the cup to his hands still cuffed along the edge of the table. Inch by inch, her eyes drifted up the sinews of his left forearm to the cut of his flexed biceps and stopped at base of his tattooed dragon tail.

Her lips parted.

Heat burst from his belly and spread out to every limb and — *not again.* He dropped into his chair and creaked the legs across the floor, shoving his lower half under the table.

She shook herself out of her zoning and stared wide-eyed into the fireplace. Rose-colored splotches bloomed on her cheeks.

He absolutely was not going to let himself read too much into whatever her thick, heated gaze meant. Or address his sudden lack of bodily control. He would, however, let honest and blunt Danny out to play.

"Did you think I was embarrassed by your dancing?"

She stiffened and darted a quick glance toward him. "You wouldn't be the first."

His jaw ticked. Who was the first? He sure as hell hoped it wasn't Brandon. "I grew up around Ian, who insisted on learning traditional Scottish jigs. There is nothing you could do to embarrass me. Besides, you said you were having fun."

"Yes, I did. But maybe a bit too much."

"No such thing."

Her posture softened, and a smile formed on her mouth. "I've always felt that way, but . . . " She let the rest of what she thought drift away and brought the rim of the teacup up and sipped. "Royal Milk Tea is delicious. How do you make it?"

"I could tell you, but then I'd have to kill you."

She chuckled, and he smiled, fully relaxing again. He liked making her laugh. "It's really easy. You make it on the stove. I'll write down the recipe."

"The stove?"

He took in the note of panic in her voice and slowly said, "Or I could just show you sometime. If you want."

"You'd do that?"

"Of course—"

The front door gusted open, and Merv came in, followed by George. Danny waved to them and smiled at their predictability.

They lived on two different sides of the island yet showed up at the same time. Always played chess. Always bickered at each other, but never stopped hanging out.

George stumbled to a stop when he saw Claire. "Mother?"

Merv snickered and smacked his back. "She ain't your mom, George. I've been telling you for years you need a new prescription for those glasses."

"Hello." Claire waved. "Thank you for helping me find this place the other morning."

"S-Sure thing, ma'am."

Danny sat, stunned. In all the years he'd known George, never had the retired veteran turned that shade of red or stuttered. He watched in increasing amusement as George shrugged off his friend's taunting back slap and mumbled, "*fika*," to Emelie.

"What does that say?" Claire brought back Danny's attention and pointed over his head.

"The words above the bar? *Välkommen Familj* – Welcome, Family."

Her breath hitched and her eyes glistened. What did he say wrong?

"Are you alright?"

She swiped quickly under her eyes and cleared her throat. "Yes. I'm fine. I like that."

He looked over his shoulder again. What about the sign made her tear up? "It's old. Probably need to replace it."

"Don't you dare."

He whipped back to find her smile returned. "This place has a great atmosphere, Daniel. Don't change a thing." She held up her journal and flipped through the pages. "You have no idea how important it is for a writer to find the right kind of atmosphere to write in. I haven't gotten this many words down in one sitting for ages. My muse likes it here."

"Well, your muse is welcome anytime. You could tag along, too, I guess."

She laughed in her cup, and tan-colored bubbles popped up.

He grinned, hoping to keep finding ways to make her laugh, and took a long, satisfied drink from his mug. "Didn't you say you needed to ask me something?"

"Oh, yes." She placed her cup down and unbuttoned her cloak. Peeling it off her shoulders, she twisted to hang it over the back of her chair, having no idea she made someone's day.

The lifting of her arms lifted the hem of her sweater and Danny tilted his head, watching the lines around her navel shift and flex. She turned back around, and he plastered his eyes to hers, commanding them not to drop and keep exploring.

"I needed to ask if I could have your wood."

Danny choked and coughed, delicious tea making a raw reentry through his nose. "Excuse me?"

"Wood? Gertrude said I needed to see you if I wanted to buy some for my cottage."

"Oh, firewood." What was he, fifteen again? How the hell did his mind drop in the gutter so fast? If there was one thing he prided himself on, it was his control over himself. Since meeting this woman, he seemed to have lost it all. "Of course." He wiped droplets from his shirt, silently cursing himself. Mustering up one last drop of dignity, he casually pulled out his phone. "Where are you staying? I can get some out to you this afternoon."

"Oh, you'd bring it?"

"I usually deliver it. Is that a problem?"

"Well . . . " Her eyes darted around and settled on Fin, who made another loud bang when he dropped a tray he tried to balance.

Emelie stood in front of him, tapping her foot. "Get it together, Finney."

"It's Finlay," he mumbled.

"I'm sure you're going to be busy here," Claire said. "I can arrange for someone else to bring it. I'll pay extra for any inconvenience."

Danny dropped his eyes and swallowed. "No need. First cord is on the house. If you really prefer I not deliver it, you can give Fin over there your address, and I'll have him deliver it instead." He glanced back up, hoping he was wrong, but her face washed with relief.

"Oh, could you? Yes, I'd much prefer that. Thank you, Daniel."

He shoved up and ran a hand through his hair before jamming it into his pocket. "Sure. Yeah. No problem." He couldn't look at her. "I should probably get back to work. Things get a little crazy on Saturdays. So, um . . . bye, Claire." He hurried around the corner.

Instead of going to the kitchen where he knew he'd be met by Emelie's grinning face and million questions, he ran up the stairs to his apartment. Closing the door, he smacked the back of his head against it.

It felt worse. Her words stung so much worse than they should, and it was nobody's fault but his own.

He banged his head again and covered his face, sliding to the floor with a loud groan.

Just Friends?

IAN ARRIVED FOR HIS weekend visit an hour after Flygande opened. He entered through the heavy door and blinked hard, adjusting to the dim light.

"Are you sure?" said a familiar young man's voice, and he spotted his cousin, Fin, talking to none other than Claire. "You don't want to just give me your address? Danny said I needed to make sure it was stored properly on your property."

"Yes, I'm sure." She smiled, pointing out a small road on his phone map. "Here, under the lean-to, is fine, thank you."

Fin shrugged and turned, nearly running Ian over. "Hey, man. What's up?"

"The sky, the clouds, this roof."

"That joke was never funny, even from Grandad."

Ian smirked and shooed him off with a jerk of his head. "Do a good job. Make the McClellans proud."

"I wouldn't dream of disgracing our name with a firewood delivery."

"Wiseass." Ian smacked the back of his head and smiled down at Claire. "You had *fika* at last, I see."

"There's still some left if you're hungry."

"Always." He turned a chair, straddling it backward, and took a spoonful of *kladdkaker*. "Mmff-avorite."

"I don't speak chocolate cake." She grinned and tucked her journal away.

Ian used his tongue to dislodge the moist crumbles from the roof of his mouth. "You leaving? I just got here."

"Afraid so." She glanced around as more bodies started piling through the door. "I'm not so great with people. Or rather, some people are not so great with me."

"Nonsense. You're amazing. Who cares what anyone else thinks?"

She dropped her chin, hiding a small smile. "Thank you for that, but I meant if they know who I am, they may cause a riot in here."

Ian shoved the buttery cheese into his mouth. "Now I'm intrigued. Do tell."

She paused and gave him a thoughtful look. "You know what? I don't think I will. I'm kind of liking this not-being-known thing."

Ian smiled and pointed to an uneaten cinnamon roll. She nodded.

"You shouldn't get used to being unknown," he said. "Most people live here because they value their privacy, but that doesn't mean they won't be curious about someone who's hanging around for a while." He lifted an eyebrow, wondering if she caught his non-question, question. She didn't answer so he asked outright. "Are you staying for a while?"

"Three months. At least."

"Then it's best to nip their curiosity in the bud. Do you have plans for tonight?"

"Oh, um." Her lips vibrated as she blew out. "Not really. Why?"

"You should come back. Not to write, but to have fun and meet some locals. I promise they're worth meeting and won't mob you."

She looked around again. "I-I don't know about that."

He reached out and patted her hand. "No pressure. Just giving you an open invite to meet some of my favorite people if you want. Maybe they'll even inspire whatever you're writing."

"You do make a tempting case, Mr. McClellan."

"I am hard to resist." He grinned. "So that's a yes?"

"How about we'll see."

"I'll take it."

She closed her clutch with a snap and that's when Ian noticed the double cups, double plates, double pastries, double everything.

"Did Danny have *fika* with you?"

She smiled with a nod and waved as she went for the door. He couldn't help but wonder if the extra color on her cheeks was because of the fire or Danny. Stuffing the cinnamon roll between his teeth, he gathered the tray to take to the kitchen.

"Where's Danny?" he asked Kevin.

He shrugged. "Last I saw, he was talking to some hot chick."

Ian set down the tray with a clang. "You can call her a woman. You can even call her a beautiful woman. Never hot chick. Don't let me hear you say such a dumbass thing again."

"You got it, boss." He saluted with a mocking smirk. He was seventeen, so that was a wasted conversation.

Ian whistled a cheery tune and made his way to the bar, checking glasses and liquor stock. He peeked into Danny's empty office and headed down to the cellar where the kegs were stored. Still no Danny.

He hopped two steps at a time to Danny's apartment and knocked. No answer came, so he opened the door. "Oi, Danny?"

"Living room."

Through the French doors of the living room, Ian spotted him, book in hand. He'd hoped to see him smiling.

Danny wasn't smiling.

"You're never up here after you open," Ian said.

"I was checking something." Danny put the book away. The dictionary, to be exact. He was reading the dictionary?

"Saw Claire and I—"

"Look, I don't want to talk about it, alright?"

Ian's eyebrows shot up. "I was only going to say I saw her. But now it looks like we're going to talk about it."

Danny shook his head and walked to the wall-lined bookshelves, mindlessly scanning the old spines. He pulled out a thesaurus.

Ian rubbed his forehead with a sigh. "What happened?"

"Nothing." He shoved the book back into place. "Let it go."

Like hell he would. "My cousin is getting ready to deliver firewood. I thought you did that."

He swung toward him. "She didn't want me near her house, alright? *Me*." He jammed a finger into his chest. "Anybody but me."

"That's not true."

Danny held up both hands. "Ian, don't give me anymore bullshit. I'm sick to death of bullshit messing with my goddamn head."

"Danny?"

"*What*?"

"Finlay isn't taking it to her house."

"What do you mean?" His eyes bulged. "I specifically told him—"

Ian held up a finger and Danny stopped. "He knows and told her that, but she didn't want him to bring it to her house. Asked him to drop it off in some area—" He paused, thinking about the familiarity of the location he saw but wasn't close enough to see the name of the road.

"Well?"

He shook the thought away. "To leave it under a shelter off a road, not her house. She asked Gene to do the same thing when he delivered groceries. It's not just you, *bràthair*."

Danny's shoulders drooped with a heavy exhale. "I don't understand. Why wouldn't she want anyone at her house? She's renting."

"She seems to be a pretty private person. Told me if people knew who she was, she'd be mobbed."

Danny plopped on the couch with a long sigh. "Well, I can think of one person who'd mob her if he knew who she was."

Ian joined him on the other end of the couch and stretched his legs on the coffee table. "Who's that?"

"You."

"Me?" Ian laughed. "I know her and I'm not freaking out."

"What's your favorite novel?"

"*Ghost Crossing*. You know that. Takes place a few miles from where my ancestors are from."

"By M. C. C., right?"

"Yep." He entwined his fingers behind his head, unsure of why Danny brought that up. "The man is a horror-writing genius."

A slow smirk rode up Danny's cheek. "Did you ever look up a picture of *him*?"

"Are you kidding? I'm part of his fan club. The true fan club that took a vow to never dig into his identity."

Danny snickered and Ian glared. "Laugh all you want, but after signing our 'vow,' we get exclusives and sneak peeks for his upcoming work. He's got a new one coming out next year. Untitled, but we're going to get a chance to vote on it. Plus, we're the first to know when he makes a rare appearance at a comic-con so we're the first to get tickets. Obviously, he never attends in person, but he does an over-the-phone live Q&A with his fans using this crazy-ass voice distorter."

Danny grinned wider and Ian got nervous.

"I'm sure if you looked him up, you'd get a hell of a surprise."

Ian dropped his feet with a thud. "What does any of this have to do with Claire?"

"Madelynn Claire," Danny reminded him. "From the old-money family of Cooke."

Ian's mind blanked for a solid minute as he gulped air like a guppy. "Sweet mother of God," he breathed out. "Are you shitting me? Don't shit me, Danny. He's a she?" His voice rose an octave. "And *she* was sitting across from me a minute ago?" He couldn't feel his face. His palms squished his cheeks so hard he had fish-lips. "*Danny?*"

Danny leaned forward, shoulders shaking. "My God, man, you should see your face."

Ian continued to freak out in girl-pitch-level shrieks, and Danny fell to the side of the couch, rumbling with laughter.

"I can't—" Ian jumped up and paced, still holding his face. "How can she . . . wait . . . does she know who I am? No. How could she know. Oh, sweet Jesus. He's a she and she's here. *In Solsken."*

Danny wiped his eyes and tried to sit up, but fell back down when Ian shrieked again.

"I've always wanted to meet him . . . er her." Ian managed to lower his voice half an octave but continued to pace. "That last Q&A I went to was the longest conversation I've ever had with her. D-Do you think . . ." He stopped short and faced Danny. "Do you think I'll sound stupid if I tell her how her first novel saved me?"

Danny managed some composure and sat up. "I think she'd love it. Just don't scream again."

"You're right." Ian wheezed one more deep breath and finally regained some control. "Freaking M.C.C. I wonder if that's why she hesitated when I asked her out tonight."

Danny's laughter abruptly stopped. "You asked her out?"

Ian gave him his best *are you kidding me?* face, but inside he was smiling. The little green monster was a good sign. He pointed to his own chest. "Priest, remember? I asked her out here tonight for a chance to get to know the residents. You know, before they start getting curious about the new person who's hanging out in Solsken for three months."

"Three months," Danny repeated, staring straight ahead. "She's staying for three months?"

"Yes, at least. Plenty of time for more *fikas."*

"Don't start."

"Danny." Ian sat back down. "You literally grabbed the first book you saw when I came up here and it was a dictionary. Just to avoid talking about her."

He opened his mouth and closed it — opened — closed. He had nothing and rubbed the back of his neck. "What's wrong with me?"

"Nothing. She's gorgeous."

"I don't need a rebound."

"That's what you think this is?"

He looked him in the eye. "What else could it be? It's too soon."

"Did Claire hit on you?"

"*No.*"

"Did you hit on her?"

"Ian," he said with warning.

"Point is, if one or both of you was trying to rush into a relationship, I'd agree with you, but you, and it seems she, are trying to avoid one. Which can only mean one thing."

Danny stared, waiting.

"You both like each other for real. Not a rebound."

He blinked. Blinked again, and again, then turned away. "But I can't do another relationship right now."

"Who said anything about a relationship? At least not a romantic one. I've already told you, I'm not pushing you. But it kind of seems you guys like hanging out together. What's the harm in being friends?"

"Friends?"

"Yes, friends. She's not pressing for more and you're not pressing for more." Ian shrugged. "So, friends."

"But—" Danny rubbed his brow and side-glanced at him like he wanted to argue something.

"There's no 'but,' just friends. Unless that makes you uncomfortable."

Danny shook his head and picked at a piece of dirt on the edge of the coffee table. "I think I can do friends."

II

To Stay or Not to Stay

SHE WAS BEING RIDICULOUS. Claire's feet followed a figure-eight trail from kitchen to living room, back to kitchen as she argued with herself.

Of course she should stay home. Stick to her plans of avoiding crowds and establishing her independence.

But wouldn't it be rude of her to turn down a personal invitation from Ian?

Back in the living room, she sighed. She knew full well that her hesitancy had little to do with whether or not it was proper or improper to answer the invite, and everything to do with a certain bearded, tattooed man.

She rubbed above one manicured brow, remembering how distracted she'd gotten by the taut cords of muscle along Danny's forearms while he'd gripped the edge of the table.

It'd been so long since she felt that tight coiling in her belly, that bloom of warmth. For years, she thought that part of her had died with her relationship with Brandon. But when her eyes had tracked the curve and cut of Danny's bicep beneath the curling tail of a dragon, a thick band of desire snapped so fast and tight, she'd been immobilized.

Then he'd noticed her gawking.

Heat sprang to her cheeks, and she picked up a paper, fanning her face. Moving to a different part of the cottage, she grabbed her journal. She should definitely stay home and work on writing or drawing Maddy.

Definitely.

She looked down at what she'd doodled. It wasn't a little girl staring at her, but a bearded man's face—smiling.

"That's not helping." She sighed but then laughed. Tilting her head, she thought over the quandary of Danny's features.

The hard jawline and all the black ink over a powerful broad frame didn't match the gentleness in his deep voice. And when he smiled? Two deep creases on either side of his mouth erased his hard edge. Like turning on the sun on a cloudy day.

His eyes puzzled her the most. So bright and clear and open. When they locked on to her, everything dormant inside of her burst to life.

Kind of like it was doing now. She gripped her fluttering stomach and fanned herself again. "Maybe I should go just for a little while," she said out loud. "But all those people." Her entire life, her family's name put her unwillingly in the public's eye. She hadn't lied when she told Ian she enjoyed not being known this week.

The only way she'd kept some mystery around her through the years was the reader fan club she started that vowed not to dig into her true identity.

Smiling to herself, she remembered the last Q&A she'd had with them. One eager fan delved so deep into her novel, he'd discovered all the details she'd hidden in it. She loved giving her fans small pieces of the real her. Even if it was in secret, it was a truer connection to people than she had in real life.

She sighed again. Maybe it was finally time to connect with people in person.

Her phone buzzed with a text from Greyson. WHEN ARE YOU LEAVING THAT ISLAND?

It wasn't the question that bothered her, it was the fact that he asked. Like she hadn't told him how long she'd be here.

She should've expected it. It'd been a year of him barely responding to texts, making her fear that he deleted the messages without reading. All because of *him*—the man she thought she was done being afraid of, but who had somehow started haunting her dreams again.

Saliva grew thick on her tongue and her fingers massaged the cold wrapping itself around the scar on her wrist.

"He's not here." She closed her eyes. "Breathe." With a hard swallow, she forced the emotions back down.

Picking up her phone, she typed, I'M HERE FOR A FEW MONTHS, BUT I MIGHT STAY LONGER. IT REALLY IS BEAUTIFUL HERE, AND THE PEOPLE ARE SO NICE. I'M ACTUALLY ABOUT TO MEET UP WITH SOME OF THEM. She took a deep breath before adding, I WISH YOU WERE HERE WITH ME.

He didn't answer, and the small hope she'd told herself not to have popped like the delicate bubble it was. She brushed a shaking finger over his name. It was nobody's fault but her own, though.

A gust of wind shuddered against the front door, interrupting her thoughts. It quieted as quickly as it came, and she shook herself from the unsettled feelings. She didn't know if she'd ever get used to the strange wind here.

Heading into her bedroom, she scanned through her closet of tailor-made clothing. She hummed as she laid out several outfits across the bed, each one a different style from a different decade. Her love of vintage clothing had started with reading classic literature, wanting to have a piece of those stories to live inside of.

A rumble came from outside, and she turned toward her window when it started to rattle. It stopped. With a roll of her eyes, she turned away. Taking the monumental step to go out tonight called for her favorite dress.

"Ma-adelynn . . . "

She gasped and held the dress against her half-naked body. "Who's there?" She darted her gaze around, looking over the empty space of her room. The wind vibrated her window again, but nothing more.

"Calm yourself." She rubbed her temples, taking a deep breath. "You just need protein. You haven't had any this week and you're hearing things."

Still, she hurried to pull on her dress. The wind blasted against her window again, and she squeaked, rushing into another room, closing and locking the door behind her.

The wind quieted, but her thudding heart didn't. She hadn't meant to come in here.

She hated bathrooms. At least bathrooms with bathtubs in them. And this one had a long cast-iron tub inside. It didn't matter that she froze every morning when she showered in it. She refused to close the shower curtain.

Forcing herself not to look at the tub, she finished getting dressed. She curled and pinned her hair into vintage waves, keeping her makeup simple as she normally would — light blush along her cheekbones, eyeliner, and mascara. But tonight, she decided to break out her favorite crimson lipstick.

She smacked her lips and stared at her reflection. It'd been a long time since she'd worn this color. A year, to be exact. A year of wearing black and no lipstick. Because lipstick meant fun — meant she didn't care and was moving on.

"What am I doing?" She tore off a tissue and froze with it hovering over her mouth. Was it wrong for her to want to move on? To enjoy a night of being around someone who made her skin heat and her mind go quiet?

She closed her eyes. That's really what it was. Whenever Daniel was around her, the inner critical voice stopped speaking. She forgot all about the social rules she'd been forced to memorize as a child, and that one shouldn't make bubbles in their tea when laughing. Most importantly, she forgot about being Madelynn.

One more look at her red lips and she tossed the tissue. This night would be nothing more than meeting some nice people, and the lipstick meant nothing. She pinned on her hat and glanced down at the large diamond ring attached to her diamond-studded wedding band.

She toyed with them for a few moments before twisting them off. Holding them firmly in her palm, she entered the bedroom again and gently placed the rings in her nightstand drawer.

"I know what I promised," she whispered, running her fingers over them. "But I hope you understand."

A cold wind burst into her room and swept up her hair. She gasped and clenched her eyes closed as a rattling noise came from her window again.

Whispers crept up behind her and she yelled out, whipping around.

Her window was halfway open.

She screamed and ran to it, slamming it shut. Her fingers scraped and pried as she cried out, trying to force the lock in its place. It jammed a quarter of the way in.

"Protein," she said, backing away until she reached her doorway. She spun on her heel, forgetting her cloak, and ran for the foyer.

At the door, she stopped and laid her ear against the pink monstrosity. Everything quieted outside. She eased out a breath and flipped a switch to ignite a warm glow over her head. Such a childish thing, she knew that, but it worked. As long as there was light, the monsters of her imagination stayed away.

The angry wind didn't return, and when she cracked opened the door, only the comforting sound of waves crashing a hundred feet below greeted her.

Slowly, she inched along the rotting front porch to the edge of the house and peeked around the side where her window was. Nothing but an empty landscape of grass-covered rocks and swaying branches. She exhaled, rubbing her arms.

Silly, foolish Claire. She was even more certain that whatever happened a minute ago was perfectly explainable. It had to be. The implication of it not being so was more than she could bear. That perhaps all she'd been through this past year had done more damage to her mind than she realized.

Her eyes closed on an exhale. She wouldn't dwell on that.

She didn't take her time leaving. Rushing on the balls of her feet so her heels wouldn't slow her down, she hurried until she set eyes on Flygande.

While she steadied herself, brushing off any signs of her rushed trek, the din of voices floated out to meet her on the path.

Heavy footsteps came from outside the wall and Claire went still. It was the way the feet hit the gravel road, forceful, steady ... *motivated.* She held her breath as the large form of a man stopped in the shadows outside the gate.

A flat cap covered his head, and his silhouette hid behind an upturned collar. Slowly, his head turned. She couldn't see him, but she knew he was staring directly at her.

For an endless moment, neither moved. Breathed.

He reached up and tipped his hat to her.

Her breath released, and she internally rolled her eyes at her paranoia. Just an islander out for a walk, who now probably thinks she's weird for staring. She attempted to recover her poise, and with a nod, she returned his greeting before pushing her way inside Flygande.

12

The Wind Blows in
Treasures and Ugly Sweaters

PIPE SMOKE AND CLANKING glasses sifted between the din of chatter. Saturday nights behind the bar were always insane. With Sunday being the only day Flygande closed, everyone flocked to get drinks, and Danny was grateful for the distraction.

Even if it didn't help much.

His eyes drifted to the front door again. Ever since Ian had said Claire might show up, he'd been stupidly glancing there every five seconds.

She probably wasn't even coming.

He and Ian scurried past each other, taking orders from those who sat at the bar and from Emelie and Fin.

Occasionally Ian had to calm Fin, whose periodic hyperventilating told him he may not be cut out for this kind of work in the long run.

"We should hire an extra pair of hands for the next few weekends," Ian said when Danny passed behind him with three beers wedged between his fingers.

He handed them off to waiting customers. "Because your old ass can't keep up?"

"*Old* ass — we're both thirty."

Danny smirked.

A shipping box plunked down in front of Ian.

"Truce," a man said from behind it.

Ian peeked over the top and glared at the smiling, dark-haired little man. "I'm busy, Marco. Go away."

"Macallan's eighteen years with single malt, yes?"

Those badly worded whisky specifications got Ian's attention.

"I brought this to make up for the uh," he rolled his hand, "misunderstanding."

"*Mis*understand —"

Danny rammed an elbow into Ian's ribs, and he bit his tongue.

Marco swung the same hand between them. "Yes, this is me trying to end a twelve-year *misunderstanding*."

Danny swallowed a laugh. The Italian may be short, but he had balls. Ian's veins were bulging on his neck. Danny clapped Ian on the shoulder with a hard squeeze, and he closed his eyes, taking a deep breath. "Fine."

"What was that?" Marco smiled and cupped his ear.

"Pushing it," Danny said under his breath, but Marco only grinned wider.

"I said, *fine*." Ian glared. "Truce."

"Friends then?"

"Too far."

Marco laughed and, with a wink, turned and whistled all the way out the door. Ian released a long, grumbling breath.

Danny fought a smile. "Proud of you right now."

"Don't start."

"He brought a case of whisky?"

Ian grinned, moving the box to the back counter and tore it open. His smile dropped.

Danny barked a laugh. "Holy shit, he didn't."

"Oh, I think he did."

Eleven bottles of Macallan, not twelve, filled the slots. In the twelfth place sat the same type of Chianti he'd left under the vat he'd tampered with. Attached to it was a note reading: **For the last bottle, you have to come to De Luca's for dinner sometime. Ciao!**

A barstool scraped, and Danny did a double take. Not Claire. But the way the blond leaned her bulging chest over the bar and ate Ian up with her eyes, Danny had to stifle a laugh.

Ian hissed. "That son-of-a—"

Danny bumped his arm. "I think you've got an admirer."

Half-scared, Ian slowly turned, swallowing.

"Can I get a Cosmopolitan, pretty boy?"

Danny coughed "pretty?" into his hand, and Ian's boot tip connected to his calf. Danny didn't stifle the laugh this time and started slowly backing away.

"Get your ass back here," Ian whispered out the side of his mouth.

It'd been way too long since Danny had such a golden opportunity to harass his best friend. The local women knew better than to try to flirt with a man who'd already taken a vow of celibacy.

Not mainlander women though. So he'd happily take this distraction—he needed a distraction—to take his mind off things . . . off *her*.

"A Cosmopolitan is this man's favorite drink to make," Danny said.

"Oh, really," she said with a slow smile.

Ian's head whipped toward him and didn't move, openly glaring at him while mixing and pouring her devil's brew with zero finesse. Danny's shoulders shook as Ian kept his death-stare glued to him and slid the glass across the bar with one hand, holding up a middle finger with his other beneath the bar.

The woman's hand slipped over Ian's. "Wanna have some fun later?"

His eyes went wide and the teasing died in Danny's throat. Clearly, she hadn't caught Ian's not-so-subtle hints of "not interested."

"Look, nothing personal," Danny said. "But a guy like him isn't going to be much fun for you."

Ian slid his hand from under hers, but she snatched it again.

"Oh," she said. "I highly doubt that."

"He's a priest."

"That's okay."

Dear God, this woman. "He's celibate."

She blinked.

"No sex."

Her hand sprang open, and she coughed up her drink. "What?"

Ian nodded, wiping his hand off on his pants. Not bothering to correct the fact that he wasn't a priest just yet. She stumbled off the stool like his unavailability was contagious.

"The bridge closing snow can't come fast enough," Ian said through gritted teeth as they watched her practically sprint to another table. "Thanks for nothing, dipshit." He sucker-punched Danny's arm.

"She just wanted some fun, pretty boy." Danny dodged another fist with a laugh.

"Even though you're an *ass*," Ian cleaned his drink shaker and nudged him, "it's good to hear you laugh again."

Danny had nothing to say to that.

"Can't believe there was a time we couldn't wait to work here because we wanted that to happen," Ian said.

Danny moved toward a man flagging him down for a drink. "Yeah, then Molly showed up and snatched you without even trying to seduce you." Danny winced when he noticed the falter in Ian's steps. He hadn't meant to bring her up. He'd only wanted to distract his own mind from latching on to the last time he himself bar flirted.

"Psst," Ian said, nodding toward the door.

Review Jackass from the other night strutted in, glanced at the bar, and bee-lined for a table of other young men dressed just like him. Lots and lots of polo sweaters and boat shoes.

Danny had seen it many times. Trust fund kids let off their parental leashes, wanting to have a bit of fun. All barely over legal drinking age with too much money in their pockets.

Ian let out a long sigh. "You should know, he needs to stay away from Emelie."

Danny paused mid-pour of a cocktail, eyes snapping up. "What aren't you telling me?"

Ian held up a hand. "Nothing she couldn't handle. But he was a giant prick about it, and that's why I cut him off last time. I'd be happy to throw him out again."

"Throw who out?" Emelie ducked under the bar to snatch a few of Ian's cocktail olives and a breather.

Why hadn't she told him about it? Danny didn't like the idea that people might be hiding things from him, thinking he was too delicate to handle it. He pointed an accusing finger across the room.

Her eyes snapped to the dining room before she eased into a casual shrug. "Wouldn't be worth it. He's leaving tomorrow."

"He's staying at the family inn?" Danny asked as he pulled an ale.

She scuffed the toe of her shoe. "Yep."

"Did you tell Uncle Nils about him?"

"Are you kidding? Pappa would have brought you and Johan in for a massive Viking scare."

"Aye," Ian looked at the ceiling wistfully, "that would've been grand."

Danny wasn't buying the lighter tone in her voice. Nor did he think she realized her arms slid protectively around her middle.

"Let Fin take care of his table," he said.

She uncrossed her arms. "I don't need the extra testosterone to deal with him. I can take care of myself."

"No one is questioning that." He stirred an Old Fashioned. "But he's not alone, and you should be free to do your job without worrying about harassment from a bunch of jackasses." He nodded his chin toward the tavern room. "Tell Fin I want to talk to him before he goes over there."

He let out a small breath when she didn't argue and actually looked relieved.

"What's up?" Fin came, panting and red faced. Ian handed him a water.

"See the table behind you?" Danny pointed, not caring if they saw him. "That man in the blue sweater was kicked out of here earlier for harassing Em. It's your table now."

Fin grew about three inches and suddenly wasn't winded anymore. "He messed with Emelie?"

"Simmer down." Ian snapped a finger in his face. "Ugly Polo is leaving tomorrow, and we just need you to wait on them so she doesn't have to. I know it's a bigger table than we've given you all night, but do you think you can handle them?"

He huffed and cracked his knuckles. "Hell yes, I can."

Danny smirked, and Ian gripped Fin's shoulder. "No need to do anything but take their orders for now."

"But you see any one of them try anything with her," Danny cut fingers across his throat, "they're done. Ian and I will help."

He nodded stiffly and broadened his lean yet toned twenty-year-old body as he marched over.

They watched as Jackass pointed to Emelie heading for the other side of the dining area and made cupping hands in front of his chest. His friends laughed and high-fived him.

"That better not have meant what I think it meant." Danny's voice rumbled deep in his throat, and Ian's hands curled into fists.

Danny wouldn't step in, though. Not unless he had to. Like the time that Seth prick put his hands on her.

Because he knew the reason his cousin felt the way she did about men. The way her father, but mostly her brother, treated her ever since their mother had a stroke. Like when Aunt Mathilde wasn't able to speak anymore, they lost their guiding sail and fell back to the old hard-ass Larsson ways. Ways born out of years of hardship from a cold, isolated island.

Emelie's father and brother, intentionally or not, were too hard on her, making her feel less than. And Danny would be damned before he made her feel the same way.

The table's laughter abruptly stopped when Fin appeared, legs planted wide, arms crossed, dark hair hanging over glaring, green eyes. "Something funny to you?"

Their silence was beautiful.

"I think I'll give him a raise." Danny stretched his neck until it popped and passed behind Ian to take a local's drink order.

"Don't you dare. It'll go straight to his head." Ian handed a different man a double McClellan, commenting on his good taste. "Besides—"

The door opened and Danny froze mid-pour of an ale. A head of honey hair stepped inside with bright-red lips.

It was like Claire stepped off the set of *Casablanca,* and Humphrey Bogart was about to come in behind her. A black, wide-brimmed hat dipped low over her right eye and a gray, knee-length wool dress was tailored to perfection over her hourglass form. Long, black gloves covered hands that held a small clutch against the simple front of the dress.

But then she turned, scanning the tavern room, and he blinked. The back was anything but plain. Almost like it was put on backward, the top was open to the middle of her toned back, where it met a row of wooden buttons that trailed over the curve of her backside, down to a flared hem. A pair of sheer vintage stockings snagged his eyes where a sexy black line tracked down the center of her calves. He swallowed hard.

Holy hell.

Ian cleared his throat. "I think ale tastes better in a glass than off the floor."

"What?" Danny did a double take of his hand, empty of the glass and curling around air. Said glass lay shattered on the floor by his feet, and the ale he'd been pulling splashed against the drain and over the lip of the bar. "Shit."

He released the tap and dropped behind the bar so fast the room spun.

Ian laughed, meeting him down there after replacing the man's beer, and handed him some towels.

"Did she see me?" Danny picked up pieces of glass, deciding right then that he'd stay crouched for the rest of the night. Maybe his life.

"Nah," Ian said. "Emelie found her and dragged her to the table you reserved by the fireplace."

"You reserved it."

"I'm your manager. I work on your behalf."

Danny grumbled under his breath.

"So what's the plan?" Ian said. "We hang down here until she leaves?"

"Thinking about it." Danny glanced up, then added with a small smile, "Or at least until the urge to buy a fedora leaves me."

Ian snorted and Danny smiled wider, sweeping up the rest of the glass from the floor.

"You need another minute?"

Danny nodded and dropped the mat. "Might as well check the keg levels while I'm down here."

Emelie leaned over the bar. "Why you guys on the floor?"

Danny quickly ducked inside a storage cabinet and Ian shot up. "You need something?"

"Claire's here."

"Oh, is she?"

God, they were pathetic. Ian shifted on his feet, probably nervous about talking to his favorite author, while Danny stayed hidden inside the cabinets.

Emelie clearly didn't buy their fake ignorance and slowly smiled. "You guys gonna come say hi?"

"Sure, sure." Ian nodded and Danny kept crouched, opening more cabinets and rattling kegs.

"When can I tell her you're coming to talk to her?"

"Who?" Ian and Danny said at the same time, like idiots. One winced, the other rolled his eyes.

"Can't believe it." She shook her head. "Two grown-ass men. One of you fan-girling so hard you can't see straight, and the other dropping shit because one look at her turns him inside out." She laughed. "Should I give you two some time to center yourselves, maybe take up meditation? I'll go find out what she wants to drink."

"She likes dry, Italian red. Grab one of De Luca's imported Barolos," Danny said, then froze when Ian and Emelie slowly turned toward him.

He cleared his throat. "Look at that. One keg's nearly empty."

Danny deserted the awkward moment, rushing away while rubbing the back of his neck. How many times had he told them it doesn't mean anything—she doesn't mean anything? And there he goes blurting what she likes to drink.

He grumbled curses all the way down to the basement where the kegs were stored.

"Get a grip." He took another deep breath before he lugged the keg he needed. The stairs groaned under the weight.

With one last inhale, he entered the bar and overheard Ian saying to Emelie, "What did you mean I was fan-girling . . . er boying?"

Emelie only smiled again.

Danny slid the old keg out and tapped the new one before he finally forced himself to square his shoulders and look Claire's way.

He went still, and Ian and Emelie went quiet, following his narrowing gaze across the dining room where a bright-blue polo sweater plopped a chair next to Claire. Her eyes grew wide when his look-a-likes brought chairs to surround her.

Emelie hissed. "He wouldn't dare."

"I think he would dare," Ian said.

"I think you need to leave." Danny read Claire's lips clearly. But Polo Man only moved closer. Feigning reaching for his beer, he grazed her chest.

Danny plowed under the bar.

"*Oi*, wait," Ian said.

He didn't wait. Couldn't wait. The flame he thought died after Jessica's bullshit licked up his insides. He may not be ready to feel some things, but this? This roiling anger filled every inch of him. This he'd happily *feel*.

13

Sometimes the Plot Twist
is in the Writer

THE YOUNG MAN DIDN'T leave like Claire asked, and his expensive cologne choked out her nose when he hopped his chair closer.

"You know, you look familiar," he said. "Do I know you from somewhere?"

At first glance, he also looked familiar, but Claire didn't want to risk another look his way. If she did know him, he couldn't be one of the locals Ian wanted her to meet. Which meant he could be from her home. She swallowed and dipped her head, hoping the brim of her hat would shadow her identity. "I don't think so. What did you say your name was?"

"Trevor Winston." He leaned even closer. "And I'd be happy to take you to my yacht on the mainland and get to know you."

"No, thank you. I'm meeting someone here."

"Yeah? Who's that?"

"Me," a deep voice rumbled, and Trevor jumped when a broad, tattooed frame towered over them.

"Daniel," Claire breathed out.

His eyes snapped to her. Green overtook the blue in his eyes as they dropped quickly over her before cutting back to Trevor. "The woman asked you to leave." His fingers curled into his palm. "I'm not gonna ask."

"You realize," Trevor leaned back, arms crossing, "I could destroy you with one post online."

Danny's voice dropped low and eerily quiet. "Should I spell

my name for you again?"

"Wine for two." Emelie arrived, eyes dropping to Danny's hands before setting down the wine on the table. Claire followed her gaze and saw them twitching.

"This her?" one polo-shirt man asked. The beer in his hand sloshed as he turned, eyeing Emelie's chest. "You're right. At least a handful."

Did he just —

Danny lunged forward, but Emelie clamped onto his arm. "He's not worth it," she whispered with a smoothing pat. "I'm okay."

"Excuse me?" Claire said. "Is this how you were raised to speak about a woman?"

Trevor and his friends snickered, and a memory of Brandon snickering whenever she'd offered an opinion snapped in her mind. Heat swelled deep in her belly.

"Get. Out," Danny said between clenched teeth. "Now."

"You should also know, *Larss-son*," Trevor mocked. "Been talking to the old man, and he's interested in buying half this island. Good revenue." He smirked. "Maybe I'll have him start with your place."

Danny's black t-shirt stretched and strained as his arms slowly curled over his chest, jaw locked. "Not for sale."

"Won't matter when he takes over all the other businesses and forces you to sell."

Danny spun toward Emelie and she shrunk back. "This is why you didn't say anything to me or Uncle Nils? He threatened you with taking the inn away?" His normally smooth voice graveled. "Did this asshole force you to do anything?"

Claire squeezed her fingers together, watching humiliation color Emelie's cheeks, desperation rolling off Danny. The heat in her belly rose, setting her face on fire.

"Don't worry." Emelie dropped her eyes. "He never touched me."

"Yet."

Danny whipped back to Trevor. "I'm going to break every

bone in your goddamn face."

Emelie frantically waved toward the bar as Trevor huffed, straightening in his seat. "I'm not afraid of you."

The chair in front of Trevor flew to the side with the man on it. Trevor yelped, climbing into himself.

"Hold up." Ian appeared and wrapped around Danny's middle, heaving him back.

"Winston, did you say?" Claire's icy tone rose over the noise, and everyone stopped and turned toward her. She leaned into the years of control forced on her as a child and meticulously tipped the wine bottle over her glass, pouring with a twist.

Not a drop dripped down the outside. Her hands steady and smooth as she cupped the bottom of the wineglass, swirled, sniffed, and swirled it again, glancing at Trevor. "Would this happen to be Sebastian Winston of Winston Enterprises?"

"Yeah." His mouth twisted. "My father owns it."

"Ah." She sipped. "Mm, Emelie, this is delicious, thank you. Did you choose it, Daniel?" No one moved, but he managed an awkward nod.

She ran a finger around the rim of the glass, holding the tension in the room for another moment. "Tell me, Trevor, is it okay if I call you Trevor? Where did your father get his start in business?"

He puffed out his chest and helped himself to the extra glass, reaching for the wine. She gripped the neck of the bottle and shook her head.

"Please, answer me first."

"He was one of the privileged few to intern with *the* Gregory Cooke. You might have heard of that family."

Her eyes flicked up to Danny, then to Ian, whose hand squeezed Danny's shoulder. Danny eased back — slightly. She looked back at her glass. "That's correct," she said. "Sebastian interned and then was given Cooke's Holdings off the East Coast to manage. He doesn't own them."

"Are you kidding?" Trevor stopped being cute and his pale face shaded on the edge of purple. "They're in his name. Of course he owns them."

"Not yet, he doesn't. If I recall . . . " She pulled out her phone and flipped through her calendar. "Ah, yes, here it is. The end of this month, final negotiations are scheduled." She turned it off and placed it on the table. Picking up her glass again, she swirled and sipped. Every movement, every word, purposeful and deliberate. She'd hold this control, knowing what she had — what he didn't.

When Trevor wiped a bead of sweat from his brow and squirmed, she lightly smiled. "I wonder how your father would feel if he found out he lost the biggest business deal of his life," she continued. "That what he's worked so hard for — sacrificed so much for — was taken away because his son threatened Gregory Cooke's daughter just to show off to his friends."

He scoffed, thumbing toward Emelie. "She could never be a Cooke."

Danny took a step, but Ian gripped his shoulder again. Claire hated the twist on Danny's face. The mortification coating Emelie's cheeks.

She turned her entire body toward Trevor. "But I am."

Color drained from his face. "Y-You?"

"Madelynn *Claire* Cooke, Mr. Winston. And not only did you not leave when I asked, you abused power you don't have to threaten the kind owner of this establishment. An establishment I've come to adore.

"Not to mention you've embarrassed and humiliated my friend Emelie here. All for what? A few laughs with these other spineless, affluent leeches?"

Trevor's chest heaved as more beads of sweat dripped down his temples.

Claire picked up her wine again. "What would Father say if I told him how unhappy you've made me?" Lifting her phone, she went through her contacts. "Let's see. If it's eight o'clock here, that would make it what time over there . . . " She tapped her fingers, calculating.

Trevor shot out of his chair, shoving a finger in her face. "Don't you dare."

She glanced down at his finger and back up at him. "Or what? You'll continue to show everyone here all the money your parents wasted on your useless education when they should have spent it on teaching you how to be something other than a pathetic, womanizing waste of oxygen? Yes, indeed. Please threaten me with your gutless bravado and ugly, manicured fingers. Where do you get them done, by the way?" She tsked, wrinkling her nose at his nails. "Honestly, even without everything else you've done, you deserve a fist into that weak chin for such a disgrace. But," she dramatically sighed, "no need for violence when I can settle this with a simple phone call. I'm sure Sebastian will appreciate all his hard-earned money going toward his half-wit brat who lost him the business deal of a lifetime."

His friends yanked Trevor back. "Come on, man. Don't be stupid. Let's go."

"You should listen to them." Claire sipped her wine. "They seem a tad more intelligent than you."

"You *bitch*."

"Yes. But I can afford to be." Slowly, she lifted her eyes to his and smiled. "Can you?"

He reared forward, and Danny stepped in between, shoving him back. "Give me a reason. Please."

"If I were you, I'd leave tonight." Claire peered around Danny. "But before you go, you better beg Emelie for forgiveness. I'll make sure it's a stipulation in the agreement that if you set one foot on this island again, the business deal will become null and void. Have a pleasant journey, *Mister* Winston. Ah, ah, gentlemen," she said as his friends pulled him to leave. "Apology first."

Trevor's nostrils flared as he gritted his teeth. "I'm sorry."

"I think on your knees is best." Claire tapped a nail on her phone. "And with more sincerity, if you please."

He cursed as he kneeled. "I'm sorry for making you lift your shirt."

Ian blocked Danny's forward lunge as Trevor tore out of Flygande with his minions behind him.

Claire slowly let out a deep breath. Her insides still burned. Reaching out, she caught and squeezed Emelie's hand. "I'm so sorry he did that to you. Are you alright?" Emelie nodded with wide eyes, and Claire straightened her posture again, sniffing. "I've always hated the Winstons." The hat brim covered her right eye as she glared out toward the front door with her left. Anger cut into her voice as she said, "Stupid manicured nails." She tipped up her glass and finished in one gulp.

14

Not All Family is Blood

DANNY'S EARS RANG, EYES blinking fast. Never had he ever witnessed such a perfectly executed, verbal bitch slap.

A smile tugged at the corner of his mouth as he slowly took Claire in with all new eyes. The straightness of her spine. The hat brim putting an edge into her features while the point of her nose tipped up. That blood-red mouth pursed as she glared at the front door.

This poised, sophisticated woman just decimated a man without lifting a finger. Without spilling a drop of wine.

Who was she, really?

"Oh. My. *God*." Emelie squealed, startling all of them from their shock. She threw her arms around Claire's neck, tipping her backward.

Danny caught the chair, and Claire's hat collided with his stomach, knocking it sideways. "Sorry."

She smiled up at him, pulling out pins before removing the hat. More caramel waves tumbled down over her shoulders, and Danny took a step back, swallowing.

"Thank you, thank you," Emelie continued squealing and hugged her again.

Claire laughed into her shoulder, the sound huskier than usual. "I can honestly say the pleasure was all mine."

"You're everything I knew you would be."

"What on earth do you mean?"

Emelie released her and cupped her shoulders. "You, as a woman and successful writer, really inspire me."

"Wait," Ian said. "You know who she is?"

"You wouldn't shut up about her books, so I read them."

"You listened to me?" He looked up, circling his eyes around the ceiling. "Are pigs flying?"

Danny continued studying Claire as her smiling eyes bounced back and forth between Ian and Emelie's banter.

"But how did you know *she* was *her*," Ian asked Emelie.

"I looked her up on this thing called the internet."

He gasped. "You're not a true fan."

A small laugh came from Claire, and Emelie bent down, taking her by the shoulders again. "You, my author heroine and now best friend, are so badass."

Claire's smile wobbled. "Oh, I don't know about that. I just know men like him, and it was nice to use that useless knowledge for something useful for a change." Her fingers vibrated as she reached for the wine bottle.

Danny caught it first. "May I?" he said.

She nodded, and while he poured, her tentative eyes lifted to him and stayed.

He wanted to tell her how grateful he was for what she'd done for his cousin. For him. But the adrenaline still coursing through his body stole all his coherent words.

He'd dealt with pricks like Trevor before, but always managed the situation with better control. He didn't normally let them get under his skin while he threatened to break their faces. He'd only silently, and if necessary, physically removed them from the premises.

Something twisted in his stomach. What if he was permanently broken now?

Ian suddenly blurted, "You're my favorite writer."

Claire fumbled her wineglass, and the tension in her shoulders left as she laughed. "So you're a *true* fan?"

"I'm a ridiculous fan. Ask Danny." He dropped to his knees

in front of her and cradled one of her hands. "I've been to every comic-con and Q&A you've been to. You may or may not remember the dork who's asked a million questions at each meeting."

"Wait, you're the Raging Scotsman?"

He grinned despite several snickers around him. "That I am, lass."

"You found all my Easter eggs." She squeezed his hand. "You know, it's because of you that I spend so much time trying to hide them."

"Because of me?" His voice cracked.

"There you go, making him fan-girl again," Emelie said. "Now he'll never shut up about this."

"You're just jealous." Ian grinned, keeping his eyes on Claire. "I've always wanted to meet you and thank you in person. Your first book saved my life."

Danny slowly inhaled, the memory of that time still tightened his chest.

"How is that possible?" Claire gripped the front of her dress.

"It's a long story." Ian waved a hand. "Some other time, maybe. But for now?" He stood and planted a loud kiss on her cheek. "That's for who you are and what you just did. God, it was beautiful. I only wish I had it on video so I could watch it several times a night. I'd have the best of dreams."

"I'll send it to you," Fin said, holding up a phone, grinning. "Seriously, Ms. Cooke, that was priceless."

"Finlay?" Ian asked. "If you're here, who's tending bar?"

"Oh, shit." Finlay raced back to the confused patrons looking left and right for service.

Danny started to make his way there too.

"I got it," Ian said. "Relax and have some wine." He winked.

"Just friends," Danny mouthed, and Ian grinned.

Emelie said, "I'll help too."

"Hold up." Danny caught her arm. "Sit for a minute. I want to talk to you."

All lightness left her eyes and she sighed. "Look, I know it was stupid not to tell anyone he threatened me, but Pappa's worked so hard for that inn."

He took her hand in one of his and covered it with his other. "Em, Solsken hasn't been able to stay a simple town for all these years because no one has tried to buy it out before. We have laws in place to preserve the history. No out-of-town businesses allowed. Only residents can own businesses, and no one can become a resident without the town voting them in. It didn't matter how much money that bastard had. He couldn't do what he threatened."

She jammed her long nails into her hair. "I'm such an idiot."

"No, you're not. I only know because I had to learn all the laws when I took over this place." He touched her cheek. "You're extremely intelligent, strong, and capable. I couldn't be doing any of this after what happened if you weren't here helping me." He wiped a tear off her cheek with his thumb. "I love you, kiddo. I only wish I could have hit him at least once."

Releasing a small, watery laugh, she threw her arms around his neck. "I love you, man-ape." She kissed the side of his head before bending to his ear, whispering, "Besides, she punched him where it really counts. Pretty amazing, don't you think?"

"Just friends," he whispered back.

She grinned as she left.

Danny shook his head and turned toward Claire, ready to ask if she needed another glass of wine. She quickly looked away to the fire, wiping under her eyes.

"Hey, you alright?"

She nodded and cleared her throat. "You have a wonderful family. Do you have siblings too?"

"Yeah, an older sister. She married a Faroese man and moved from this island to that one."

"Oh, I've been there. Beautiful rocky cliffs and ocean view. Kind of reminds me of Solsken."

"But with far fewer trees."

"And a lot more sheep."

"More sheep than people, I hear."

She laughed and finally faced him.

His smile dropped when he saw the glistening of her eyes. Out of nowhere, he had the urge to touch her face, and his grip tightened on the edge of his chair. "How about you? You're close to your dad, right?"

She shook her head. "Only child. And the truth is, I owe you an apology. I wasn't exactly honest about my relationship with my father."

"You don't need to apologize for anything you said or did."

She lifted her glass, but instead of sipping, she studied the drips running along the inside as she absently swirled it. "I can't do what I threatened because I didn't follow in my father's footsteps. More like ran from it into a marriage—" She paused, like she hadn't meant to let that last line out. Then cleared her throat. "Anyway, he's never forgiven me." She stared off into the fire.

"For choosing to be a writer?"

"Yes." She sighed. "Not a Cooke profession. But I knew Trevor wouldn't know any of this, so I figured the threat would work."

Daniel began putting some of the fragmented pieces that were Claire together. The *familj* sign over the bar. Her reaction after he spoke to Emelie. She had a family yet came here alone.

"You know, not all family is blood."

She met his eyes and searched them.

"Take Merv and George, for instance." He motioned to them sitting across the room, playing chess. "They came to the island in the mid-seventies. Merv is a retired combat medic. Saved George's life in Vietnam. Both of them are widowed, fight like cats and dogs, yet they're always together. Closer to each other than their own kin.

"And see that group of three over there by the dart boards?" He pointed. "That's Clark and Ian's aunt, Annie, the doctor and nurse here. They always wanted children but couldn't have any. Yet they helped raise more children than most here on Solsken through fostering, medical care, and donations to the school. And Gene there with them had two sons, one died in Afghanistan, the other to cancer. Annie and Clark took him in and they became his family."

"Oh, Daniel," she said breathlessly. "What stories."

"Families aren't always born, Claire." He cautiously reached out and covered her hand. "Sometimes they're made."

She glanced down at his hand, and for a moment, he thought she'd pull away. Instead, she flipped her palm up and wrapped her long fingers around his before locking soft eyes onto him. "And sad stories can change," she said. "Even if we've made the wrong choices."

Blinking fast, he cleared his throat of the sudden emotion. Slowly, he pulled away and grabbed the bottle. "You need more wine?"

"Only if you join me." She smoothed her hands down the lower half of her dress and his eyes tracked the movement. "You don't want to see what happens if I have a whole bottle to myself."

He paused with the bottle hovering over the second glass. "Actually, I do."

She laughed and snatched the bottle from him. "*No.*"

"Damn." He smirked, loving that he made her laugh again. "So, Ian invited you here to get to know some of the locals. Who first?" He gestured to Merv and George. "Now their game of chess can be brutal, but they're always up to showing a 'young-in' how it's done."

She bit her twitching lip.

"Or if you're more of a throw-sharp-objects-into-a-corkboard kind of gal, then that group by the dartboards is always up for fresh blood."

She chuckled.

"Or, if you'd like, tomorrow I can take you for a walk downtown. We can hang with some locals at Ylva's bakery while you sample more of her pastries."

She slowly smiled and touched the rim of her glass again, making her finger run along the edge. He watched the slow movement, remembering the first time he'd seen her do that in

The Pit. The scar he noticed on the plane slipped out again below her sleeve. The jagged pattern of it didn't sit right with him.

He went still. Nothing sparkled on her left hand anymore. *Does that mean —*

"I'd like that." She interrupted his thoughts. "Any of it. All of it. If it's no trouble."

"I asked, didn't I?" He tore his eyes away from her empty finger and shifted in his seat. "Besides, what are friends for?"

"Friends?"

"Is it okay if I call you that?"

"Yes." She took a long sip of wine and stared at him over the rim. "I think I'd really like that."

He smiled fully and drank from his glass, enjoying the warmth of the fire and her lingering gaze. A loud gurgle went off in her stomach and she gripped over it.

"Are you hungry?"

She looked up through her lashes. "Maybe a little."

He sat up straight. This was something he could fix. "What do you like? I have chicken or beef. Hell, I'll even go out to Solsken farms and kill the fatted pig if you want it. We kind of owe you."

She chuckled. "Chicken is fine."

"Chicken it is. Come hang out with Merv and George while I make it." He stood and held out an arm for her, and she slipped a hand around his bicep.

He had to swallow ten times in a row when her fingers touched and made light circles on his skin. Spontaneously flexing, he found himself gently squeezing her soft fingers between his side and arm.

Just friends, he reminded himself.

"How's our hero?" Ian asked when Danny pushed through the kitchen door.

"Hungry." He peeked into the freezer, then the fridge, and shook his head. "I'll be right back." He ran up the stairs to his apartment and was down moments later with fresh chicken.

Ian didn't say a word while watching him pull out pans, fresh butter, dried thyme, mushrooms, and garlic. Flygande didn't make fried food because Danny couldn't cook. He was great at it—he just didn't want the stress of cooking full-time.

He placed the pan over the flame. "What fruit do we have?"

"Citrus mostly. A few winter strawberries from down south too."

"We still have *vaniljsås*?"

"Yep." Ian pulled the small pitcher of vanilla sauce from the fridge.

"Where's Fin?"

"Mattie and Dean stopped by and said they'd help him take out the trash."

Danny peered over his shoulder. "When have you ever known Mattie and Dean to be helpful?"

"It surprised me actually. They were even excited about—" Ian smacked his forehead. "Oh saints, they were excited. He must've texted them about Trevor."

Danny flipped off the flame and shoved the pan from the heat. They both rushed toward the back door just as Fin waltzed in, rubbing his knuckles.

"Finlay?" Ian said. "What were you doing?"

He shrugged and edged around them. "Dealing with the trash."

They both eyed the bruising of his jaw, the bleeding cracks on his knuckles. "Trash, huh?" Ian side-glanced Danny, who hid a small smile beneath his hand.

"Hey," Danny called, and Fin spun around. "You may or may not see something extra in your paycheck this week for your . . . *trash* duties."

He grinned.

"But don't make it habit," Ian added.

"You got it, bosses."

He left, whistling, and Ian turned to Danny. "You know that bonus will only encourage him."

"Yeah, but Trevor now has another reason never to come back to Solsken."

"Aye. I might be a tad jealous the kids got to beat him and

not us."

"Aren't your fighting days over, priest-to-be?"

Ian crossed his arms. "Saint Nicholas once punched a man as a bishop."

"I thought it was a slap."

"I prefer the embellished version."

"You aiming to be the next Santa Claus?"

Ian shrugged. "A man has to have goals, Danny."

He laughed and flipped the chicken.

With the food plated, they made their way to the dining area, and Ian grabbed a few more bottles of wine as they went. They both stopped short when they noticed everyone had cleared out except a horde of locals surrounding Claire.

"Crap," Ian said. "You think she's overwhelmed by all of them?"

"No. That's her real smile."

Ian did a double take of him. "Real smile?"

Without answering, Danny squeezed between bodies and placed down his simple masterpiece in front of her. Sliced grilled chicken with wild mushrooms smothered in herbed white wine and butter sauce. Next to it lay a pile of glazed baby carrots and a glass bowl filled with cut-up strawberries in vanilla sauce.

She clapped her hands together. "Daniel, this smells delicious. Thank you."

He smiled and pulled a chair up behind her, forcing his eyes not to linger on the soft valley between her exposed shoulder blades. She wasted no time digging in.

George crossed his arms. "How come you never give us food like that?"

"'Cause you ain't as pretty," Merv said.

Danny's eyes snapped to Ian. Rumors were about to soar.

"Actually," Ian said. "This meal is a thank you for helping to rid Solsken of ugly polo shirts."

"Good riddance," Annie said. "One of them brats came through and smacked my ass."

"What?" Clark bolted upright. Even for a man of sixty, no one on the island would ever dare challenge him in a fight. He stayed physically fit with a punching bag, running five miles a day, and climbing the cliffs of Solsken for fun.

Ian waved his hand and got Clark's attention. He pointed at Fin, who grinned and held up his scabbing knuckles. Emelie did a double take, and Fin quickly dropped them.

Clark grunted his approval. "I think this calls for more beer."

"Whisky." Gene held up a glass.

"Ale," George and Merv chimed in.

"Water," said Annie, and they all grumbled at her. "What? Someone has to get up and do the Lord's work tomorrow."

"And I love you for it." Clark slid his arm around her and gently patted her rear-end, whispering in her ear. She flushed and nudged him with a chuckle.

Claire picked up a bottle of wine and filled a second glass, handing it to Danny. His fingers brushed hers as he took it, eyes snagging on the color flushing up the curve of her neck to her cheeks. Clearing his throat, he inched his chair closer and leaned over her shoulder. "Is the food alright?"

She turned and their noses bumped. Her eyes dropped to his mouth and his followed, but neither of them moved to separate.

He should probably move to separate.

"I've never had anything more delicious in my life," she whispered, still staring at his mouth.

Just friends, he told himself, as he absolutely didn't move an inch.

Whispers in the Wind

"YOU SURE YOU DON'T want me to walk you home?" Danny asked Claire while leaning on the squeaking gate. The last of the residents were waving their goodbyes as they walked down the lamp-lined main street.

"I'm sure." She smiled down at her feet. "Are you still wanting to show me around town tomorrow?"

"Of course." He gripped the spokes on top of the gate, swinging it back and forth. "If you want to."

They were like young kids, stealing glances at each other, rosy-cheeked. Danny, fidgeting and nervous, stuffed his free hand deep into his pocket, while Claire stood swaying a little, clutching her small purse.

"What time should I be here?" she asked.

"Well, Ylva's opens at seven, but if that's too early, any time after that works."

"Seven is fine. I'm usually awake by then anyway."

The gate creaked in Danny's hand again. "I'll see you at seven then, Claire," he said her name slowly, savoring the taste of it.

She tucked a hair behind her ear and smiled. "See you then, Daniel."

He swung the gate wide and held it open as she waved and walked the unlit, opposite direction as everyone else. He watched as she turned the corner and became lost to the darkness.

"You give her that flashlight?" Ian came up behind him.

He didn't turn but continued to watch where she disappeared. "Yeah. I still don't like her going alone this late."

"At least there aren't any bears out here. The worst she'll see is a raccoon."

"Or a tourist."

"Finlay said they scared Trevor and his friends off the island by egging their Beamers all the way to the bridge. The rest of the tourists will be gone when the snow hits. Besides, she handled herself well tonight."

"Yeah, but . . ." His eyes roamed the darkness as he rubbed the back of his neck. "Ever get the feeling you're being watched?"

Ian glanced around them. "Out here?"

"Yeah? No?" Danny scraped a hand over his face. "I don't know. She'd hate me if I followed her, though, wouldn't she?"

"I don't know about hate, but she probably wouldn't like it."

He sighed. "How's your gut?"

He wasn't asking about Ian's digestion, but the developed sixth sense he got from his childhood when something wasn't right.

"Fine, but if you want, I can ask Finlay where he delivered the firewood. Maybe it'll help knowing the area where she's staying, so you can know what neighbors are close by. Might even be George since he met her first. He's got a small arsenal."

"Yeah, would you do that?" He ran a hand through his hair, glanced once more down the road, and with a heavy breath, made his way back into Flygande.

CLAIRE COULDN'T FEEL THE rocks crunching under her feet or the icy wind biting her face. Only the warmth brimming inside her.

Danny had no idea how much his dinner meant to her. No one had ever cooked for her just because. Not unless they were paid to. And through that one small gesture, she felt taken care of—cared for. For the first time in over a year, a heavy weight eased from her shoulders.

Even the wine she was served was thoughtful. She hadn't thought he'd heard anything she said at the airport bar, but he must have listened to the type of wine she liked because Emelie brought her one of her favorites.

She rubbed a gloved hand just below her ear. The heat from his mouth when he talked to her still lingered. First when he asked about the food, but then he continued, inputting comments about the residents she spoke to. Helping her fully understand all the conversations going on around her.

Every time he leaned in, she let herself imagine that he did so because he wanted to be close to her. It was foolish, of course, but she enjoyed letting herself think about it.

She hopped over a rock and nearly twisted her ankle.

"I need different shoes," she mumbled and remembered Danny's boots. Thick-soled, black-leather boots that slid to either side of her chair while he sat behind her, making her feel encompassed in a hug. Even safe, somehow, secure. How could one man's boots make her feel all of those things?

When they'd bumped noses, she lost all reason. Her only thought—all she could focus on—was how much she wanted to know what his full lips felt like.

Skidding to a stop, she released an exasperated sigh. "Kiss him? Really, Claire?"

She shook her head but couldn't keep herself from smiling. She was happy, truly happy. Not only from his attention and thoughtfulness, but from the new friends she made. Wonderful friends whose kindness and welcoming made her heart full and ache at the same time.

She sighed into another smile. The food, the wine, the fellowship—his breath on her ear. This night would be marked as her favorite.

Maddy bubbled up inside her mind. Tonight she'd write a happy story. The little girl who was too much for most people would find a loving home to go to, large enough for all her bigness.

Anxious to write the words Maddy needed to speak, she

picked up her pace and came around the bend to the cottage.

She stopped short. The house was dark and the cozy light she'd left on no longer glowed.

A cold wind whipped around the corner, and it all rushed back with the sudden chill. She'd forgotten all about her experience before she left.

Needing to hold on to the warmth of her recent happiness, she rushed forward, up the creaking stair, and placed a shaking key near the lock.

"Ma-adelynn . . . " a voice whispered from her left.

She swung around, clicking on the flashlight. "Who's there?"

"You promised me . . . " the voice echoed behind her, and she jerked that direction, beaming the light over open swaying grass and rock piles.

Nothing was there.

She whimpered and the key in her fingers rattled against the lock. The wind shifted directions, bringing another whisper, and she fumbled the flashlight until it fell with a loud thump.

"Replaced me with the Viking *already-y-y?*" The voice crept like barbed tendrils up the hairs on her neck.

With a small cry, she used her other hand to steady her shivering one and jammed the key into the lock. The wind shifted again, gusting into her right side and she screeched, twisting the key. The door swung open, and she slammed it shut, gripping her chest. "It can't be real."

Her breath came out in short puffs of white air. The cottage was so cold. Skittering her fingers along the wall, she found the switch. It was down, not up the way she left it. She flipped it, flooding the cottage with light, eyes darting around the interior. Nothing out of place.

Maybe she hadn't left the light on. She rubbed the side of her head and groaned. "Or maybe I'm losing my mind?"

Sliding the chain lock into place, she shivered and hugged herself as she made her way to the living room fireplace. Light and heat. Those things were real.

The crackling flame warmed her face and hands, but it didn't warm the aching chill in her bones. "Everything's fine. You're fine, Claire." But no amount of self-soothing calmed her.

Still shaking, she started rushing around her home, flipping on lights. All the lights. She didn't care how ridiculous it was, she'd sleep with every light on.

Finishing, she double checked the chain lock and listened for any disturbance on the other side.

All was calm.

Dancing from foot to foot on the icy floorboards, she changed into pale-pink, satin pants and matching camisole top, making a note to buy something warmer before she froze to death in her sleep. With one last glance at the jammed lock on her window, she leaped from where she stood to the bed, avoiding more cold floor. She wriggled under the electric blanket and pulled a thick, down-filled blanket on top.

In the quiet, her mind went back to what she'd heard outside. She couldn't have imagined it. The voice said too much — personal things — and was unmistakably male this time.

But no one had been close enough to whisper in her ear.

She yanked the covers over her head, determined to keep her eyes open all night if she had to.

The sound of distant crashing waves and the warmth of double blankets lulled her. Soon her eyes drifted shut. Danny's smile in her mind's eye followed her to sleep.

"MADELYNN," HE CALLED from a distance.

She hummed and nuzzled into a soft pillow. "Yes?"

"Madelynn." His voice was closer. "Wake up."

Her eyes fluttered open to darkness. Her mind groggy and disoriented. "Brandon? Where are you?"

"I'm in the bathtub."

Half-dazed, she eased up and yawned. "Did you just get home from a meeting?"

"Yes, come talk to me."

She rubbed her face and let her feet fall off the side of the bed. They hit a cold floor, and she jolted, blinking hard. Everything was dark.

Everything was — *dark.*

It was dark.

Her heart smacked against her rib cage and her breath came out in wheezing bursts. All the lights were off.

"What's the matter, Ma-adelynn . . ." A deep rumbling laugh shook the outside wall. "Scared?"

Her window flew open, and she screamed, falling out of bed. She hit the end table, making it crash, and see-sawed up. Her head swam.

"You took off my ring-*ing-ing*?" His echoing voice came from her right and she veered left, slamming into the wall. "Don't you remember? 'Til your death do us part."

She screamed again. Throwing her palms over her ears, she rushed forward, colliding with the front door. Icy air smacked her back and goosebumps exploded over her exposed skin.

"The curtain, Madelynn. Come look behind the curtain."

"Leave me *alone*." She pawed the wall for the light switch and flicked it up.

Nothing.

Up, down, up-down-up-down — no light came to save her.

"The curta-ain . . . " the voice whispered up her spine.

She should look back. Face this phantom straight on. But if it was him, if she saw those hollow, gray eyes —

The chain on the door clinked and vibrated under her shaking fingers and jammed. "No." She pounded her fist against the door. The chain loosened and she flung it open.

"Where you go-o-ing?" the voice sang.

She shrieked and plowed forward, tripping over the forgotten flashlight. Feet caught the single stair, and she crashed down, face colliding with sharp rocks.

Tears blinded her as she pushed up on wobbly arms and fell

again, slicing her left shin.

The voice rolled in deep laughter.

Yelling out, her bare feet finally found their footing, and she blindly ran, stones biting into her feet. Warm liquid oozed into her eye. Swiping it, she looked down and screamed. Her hand was covered in blood.

The laughter grew distant, but still she cried and ran—screamed and ran.

Ahead of her, a familiar dark building took shape and soft light floated out of a window above the door. She followed the light like a beacon and smacked face first into a gate. The force flung her body backward. Cold wind whipped up behind her and she screamed again. The curtain in the window above the door swiped to the side.

Dragging herself up the peeling gate, she gripped the spokes on top, violently shaking them. It popped open and she tripped. A pebble wave whooshed over her body. Her hands sank deep as she pushed up her vibrating body. Stumbling up the stone steps, she threw her fists against the door.

"*Help* me."

Heavy thudding came from inside and the door swung open. She plowed forward and collided with a hard body.

"CLAIRE? *CLAIRE.* WHAT'S WRONG?"

"Don't let him in."

Danny wrapped himself around her, twisting her away from the opening. The door slammed shut. "Don't let who in? What's happened?"

She clawed at his bare chest and burrowed her face like she was trying to crawl inside his skin.

"I didn't know," she cried. "Tell him I didn't know."

"Tell who?" Danny took her by the arms, easing her back.

Blood. There was so much blood. "*Shit.* What happened to your face?" He cupped her cheeks, tilting her head back. His eyes ran wildly over her face. "Who did this to you?"

"What's going on?" Ian came into the mix, disheveled, with a baseball bat in his hand.

"Look at me, Claire," Danny said, voice rising. "Talk to me. Who did this to your face?" He got louder and louder with every word. Big as he was, Danny only ever yelled when he was afraid. And with his current volume, Ian raced outside, bat held up.

Moments later he came back. "I didn't see anyone."

Claire's mouth vibrated as she peered up at Danny.

"I didn't know." She whimpered. "He was behind the curtain, and I didn't know. I don't want another curtain. I can't look behind the curtain."

Danny wasn't having any more of it. He swept under her legs, lifting her into his arms. Running up the stairs with Ian behind him, he kicked the door open and rushed her to his living room, carefully placing her on Ian's couch bed.

Clutching her face between both palms, he looked it over. "Did you hit your head, Claire? Did somebody hit you on the head, Claire?" He felt the need to repeat her name, hoping it would draw out some answers.

Ian handed him a wet washcloth and Danny swallowed down nausea as he wiped crimson drips off her face. He eyed the cut on her forehead and let out a breath. The amount of blood made it look worse than it was. But, God, her terrified face.

"What man was behind the curtain?" His voice rose again. "Did he attack you?" She still didn't speak, and he began carefully running his hands over her body.

Danny checked under her arms, on each side, and down her legs, looking for more abrasions. He found blood on her shin, and as he went to clean it, he realized she shivered in nothing but thin sleepwear. *Revealing* sleepwear. He tore his eyes away. "Ian, a blanket." Focusing on the cut, he blotted it as Ian tucked one around her.

"Did someone push you or did you fall?" Danny tried to quiet his voice, but it was a losing battle. His hands were shaking. "Can you answer me, Claire?" He got loud again. "I need to know. Is someone coming here for you?"

"Don't let him in." She bolted halfway up, eyes wide. "Don't let Brandon in."

"Brandon?" He caught her shoulders. "Claire, he isn't here."

"He was in my cottage, an-and he laughed." She gripped his arms and yanked him forward. "He knew I took off the rings."

"It doesn't matter if he knows. He's dead."

She broke into fresh tears, and Danny released her, gripping his hair. "I'm sorry. I'm not trying to be insensitive, Claire. I—"

She hiccuped and fell back, covering her face with her hands.

He slowly turned toward Ian, teetering on the edge between desperation and exploding.

Ian held up a hand, telling him to let him try. "Claire," Ian said quietly, and she uncovered her face. "Did somebody hurt you?"

She shook her head.

"Did somebody scare you?"

She nodded and her bottom lip lost control again. "He came through my window." She blinked fast as more tears spilled. "The curtain. He was behind the curtain, and I didn't know—but he'll never forgive me."

Regardless of what did or didn't make sense, a man breaking into her house was something tangible Danny could work with—and he desperately needed something to work with. "Where are you staying?" he asked.

She bit her lip but didn't answer, and all the control he barely held on to broke. "Now's not the time to be *private*, Claire."

She shuddered, and he tore away from her, gripping his hair again. Closing his eyes, he took a deep breath, trying to regain control.

"Hang on," Ian said. "Let me see if Finlay ever messaged me back." He pulled out his phone and opened the unread message, tilting the screen toward Danny to read.

I DROPPED THE CORD OF WOOD OFF NEAR SVEN'S PLACE, BUT

ON THE SIDE OF THE ROAD. WEIRD, HUH? NOT SURE WHY SHE WANTED IT THERE. NOT A HOUSE FOR MILES, EXCEPT FOR GERTY'S. BUT, YEAH, SVEN'S LANE.

"Sven?" Danny spun toward her.

Ian crouched down and smoothed a touch over her hand. "Claire, are you staying in an old cottage? Red roof? A bit run down?"

She slowly nodded.

Danny snatched the baseball bat out of Ian's hand, and his feet pounded down the stairs. He wasn't buying a ghost haunting, and whoever did this was going to feel how real his bat was.

A Message from Beyond

IAN RAN WITH ONE of Danny's shirts in his hand, hoping to find him before he caught whoever did this.

Danny had always been the calm one and Ian the reactionary one. This recent switch in Danny, twice in one day, could only mean one thing. He was beginning to feel things he never thought he would again.

As wonderful as that was, it scared Ian. What happened with Jessica changed Danny and this new side—this edgier, unhinged side—was something Ian didn't know how to handle.

If he couldn't catch him, if someone died, Danny would not only lose the life he was trying to rebuild, but Jessica would win twice by taking both his dignity and future.

"You know?" Ian looked to the sky as he panted, wishing he'd kept up with track and field practices. "I know there's a whole *your will not being my will* thing, but maybe, just this once, our wills could be the same?" He puffed clouded breaths. "We both know him losing it would be a bad thing, so maybe giving him a dash of patience wouldn't be a bad idea?"

He sprinted around the bend to the silhouette of the cottage and squinted, trying to see movement.

A scuffle to his right dropped him down as a wooden bat swung over his head. "Danny, it's *me*."

"Shit. Ian? Announce yourself next time."

"Is that before or after you knock my head off?" He crab-walked toward Danny, throwing the shirt at him and murmured to the sky, "Perhaps a tad more patience than that."

Danny tugged on the hem of Ian's sweater and pulled him behind the large rock he'd been hiding behind. "What are you doing here?"

"What's it look like I'm doing? Keeping you out of jail."

"You shouldn't have left her. What if whoever did this figures out she's there and tries again?"

"You know what? You're upset. So, I'm going to pretend you didn't just accuse me of leaving her alone." Danny opened his mouth to speak, but Ian stopped him. "Emelie is with her, and Doc and Auntie are on their way to do a more thorough examination."

He let out a long sigh.

"Anything yet?"

"Nothing." He pointed toward the house with the bat. "The door keeps swinging open and closed, but other than that, I haven't heard or seen anyone sneaking around." He gave another tug on Ian's shirt and nodded in the direction he was going. Ian followed until they reached the next boulder.

Danny rubbed his forehead. "How was she when you left?"

"Quieter. A bit embarrassed by the state she'd arrived in. Kept apologizing. Wanted me to be sure I told you that she was sorry."

"What the hell does she have to be sorry to me for?"

Ian took a deep breath and braced for his reaction. "She said to tell you she was sorry she upset you again."

"*Fuck*." He jammed fingers into his hair. "I'm not upset at her, for shit's sake. I didn't mean to yell, and I sure as hell wasn't yelling at her."

"I know that and told her."

"But you saw the look on her face, right? I scared her." He gripped and yanked on his ponytail. "She'll never speak to me again after this."

"She's not Jessica." The words flew out of Ian's mouth before he could stop them, and Danny's narrowing eyes told him he'd stepped over the line. "Look." Ian held up both hands. "What I meant to say is I think there's a lot more going on here and a lot about Claire we don't understand. One minute she's timid and shy and the next she's throwing down Polo Boy.

"She's struggling with something and it's not just grief. Everything she said tonight, whether it made sense or not, had something to do with her husband. And alive or dead, whatever happened in this place was very real to her." Ian rubbed his tingling thighs, numb from crouching too long. "It's clear that—" He stopped and side-glanced Danny.

"Just say it, Ian."

He pushed out a breath. "It's clear she cares what you think about her because in the short time I've known her, upsetting you has always upset her. That's why I don't think you're going to get the silent treatment."

Running steps sped down the lane, and Danny jumped up again. Ian clamped over his arm. "It could be Finlay. I told him we might need an extra hand."

"That's more than one person."

"I may or may not have told him to bring Dean and Mattie."

Danny dropped down. "And you're worried about *me* going to jail? With them, someone is guaranteed to go."

"Are you kidding? They're Solsken's finest troublemakers, and troublemakers are what you want when someone is causing trouble."

"Ian?" Fin whispered.

Ian waved his hand and they crouch-ran toward them.

"Is it true?" Fin asked when he reached them. "Is she really living here?"

"We haven't gotten inside to check for sure," Ian said.

"Damn. Living here?" Mattie shook his head of thick, black curls. His bruised eye was visible from his fight with Polo Boys. "With that video of her tearing that dude's balls off and serving them back on a silver platter—just damn. I want to meet her."

Danny gave Ian a pointed glare and Ian smirked.

"What's the plan?" Fin asked.

"We need to circle around the place and look for any signs of tampering," Danny said. "Whoever scared her knows the area, so check for footprints too. Look for any sign that they may still be around. If no one finds anything, we meet up inside the house and see what's there."

Dean, built like an offensive lineman with a buzz-cut, had been silent up until now and cleared his throat. "I hate to state the obvious, but what if it really is a ghost?"

Danny rolled his eyes and cursed, taking off around the right side of the cottage, with Ian following. The other three went left.

Halfway around, Danny stopped with a frustrated sigh. "I don't get it. Why is she living here? It's not like she's poor and has no other choice."

"Other than the state of the house, it's the prettiest spot on the island."

"She does love atmosphere."

Ian hid a smile.

Moving forward, Danny circled around to where the other group should be.

"Psst." Fin came up to them. "There're some broken branches along the west side opening up to a rough-cut path. Dean and Mattie are checking it out."

Danny nodded, and they crept farther along the other side of the house. He tugged on Ian and pointed out an open window. Ian nodded. Lifting his bat, Danny tapped the outside, hoping to spook someone. They heard nothing but the *creak-creak* of the front door swinging on its hinges.

Danny slowly stood, eyes peeking through the window. "Where are you, asshole?" he whispered.

Ian handed him his phone with the flashlight on, silently telling him that he and Fin would go to the front to catch them if someone ran out.

With a nod to Fin they both braced on either side of the open door. Another banging came from the back of the house as Danny yelled nonsense. Nothing came out. Slowly, they both peered around the doorframe before stepping inside.

Ian sighed. "Danny? House looks empty."

There was a heavy thump on the front porch followed by a loud crack and a, "Mother*fucker*."

Ian leaned out of the doorway, grinning. "Not your night, is it?"

Danny glared up at him with his left leg swallowed inside a hole. Ian grinned wider and reached out, pulling him up. "Two f-bombs in less than an hour too. Impressive."

Danny ignored him, eyeing the porch planks, daring them to give out on him again.

Ian reached for the light switch and flipped it. Nothing came on. "Has she been without power too?"

"I'll check the breaker." Fin hopped down the front step and disappeared around the right side of the house.

Danny eyed their surroundings. "The Island of Sunshine. Jewel of the Atlantic. And all we have to offer her is shit to live in?"

"Look at it this way," Ian said. "Now you know why she didn't want you to see where she lived. I imagine she's embarrassed by it."

"We're the ones who should be embarrassed."

"You said she came from old money, right? What if this has nothing to do with us? What if this was some sort of rebellion against her family?"

The lights blinked on—every single light—and Danny and Ian took in the place, checking for any signs of disturbance. When they didn't find anything, Danny zeroed in on the rotting interior. "The ceiling is sagging here, and look at this." He touched part of a wall and the plaster crumbled. "I can't believe she lives here."

"Saints." Ian pointed. "Did an animal rip apart the couch?"

"And instead of buying a new one, she fixed it? I don't understand."

"Are you sure she's got money?"

Danny arched a brow. "Like ridiculous amounts."

"What if her family cut her off financially?"

"Her husband was well off too."

"She could've had some complications with his will."

Danny stared at him for a moment and blinked twice. "She's made more money off her books than you and I have combined."

Ian blew out air. "Well, beats the hell out of me then."

Danny stopped at the stove and snickered.

"What?"

He pointed to a drawing of an oven in the shape of a dragon spitting fire at a woman who held up a pot. The woman had a dialogue bubble. Danny read, "All I wanted was to make macaroni and cheese. Is that too much to ask?"

Danny ducked down and looked under the burners. "This is so old it doesn't have a pilot light. Probably had the gas too high when she tried to light it." He held up the picture once more and smiled before placing it back where he found it.

They made their way down the hall to the bedroom. Danny pushed the door open with the bat and it slid through his hand, hitting his foot. "Dear God." Pillows lay scattered on the floor near an upturned nightstand with a shattered lamp. The bed blankets lay twisted, half hanging off the bed near a pile of disheveled journals.

He pointed to the window. "There's no curtain. Didn't she say he was behind the curtain? Did you see any curtains in the house?"

Ian shook his head, chewing the inside of his cheek.

"Ian? Danny?" Fin's voice shook. "You guys better come see this."

They rushed to the bathroom.

"What kind of psycho shit is this?" Fin pointed to the side of the bathroom, and Danny and Ian followed his finger. "Is that written in blood?"

Danny jumped back and Ian crossed himself. A threadbare shower curtain stretched across a tub full of water and behind it, a tiled wall was covered in dripping red words. Danny used his bat to pull back the curtain and they read:

Tsk-tsk you should have looked

Behind the curtain on a hook
The water's turned cold
My actions now bold
To get you to see
You'll never be rid of me

Ian gripped Danny's arm and pointed at the drain plug where a picture of Claire and her husband on their wedding day floated, tied to a rock at the bottom.

The words, **Until your death do us part**, were scrawled across her face in permanent marker.

17

The Unexpected Isn't
Always Unwelcome

DANNY THREW HIS SHOULDER into Flygande's heavy door, yelling, "Claire?" He took two steps at a time up to his apartment. "*Claire.*"

"Quiet, Danny."

"Don't shush me, Em. Where is she?"

"Clark gave her something to calm her. She's out cold in your room. What's going on?"

Danny burst through his bedroom door, and it wasn't until he saw her, surrounded in every pillow he owned like a pillow fortress, that he dropped his hands to his knees, heaving for air.

That damned, twisted message. He hadn't stopped running since he read it.

"I called the police," Ian said from behind him.

"Is someone going to tell me what's going on?" Emelie said.

Ian pulled Emelie aside while Danny stayed in his room, catching his breath.

"*What?*" Emelie boomed.

Danny shut the door against the noise and stepped quietly back to Claire. He checked her bandaged shin propped up on a pillow and took a closer look at the single butterfly suture on her forehead.

"I'm sorry," he whispered, crouching beside her. "I didn't mean to yell at you." He moved a strand of hair out of her face and his fingers grazed an icy cheek.

Until your death do us part . . .

Danny snatched her wrist. A steady, resting heartbeat pulsed under his fingers, and he let out a long breath. He had to calm the hell down and think.

Pulling a thick blanket from his closet, he moved to drape it over her and froze, realization slowly trickling in. She wasn't in her muddied sleepwear anymore, but wearing *his* clothes. Only a t-shirt to be exact. The hem rested against her upper thigh, hovering at the curve of her backside. His belly clenched, and he quickly tore his eyes away, securing the blanket.

He had no idea how long he stayed there, watching the slow rise and fall of her back.

Ian came in and handed him a cup of strong tea. "Officer Murphy is here. He wants to talk to us."

Danny double checked her blanket before leaving the door open a few inches in case she woke up.

They went to his open kitchen where the chief of police, Tom Murphy, sipped coffee. Emelie, Fin, Mattie, and Dean were all around the oval wooden dining table.

"What'd you find?" Danny said.

"These two found a container of pork blood at a small campsite near her house." Tom nodded to Dean and Mattie. Even though they were innocent, they had a look of guilt on their faces. Probably from their many run-ins with him.

"There were no fingerprints on the container, but it's the same variety used for traditional island blood pudding," Tom continued. "I'll send it to the mainland lab with some samples from her bathroom to see if they match. Hopefully they do."

"And her window?"

"Fishing wire rigged to open yet stay unseen. We're currently fingerprinting the house. If she—"

"She's asleep," Danny and Emelie said at the same time.

"Doc gave her something strong," Emelie added. "She won't be awake for a long while."

"Bring her over to the station as soon as she's up tomorrow. I'd like to talk to her. Is there anything else you can tell me that might help figure out who's doing this?"

"She writes horror novels," Ian said. "This reminds me a little of one of them. Where the husband haunts the wife because some creep is stalking her."

"*Phantom Love*." Emelie snapped a finger. "Only that was more of a love story like the movie *Ghost*. The husband didn't threaten her, he protected her."

"Horror?" Tom made some notes. "Any violent ones?"

Ian huffed. "They're all a bit violent but really, really good."

"No one is questioning her writing abilities, McClellan. What about her fans? Any crazies?"

"They're all a bit nuts," Danny said, and Emelie and Ian protested with middle fingers. "She also comes from a well-known wealthy family and her late husband was famous. Not sure if any of that has anything to do with this."

Tom kept writing. "What happened when she came here tonight?"

Danny and Ian gave their versions of the story. "Oh, and there were these guys who were kind of pissed at her before they left last night." Danny crossed his arms. "One was named Trevor Winston. Not sure of the others."

"I have their license plates," Mattie said. "Memorized them while I was egging them."

Tom raised an eyebrow.

"We were throwing them off the island," Dean added, not helping. "For harassing Emelie like that Seth prick."

Tom turned to her, and she glared at Dean. "It wasn't like Seth." She sighed. "I'll tell you what happened, but not here."

"If there's nothing else anyone can tell me, I'll be on my way. Call me if anything comes up." He motioned to Emelie to follow him down the stairs.

"Got any ale we can have?" Mattie asked Danny.

He shrugged. "Help yourself."

"Sweet."

Ian stepped in front of them. "No."

"But Danny said—"

"Nuh-uh. I banned you from drinking here for a reason. Drink and do dumb shit with your own ale."

"Epic fail," Fin mouthed to them, shaking his head.

"We appreciate your help, though," Ian said, ushering them out. "Free meal, *without* alcohol, the next time you're here."

Emelie came in after them, shoulders hunched forward. "Officer Murphy is going to escort me to pick up some clothes for Claire."

"Em?" Danny said. "You alright?"

Her eyes pooled before she dropped them. "I wish I would have said something, *anything*, sooner. If I find out Trevor had anything to do with this, I'll—" She grabbed around her middle.

Danny's chair scraped across the floor, and he took three wide steps, wrapping his arms around her. "Listen to me. Trevor isn't your fault, understand? Don't let another man's abuse of you make you feel guilty. Not Seth, not Trevor, no one. You hear me?" She curled into him, and he squeezed her. "I'm here for you, Em. You can come to me anytime. Especially with things like this."

Her voice came out as a whisper. "But you nearly killed him, Danny."

"Look, what happened with Seth—"

"If he had, it'd been worth it." Everyone snapped toward Fin. "The fact that the bastard got to live is bullshit."

Danny and Ian glanced at each other.

"What's your problem, Finney?" Emelie said.

Fin crossed his arms and looked away from her, jaw welded shut. "Nothing."

She snatched her purse. "I better go. Officer Murphy is still waiting."

Danny caught her arm. "Thanks for coming in the middle of the night to stay with her."

"I just hope she's alright."

"If you want, you can sleep on the air mattress in the guest room so you can see her first thing tomorrow." Danny rubbed his face. "Or should I say later this morning."

"I'll stay, too, in case Creep decides to stop by." Fin edged past Emelie without looking at her.

Exhausted, Danny and Ian moved to the living room and plopped down on the couch with loud groans.

A piercing shriek came from Danny's room, and they rushed across the hall and through the door. Curled in a tight ball, Claire gripped and wrestled a pile of pillows, fisting the fabric. "Don't touch me."

Danny swept the pillows aside, and she gasped. "The curtain."

"Hey, shh." He dropped to his knees and brushed hair out of her face. "It's okay. There's no curtain."

"Danny?" Ian whispered, pointing to her shifting eyelids. "She's not awake."

"Curtain." She groaned. Her body rocked back and forth.

"It's okay, Claire." Danny smoothed a hand over her hair, down her back, and rubbed gentle strokes up and down. Her breathing began to quiet and when she went still again, he slowly eased off. She yelped and her arms sprang out.

"Shh." He took both her hands in one of his and rubbed her back again. "You're okay."

She whimpered and her body curled into itself. "No curtain."

He laid his upper half on the bed and placed his face next to hers. Reaching for another strand of hair, the back of his fingers brushed her cheek. "No more curtain," he whispered.

She shifted and her face inched toward his voice. When the tip of her nose touched his cheek, she nuzzled under it. His wide eyes tracked over to Ian who unhelpfully shrugged and grinned.

Claire hummed, and her body slowly unfurled. Her soft arms wormed out and around him, locking at his back. Danny's wide eyes met Ian's again.

"She looks cozy," he mouthed.

"Ian."

He stifled a laugh. "Try seeing if you can replace yourself with those pillows."

Danny lifted the biggest he could find and unhooked her arms.

She shuddered and re-locked her arms around him.

"What do I do?"

"Maybe stretch out with her for a few minutes, see if she falls into a deeper sleep."

"You think so?"

Ian gave him a thumbs up.

Danny carefully lifted the bottom half of his body onto the bed and looked up at Ian, questioning the large blanket he pulled over them.

"She looks cold."

"Ian, get back here."

"She needs quiet, Danny." He tiptoed backward, not fooling anyone, and grinned before slipping out.

Claire shifted again, silencing Danny's protest. He repositioned her head inside the nook between his arm and chest so her neck wouldn't cramp. Her hold tightened, pulling her body flush to his.

He froze and blinked slowly. Dear God, he could feel every curve—every soft curve. And against all the warnings going off in his head, he melted into her, sliding an arm over her waist.

Only until she's in a deep sleep, he told himself and rested his cheek against her hair.

The scent of her traced memories from the night before into his mind. He'd kept coming up with excuses to be close to her, to talk in her ear. Maybe because he rode high on what she'd done for Emelie, or maybe he'd had just enough wine not to care. He wanted to catch the perfume of citrus flowers on her skin and feel its softness whenever his nose bumped her while he talked.

His hand rubbed along her back. He wasn't sure when he started, nor did he seem to care.

Only while she slept had Jessica ever let him cuddle. Their physical connection began and ended with sex. Another bad sign he'd ignored. Here, with a woman he'd only recently met, he felt more comfort from her closeness than he'd ever had in his entire relationship with the woman he married.

Claire nuzzled deeper, bringing back his thoughts.

It all fell away then. The willpower to listen to the million reasons why he shouldn't pull her closer, shouldn't let himself put to memory every line, every freckle of her face.

Nor did he notice the drooping of his eyelids.

18

Deparate Times Call
for Pleasant Measures

A LEG DRAPED OVER his hip and soft skin rested under his hand. So soft and warm, he slid up the long, smooth thigh, wanting to feel more. Her leg responded, sliding along his side, making his journey to the underside easier.

Flattening his palm, he deepened the pressure, kneading his fingers in small circles as he went. Her leg slid further up, then down, up, then down again, following his slow circular motion.

Lace underwear interrupted his movement and without hesitating he slipped inside welcoming the fullness that filled his hand. She responded with a small hum, and he gripped harder, pressing her firmly against him.

Her leg locked around his hip, keeping the pressure there as he slipped out from soft lace to roam higher. The tip of his nose brushed along the curve of her shoulder, following the scent of citrus groves. While his hand glided over the contours of her hip — her waist — higher.

Sinking into the curve of her neck, his lips parted once, twice. The third kiss brought a sweet, gentle noise from her mouth telling him more — she wanted more.

Pushing up material blocking smooth skin, he found and circled a full breast, then another. Gentle strokes and soft pinches, he alternated, enjoying the feel of them responding to the lightest of touch.

The leg that held him squeezed and she rocked forward — she

wanted him. Wanted him so much she rolled into an arch, pressing up into his hand.

He nipped firm lip pinches from her neck down her collarbone, heading to where his hand still played. Her louder hums asked him to do this — needed him to do this.

He was going to do this.

He. Was. Going. To. Do — *this*?

Danny's eyes sprang open before his mouth got there, and what a hell of a view greeted him.

"Shi-it," he whispered, suddenly aware that he hadn't been dreaming and his hand filled with something warm and soft. His wide eyes parked over said hand, cupping an ample breast.

It didn't help his already interior freak-out moment when his view continued to dart all over what he could only describe as the nearly fully naked body of an incredibly beautiful woman.

But he didn't have a woman — she'd divorced him — yet here he was about to make love to one. His eyes shot up to the face, and he lost the ability to breathe.

Mostly naked, Claire lay in his arms and under his hand.

"Shit," he whispered again.

How the hell did this start? He blinked hard, trying to remember what he'd been thinking, but he hadn't been thinking. He just did — er, is still doing. He stared again at the hand cupped to her and trailed his eyes down to the very real black lace panties he'd been inside of. They were still pushed up, exposing half of a perfect ass.

"Shit."

He fought hard to think of who he thought he'd been touching. Did he know it was her? Did he think it was Jess?

Her shape felt nothing like Jess and if he was completely honest, he knew for a fact that he never once thought of Jessica.

Double shit — triple shit.

Clouded memories cleared and he remembered why he laid there. How he'd tried to calm and comfort her the night before, but that's all he planned to do. Not this.

He glanced back up at her angelic face, hoping the sleeping medicine stayed in effect. That the small sounds coming from her mouth didn't mean she was waking.

Her golden-brown hair splayed in waves over his pillow. The way he'd have loved to imagine her in his bed, if he had had the time to imagine her before seeing her.

She clicked her tongue on the roof of her mouth, snapping him back to the moment just in time to watch her arms stretch above her head, elongating her lean, toned figure, and pressed her breast further into his hand.

If it was hard before now, this was impossibly hard for a man who was trying to find the will to let go.

She released a sing-song sigh, and her brow furrowed, eyes still closed.

Was that a *why is someone touching me?* Face, or a *why did someone stop touching me?* Face.

Idiot. Of course it wasn't the latter. She didn't know he crawled into bed with her. He did all that stupid on his own. He'd smack his own head if his one hand wasn't keeping him from seeing an eyeful and the other wasn't caught under her neck.

He shimmied, trying to get the shirt to fall over the other breast that he hid against his chest and unknowingly caused friction.

She rocked her hips into him, and he froze. That didn't help.

He needed to let go. Yes, he absolutely needed to let go. That and stop loving how she reacted to his every touch, encouraging him to do more.

It may have seemed like an easy thing — letting go — yet his sleep-drunk, racing mind stuttered, restarted, then froze. Maybe if there was a manual on how to unstick your hand from where you didn't want to, this would be easier.

One thought managed to get through the traffic jam. An anxiety-filled one where she suddenly woke and screamed when she saw him.

Yep. That did it. He forced his eyes closed and opened his hand, reaching for her shirt. His palm grazed over a perky breast, and he cursed, making silent pleas with God that if he wanted him to do the right thing, he needed to stop throwing impossible temptations like eager boobs at him. He blessedly found the shirt and lifted it high to avoid any more mind-numbing grazing and yanked it down.

He took a moment to breathe.

How could he get his arm out from under her neck without waking her and causing the panic he previously imagined?

Sliding back, he inched his arm as he went, laying out the fleece before the Almighty to get him out of this without waking her. Her leg slid off, and in another few inches, he was free. So free, he lost his balance on the edge of the bed and ugly fell to the floor with a hard thump.

"Shit," he groaned. It seemed shit was the only word he could say anymore.

Without moving, he waited on the floor when she stirred, hoping she wasn't waking. When she stopped moving, he slowly lifted his head, peeking over the mattress, and found himself at eye level with a set of full rosy lips.

All of that just happened, and he still hadn't kissed that mouth.

He forced himself up the rest of the way and decided against tucking her under the blanket. He'd already pressed his luck and needed to get the hell out of there.

She stirred again with more quiet hums and reached out, running a hand over where he'd just been.

Would you touch me like that if I were still there?

That damn thought made his brain stutter. He snatched a pillow from the floor and plunked it over his screaming lower half, tiptoeing backward. He gripped the doorknob, slowly opened it, and thanked heaven he'd greased out the squeak it used to have.

Like an escapee from a bad one-night stand, Danny backed out ass-first. When he cleared the door, he shut it with a quiet click and pressed his forehead against it, sighing.

"Good morning."

Danny whipped around to Fin and Ian casually leaning against the wall. "How long were you there?"

"Heard a noise." Fin smirked

"More of a loud thump," Ian added, the corner of his mouth ticking. "She kick you out?"

Danny glared with all he wanted to say but couldn't form the words. "Why didn't you wake me?"

"You looked too cozy," Ian said.

Fin glanced down. "Nice pillow, by the way."

Danny's tingling face burst with heat.

"Oops." Ian interrupted his soon-to-be outburst and held up a finger, bending his ear toward the door. "Sleeping Beauty is stirring."

"Might I suggest a cold shower?" Fin said.

The sound of the bed creaking sent Danny stagger-running to the bathroom, pillow still intact. He kicked the door shut on Ian and Fin back slapping each other in silent laughter.

DANNY DRAGGED TIME OUT as long as possible in the bathroom, trimming his beard and hair. Going back and forth between wanting to avoid seeing her and not being able to wait another minute until he could.

He wasn't sure what was worse, the idea of her acknowledging what had happened or acting like nothing had.

When she still hadn't come out of the bedroom, he avoided Ian and Fin's smirks and plastered himself in front of the sink, taking his nerves out on scrubbing dishes.

"Morning, Claire," Ian said loudly, and Danny jumped.

"Hello," she said, and when her eyes met his, he didn't move. Waiting. Hoping. Freaking.

Then she smiled. Not full, but not fake. She wasn't running, so he'd take it as at least positive.

Stepping further into the space, she took in his simple kitchen, eyes pausing on small details, while his paused on her fitted wool jumpsuit, slowly moving up to the perfectly messy bun she sported.

"It seems I've taken over your home, Daniel."

"Nah, it's okay." He busied himself again, washing the few dishes left in the sink. "Tea?"

"That would be lovely. That medicine made my head quite foggy this morning."

Danny grabbed a small pot, measured out two cups of water, and set it on the stove to boil. Then he went to the fridge and measured out equal parts milk. God, his hands were shaking.

"Royal Milk Tea?" she said by his ear.

He startled and hot liquid splashed onto his hand.

"Did you burn yourself?" She touched his arm.

He yanked away and ran his still shaking hand under cold water. "It's fine." He forced a smile. In his nervousness, he forgot to answer her tea question and continued by adding tea leaves to the mixture and turning the heat down to a simmer.

"I-I'll leave soon, I promise."

He twisted around. "Who asked you to leave?"

"Well, I . . ." She touched the suture on her forehead. "No one did."

Danny, thinking the matter was settled, nodded and turned back to the sink.

"Oh my God, why is there no coffee?" Emelie shuffled in from the hallway.

Fin's cheeks tinted, brightening the top of his ears, and he did a quick scan over her low hanging pajama pants and cropped t-shirt. Danny caught Ian's knowing look and they both smirked. He was a goner, and Emelie was clueless.

"Claire." Emelie went toward her, arms out. "How are you so pretty first thing in the morning?"

"Oh hush." Claire wiped a wisp of hair out of her face. "You're always gorgeous."

Emelie snorted and squeezed her. "How are you feeling? Did you sleep alright?"

Shit. Leave it to Em to be the first person to ask her what they all should have asked right away.

"I think so. I can't quite remember, except for a few vivid dreams."

Danny stiffened. Peeking over his shoulder, he watched her fingers slide up the side of her neck where he'd kissed her.

Dream. To her, it was a dream? He thought knowing that would bring him relief, but his stress level peaked. Was it a happy dream? A bad dream — he lost feeling in his cheeks — a nightmare?

"Good dreams?" Emelie asked, wiggling her eyebrows.

Danny peeked back over his shoulder.

She didn't answer at first, and his stomach curled in on itself. She glanced up, locking onto his eyes for a brief moment, biting her lip. "Yes, quite good dreams." She dropped her gaze, touching her neck again.

With his back turned to all of them, Danny smiled.

"Did you get my things?" she asked Emelie.

"Yeah, thought you'd want to have them with you."

"Thank you, but you didn't have to bring all of it. I'm not staying long."

Danny clunked a mug against the table, and cream-colored liquid swished over the edge. "Where are you staying then?"

"The cottage?"

He felt the shift. The moment all nervousness evaporated, replaced with something else. Something that burned in his stomach and made his skin tight.

"You can't," he said slowly. "It's a crime scene."

"A what?" Her face blanched. "But it was all in my head. Nothing happened. I was clumsy and tripped."

"Clumsy?" His voice strained. "No, Claire, you're not clumsy. And there's not a damn thing that happened to you that was just in your head."

Ian touched her shoulder. "Did you go into the bathroom?"

"No, why?" She rubbed over goosebumps on her arms. "I don't like to go in there unless I have to. It's a long story."

She straightened her posture, hand pressed to her stomach where her body now trembled. She was trying to mask it? Trying to convince him she wanted to go back when she clearly didn't? Why?

A tremble of a different kind took over Danny. His forefinger pressed into the table until it bleached. "Someone very real was in your house, Claire, and left you a message in the bathroom."

"What did it say — no wait, don't tell me." She closed her eyes and took a deep breath. "I'm sorry to have bothered you all with this. I should just go."

"Hey." Emelie stood and dragged her into a hug. "No, come on. Don't leave."

Claire melted into the affection. "But it's for the best."

"For who?" Danny said, sharp. "You think the shit that happened at Sven's isn't going to follow you?"

"It didn't start until I came here, so it should stop when I leave."

"I don't think so." His lips flattened against his teeth. "I think that 'You'll never be rid of me,' written in blood, means just that."

"Wha-what?"

"Danny," Emelie snapped. "She said she didn't want to know."

"Right." His face twitched. "We should definitely keep it a secret that some sick bastard drowned her picture, with 'Until your death do us part' on it."

"Don't be an asshole."

But Danny's attention was solely on Claire. When he'd said it, she'd avoided eye contact with him.

The twisted marriage vow wasn't a surprise to her.

He took a step toward her, zeroing in. "Who's threatening you, Claire?"

She shook her head. "If I tell you, you'll think I'm crazy."

"No, what's happening to you is crazy. Try me."

More wisps of hair dropped around her face as she met his gaze. "Exercise and proper diet were more important to Brandon than to me. He used to tease and say he'd outlive me and that our vows should have said, 'Until your death do us part.'" She puffed a small laugh.

"Who the hell tells their wife that?" Fin said.

She graciously smiled. "He was always a bit brash with his humor."

"Did you like that kind of humor?" Emelie frowned.

She shrugged. "I just took it for what it was—Brandon."

Danny, now securely in the *I hate Brandon* corner, swallowed everything he wanted to say and instead said, "But this wasn't a ghost, Claire. Whoever did this rigged your window to open, came into your home, and threatened you."

"It has to be." Her eyes shimmered. "Only Brandon knew of that vow joke. If it's not his ghost, then I can't even begin to think of who it is. And the best thing for me to do . . . " She stepped toward him, and he straightened. When she took another step, his eyes betrayed his sudden distracted thoughts and ran down over her. Was it just two hours ago that he'd held her?

"The best thing for me to do," she repeated and stopped in front of him. "Is to leave this island and deal with this alone."

He searched the entirety of her face. "Why alone? Why is everything you do alone?"

She lowered her head and swallowed. "Because that's what I deserve."

"Bullshit."

"Excuse me?"

"You heard me." He plunked down his tea mug and picked up hers. "Bullshit that you deserve this and bullshit that you're doing this alone." He took her hand and curled her fingers around the handle, nodding to her cup. "Drink your tea. It'll help with the headache."

"How do you—oh." She dropped the fingers rubbing her temple with a sigh and slowly lifted the mug to her mouth. "You can't just 'bullshit' me into staying, Daniel."

He stepped into her space and her lips froze on the rim of her cup. Dipping his head, he said in a low voice, "Bull. Shit. That you're leaving this island." He twisted around, throwing open the door, and thundered down the stairs.

19

What Are Friends For?

"WELL, I . . . " CLAIRE PUFFED out a breath and stared at the three people holding back smiles. "Why did he leave in the middle of our conversation?"

Ian cleared his voice. "He was done speaking."

"And said bullshit, so . . . " Fin shrugged.

She blinked once, twice, the third time a spark ignited. "I wasn't finished, though."

"Maybe go tell him that then." Emelie pointed to the door.

Claire propped her hands on her hips and shifted front and back — Madelynn and Claire, propriety and passion — playing tug of war. Brandon never let her win an argument. Always talking over or around her. Danny did neither of those things, still, somehow she'd lost. Her cheeks burned.

"You know what? I think I'll do just that." Claire marched down the stairs. Her mind running too fast to register the three cheering voices behind her.

Danny's voice drifted from behind a closed wooden door, and she stopped in front of it. He had time to talk to someone. Clearly.

What was happening to her? Was it just the trauma from last night? She felt a little wild. Unhinged in the middle. Her fingers went numb curled around the doorknob. And for the first time, Claire didn't weigh what was proper and what wasn't.

She threw open the door.

DANNY FROZE MID-SENTENCE and did a couple of double takes. He'd hoped his bluntness would light the fight he'd seen when she confronted Trevor. But nothing could've prepared him for what simmered at the entrance of his office. Claire. Hands squeezed tight at her sides. Eyes like a burning pyre.

Nor did he realize he'd enjoy it so much.

He cleared his throat and glanced down, making a quick, hidden adjustment below the desk.

She opened her mouth to speak, and he held up a finger. "That's what I thought. Okay, yeah, it'll take a bit. She hasn't eaten yet." Unable to stop himself, his eyes slid back to her. She still burned. "But I'll bring her over as soon as she does. Thanks, Tom." In one slow, controlled movement, he placed the handset on the receiver of an old landline phone and swiveled his chair to face her. Steepling his fingers under his chin, he said, "Yes, Claire."

"We weren't finished talking."

"Weren't we?"

"Why is there a rug here?" She pointed down at the doorway.

"My Grandfather started it. You wipe your feet before you come in to say what's outside the door stays out there. You wipe when you leave to keep what's in the office, inside."

"Well, in that case." She hopped over the rug, bringing it all in.

He hid a smile behind his fingers. "Might want to grab your cloak."

"Oh." Disappointment flashed in her eyes. "Okay. It'll take a minute to pack. But if you drive me to the airport, I can take care of everything else from there."

"I'm not taking you to the airport."

She stopped on her way to the doorway, still avoiding the rug, and spun around. "But I told you I'm leaving."

"And I said bullshit." Her eyes bulged, and he fought another smile, quickly adding, "But also, Officer Murphy needs to speak to you."

She pointed to his phone. "You called him on purpose. You knew he'd say that."

"Yes, I did."

His directness stunned her momentarily, but then she straightened her spine. Her face bending down halfway, she glared out of the tops of her eyes.

Shit. The fire he lit in her blazed as she slowly, purposefully — one foot in front of the other — stalked toward him.

It threw off his game. Hell, it threw off every thought in his head except the swing of her hips and how much he wanted to get a firm hold on them.

She slapped her palms down on his desk, snapping his brain back, and leaned halfway across. "You can't force me to stay here, Daniel."

He arched back in his seat, taking all of her in. "I'm not. Officer Murphy is."

"I didn't come here to have another parent, agent, or *man* tell me what I can and cannot do."

Danny placed his hands on either side of hers and stood, meeting her at her level. "Good. We're in agreement then."

"You're," her view dropped to his mouth, "taking me to the airport?"

"No."

Her eyes ticked up and narrowed further. "You. You were the *man* I was referring to, in case that wasn't clear."

He slowly smiled. "Look me in the eye and tell me you want to leave Solsken because you hate it here, and I won't stop you." He inched closer until he felt her rapid breathing on his face and lowered his voice. "But if you're leaving because you're being bullied away from where you want to be, then I'm not letting you go."

She closed her eyes with a deep breath, and to his great disappointment, backed away. "You don't understand."

"Then tell me."

"He knew we were together last night."

Their "together" from this morning flashed in his mind, and

he circled around the desk. "I didn't—we didn't—nothing happened, n-not really, not on purpose." He blew out air.

"I know that. We just had wine and talked."

Ah, yes, *last* night. That's the together she meant, dummy. He cleared his voice. "So, you're going to let some bastard threaten you for talking to me?"

"It's not that."

"Then what is it?"

"I can't . . . I won't . . ." She took a deep breath and tried again. "I won't bring you into my mess, Daniel."

He stepped closer. "What if I want to be there?"

"No." She shook her head. "Trust me, you don't."

"How many friends do you have, Claire?"

"I beg your pardon?"

"Do those friends usually let you handle ghost-threatening assholes alone? Because I can tell you one thing, if someone threatened me, Ian would beat them to an inch of their life and go back to do it again. Don't even get me started on what Ems would do, or what I'd do for either of them."

"People like me don't have friends like that."

He pressed his tongue into his cheek, studying her. "I thought we established that we're friends last night."

"Daniel—"

"You said you don't want anyone else telling you what to do, yet here you are doing exactly what this bastard wants." He curled his arms over his chest. "Do you hate it in Solsken?"

"No, I love it."

"You feel unsafe with me then?"

She dropped a long look at the dragon hurling fire over his flexed arm. "I-I feel quite safe with you."

"Good." He edged around her. "Grab your cloak. We're headed to the station." He walked out without wiping his feet. He wanted what was in his office to follow him out.

She did.

Danny ignored all three eavesdroppers scurrying away from

his office and into the bar area pretending to clean, and smiled when he heard, "You know, I can get to the airport without you."

"I'm sure you could." He made his way up and into his apartment. "But you're not going to," he called.

She followed, feet stomping all the way up. "Do you boss around all the residents here, Daniel? Are you like a king and all of us peons must bow and obey?" She kept stomping and his smile grew. "I have news for you."

She paused in the stairwell, and he half-turned toward it when he heard a deep breath. Like she gathered up air to control herself again.

No, let it out for me. He startled at his own thought.

"Friends," she said, voice more calm but razor sharp. "Do not let *friends* get into crap with them."

Danny grinned widely. "Actually, that's the very definition of a friend. To drive straight into a great big pile of shit, *together*."

"Oh yeah? Well—" She hopped over the top step and plowed right into him. She went very still, staring at his chest. Her gaze a little dazed like she was lost in a memory. Then slowly, her hand drifted to the side of her neck where he'd kissed her.

Did she still think it was just a dream?

"Found it," he said, and she blinked. He held up her cloak hooked on one finger. The point of her turned-up nose lifted, ready for more fighting. "I promised you breakfast and a tour, remember?"

"Oh." All the fire smothered in her eyes, replaced with disappointment. "I forgot about breakfast, and it's getting late."

"Not too late. We can still go." He tipped his head. "That is, if you're going to stay for a while longer."

"*Please*, stay," Emelie yelled as she, Ian, and Fin ran up the stairs, making their stairwell eavesdropping known.

Claire spun around. "But where would I stay?"

"Normally, I'd say you could stay at the Solsken Inn, but when Trevor and his friends left, their rooms were taken by some long-termer who seems to be hibernating in as much space as he can get." Her face brightened. "Danny's got a spare room though."

Ian's eyes snapped to him, probably waiting to see him panic. It was there. Sitting like a heavy fist in his stomach.

"O-oh, no," Claire said. "I couldn't stay here."

"Yeah, you could," Fin said. "We all did last night."

"But—" Her eyes slid to Danny, and he remained silent, studying her. Waiting to see if she was actually against the idea, or trying to be polite.

"Look at it this way," Ian chimed in. "Flygande has the best security system on the island. A genuine Jake Matthews' System."

"Oh, a Jake Matthews?" Tension eased out of Claire's expression. "Yes, I'm familiar with them. His systems are the best that I know of."

"It helps that the man is stupid rich and has a pretty face to back them up too." Emelie sighed. Fin crossed his arms, rolling his eyes.

"Danny had it installed before he left," Ian said. "Because while he lived here, well," he gestured to Danny, "he *was* the security and no one but dumb kids ever tried to break in."

"But why are you all doing this for me?" Claire looked to each of them. "You hardly know me."

"Purely selfish reasons," Ian said. "We want bragging rights for having your next novel written here. Hopefully bring more ugly polos to Solsken."

She laughed before facing Danny. "You sure you're okay with this?"

He nodded, quick and short. The reality of being close to her every day slowly closed in, scaring him shitless. But Ian was right. Flygande was one of the safest places on the island.

Just not the safest place for his heart.

"Then if I do stay," Claire said. "I stay in the guest room. I'm not taking your bedroom from you."

"Sure." His jaw ticked. "Absolutely." Nope. Absolutely not.

"And it's only until things get sorted. Then I'll go back to the cottage."

"It's whatever you want, Claire."

A slow smile lifted her cheeks and she whispered, "Bullshit."

He belted a surprised laugh, and Emelie cheered, throwing her arms around Claire. "Danny's right, you know. This is what friends do."

"Friends," Ian announced, surrounding them both in his arms. Claire and Emelie squeaked when he squished them together.

Behind the Curtain

"DON'T YOU WANT A coat?" Claire eyed up Danny's t-shirt as she slipped on her gloves.

"Nah, but hang on." He went to his room and she winced.

"I'm sorry," she called, thinking of the underwear she'd tossed on the floor. "I forgot to clean up my-my stuff."

Danny's throat cleared before, he said, "Not a problem."

He came back out with a navy slouchy beanie, his cheeks a little more rosy. "My ears are the only part of me that gets cold in this mild weather."

Maybe that's why his ears were red too? They were hit with a blast of cold wind.

"Mild?" Claire said.

Danny grinned and tapped a fist on his chest. "Solsken Viking, M.C.C."

She laughed, and he held the gate open for her, motioning in their direction.

The first thing they came upon was what looked like multiple homes built into each other. Each one was a different size, starting with a small stone cottage on the left and ending with an estate-looking building with three high columns guarding the entrance.

"Solsken Inn," Danny said. "Another Larsson establishment." He waved to an older man walking behind a frail-looking woman in a wheelchair. "Good to see you, Uncle Nils. How's Aunt Mathilde this morning?"

"Having a good day, Danny. Having a good day."

"Is your aunt alright?"

"She had a stroke some years ago," Danny said quietly as he watched his uncle wheeling her along a winding path. "Left her paralyzed on her left side and her health's deteriorating."

"Isn't there any place that could help her?"

"On the mainland, but my uncle never admitted her. Said she'd never forgive him for taking her off the island. So," he sighed, "he left his children to run the inn while he takes care of her. Well, more like Em runs the inn while her brother Johan does whatever the hell he wants. I do what I can, when I can, to help her though."

Claire went quiet, studying him. He was an endless well of goodness, she decided. The kind of rare, pure goodness just because. Not expecting anything in return.

Following down the twisting, unpaved Main Street, Danny pointed to a small barn next to Solsken Medical Center where a giant dappled gray head poked out, chewing hay. Claire cooed and stepped toward him.

Danny touched her elbow, easing her back. "Don't let that sweet face fool you. Gus is a biter unless you're Annie. He's her pet and the literal horsepower of our ambulance sleigh when the snow gets too deep. So, he may be a cranky old bastard, but he's dependable."

Across from the medical center in the town center, he stopped next to a tall tower made of stacked dry stones with a weathered bell crowning the top.

"This here is Old Governor." Danny rested a hand on one of the gray stones. "The oldest piece of construction on the island. During the busy tourist months, we have a temporary doctor that helps out at the medical center. But Doc Clark and Annie are the only ones who live here year-round." He looked up reverently. "In the winter, when the bridge closes, this bell is how we sound out emergencies because cell phone towers are unreliable in severe weather and not everyone has a landline phone. It's saved many lives over the years."

Claire patted the old giant. "I like you," she whispered, and Danny smiled.

They came upon a large facility with a bank of thick glass panels lining the front. Magnificent copper stills in a row stood like silent watchmen behind them. "McClellan Distillery, or Ian's second home," Danny said. "If you ask, he'll give you a very detailed, very lengthy tour and insist you try all the whisky."

She covered her mouth, whispering, "Don't tell him, but I don't like whisky."

"Pretty sure even that wouldn't change his mind about you being his favorite."

She laughed and wiped fake sweat from her brow. "Where's his first home?"

"It's on the other side of the island." He went quiet for a long moment. "But he mostly stays with me when he's not at seminary."

Claire sensed he was holding back information but respectfully didn't push for more.

"Here we are."

They came around the winding main street to Ylva's Bakery & Café. A quaint cottage made of gray stone, adorned in bright-blue shutters with painted yellow flowers. Matching empty flower boxes sat under each windowsill with electric candles behind the divided light windows. A weathered Swedish flag and a newer American flag flapped on either side of the door.

Claire clapped her hands together. "Could this place be any cuter?"

Danny pointed out a Swedish word etched over the doorway. "Recognize that?"

"That says, welcome. Right?"

"*Mycket bra.*" He smiled. "Very good."

"Do all you Larssons speak fluent Swedish?"

"Normally, yes," he said. "My dad spoke it occasionally, but my mom, who's half English, chose to only speak English. So, I understand more than I speak."

She gestured to the café. "And is Ylva your cousin too?"

He shook his head. "Ylva is one of Solsken's many transplants. She grew up in Sweden."

A bell jingled as he pulled open the door, letting her walk in front of him. Claire gasped, taking in the rustic wooden tables and wrought-iron chairs filled with rosy-cheeked customers chatting happily over steaming mugs of coffee and plates full of baked goods. Tealight candles in snowball shaped glass sat at every table, and paintings of bright yellow fields beneath clear blue skies hung over them.

"*Hej*, Daniel." A middle-aged woman with cropped, golden-blond hair smiled at them from behind a glass counter.

Danny waved. "*Ylva, roligt att se dig.*"

Her clear blue eyes fell on Claire and brightened.

He introduced her. "I was giving her a tour of the island. She loves your baked goods."

"*Tack så mycket.*" She smiled at Claire, and to Danny, she raised one eyebrow.

Claire smiled back and turned to take in more of the café.

"*Hon är väldigt vacker,*" Ylva said to Danny.

"*Ja.*" He cleared his throat. "*Men hon är bara en vän.*"

"Just a friend, indeed," Ylva said under her breath.

Danny pinched his lips closed when Claire faced them again. "What did you say?" she asked.

Ylva smiled. "That you are very beautiful."

Claire's cheeks warmed. "Oh, thank you." She'd never been great at compliments and refocused on the painting of a Swedish countryside.

"*Vad kan jag göra för er?*" Ylva asked.

"We too late for breakfast?" Danny said.

"Never, *välkommen.*" She showed them to a two-seater table. "Sit, sit." She motioned to the chairs and placed down a small basket with hard crisp bread and *limpa* inside with a bowl of butter. "*Varsågod.*"

Danny pointed at the tabletop menu. "She has more than

Swedish foods here. There's also a full Scottish breakfast, or eggs any way you like, with fruit and oatmeal if you prefer."

"All of it." Claire grinned. "I can't eat it all, but I want all of it."

He laughed and ordered a total of three breakfasts with a serving of *kanelbullar*. "I can see that feeding you is going to be a hell of a lot of fun."

She smiled, but his faltered, his fingers going to the slouchy with a small tug.

"Daniel I . . . you're under no obligation for me to stay with you."

His eyes snapped to her. "You're having second thoughts?"

Second, third, and even tenth thoughts. "Are you?"

His steady gaze remained on her. "No," he said. "I'm not."

Breakfast came, breaking the moment, and Claire welcomed it with a small clap of her hands. "Ylva, this looks delicious."

Ylva beamed with a small bow of her head and ordered for them to "Eat, eat."

"Oh, I forgot to ask for extra plates." Claire peered around, looking for Ylva, who disappeared into the kitchen.

"We can share."

She went still. She'd tried that with Brandon, once, on their honeymoon. The night she'd also unknowingly conceived Greyson. She'd been so happy. Finally loved. But he'd been so repulsed by her doing that, he refused to eat the rest of his food. "It doesn't bother you if I touch your plate?"

"Did Brandon—" His mouth snapped closed, and he blinked away, rubbing the back of his neck. "I don't mind, if you don't."

To prove his point, he took a large bite of oatmeal topped with walnuts and raisins and offered her the bowl.

She wasn't sure what to make of him, but when she searched his eyes, he only smiled with a nod. Cradling the bottom of the spoon, she gently blew away the steam and curled her lips over it. Honey with nutty sweetness melted on her tongue, and she closed her eyes. "Mmm."

When she opened them, Danny's frozen gaze on her mouth quickly dropped, and he cleared his throat.

"Okay," he said. "I have to ask." He dug into the oatmeal, right where her spoon had been. "The note on your stove with the dragon. Was that because the flame burst when you tried to light it?"

"Yes." She leaned over the table. "It was awful." And so, so scary.

The corner of his mouth lifted as he scooped some eggs. "I'm assuming you've never cooked on something that old before. It's tricky." He held out the plate of eggs to her.

She took them with a wince. "I haven't really cooked on anything before."

"You eat out mostly?"

"Actually no, but I'm afraid my reason is going to make you think I'm quite a snob."

"You seem to think I'm thinking a lot of things I'm not."

She didn't know how to answer that.

He forked some black pudding and said, "What's your reason?"

She covered her lap in a napkin and fingered the edge. "Well, growing up, we always had a cook. It was considered improper for me to learn to cook or clean, but I'm trying." She met his eyes and dropped them again. "I also had a maid, a nanny, and a driver."

She paused, glancing up again, and he tilted his head, waiting for more.

"When I married Brandon, it stayed the same. So, I never learned to do any of it. When I came here, I thought I could magically learn to do those things on my own." She sighed. "But I couldn't even make macaroni and cheese."

Incapable Claire. She lost her appetite and laid down her fork.

Daniel stopped chewing and rested his elbows on the table. "Still waiting for the snob part."

"I just told you. I had a cook, maid, nanny, and a driver."

"With the amount of money you grew up with, that's normal right?"

She nodded.

"Being born into a wealthy family doesn't make you a snob. But what I'd like to know is . . . " He wiped a napkin across his mouth.

She held her breath. It was coming. The interrogation about her upbringing. The questions of what it was like to be so "pampered." Which would lead to her having to disclose how her family was nothing like his. Being a Cooke meant a name and status, not affection or a support system. Then his criticism would kick in and—

"Claire?"

"Huh, what?"

"You alright? Still have a headache?"

She dropped the hand rubbing her temple. "No. I'm sorry, what did you say?"

"I asked you if there's anything you wanted to learn to do that I could help with."

It took her a few moments of stunned silence for her to realize she never answered. "Oh, um, macaroni and cheese. Do you know how to make it? It's my favorite."

He slowly smiled. "I think I know what's for dinner."

DANNY TORE OFF HIS beanie when they entered the police station and ran a hand through matted, blond strands. "I'll be waiting out here when you're done." He looked for a chair.

"Oh." She stopped short. "Are you not coming with me?"

He shot back up from his seat. "Do you want me to come with you?"

"You don't have to." She placed her feet together.

"I know I don't, but I will if you want me to."

They were back to shifting feet and hands jammed into pockets with stolen glances.

Claire forced a smile. "You've done enough for me, thank you."

Officer Murphy cleared his throat, and they both turned. A small smile twitched under his bushy mustache. "You're not under any investigation, Ms. Cooke. Or do you prefer Mrs. Johnson?"

"It was Cooke-Johnson, so Cooke is fine."

He nodded. "Danny can come along unless you prefer to keep this conversation private."

"Oh, no. I'm okay with it not being private, if he wants to come."

Danny ended the misery for both of them and stepped up next to her.

Tom went down a yellow-stained, linoleum-clad hallway where one florescent light in the middle flickered.

"Are you sure you don't mind?" she whispered.

"I'm sure." The warmth of Danny's hand soaked into the small of her back as he directed her in front of him. When his fingers dropped away, a small part of her withered. It was getting harder and harder to convince herself that being alone was best. And how much harder was it going to be staying with a man whose touch did that?

She sighed.

"Have a seat." Tom motioned to chairs in front of his metal desk. "Do you need anything to drink? Some water? Coffee?"

She shook her head. "I'm fine."

He rested his elbows on the desk and his intelligent, kind eyes studied her. "How are you feeling?"

"Better."

"Good. Well, I won't keep you long. With the evidence we've collected, it's clear the break-in was intended to frighten you and maybe even harm you." He looked up from his notes. "Do you know anyone who'd want to do that?"

She rubbed her palms together, skin suddenly clammy. Her mind raced to where she never wanted to be again.

The weight of his body . . . the stench of his breath . . . pain slicing through her wrist . . .

"Claire?"

Danny's whisper tore her from the memory, and she dropped the hand rubbing her scar and slid it over her phone. The true assurance she had that he was gone. "Alive? No."

Tom's eyes flicked to Danny, who stayed quiet. "You think someone who's dead is doing this?"

"I only know that whoever did it said things only my deceased husband knew."

"Like what?"

"Like the promise I made when he died that I'd never take the wedding rings off."

She removed her gloves, and Danny's expression shifted into something unreadable. His gaze glued to the large diamond on her finger.

Tom leaned back and studied her. "Even if that's true and this was a phantom, I think whether you wore a ring or not would be the least of his worries."

"I know how this makes me sound." She swallowed and spun the ring on her finger. "But when this person or spirit spoke, his voice was everywhere yet nowhere at the same time. Sometimes it was beside me, then behind me. Other times all around me. I looked, Officer, no one was there. But when I went out the door, the voice still followed me. Can someone alive do that?"

Tom's bushy brows shaded his eyes. "How long did the voice follow you?"

"I'm sorry, I don't know. I was yelling so loud, I-I didn't notice when it stopped."

Tentative, warm fingers slipped over her shaking ones, and when she looked up, Danny gave them a gentle squeeze.

"I don't know how he spoke to you like that." Tom folded his fingers together. "But I'd bet my entire career that it's flesh and blood, not a ghost."

Claire dropped her eyes to her hands.

"I know this is difficult, Ms. Cooke, but in order to understand why someone would be threatening you with something your husband would say, I need to talk about your husband's death."

A shudder ran through her, and Danny's hand squeezed. "What do you need to know?"

"Well, anything that may point us to why this is happening."

"It's happening . . . " The words came out strained, and she closed her eyes, forcing the rest out. "It's happening because it's my fault he died."

She felt a jolt in Danny's hand and quickly pulled away before he could.

"Ms. Cooke, there's no record of foul play in your husband's case. I read it. It said it was accidental."

"Yes, it was." She stared down at her fingers, pinching and squeezing the tips. "He had a hard day and took some extra anti-anxiety medicine to relax. He fell asleep and drowned in the bathtub."

"How is it your fault, then?"

In the slow parting of his lips, Claire knew Danny had put it together before she even said the words.

"Because I didn't look behind the curtain."

Helpful Kenneth

THE CURTAIN. DANNY'S HEART pounded in his ears, muffling Tom's voice asking Claire to clarify.

"He was quiet, and I didn't want to disturb him," she whispered, swallowing. "He drowned because I didn't look."

A knot formed in Danny's stomach, and his eyes slid closed. He forced a calming inhale. Her jumbled words from the night before. The grief and panic on her face. Everything she said and did finally made sense.

She blamed herself for it all.

Claire glanced at him, and for some reason, her eyes went wide when she saw him. He quickly adjusted his expression, not sure what she read from it, but it was too late.

She turned to Tom and asked, "Are we done?"

Tom looked from her, to Danny, back to her again. "Yes. For now."

She rushed out of the office.

"Claire?" Danny chased after her into the icy wind and yanked his slouchy over his ears. "Hang on."

"Don't worry," she called without turning around. Her feet made quick work of the ground beneath them. "I'll find another way to the airport."

The knot in his stomach tightened. "We back to the airport thing again? Why are we back to the airport thing?"

"I'll call Kenneth and he'll come get me. Don't worry."

"Kenneth?" He stopped and screwed up his face. "Who the hell is Kenneth?"

Instead of answering, she went faster, and he took off after her again.

"Are you always going to run away from me instead of telling me what I did to upset you?"

She slowed a little, and he caught up to her. "It's okay, Daniel."

He gulped a breath. "It doesn't seem okay."

Taking off again, she said, "Don't know why I didn't think of him before."

"Him who?"

"Kenneth."

He panted behind her. "Friend?"

"No. Cab driver from the airport."

The hair on the back of his neck sprang up, and he slowed. *Cab driver?* She gained too much distance, and he started up again. "Claire, hang on. There aren't any cab drivers at the airport. It's too," he gulped another breath, "small. You rent a car or have someone pick you up."

"Well, he had a cab."

God, he was tired of having a yelling conversation while running. "What did you say his name was again?"

"Kenneth Greene," she yelled over her shoulder, "and he was very nice."

"Oh, I bet he was." He gripped a side-stitch. A cramp was forming in his thigh. "Crook more like it. Did you pay cash or card? Claire, slow down."

She didn't slow. "Usually I pay cash for everything, but I didn't think he'd have enough change." She wasn't even winded while talking. "Why is that important?"

"Because a card would have your name on it, and he already knows where you're staying."

She skidded to a sudden stop, and Danny groaned in relief.

"Why had he been so conveniently where I needed him to be?" she said, more to herself than him, then whispered, "Couldn't be."

"Care to let me in on what's going on inside that head?" He bent over, grabbing his knees. She took off again.

"Dammit." But he followed.

The gate at Flygande slapped open, and she jumped down the one step. Her feet swished into the tiny pebbles as she ran to the stone steps and up to the door. She jiggled the handle, but it was locked.

"Come *on*." She kicked it.

Unused to hearing her yell, Danny eased onto the first step. "It's solid oak. Kicking it will only break your foot."

She let go of the door and hugged herself.

"Whatever you thought or think I'm thinking about you." He took the next step. "It isn't true."

Her shoulders dropped.

"That's it, isn't it?" He took the third step. "Something in the look on my face at the station made you think I was upset at you, but I'm not. How could I be?"

Puffs of her clouded breath increased, puffing faster and faster and he knew he was right.

"I prefer a kick to the face, Claire," he repeated her words from the airplane. "And I'm not the backstabbing type."

"We'd had another argument," she said, quietly. "That's why he took the extra anxiety pill. *Me*. I was just so glad he'd stopped yelling, I didn't . . . " She swallowed and turned, tucking her face into the alcove of the doorway. "I should have checked on him."

"Everyone fights," Danny said carefully. "His death was an accident."

She shivered and rubbed her arms.

Because that's what I deserve. Her words from earlier hit him. Seeing her now — hiding, shoulders rolled forward, body curled into itself — she actually believed it. He took the last step and planted his wide frame behind her, blocking the wind.

"Claire, look at me." He touched her shoulder, and she shook her head. "Please."

She turned, clamping hard on her bottom lip, looking everywhere but his face.

"It's not your fault."

Her entire body began to vibrate. "But I-I should have known."

"How, Claire? How could you have known?"

"Maybe if . . ." Wet drops spilled over the rims of her eyes. "If I just—" Her face crumpled, and a sob burst out.

His body reacted without him. Careening forward, his hands sprang out, but he stopped short. What if she shoved him away?

"Claire." His voice was unsteady. "Would you mind if . . . could I please . . . " Slowly, he stretched his arms out toward her again and whispered, "Can I hold you?"

She plowed forward, colliding with his body, and buried her face deep in his chest. He finally breathed, arms encircling her.

"It wasn't your fault." His hand glided down loose strands of her hair.

"Then why is this happening?"

"I don't know." He rubbed small circles on her back, folding her further into him. "But I'll help you figure it out, okay?"

A small movement stilled him. Hands tightly tucked against his stomach slowly slipped out and inched around his waist. Like she was testing his reaction. He kept still as slender fingers reached his back and spread out against the contours of his spine.

Everything shifted. He was no longer the one holding her, but she him. And with a simple press of her fingers, a gentle touch, weeks of tension and stress started to ease.

Then her hands began to move.

The cold wind faded into the background and he with it. He was in his room again, and she was in his arms. Everything he'd seen, done. The feel of her. Her responses to his touch.

His heartrate jumped, and his palms throbbed with the ache, the echo of her still in them. Her taste, her skin on his lips—

He squeezed his eyes closed. He couldn't let go like this. Not again . . . not with her.

Rummaging for another thought besides her half-clothed body stretched out in his arms, he pounced on the first one he found. "No more airport."

She giggled and the thickness of the mood lifted.

"I mean it." He smiled. "No more trying to escape to the airport or talks of creepy Kenneths. You stay and we figure this out."

"Creepy Kenneths?" Her giggle turned into a chuckle, shaking her body. Oh, how he loved making her laugh. But to his great disappointment, her arms dropped from around him. "Okay, no more Kenneth."

"Good." He inserted his key and held the door open. She continued to laugh as she walked over the threshold, and he used the moment of turning off the alarm system to get his head on straight.

It had happened so fast—his shift from enjoying an embrace to wanting her—and he knew what that meant. Knew that he needed space from her to keep those desires under control.

How the hell was he going to do that with her living here?

"Hey, how'd it go?" Ian's voice came from the stairs, with Emelie behind him.

Danny removed his hat. "He has what he needs for now. Where's Fin?"

"New batch of whisky is going into barrels."

"Should I tell Officer Murphy about Kenneth?" Claire pulled out a business card and held it up.

Danny snatched it and flipped it back and forth, one eyebrow raised. "Cab driver from the airport that only leaves you a phone number and a motel address?"

"Oh, my goodness." She covered her face. "That makes it sound so much worse."

"But there aren't any cab—" Ian went quiet at Danny's, *yeah-she-knows-that-now* look. Ian said, "How about I call Tom about Kenneth while you put your signature down on that paper?" He steered Danny toward the bar. "It's Nordic Dive time."

Danny rubbed the back of his neck. "I don't know. I'm not feeling up for it this year."

"Perfect. Happy to take your trophy."

"Over my frozen body."

Ian grinned, and Danny marched over and started writing his name. Citrus flowers drifted over his left shoulder, and he smiled at the beautiful face peeking behind it. "You don't want to know."

"Oh? I think I do now."

He held up the paper. "Every year when the temperature drops, a bunch of crazy-ass men strip and dive in the ocean."

"Only men?"

"Solsken women are smarter than that," Emelie said.

"Wait." Claire's brow lifted. "Did you say strip?"

"Most wear swim trunks," Danny said quickly. "But there are a few purists who think that to embrace the true Nordic Spirit, you have to dive in stark naked."

"Which one are you?"

He was so unsure of how to take her question, he literally sputtered and never answered.

"You've stunned him, Claire," Emelie said in a deep announcer's voice, holding a fake microphone to her mouth. "The man now wants to know if you're picturing him naked." She held the fake microphone to Claire's mouth.

A towel smacked Emelie's ass, and she squealed and ran as Danny chased her, whipping her. She grabbed her own towel and Claire laughed, watching them dodge each other's whip-slapping towels.

After a loud crack, Emelie yelled, "Uncle," and flipped him off. "Yours was wet."

Danny grinned, holding his hands up in victory as he strutted to the bar and tossed the towels in a bin.

Claire followed. "That wasn't fair, Daniel."

"This is Solsken, M.C.C. Life isn't fair." He laughed when her finger poked his chest. He backed up, hands in the air, as she continued to poke him. "Look." He grinned at her adorable faux glare. "If I hadn't cheated, she would've."

"Man-ape," Emelie yelled. "You left a mark." She gathered another towel, rolling it slowly.

"You said 'Uncle.' No take backs."

Emelie made a show of dipping it in water.

"Shit," Danny said. "Quick, Claire. Grab two towels." He smiled when she giggled like a little girl and did as he said. With her crumpled face full of tears still in his mind's eye, he'd keep this going as long as possible. "Keep an eye on your flank. Ian also cheats."

She squealed and turned to Ian.

"I would never," Ian said.

"He's lying," Danny whispered in her ear. "He's holding a towel behind his back."

Claire jumped back straight into Danny's front. He swallowed a grunt, hands flying to her waist without a forethought.

"Are we about to go to war, Daniel?" she asked without looking back. Towel slowly twisting in her hands.

He was. But not war with towels or friends and family. He took a step away from her, dropping his hands. This was a battle he wasn't sure he'd win.

Claire laughed as Emelie and Ian slowly advanced. Her butt did a little wiggle as she positioned herself to fight.

No. He was sure of it. He'd fallen into ease with Claire without trying. Without fighting for it like he had to with Jessica.

But just like then, he knew, no matter what happened, he'd be coming out on the other side of this a loser.

22

Maddy's World

DANNY ICED A WELT on his thigh. Claire, unsurprisingly without a scratch, insisted upon it.

And now, in the quiet of the pub, he wasn't sure if he felt more relieved or anxious now that Emelie and Ian left and he faced his living situation with Claire. Even with Ian's joking parting words of, "keep our new friend close. But not too close," which earned him a firm head smack, Danny went back to being awkwardly nervous around her.

"So, um." He coughed. "Hungry?"

"Not yet."

He shifted the ice. "Okay, uh . . ." If this didn't stop soon, he'd be falling apart by dinner time. Claire's phone thankfully buzzed, saving him from saying anything more stupid.

"Oh, this is my agent. I should get it."

"I'll just be upstairs if you need anything." He hurried toward the stairs, tossing the ice, and stopped when her voice came out in stutters.

"I-I . . . yes, I know the deadline is coming up. I'm sorry, things have been a little crazy . . . y-yes, I remember what you said . . . yes, I've dropped the silly side project."

Danny bristled. Was this "silly side project" the one she'd excitedly worked on while on the plane? She'd said she no longer wanted parents, agents, or men telling her what to do, but now she wasn't fighting for it anymore. Why?

Perhaps he'd stick around and check liquor stock.

"I know you have my best interest in mind . . . of course," she said. "Yes, I'll have something to you in a couple weeks. Yes, thank you, Allen." She hung up and leaned her forehead against the cold fireplace stone, groaning. "What are we going to do now, Maddy?"

"You normally thank people for taking away what's important to you?"

She spun around. "I beg your pardon?"

Danny crouched and started stacking dry wood into the fireplace with heavy thuds. "I said, are you going to let him take away what's important to you?"

"I heard what you said, I just . . . " Her eyes flashed, and he held back a satisfied smirk. There was his fiery Claire.

Wait—not his.

"He's only trying to foster my talent."

"So, he fosters your talent by squashing it into the box he thinks you should be in."

She huffed and his smirk rose higher.

"He knows the industry better than I."

"Maybe. But you know *you* better than he does. Do you like writing horror?"

Her defiance dropped with her head in a deflated sigh. "Yes. No." She shrugged. "I used to love it."

"How long do you think you can succeed in something you don't like doing?"

"But if I don't, my contract could be forfeited."

He swiveled toward her, holding up a stick and lightly poked her thigh with it. "I didn't realize Allen was the only agent out there."

Her expression tightened with all the things she wanted to say, and he smiled again. She smacked his stick away. "He's not, but he helped me get out there and obtained all my publishing contracts."

"That's his job. You don't owe him for that."

"But what if he's right and no one buys it? I-I mean I'm no J.K. Rowling."

"What if he's wrong? And I'm pretty sure even J.K. Rowling didn't think she'd become J.K. Rowling."

The corner of her mouth slipped, but she forced it back down. "Writing children's books has very little chance for success."

"Wait." He put it all together. "Maddy is short for Madelynn and that's a children's book?"

"A series of books, actually." She dropped her hand off her hip and chewed on her lip. "And yeah, she's the child inside me that never really had a chance to get out." She awkwardly hugged herself. "Weird, huh?"

"No." He stood and stepped back from the blazing heat, wiping dirt from his hands on his jeans. "As a matter of fact, I'm thinking these books need a second opinion."

"From whom?"

He poked his chest.

"You want to read my books?"

"I kind of want to meet this child Claire that never made it out in the open." He smiled and watched hers fully bloom. "If you don't mind."

She shifted her feet, placing them close together and perfectly aligned. He didn't know why she did that, but it was another layer of her he wanted to understand.

"Well, I think that would be okay." She chewed her lip again. "But you probably won't like it."

"I highly doubt that."

"It's unedited."

"I'm making tea."

He felt her smile on his back as he made his way to the kitchen. When he returned, she'd settled into what he now considered her chair and table, hugging one knee to her chest. His eyes wandered from her rosy cheeks to her hair re-piled on top of her head in a messy bun. She looked completely at home, chewing on a pencil with her shoes off and her sock-covered toes wiggling.

How had he been nervous around her only an hour ago?

"Okay, I'm ready." He set down the tray, pulled up a chair, and held out beckoning fingers.

Her face blanched. "I couldn't possibly sit here while you read it."

"Why?" he asked slowly.

"I couldn't stand it if you made a face."

"I'm not going to make a face."

"You might, and I'll misunderstand you again."

He couldn't exactly argue with that. "Where do you suggest I go, upstairs?"

"No." She gnawed on her thumbnail. "I mean, only if you want to."

"What if I sat behind you here at this table? Still close by, yet you can't see me."

"Yes, that should work. And I promise I'll do my best not to ask you what you think every three seconds."

He laughed, and she stared wide-eyed. Apparently, she was very serious. He picked up his mug and held out gimme fingers again.

She hesitated with her hand at the bottom of a stack of journals.

"It'll be fine, Claire."

With one more long breath, she pulled it out and handed it to him with shaking hands. He felt the weight of how precious of a thing she gave him and let his fingers touch hers as he took it. "Maddy's in good hands."

"I trust you, Daniel."

That statement knocked him back and swelled inside him. She trusted him. What did he do to deserve something that special? Taking a breath, he left her with a final reassuring smile and slid onto the bench.

She spun in her seat, facing him. "Daniel?"

"I haven't opened it yet."

"I wanted to ask you something." She tapped the pencil on her chin. "I'm wondering if I stopped liking what I wrote because

I didn't want to lose Maddy. Does that make sense?" Before he could answer, she continued, "After hearing how much Emelie and Ian love my work, I really don't want to let them down. I love all my fans and I love doing my live Q&A with them. I'm just not sure . . . " She never finished her thought and rolled the pencil between her teeth.

"Is there any reason you can't do both?"

"Both? I guess I've never thought of that because they're so different, and well, because Allen said —"

"Where did you find this agent?"

"He was a friend of Brandon's."

Danny had to start and stop half a dozen times to keep from saying his honest opinion about any friend of Brandon's. Instead, he said, "When I finish here, I think we should try to find a way to do both."

"I'd like that." She dropped one more nervous glance at her journal before tearing away with a deep sigh.

He gently untied the leather wraparound strap and kept his eyes on the back of her head. He expected another interruption, but she didn't move.

Opening the front flap, he read, **Hello, I'm Maddy**, and smiled. In front of him was a sketch of a waving, wild-haired little girl with freckles, patched skirt, and mismatched striped socks, standing in front of a sign saying, "Home for Girls." Her button nose scrunched as if she tried to peer through the page to see him.

"Nice to meet you, Maddy," he whispered back.

Flipping pages, Danny followed her journey through adventures and mishaps. She talked about desires for a family while splashing through mud puddles and her dreams for a prince while kissing a frog. Castles were built out of old boxes and chores were turned into imaginative games in faraway lands.

But those games always got her into trouble. Mud tracks tarnished the halls. A frog landed in a bowl of cereal. A stack of plates crashed to the floor from a zealous mop swing.

A faceless adult appeared, tapping their foot and pointing

a finger, telling her if she didn't shape up, no one would ever adopt her.

Danny knew this wasn't an exact replica of Claire. She was wealthy and not an orphan. But the more he read, the more he saw a pattern. Maddy was highly misunderstood by the adults around her, and more than once it broke her heart — which broke his.

Near the end, he paused on an image of Maddy being groomed for a potential family. Her unruly hair was tamed, mismatched socks aligned. Her hands and face were scrubbed clean.

Feet together, Maddy. Don't slouch. Don't speak unless spoken to, and when spoken to, remember your proper words or no one will like you.

Claire shifted in her seat, and he glanced up, watching her fiddle with a loose strand of hair at the base of her slender neck. This part of Maddy's story, he realized, was a clear view into Claire's childhood. Why she stood the way she did and spoke the way she spoke — and why she believed people like him so easily thought the worst of her.

He took a deep breath and turned the last few pages. As Maddy was introduced to potential families, one thing after another went wrong. She fumbled her words, dropped a plate on a man, and accidentally laughed when her pet frog leaped from her pocket into a woman's mouth.

In the end, no one wanted her, and when Danny saw the sketched tears rolling down her plump cheeks, he was ready to jump into the book and adopt her.

Turning the last page, Maddy was Maddy again, disheveled and adorable. She "psst" at him with a curled finger. **Chin up. Don't fret**, she said. **It'll get better, you'll see.** She smiled with two front teeth missing.

Her image blurred in his vision, and he closed the journal, rubbing his forehead. He hadn't been ready for that. Little Maddy, with her joy and childlike wonder, reminded him that his recent marriage break meant his dreams for his own family were also broken.

He pinched the bridge of his nose and swallowed repeatedly.

A crackling log snapped, and his attention came back to Claire. He didn't bother telling her he'd finished, but instead, watched her twist more strands of hair around her fingers. Firelight danced and flickered over her profile, and he found his breath again.

She calmed him, somehow. Not by anything she did particularly, but by the fact that she was here with him, quietly soaking in the heat from his family-built fireplace.

He cleared his throat, and she slowly peeked around. "I have one question for you."

"Oh, a question? Sure, what is it?"

"How many more books of Maddy do you have?"

"Six. But one is unfinished."

"Good." His fingers absently traced the outline of the journal. "Because I need more of her."

A mix between a laugh and a cry gusted out of her. "You liked her?"

He scooted to the edge of the bench, and against everything in him yelling that he shouldn't, he leaned forward until only a few inches lay between them. "No, not *like*, Claire, *love*. I love Maddy, and I may have to fight this agent of yours if you don't try to publish her."

She pressed a hand to her cheek. "Do you really mean that?"

"I really mean that." He held out the journal between both hands. "I think it's time you let your inner child run free."

Roomies

CLAIRE DIDN'T KNOW HOW to react. Whether this was one of those social situations where throwing your arms around someone's neck is too much or not.

Danny stood before her with a case, not a box or two, but a case of her favorite boxed macaroni and cheese. The one Gene didn't have in stock when she'd bought some. The same one her favorite nanny used to sneak to her when she found out she'd never had any.

"How did you . . . " She couldn't hide her exuberant smile, and with a clap of her hands, she let out a louder than normal, "Thank you."

Danny smiled, opening one of the two bottles of Italian wine he brought up from Flygande before setting out milk and butter. "You ready?"

"Will you let me do most of it? And just tell me how I'm messing up?"

He stepped back, gesturing to the pot. "It's all yours, and you're not going to mess it up. First, you want to get your water boiling."

"How much water?" She picked up the box and looked at the back. "It says six cups, but you opened two boxes. Will this pot hold twelve cups?"

"You only need enough to cover the pasta. Mostly full should do it."

"Are you sure?"

He fought back a smile. "I'm sure."

She struggled to trust him over the box, but in the end, determined to do it with a firm nod. "Mostly full."

With wobbling ripples of water, she carried the filled pot to the stove.

"Now for the fire."

She stepped back. "Will it explode at me?"

"I promise there's no dragon in this stove."

She groaned. "That note must have looked so stupid."

"It was cute, not stupid." Heat flushed her face, and he cleared his throat, rubbing the back of his neck. "This is a fairly new stove and has a built-in pilot light. All you have to do is turn that knob." He pointed out which one to turn. "And ignite."

She gritted her teeth, and with a faint squeal, started the flame. "How long does it take?" She checked and rechecked the pot.

"From start to finish, about twenty minutes."

She wondered if there was a way to make it longer. Especially since Danny positioned himself just behind her. Close enough to feel his body heat against her back, but not touching.

"Now add the pasta."

She did so with gusto.

Danny yanked her back, arm gripped around her waist. "Careful or you'll burn yourself."

Claire was too happy making her favorite food to feel embarrassed. Or maybe it was the distraction of his arm still around her doing things to her. Beautiful things. Foolish things. Things like making her want his hand to slip under the hem of her shirt and touch her skin like she dreamed he did this morning.

He went still. Did he feel her thoughts? Her rapid breathing? Or was it because her fingers had brushed the edge of his hand?

A warm, gentle breath moved along her shoulder and without a forethought she tilted her head, exposing her neck. His grip tightened, putting her body flush with his and when his breath feathered closer to her pulse, her eyes closed.

Replaced me with the Viking already? The phantom's words iced over her, and she went rigid.

Danny dropped his arm and took a few steps back, running a hand through his hair. "Uh, next we make the sauce." He told her how to strain the pasta and mix the milk, butter, and cheese. All while maintaining a greater distance.

She'd ruined the moment. Or maybe she'd misinterpreted what his closeness, his touch, had meant.

Over her shoulder, she watched him walk away with his bowl of food and disappear into the living room. She closed her eyes, letting out a frustrated sigh as her fingers brushed where his breath had been.

WHAT THE HELL WAS he thinking? God, he was stupid. He'd been so damn close to tasting her again and ruining everything.

Danny turned on some music and plopped on the couch with a quiet groan. She was here because of his security system. For a friend like he promised. And if he wanted to keep that promise, he needed to stop reliving their morning together in his head.

He pushed cheesy noodles around his bowl and took a nibble here and there. To be honest, he wasn't even seeing the food. Just her. The pulse in her neck. Soft skin.

"Stop it," he whispered and snatched his wine.

A gentle knock on the glass pane made him look up. Claire peeked through one of the windows, doe-eyed and chewing on her lip. Even though the other door was wide open, she acted like she was trapped on the other side. Her wary expression wasn't helping how cute she looked.

"You need something?" he asked.

She shook her head but didn't move.

"You can come in if you want."

"I didn't want to bother you."

"You're not."

Her foot came first, then the rest of her, slipping around the door. "Is it okay?" She pointed to his still full bowl.

He quickly forked a large bite. "It's delicious."

She remained awkward and shifted her feet. Looking around his room, she ended on the old turntable. "What is this song called?"

"'Eleanor Rigby.' When my parents moved away, my mom left all her old Beatles albums."

Her head cocked to the side as she moved toward the speaker and lowered to her knees. He watched her—eyes closed, mouth pursed—feeling every word until it ended.

"Drive My Car" blared, and she jumped with a giggle. She thumbed toward the speaker with another laugh. "That's me."

Confused, he zeroed in on the lyrics and smiled, shoveling more food. He was pretty sure "Eleanor Rigby" was her too.

"Excuse me, sir," he said in a high voice. "Will you drive my car?"

"More like, 'Ahem. I'm ready to go. Get the car ready.'"

He winced. "Ouch. Yes, ma'am."

"See?" She pointed to herself. "Snob."

"You like the Beatles, so you can't be a snob."

Her humor dropped as she stood and cautiously walked toward him. "Do you normally eat in here?"

Crap. He didn't want to ruin the lighter mood by saying he was hiding from his stupidity. "Sometimes."

"I didn't mean to intrude on you."

"You're not intruding." He scraped the last bite out of his bowl. "This is your home for now too. You should feel free to go wherever you want."

"But will you tell me if I ever bother you? Or do anything to make you uncomfortable? I know how much of a sacrifice this is for you." He opened and closed his mouth several times, but she kept talking. "I mean, we only just met, and then I crashed your home. Literally. I'll pay for the food and of course all this wine you've given me and whatever extra for rent or mortgage. I won't be a burden to you, Daniel." She finished with a deep inhale.

He set down his bowl and said, "First of all, I invited you to stay, and I don't pay rent or mortgage. I own the place. I'm also drinking this wine and eating this food, so you don't owe anything for it." Stretching out his legs, he added, "As for bothering me, I'm pretty open about things that bother me, and you're not on that list. And you don't make me uncomfortable." He sucked in his nerves and rushed out the last words. "But I made you uncomfortable and for that, I'm really sorry."

She straightened. "Uncomfortable? You've never made me uncomfortable."

"But," he blinked a total of three times, fast, "out there, when I held you for too long?"

Her eyes dropped and she lined up her feet. "That didn't . . . " She paused. "That didn't make me uncomfortable—you don't make me uncomfortable." She scratched under her suture. "You are an incredibly generous, thoughtful, and kind man, and I don't want to take advantage of your goodness."

He let everything she said warm over him and held her eyes. "You're not taking advantage."

"I think I was." She nodded toward the door. "Out there?"

Did she mean when he held her or the cooking lesson? Either way, neither took advantage of him. "Maybe we agree to disagree on this and have more mac and cheese with wine."

She slowly smiled. "Only if we listen to more music?"

"Done."

The soft guitar strum of "Yesterday" filled the room, and he went quiet. Claire lowered herself on the other side of the couch, watching him. He tried and failed to not let the lyrics of lost love affect him. But the growing strain of raw emotions tightened his face.

Claire said nothing, but took a deep breath and pulled up her legs, tucking her chin between her knees.

"Can't Buy Me Love" came next, breaking the tension.

"I bet Greyson, my son, would love the Beatles too," she said.

"I didn't know you had a son."

Her shoulders drooped, and a sadness tugged on the corner of her mouth.

"He's sixteen and every bit the teenager that doesn't want to talk to his mother." She laughed it off, but he knew there was more to it. "Can I ask you something?" She faced him. "I saw an old picture of you and Ian in your room. You both looked so young. Have you really been friends that long?"

He nodded and swirled the wine in his glass with a hint of a smile. "We've been friends since the day we met. He was always getting into trouble, and I was always getting him out of it."

"Ian? Really? I can't picture it."

His smile faded. "He had it rough with his dad growing up and it made him lash out sometimes." He stared into his wineglass. "He didn't know how to stop the cycle of feeling bad, then lashing out, back to feeling bad for lashing out. He struggled off and on for a while."

"How did he change?"

He set down his empty glass. "A few things happened at different moments — he calls them graces. Where he was headed in the wrong direction and one of these graces stepped in. One of them was your books."

She gripped the top of her shirt. "Is that what he meant when he said my first book saved his life?"

He nodded and poured more wine into her glass, then the last of the bottle into his.

"But how?"

"I think he'd like to tell you the full story himself. But he'd gotten into more trouble than I could get him out of and ended up in juvie."

"Jail?"

"Does that bother you?"

"No, it's not that. I guess I can't imagine him getting into that kind of trouble. He's so nice."

"He's always been nice, only dealt a bad hand and a bad temper. No one has a bigger heart than him, though. And miraculously, he managed to change because of you, his girlfriend Molly at the time, and a priest named Joe. The same priest who made him want to become one."

"And you, I think."

He shrugged, lost in all the memories. "I'm his *bràthair*."

"Scot Gaelic for 'brother.'"

"Yes, how'd you know?"

"I used it in one of my books."

"*Ghost Crossing*?"

She straightened. "Yes, actually."

Danny slowly smiled. "That's his favorite."

"I'm so humbled right now." Claire gripped her chest. "How long has he been reading my books?"

Danny looked at the ceiling, his head resting close to hers. "He got your first novel as a gift from Molly when it came out. I think he was sixteen. So, since then."

"That long? I was twenty when that released."

He did a quick calculation. That made her four years older than him. Would the age difference be a problem for her? *Dear God, stop it.* He shifted in his seat.

"How old was Ian when he moved here from Scotland?"

Danny barked a laugh. "He's one hundred percent Solsken, born and raised."

"But his speech, his accent?"

"Family pride and a long visit to the Motherland a while back. When he returned, he decided Scottish was the only way to live and speak. And I've endured years of kilt wearing and Scottish verbiage ever since." He grinned when she snickered.

"That makes him truly endearing."

"Yeah." He sipped his wine, still smiling. "I wouldn't change him for the world."

She tucked her knees closer to her chest and grabbed her toes, squeezing and rubbing them.

"Are your feet cold?"

"I thought these socks would be warm enough."

"Cotton is the worst for cold weather. Hang on." He left the room and returned a few moments later with a pair of bulky socks. "From my sister in the Faroes. They're made of Faroese wool."

"But what about your feet?"

"I have another pair that actually fit me." He pointed to the long, thin tops. "My sister forgot I don't have skinny legs."

Claire laughed and slipped them over her feet, sliding them up to mid-calf. "They're in-cred-ible," she stuttered into a long yawn.

"Why don't you head to bed."

"Where's the guest room?"

"Right there." He nodded to the door across the hall.

"That's your room."

"It's the warmest room in the house because I have a separate thermostat in it."

"But—"

"I can sleep anywhere, Claire. If you remember from the first time you walked into Flygande." He rubbed his brow and puffed a small laugh. The reddening of her cheeks made him wonder just how much of it she remembered.

"Are you going to sleep now too?"

"Not quite yet."

"Well, I can stay up for a bit longer. Unless you want some quiet. Brandon always needed his alone time."

He wasn't about to unwrap that. "I don't need to be alone, and you can stay if you want." He walked to the stereo and placed another record on the player.

Thirty minutes was as long as she lasted before her head drooped. Danny shifted, so she touched down on his shoulder and stayed like that until she fell into a deep sleep.

Slipping an arm behind her shoulders and one under her legs, he lifted her, holding her against him. She nuzzled into him the way she had last night, and he slowed his movements, taking his time, soaking in the feel of her.

When he reached the room, he placed her onto the bed and

re-tucked all the pillows around her the way she'd had them the night before, covering her with the heavy blanket.

For a few moments, he watched the slow rise and fall of her breathing. "Just so we're clear," he whispered. "I don't need space from you for quiet." Catching a strand of hair, his finger ran along her cheekbone. "You're becoming my quiet, Claire."

Things That Go Creak in the Night

DANNY'S EYES SPRANG OPEN, and his heart raced. What woke him? He blinked hard, eyes darting around the moonlit guest room, over his weightlifting bench and dumbbells, an antique armoire and upholstered chair, and stopped on a pair of thick, wool socks. He slowly traced up the length of long, bare, ghost-white legs and froze on gorgeous, sculpted thighs.

"Are you awake?"

He startled. The gorgeous legs belonged to Claire. The woman standing before him without pants, wearing only his t-shirt, again. He bolted upright. "Everything okay?"

"I heard a sound outside my window and young boys' voices. I think they're trying to break in here."

He threw off the covers, forgetting his own barely dressed state of fitted boxer briefs, and yanked on a pair of sweatpants that hung low on his hips. He did a double take when Claire cupped her cheeks, smiling a little. "How many were there? Did you see them? How old?"

"Two, maybe three. I'm not sure how old."

He ran fingers through his hair and wriggled it hard, making his thick strands stick up in wild sprouts. He passed by her with a wink. "Wanna have some fun?"

"With what?" She followed his fast steps down the stairs.

"I failed my last Viking scare," he whispered while turning off the alarm. "A Solsken tradition. Now I have some making up to do. Can you sound scary?"

"I can sound witchy."

"Perfect. May I?" He reached up to her half intact hair bun and carefully removed the band. Tucking his fingers into her hair with a much gentler tousle—*damn, it's so soft*—he made it bush out on the sides and grinned. "Here, grab this hand axe, it isn't sharpened, and I get this." With a glint in his eye, he yanked a broadsword off the wall, half the length of his body.

"Why are we scaring them?" she asked as they reached the door.

He looked back with a maniacal smirk. "Because all Solsken boys need a good scare to stay out of trouble. Ready? Follow my lead."

Inching the lock open, he listened to their whispers, "I'm telling you, he was just as scared to see me as I was him. He's lost his power, dude."

"Yeah, he's washed up," said a different voice.

"What's that above the door?" another said.

"Focus," the first one hissed. "Remember, we're going for whisky. Only one bottle. Don't be greedy."

Danny smiled widely and threw open the door. "*Vad gör du?*"

Three pre-teen boys screamed and stumbled down the steps, one of them rolling all the way as Danny stomped forward.

His bare chest heaved a low growling breath. "I said, what are you doing?"

"What is it, my dear? Little children?" Claire cackled. "Oh, do let them come in. I'm hungry." Placing a hand on his back, she peeked around him. "How about that one?" She swung out the axe, and the boy shrieked.

Danny's scowl nearly cracked. She was perfect. All that was missing was the long nose and hairy wart. "*Nej*, they need a good stabbing first." He raised his sword over his head and roared, "*Kom hit.*" The sword crashed down between one of the boys' legs.

He screamed for his mother and skid-ran to the gate, followed closely by the other two. Claire continued to cackle as Danny chased them, yelling more threats in Swedish.

Weakened with laughter, Claire plopped on a step and yanked the wide shirt over her cold knees.

Danny strode back toward her, grinning. "You've been initiated into the Viking scare, my lady."

Tears dribbled over her cheeks as she gasped for breath. "I feel awful, but I can't stop laughing. Poor things were so scared."

He sat next to her, grin still plastered on his face. "You should see some of the ones Ian and I do together. He gets this crazy-ass, wild-man look in his eye and shrieks like a banshee. The kids really think he's going to kill them." He lifted his dull blade and kissed it. "Thanks, Princess."

"Princess, huh?"

"Nobody messes with Princess."

She broke into another laugh and tried to smother it. He chuckled and took her by the elbow, helping her stand. "Come along, Witchy. Let's get you back inside before you freeze." Hand still on her arm, he reached for the knob.

A wind gusted and blew open the gate with a crack. It whip-whirled up the walkway and blasted into them.

Claire gasped.

"Guess I didn't latch the gate right. Let me—Claire? What's wrong?"

Color bled away from her face and her whole body shook. "He's here."

"Who's—" A deep, vibrating rumble rode on the wind, growing louder. Danny jumped when Claire's icy grip clutched his arm, and she pointed to the underside of the overhang above them.

Dripping glowing letters scrawled, **You'll never be rid of me.**

The rumbling wind smacked into him again, and Danny whipped back around. "Get inside, *now*." He shoved open the door and lifted her because she didn't move, throwing his entire weight against the door, and slammed it. He bolted the lock and set the alarm. "Go upstairs."

"H-He came for me here."

"Upstairs, please." He tried and failed not to yell and took hold of her arm, leading her away from the door to the stairs. "Go. I'll meet you up there."

She latched a hand around his wrist. "Don't leave me."

"I need to find out who painted that and whatever that noise was. Until I do, I want you upstairs."

The same drawn-out, gaunt expression from the night before washed over her features, and an uncontrollable surge of fear took hold of him. "Look at me." He clutched her face. "It's going to be okay. You said he's here? Did you see him?"

She slowly shook her head.

"You're safe, Claire. You hear me?" Danny gripped her hand and led her to his office and around his desk. He yanked out the top drawer and lifted a 9mm Glock, chambering a round.

The sound snapped her back into awareness. "A gun?"

"The only time Solsken gets any real trouble is when mainlander shits cross our bridge. Come. We're going upstairs."

"You won't leave me?"

"I won't leave you." He led her out of the office, keeping himself between her and the door, listening for any more sounds. Upstairs, he led her into her room and locked the door. Pulling out his phone, he made his way to the window and peeked out. The gate no longer swung on its rusty hinges and as far as he could tell, the wind noise died.

"Yeah, this is Danny Larsson. Is Officer Murphy in? No, it's in regard to his case, and he told us to contact him directly if anything else happened. Okay, thanks. I'll try him there." He hung up, dialing another number, and glanced back.

Claire sat in the center of the bed inside her pillow fortress, rocking. Her knees hugged tightly to her chest, face buried between them. She looked utterly abandoned.

"Hey, look at me." He dropped the curtain and crawled inside her pillows, lifting her chin. "You're going to be okay."

Tears rolled down, and she kept rocking. Shivering.

"No, please don't cry. Come here." He wrapped around her,

pulling her tightly curled body in and began rubbing small circles on her back. "He's not going to get you in here. Okay?"

She didn't answer, but slowly turned, tucking her face into his chest, and he squeezed her.

"This is Tom," a groggy voice answered.

"It's Danny. I'm sorry to wake you, but we had another incident with Claire's case—yeah, here at Flygande. Bastard painted a message over my door. Then some weird wind blew directly at the building instead of across it like it should and . . ." He hesitated, looking down at the top of her head before adding, "I'm fairly certain I heard a voice calling her name."

DANNY POURED FRESH COFFEE for Tom and refilled Claire's tea. She sat silently, wrapped in a heavy blanket at the table with an empty look on her face.

"There were definite signs of disturbance on the ground in front of your place." Tom looked between them. "Some rocks were dug up and moved so they could get a clear angle to the building. Probably thought no one would notice a few upturned rocks, but rocks don't just move here. There were also heavy indents in the dirt, so I'm guessing it was some sort of fan or wind machine." He took a large gulp of coffee. "I also interviewed the boys, but none of them saw anyone. Too busy running from some witch and a Viking with a sword."

Danny couldn't even laugh at that. "What about the painted message?"

"No fingerprints, but we're working on matching the paint."

He sighed and pinched the bridge of his nose.

"We haven't been able to figure out how he speaks like a ghost yet," Tom continued, sipping from his mug. "But we managed to find a footprint in the dirt. I made some calls to the county Sheriff's office on the mainland and they're sending a few deputies to help us patrol the area. This way we'll be able to monitor all abandoned roads like Sven's."

Danny, unable to stay seated, hopped up to top-off Tom's coffee.

"Hopefully, with this joint effort, we'll get him if he shows up again. Ms. Cooke?"

Claire slowly lifted her unfocused eyes, and Tom smiled kindly. "Good news about the footprint is I can assure you whoever is doing this is a physical person. Which means we can catch him.

"I also wanted to tell you that the lab test results came back. It was in fact pig's blood on your bathroom wall, and it matched the container we found, though still no fingerprints. But with this footprint of a man's boot," he pointed to a photo on the table, "it shows he's getting cocky, and cocky means he'll mess up. And when he does, we'll be ready." He took one last swig from his mug and faced Danny. "We'll be stationing someone nearby at night."

Danny nodded. "I'll be keeping my pistol on me, so let them know that they should send me a message before wandering my property."

"You got it." Tom stood, looking down at Claire's blank expression. "We don't take threats lightly on Solsken, or we never would've survived this long on our own, Ms. Cooke."

She shivered at her name and seemed to finally hear him, making eye contact. "Thank you. I'm sorry I've brought so much trouble to your island."

"Nonsense." He smiled. "We need a real case now and again to keep us on our toes. Goodnight, or good morning, rather. I'll be in touch."

Danny led him down the stairs to reset the alarm, wishing he'd sprung the extra cash for outdoor cameras.

"I almost forgot." Tom turned at the door. "Let Ms. Cooke know that we're still trying to track down Kenneth Greene. The address to the motel was a dead end. But he does, in fact, have a record." He toyed with his mustache with a hint of a smile. "Apparently, he tried to start a bingo business for retirement communities but rigged all the numbers to go in his favor. Thought no one would notice."

Danny puffed a small laugh. "They're elderly, not stupid."

"Which makes it hard to believe he'd be smart enough to orchestrate all of what's been going on here without getting caught." He paused before saying, "I'll be honest, Danny, this feels personal. She hasn't mentioned anyone else this could be?"

"No." He ran a hand over his tired face. "What about Trevor?"

"Trevor's been active on social media and posted recent pictures of him and," Tom cleared his throat, "lots of women being very attentive to some bruises on his face. Apparently, it was a party for his father's official takeover of Gregory Cooke's East Coast businesses. After looking into it, we discovered the deal went through sooner than Ms. Cooke had scheduled, so there really isn't a motive other than his pride. If he's still mad about it, he could be working with an accomplice, so I'm not ruling that out completely." He sighed. "Try to reassure her we're doing all we can."

"I will, and thanks."

Tom opened the door with a backward glance. "Snow can't come fast enough."

Danny grunted his agreement. No one but Solsken residents looked forward to being cut off from the rest of the world during winter.

He wasn't sure what to expect when he got back upstairs. But a fully clothed, hair-fixed, no-blanket Claire with a notebook, wasn't it.

"What's going on?"

"I'm making a list."

Curious, he sat next to her and grabbed his mug of tea. She spun the notebook for him to read and pointed to the top.

"Who's that?" he asked.

"The company that owns the cottage. I think it's time I put my Madelynn Cooke pants on and call them with a threat to sue. I should've done it sooner but . . . well, the reason seems silly now."

"Wanting to prove to everyone that you could make it on your own isn't silly, Claire." He pointed to the next item on the list.

"Carpenters?"

"After they sell me this scam of a cottage, below market price for my inconvenience, I'm going to fix it up the way it should be." She gave him a wary glance. "Or do you think that's a silly idea?"

He pressed his tongue into his cheek, looking over the rest of the list:

-Visit Gerty and walk Gunner

-Learn to cook more than mac and cheese

He paused on the last one.

-STOP BEING AFRAID

"Not silly. The residents of Solsken will be happy to have Sven's home fixed up." He held back on the prodding question of whether that meant she planned to stay or not. "As for carpenters, I can help with that. My cousin at the lumber yard knows the good contractors from the bad ones." He scooted his chair closer. "But I'd like you to do something for me first."

"Oh?" She sat up straight. "What's that?"

"Make a list for me of everything you want to learn to cook."

She distractedly ruffled the corner pages of her notebook. "But you have Flygande Norseman to run. I-I can just search the internet."

"Learning by doing is best, besides I thought you hated the internet."

"Yes, but—"

He stopped her with a raised hand. "I'm happy to teach you, Claire. But there's something else I want to ask you."

She let go of her notebook, giving him her full attention.

"How can I help you not be afraid?"

"That's on me, Daniel."

"You're in my home. On my island. I want you to feel safe."

Her eyes settled on the table, on his gun, and she chewed her lip. "Most of my life I've been surrounded by a team of security." She took a deep breath. "In my pursuit of independence and keeping a low profile, I left them in California. Could you maybe," she lifted her eyes to his, "teach me to shoot that?"

"Sure. When do you want to start? After breakfast?" He yawned and stretched.

She bit back a smile. "No, right now I want something else from you."

Kiss me. He shook his head fast. She definitely didn't say that. But his exhausted brain thought now would be a great time to conjure it. He cleared his voice. "What's that?"

"Sleep. I want you to get some sleep."

He slowly smiled and rubbed a sore muscle in his shoulder. "Nah, I'm fine."

"I'm sorry, Daniel, but it's not up for negotiation. Flygande opens in about five hours, and you need it. And don't even ask about me," she added, when he opened his mouth to ask just that. "I can come back up here to sleep anytime. You can't. Now go." She stood and actually snapped her fingers at him, pointing toward the hall.

Besides his mother, he couldn't remember the last time a woman ordered him around. But he had to admit, he liked it from this woman. "How about I lie on the couch instead? Just in case."

She sighed. "Alright, but I'll be checking on you to make sure you're trying to sleep."

Her no-nonsense attitude while being considerate and sweet was cute as hell. "Fine."

Stretched out on the couch with his hands behind his head, he crossed his feet at the ankles and closed his eyes. He had no intention of sleeping, only resting. Both French doors were left open in case there was a disturbance, and while his breathing slowed, he enjoyed the sound of her movements around his home.

One day, and she already filled his space, his mind and his—no, not that. Not yet.

He was at a crossroads and he knew it. Knew that the feelings he had for her were growing deeper than he should let them. But he didn't know how to tame them—stop them. Like it or not, rebound or not, he was getting attached, and that scared the hell out of him.

She'd made no promises to stay. Made no real indication that she felt the same way about him, and he couldn't, *couldn't* go down that road again without some assurances.

Knitted wool draped over him and he opened one eye, peering up at her.

"Absolutely not." Claire covered his eyes, forcing them shut. "Keep them closed."

He smirked, enjoying the feel of her hand on his face.

"Lift your head." She stuffed a soft pillow under him.

He didn't need a pillow or a blanket, but he wasn't about to say it. Not when she fluffed his pillow and tucked the blanket securely around him. Each action precise, careful, caring.

This was another missing piece from his short marriage. He'd repeatedly gone out of his way to please and help his wife, but she never once did the same for him—she couldn't, really. She was so broken and tangled in her own world there wasn't enough room for him there.

"Here." Claire carefully removed the band from his hair. "You can't sleep with that jamming into your head." She ran fingers through his thick strands, smoothing it out and lightly massaged his scalp.

He closed his eyes, pulse quickening. *Don't lean into her hand . . . don't lean into her hand.*

After another soft stroke of her fingers, he took a deep breath, shoving, kicking, punching back the urge to reach up and guide her hand down over him. *God*, he wanted her to touch him.

She removed her touch too soon and tiptoed backward. His eyes half-opened, watching her.

"Sleep," she whispered before flipping off the lights. "I'll wake you if you're needed. Otherwise, don't you dare get up."

"Yes, ma'am."

Whatever this was—whatever she was becoming to him—would have to just be for now. He didn't know how to fight it. Didn't know if he *should* fight it. And if he was being honest, he was damn tired of fighting.

25

The Heart Doesn't Always Decide

TWO WEEKS. NO WEIRD winds, painted messages, or even a hint of harassment. And all the patrols brought back negative results. The man had vanished. Or, as Officer Murphy said, more than likely gave up when he saw the patrols, or left the island due to the upcoming threat of snow.

Tom assured them, however, that even though they were easing up on patrol, the case was still open and to let him know if there were any more incidents.

Claire wasted no time on her list, especially the last item. Taking daily lessons at the gun range, spending hours rigorously practicing, Danny watched her fear slowly fade into confidence, while his grew into a formidable beast. And when she came home one afternoon brandishing a gun catalog, asking for his help and guidance on what best to purchase, Danny knew why.

It had started with the routine. The everyday domesticity. Blending and adjusting to each other's habits seamlessly. It was the one pair of shoes dwarfing the other, sitting side by side at the doorway. The shared meals.

But even more than that, it was the tea Claire had ready for him an hour before work. The meals she thought to bring down to him during his slow time so he could eat. It was the folded laundry neatly stacked on his bed, and the small notes of greetings she left on his fridge—written in Swedish. As if attempting to learn his ancestor's language wasn't barreling her straight into his sensitive center.

And now she looked to him for help on something as important as her safety—as if his opinion held weight.

Cohabiting with Claire, he alarmingly realized, had become more of a real marriage than his actual marriage had been. And the more their lives intertwined, the harder it became to draw that line separating her into the "just friends" category.

He couldn't keep blaming it on exhaustion after work every time his breath hitched when he stepped inside his apartment and smelled her perfume. Or when he walked into the living room to see the living, breathing manifestation of his every thought sitting on his couch with the lights dimmed, music playing, holding up his favorite ale for him. Claire, smiling, wearing those damn wool socks he'd given her.

Perhaps he could blame it on the night he looked down and realized he didn't remember the last time he saw her wear her wedding rings.

On the second Friday night since she moved in, "Hey Jude" drifted out of the speakers. Danny had heard this song more times than he could count, yet tonight his traitorous mind decided to morph the lyrics and associate them with Claire.

It didn't help that she sat next to him, their thighs touching, her warmth melding with his. When the chorus hit, he chanced a quick look and found her eyes waiting for him.

No, not waiting, slowly dropping to his mouth.

The air in the room grew thick and crackled, pulling the breath from his lungs. All the charged energy magnetized his body to hers, and he found himself drifting closer, eyes glued to those lips.

Just once, he wanted to let it all go and taste her.

The record skipped, snapping the moment, and Danny jumped up to change the album. When he glanced back, Claire hugged her knees tight to her chest and wouldn't meet his eyes.

He'd almost kissed her.

He'd almost ruined everything.

"I'm uh . . . " He scraped his fingers through his hair. "I'm kind of tired. So, I'll . . . um, goodnight, Claire." Without looking back, he rushed down the hall to his room. Crawling onto the air mattress, he crushed a pillow against his chest.

The music stopped, and he watched the light under the door flick off. Soft, padding footsteps came closer and stopped outside his door. He squeezed the pillow. If she knocked, if she came in, he'd—

The footsteps faded back down the hall, and he turned away, burying his face in the pillow.

SINKING INTO A FITFUL sleep, Danny floated between a dream and a memory.

Jessica straddled his hips in bed, looking down on him, smiling. "I have something for you."

His stomach balled up. He knew that smile. Glint in her eyes, mouth too wide. He swallowed and scrambled to think of which "medicine" she could be taking right now. "What is it, babe?"

She unfolded papers and held them before his eyes. Divorce papers signed and ready. "W-Wha—" Danny stuttered and stumbled out of bed.

"You know I'm a free-spirit." She waved her hands and swayed to music only she could hear.

"And I've never tried to stifle that."

"Justin said . . . you remember our neighbor? Strong jaw, nice biceps."

Because that's what a man remembers about his neighbor? At that moment, watching her touch her plump lips while describing him, he knew. Knew what she did, but he had to ask anyway. "You slept with him?"

She laughed like it was silly but didn't deny it.

"Answer me, Jess."

Her eyes, pupils blown, lifted with a smile not quite her own. "Come now, Danny. What do you think?"

"I think you married me." His shaking finger jammed into his chest. "That you made promises to be faithful to *me*."

She laughed and swayed again. Laughed so hard she rolled off the bed. "I have a list." She held up her phone, opening her notes app. "Wanna see it?" Everything was so goddamn funny.

The list, he soon found out, was every man she'd slept with not only over the past month they'd been married but the entire year they dated. Danny lost feeling in his limbs, his insides slowly caving in.

She finished with flushed cheeks. "Yes, there it is," she said, eyes drooping. "My bad energy is leaving now."

"I have more for you."

Her hazy eyes sharpened on him. "Don't act like you don't know who I am, or-or about my needs when you married me."

"Your addictions, you mean." She glared, and he released a harsh laugh. "And don't you mean who you were? Or do you conveniently forget repeatedly telling me things changed for you when you met me?" He snatched his phone.

"Who are you calling?"

"Making an appointment to get tested for some other bastard's disease. Something you should probably do."

She slapped the phone out of his hand. "You are so . . . " She never finished and started fanning herself. Her ever-struggling anxiety taking over.

He wouldn't ease it for her, though. Not this time. Instead, he spoke in a raw voice, fingers rubbing over the ache in his chest. "I don't understand, Jess. You said I was enough."

But he did understand one thing. He'd pushed her to see a doctor again. To get help for all the abuse of her past that turned into these addictions. He'd felt her closing off even then. Or maybe she'd never been open to begin with.

"You could never be enough." She got so close. The tormenting scent of her washing over him. With a scathing smile she whispered, "I used you like I use all of them. Like my medicine. To make me feel good. But I'm tired of being chained down." She laughed again. "You're nice to look at, baby, but you'll never be anything more than a nobody bartender from a goddamn frozen island."

Danny startled, eyes flying open. He didn't move. Heavy breaths lifted and lowered his chest. He pressed a hand over his racing heart, getting his bearings. He wasn't with his ex-wife, but in his old guest room. On an air mattress.

His phone buzzed, and he rolled over to see a calendar notification pop up. He cursed, scraping a hand over his face with a groan.

Maybe he'd just sleep this day away.

A gentle knock. "Daniel? Are you awake?" a soft voice asked. "I made breakfast."

Claire. The memory of last night rushed him, and he rolled to his back, staring at the door. They'd made plans to bring Gunner to Sven's property together and then stop at the fishmonger. But that was before he'd almost kissed her. Before the calendar reminded him what day it was.

If he told her he didn't feel like going, she might dig to find out why, and that was one conversation he didn't need right now.

"Yeah," he said. "Coming."

Breakfast showed no signs that Claire was upset about the night before. He should've been relieved, but he wasn't. If anything, her nonchalance only added to the heaviness he couldn't shake. He didn't want to be alone in this muck of regret.

A few times he thought he felt her eyes on him, but when he glanced up, she'd have them dutifully lowered.

The temperature now close to freezing, Danny threw on a wool sweater with his slouchy before they headed out into the blustering wind. He embraced the icy chill against his cheeks, breathing in the comforting, familiar scent of evergreens and salt water as they walked.

"What's your favorite food?" Claire held a swinging bag of fish, head bent against the wind.

Danny nodded toward Ylva's. "*Kanelbullar*, hot out of the oven. I can cook almost anything, but I'm terrible with baking."

"I see." A small smile played on her lips.

"Why'd you want to know?"

"Just curious. Excuse me a minute." She pulled out her phone and started texting someone.

The uneasiness he woke up with washed over him again. "Everything okay?"

"Perfectly so—oops." She tripped on a rock, and he caught her arm.

"As nice as your shoes are, I think it's time to head to Gene's and invest in a good pair of winter boots before you break an ankle. Snow is coming."

"Boots aren't cute, though."

"You don't need boots to be cute."

Her cheeks flushed, and he cleared his throat. He was misreading her again. Or did that blush mean something?

"We should also pick up a warmer coat and hat too. Trust me, you'll need them."

"I trust you."

That was the second time she told him that and the second time his chest tightened with the responsibility of it.

More stones threatened her trek, and he held out his arm for her. She tucked her hand inside and squeezed his bicep. *It's not because she wants to touch me – right*? God, hope was a dangerous thing.

"Is Ian coming back today?"

"Yep. End of term exams are done, and he's heading in this afternoon." He tried clearing his head by looking up at the thickening gray cloud cover. The snow may even start tonight.

"What time? Emelie and I are headed out together."

"Around two. What are you and Ems up to?"

She smiled but didn't answer. "I missed seeing him last weekend."

"Yeah, working Saturday nights without him makes me appreciate even more all the Saturdays he did this without me." *Two months ago when I left*, he didn't add.

"Tell him I'll cook dinner."

"After you're done with your mystery visit with Em?"

"Exactly," was all she gave him.

They weren't even home ten minutes before Emelie burst in. "Come on M.C.C., we've got places to go."

Danny's jaw went slack. "B-but . . ."

"Bye." Claire wiggled her fingers at him as Emelie dragged her down the stairs and out the front door with a slam.

The silence swallowed him whole.

For the first time since she blew into his life, he was alone—truly alone. And he didn't like it. Not. One. Bit.

His eyes traveled from the empty stairwell to the bag of fish still lying on the kitchen table. He'd planned to surprise Claire with a new recipe he'd looked up just for that fish.

The stupid fish staring at him with empty eyes and an open mouth.

"What are you looking at?" He shoved it into the fridge and cursed, slamming the door.

He loved his cousin, but seeing her out of her work clothes and all dressed up reminded him of the lifestyle she led when not working. A partying lifestyle. The same one that nearly destroyed her life when she'd left the bar on a night off with a stranger named Seth. The man who thought because she was drunk, he could drag her behind the Viking-shaped tavern and lay his hands on her.

The one and only time Danny nearly killed a man.

Emelie grew more cautious after that, but she still loved a bit of partying inside the clubbing scene on the mainland. Though not his idea of having fun, he understood she needed a break from island life. To blow off some steam from the heavy responsibilities put on her with her mother's condition. But now she had Claire with her.

A plate cracked between his hands. "Shit." He slammed it into the trash can. Why did Em demand Claire leave so fast? And why the hell didn't she want him to know where they were going?

It could only mean one thing. Emelie planned for them to do something he wouldn't approve of.

He stress-cleaned again. Scrubbed a pan in the sink so hard the counter creaked. The hum of the vacuum didn't quiet his mind, and the dusted, re-organized bookshelves brought no satisfaction.

"Are you kidding me?" His arms curled over his chest as he stared at the kitchen clock. It'd been hours since he started cleaning, but the clock only read thirty minutes. Thirty damn minutes of no relief from his screaming head.

All his previous doubts about Claire crashed in. Every compliment she'd given, only politeness. Every smile meant nothing. Every hug, just a hug. And that small, cherished touch she'd given him earlier — meaningless.

This morning's calendar notification popped back into his mind, and he knew it then. The hazy, happy cloud he'd lived in these past couple of weeks evaporated to the clear and ugly truth. The feelings he had for Claire weren't mutual.

Why would they be? She had a big, fancy life to live and exotic places to travel. It's not like she stayed on the island — at Flygande — for him. Who was he but a small speck on her map?

Insecurity gushed over him, pricking his skin and souring his stomach. He emptied the kitchen cabinets with loud clangs and started to scrub them. This small speck still wanted to know where she went, even if he wasn't important to her.

He froze. Is that why she didn't tell him where they went? Did Emelie drag her to one of her parties? Introduce her to some of her friends — *male friends*? That's it. That's where she was. With some twenty-something asshole grinding against her on a dance floor.

The cabinet groaned and clunked, falling lopsided on the wall. "Dammit," he hissed. Steadying his shaking body, he ducked under to see a few snapped screws from his heavy-handed scrubbing.

"It's morning, idiot." The cabinet protested as he lifted it. "Nobody parties in the morning. Not even Em."

Still, the uneasiness lingered. At least now he had a project to focus his attention on for the next several hours.

Damn his efficiency. Forty-five minutes later, he stood staring at his empty home again.

He needed to get out of there. Out of the place with little bits and pieces of Claire everywhere, staring at him. Mocking him.

Tearing around, he stormed down the stairs to Flygande. He'd get everything ready and prepared for a busy Saturday. Possibly the last busy Saturday if snow came.

He hit the bottom step and his eyes fell on her table by the fireplace, his mind conjuring images of soft hair falling around her face, brushing along her slender nape. That mouth pursed around a pencil clamped between her teeth while she focused.

He groaned, fists pressed into his eyes. There would be no escaping Claire here.

"Get used to it." Beer glasses clinked as he stacked them. She was going to leave, and this would be the rest of his life.

He stopped his fourth round of bar polishing and sank his head with a heavy sigh. It was nobody's fault but his own.

You'll never be anything more than a nobody bartender from a goddamn frozen island. He tore up the spotless rubber mats from behind the bar and slammed them down in the kitchen area.

His pride and joy had always been his family heritage. His connection to an island—to a people—that no one else had. But to someone like Claire, it was probably pointless. Small. Pathetic.

He sprayed, soaped, and violently broom-scrubbed the mats.

What about his plans to never let another woman past his barriers? The place that could destroy him. Yet there she was, dangling a finger over his bleeding center.

"At this point, I'd think you could serve dinner off these mats."

DANNY WAS SPIRALING. NOT sure over what, but Ian spotted it the moment he stepped into the kitchen to his flushed-faced best friend with wild eyes.

"Ian, what the—is it two already?" Danny looked at his watch-less arm. "*Shit*. I didn't open the doors. The chairs are still up. Where's Kevin and Fin and-and where the hell is Emelie?"

"Whoa." Ian held up both hands. "I'm early. Thought I'd surprise you and Claire. You didn't enter a time warp."

Danny didn't smile, so Ian did a few quick calculations. He cleaned things that were already clean and was pissy. He'd only left him for two weeks and he reverted back to angry, obsessive cleaning?

Only one thing could've caused this. "Where's Claire?"

"Don't know. With Em."

"When is she coming back?"

"Don't *know*."

"Ah, got it."

Danny stepped into his space. "What? What have you got?"

Touchy too. Could be pretty serious. "Nothing." Ian smiled. "Want me to take down chairs?"

"Yes." He scrubbed the mats again.

Ian spun out of the kitchen and reached for his phone, texting, S.O.S. WHERE ARE YOU?

Emelie responded almost immediately. TOP SECRET. WUZ UP?

YOU PLANNING TO BRING CLAIRE BACK SOON?

NOT YET, WHY?

DOES DANNY KOW WHY YOU'RE OUT TOGETHER?

A long line of zipper-mouthed emojis popped up in response.

EM, HE'S MAT SCRUBBING.

SHIT, REALLY? DID JESS SEND HIM ANOTHER PACKAGE?

NO, THIS IS DIFFERENT. It's worse, he keeps himself from adding.

HE PROBABLY REALIZED HE LIKES CLAIRE AND IS FREAKING OUT A LITTLE. HE'LL BE FINE.

HE'S NOT FINE.

There was a long pause, the three dots appearing and disappearing. I NEED TWO MORE HOURS. COVER FOR ME AND I'LL HAVE HER BACK THERE, WRAPPED IN A PRETTY LITTLE BOW.

Ian rolled his eyes, mumbling, "Maybe you should have let me in on this secret to begin with."

Danny kicked the swinging kitchen door open, and Ian stuffed his phone into his pocket.

"How's seminary?" Danny dragged out the heavy mats, one in each hand.

"Incredible, really. I still can't believe I get to do this. Even if I fail, it's worth it for Theology alone."

"You're not going to fail." The mats dropped with a slap, and he used his boot to position them.

"Thank you for that. Did you eat?"

"No, why?"

"I'm hungry." Ian pulled down the last chair. "How about I fry up something bad for us. Some Flygande specialties."

"Go for it, but I'm not hungry."

Ian let out a quiet sigh, watching Danny clean spotless chairs. He'd been overly optimistic about how well his best friend had been doing.

Ten minutes 'til eleven, Emelie rushed in, heading straight for Danny's office. "Sorry, I'm late."

Claire swooped in after her, covered in a thick, down coat, wind-blown and smiling. "It was my fault, I'm afraid."

At the sound of her voice, Danny visibly relaxed—for five seconds. That's all he allowed before something else took over. Something cold. Foreign. Every muscle in his body flexed and tensed the closer Claire got to him, and Ian was grateful he held a bar towel instead of a glass with his white-knuckled grip.

"Hello, Ian." She waved. "Are you hungry? Daniel and I got fish today. He was going to help me cook it."

"Don't have time now." He rubbed small circles into the wooden bar. "I open soon."

"Oh." Her smile faltered. "You're right, it's Saturday. You're always busier on Saturdays." She glanced around the spotless, empty tavern. "I can just make it the other way you taught me. Should I bring you some?"

"Not hungry." He turned from her and began re-stacking the beer glasses.

She watched him, wide-eyed, for a few painful seconds before asking in a shaky voice, "Daniel? Are you angry with me?"

"Nope. Just working."

She slowly turned to Ian. "Are you hungry?" she said so quietly he barely heard her.

He side-glanced Danny, waiting for him to stop whatever the hell part of him thought this act was a good idea. "I'd love some." Even though he just ate.

"I'll bring it down." With one more confused look Danny's way, she turned toward the apartment steps.

"The table by the fire can't be reserved tonight." He spoke over his shoulder without looking at her. "It's going to be slammed and we need the extra space."

"Yes, o-of course. I never expected you to do that for me anyway. I'll find a place." She gave him a gracious smile, but he edged around her without a glance, pushing through the kitchen door.

Ian's hands dropped to his side and curled into tight fists. "I'll save you a seat here." He pointed to his side of the bar at the very end. "It'll be open and ready for you with a cup of tea or wine whenever you want."

Her eyes stayed on the swinging kitchen door as she walked toward the stairs. "If it's no trouble."

Ian burst through the kitchen. Kevin yelped but Danny didn't flinch. He knew he was coming. "Kev, give us a sec."

"He's got work to do."

"No, I don't." Kevin held up his hands and darted around them while Ian crossed his arms, boring holes into Danny's dumb head. He wasn't going to say a word until Danny did.

"It's not her table."

"The *hell* it isn't. Why you shutting her out?"

"I just told her I needed the table."

"Daniel Mikael Larsson, if there's one thing I've never pegged you for, it's a bullshitter. And I sure as hell never thought you'd try to bullshit me. Look at me."

Danny whipped around, stepping into Ian's space, but Ian

held his ground, rising to his full height.

"You want to hear the truth? Fine, I'll tell you the truth. I can't be friends with her, Ian. I can't even let her remotely close to me."

"Why?"

He held a forefinger and thumb in his face, squeezing them together. "If I give her an inch — if I give her even a hair of space in here," he smacked his chest, "then she's all in. Do you understand me? I can't just give her a little. I have to give her everything and I can't. I can't give her or any other woman everything ever again."

"But she lives here. Are you going to throw her out now because you suddenly changed your mind?"

Danny faltered for a second, and his expression showed his inner struggle. "I wouldn't do that. But maybe I can work something out with Em until Sven's place is finished. There haven't been any more threats."

Ian deflated a little. "You don't have to do this, Danny. It's okay to be afraid."

His head snapped up, and Ian stepped back when a dead look met his eye. He didn't know what Danny was about to say, but knew he didn't want to hear it.

"I'm not playing this game anymore." His voice dropped low. "It's over. I'm done." He pushed past Ian like he wasn't there.

26

We All Have to Live
with the Choices We Make

DANNY HAD BEEN RIGHT about one thing, Flygande was packed from the time the doors opened. With snow in the forecast, everyone wanted one more outing of fun before either being trapped in their homes or leaving the island.

Emelie got wind of everything going on when the first person sat at Claire's table, and she was told to leave them there. She'd refused to speak to Danny after that except to bark drink orders at him.

Long after dinnertime, Claire still hadn't shown up. Ian chanced another look at the door leading to the stairs and caught Danny doing the same thing, his hand unconsciously going to his small ponytail with a frustrated tug.

Ian sighed. Regardless of what Danny was trying to do, the man couldn't shut it off that fast.

Half-past eight, the door slowly opened. Ian and Danny froze. Apparently, Danny wasn't the only one who'd reverted. The Claire they'd met the morning she arrived at Flygande stepped through, minus the sunglasses. From her cloche hat to her cape, down to her buckled, pointed shoes stood her exact replica.

Even though her red-painted lips said *look at me*, her eyes remained downcast as she walked on the other side of the bar in front of them. She was timid again. Reserved. No longer the confident, happy woman they'd come to know.

Danny swallowed hard and took a step back, looking her over.

"Are you cold?"

Claire glanced up, putting on what Ian now understood was the fake smile Danny had referred to. "No. If it's alright, Ian said I can sit over there."

Danny swallowed again. "Of course." He eyed the table that was absolutely hers and sighed when he saw a stranger sitting there.

Good. Let it sink in, Danny Boy.

"What are we having?" Ian said jovially, trying to ease the tension as she took her seat. "That fish was delicious, by the way. Wine?"

"I burned it."

"Nonsense. I like a good char. Wine?" he asked again.

She forced a half-smile. "Yes, I think that would be best." She opened her clutch and pulled out a hundred-dollar bill. "Keep the change. I owe a lot more."

"Don't be silly, Claire. You're family." He pointed to the carved words behind the bar and slid the money back, patting the top of her hand. He'd be buying all her wine and food if Danny suddenly decided she needed to start paying for everything too.

Ian uncorked the bottle, poured her glass, and set the bottle beside it. "What have you been up to?"

She brightened a bit. "I got a text from my son. He said he wants to visit me on his break in a few weeks." Her real smile appeared.

"Excellent. We should have a nice dinner for him. Introduce him to the town."

She side-glanced Danny, who attempted a stealth eavesdrop. "I would love that. Any suggestions where?"

"Here, of course."

Again, she looked at Danny. "I don't think that's a good idea."

Screw this. If Danny wanted to ruin things with her, that was on him. There was no way Ian was going to let this woman think she wasn't welcome anymore. "Of course it's the best. Isn't it, Danny?"

Danny spun around, and Ian gave him a stony glare.

"Yeah, of course." Danny's eyes never reached hers. He stalked back to his side of the bar, and Claire sank a little in her chair.

Ian's teeth crushed together, making his jaw ache. Being caught up in sparing himself, Danny couldn't see his "operation keep Claire out of his heart" wouldn't have the effect he wanted. He seemed to forget that the only thing this would accomplish would be to make her think she did something wrong — *again*.

"Borolo is an excellent choice." A handsome middle-aged man, clean-shaven and well-dressed, pointed at her bottle as he sat down. "My family used to travel there every year."

This. This was what Ian needed. Another man to stir the Danny dumb-dumb pot.

"This particular winery or just the region?" Claire asked.

"The region." The man smiled and casually scooted closer to her.

"Would you like a glass, sir?" Ian offered.

"Yes, please."

Ian felt Danny's hard stare on the side of his face, and it summoned a snide smirk. He would absolutely encourage this man talking to Claire. He wanted to cut her off? Then he could stand and watch how easily he'd lose her.

The man, Jeremy, seemed nice. Sophisticated. Educated. Gentlemanly — and she was a hundred percent uninterested. Pleasant? Yes. Polite? Absolutely. But she wasn't being Claire, she was being Madelynn, and that's what Madelynn did.

Keep glaring, Danny.

Jeremy settled in to talk to her. They had a lot in common. Both originally from the West Coast. Both from wealthy families with a love of Italian wine.

Danny continued to pretend not to watch them like a hawk. He did, however, come use Ian's taps instead of his own to listen in a few times.

The place grew louder, and Jeremy leaned close to Claire's ear to say something, slipping his hand over hers.

Danny went still, glass under the stout spout, but no stout

poured into the glass. Ian looked from Jeremy to Danny and waited.

His eye twitched and his fingers turned white around the glass, but he didn't move. He wasn't glaring at the man or Claire. His gaze glued to their hands, waiting to see something—but what?

It's funny how a simple thing can trigger a thought and that thought can bring a beacon of light into the darkness of a situation. Ian checked the date on his watch and cursed. Everything Danny said in the kitchen finally made sense, and he wanted to smack himself for not putting it together sooner.

Two months to the day, Danny made vows to give his heart to a woman who'd so casually, so carelessly, thrown it away.

Now he stared at Claire, with her hand under another man's hand. She may not have been Danny's—hell, he was trying to push her away—yet Ian knew he stared at their hands, silently asking her if she could easily be swayed by another man's attention.

Danny had no right to ask her that. But it was in his utter stillness that Ian knew he waited to see what kind of woman she was, nonetheless.

Without knowing the test she was under, Claire removed her hand from Jeremy's and tipped away from him, saying, "Thank you for your sentiments over my late husband, but I'm alright, truly."

Confusion twisted Danny's face as he switched back to his taps. She easily passed his test, and now he didn't know what to do with that. Nor did he have time to think about it.

The bar filled with the loud sound of squealing, giggling female voices. Ian and Danny glanced at each other before turning to see the entire front of their bar filled with women in high-heels and short skirts, removing their coats to let their gaping chests out in the open.

"Like I'm not having a hard enough time at this bar," Ian mumbled.

The woman in the center of the group had a giant pink boa

around her neck, wearing a crown and a sash reading "Bride-To-Be."

More than a year ago, this would have been a fun night — for Danny, at least, pure torture for Ian. More than a year ago, Danny would've flirted and played this group with a smooth hand. Giving out a few innocent cheek kisses and keeping their drinks filled. Getting them the tips of a lifetime.

But when Ian looked at him now, he only saw, *not this — not again,* written on his face. Memories still fresh from the time when a similar group showed up and one of the bridesmaids, after several hours of flirting with him, took him by the shirt and shoved her tongue down his throat.

Ian shuddered. He'd hated Jessica from that first moment.

Bachelorette parties happened. Flygande was known as a quirky place to have a good time. So, Ian generally let Emelie take over his side of the bar when the women got handsy or rowdy. But what could he do when neither he nor Danny wanted to serve these women? Emelie couldn't run the bar alone.

With years of bartending under his belt, Danny rolled back his shoulders and put on a smooth, practiced smile. "Evening, ladies. Congratulations to the Mrs."

"Not yet." She winked. "Shots for me and the girls."

"You got it. What's your poison?"

"*Tequila,*" they shouted in unison and ended in a fit of laughs.

Ian had no doubt they were already a little toasted. Probably came from one of the mainland's bars.

Ian helped Danny set up the shots. "Lemon or lime?" He got an answer for both and set them out, removing his hands from a couple of fingers that tried to thank him with a lingering touch.

Definitely tipsy already. The glassy glint in their eyes told Ian that he and Danny were to be their entertainment for the evening.

A woman on Danny's side licked her wrist, holding heavy eyes on him, and stretched it out toward him. "Salt it for me?"

"Don't do it," Ian groaned.

But he did.

Ian cursed and glanced at Claire. She saw it too. Of course she did. Hard not to notice what was happening with all the noise and squeals.

The salted woman smiled, drank her shot, and licked again, slower this time. Her seductive eyes said more than Ian ever wanted to know as she held her wrist out to Danny once more.

Danny's professional demeanor slipped a little. Why he thought it would only happen once, Ian didn't know.

"Please let him get his brain back," he spoke to the ceiling, hoping Danny's falter meant the mental reasoning he'd always prided himself on having returned. Danny didn't need another Jessica moment. Especially in front of Claire.

It's not that Ian hated these women. He understood. Neither he nor Danny wore wedding bands, so this was all a bunch of harmless flirting for them. But he sure as hell could hate on Danny for not giving them any hint that they bothered him — and they *did* bother him. His entire body was tense.

Jeremy laid down a business card for Claire when the tequila drinking women became louder. "Call me sometime if you're ever back west. Maybe we could have dinner."

She picked up the card, and Ian watched her questioning if she should keep it. She blinked toward Danny, who held the woman's hand again and salted her wrist. The woman licked and thanked him, this time with fingers sliding up his arm and over the head of his dragon.

"Pull away," Ian whispered under his breath.

"This tattoo is beautiful." She circled it several times, but he didn't move.

"Will do." Claire raised her voice, probably hoping to drown out Danny thanking the woman for the compliment, and dropped Jeremy's business card into her bag.

"Lick it for me?" The voice of the bride-to-be sent a shockwave through Ian — and not because she was engaged to another man.

On paper, Danny was single. But they both knew he wasn't where it really counted, and if he thought he could do this with Ian's favorite female person watching? Well, then, Ian would be putting his fist through Danny's ear.

The woman with the boa leaned over the bar, holding out her wrist, and Ian went deaf. The old familiar sound of blood pounding inside his ears whenever he was about to get in a fight. Danny stared down at her wrist, and Ian lost feeling in his tightly squeezed fingers. "Dear God, *bràthair*. Don't do it."

Danny side-glanced Claire.

His glance caught the engaged woman's attention. Clearly not used to being ignored, she gasped loudly when she saw Claire. "Oh my *God*. Look at her. Is she real?"

All the other women turned and stared. "No, she's a mannequin, I think." The closest one poked her and squealed when she moved. "She's real."

Claire fake smiled. "Can I help you?"

They broke into a fit of giggles and the bride-to-be said, "I haven't seen that shade of lipstick in years. And where did you find that hat? I've never seen anything like it. It's simply ado-orable."

Claire dropped her eyes over her clothes, touched her cloak, her bottom lip, her hat—all with a shaking hand. "It's custom made, so I imagine you wouldn't have seen it before." She tried to steady herself again and sipped her wine.

Ian remained frozen, hoping his best friend would step in and say something. Danny *always* said something if there was even a hint of someone picking on someone he cared about. But instead, he remained wordless, eyes straight ahead, jaw pulsing.

"Wine?" The bride-to-be was clearly put off by Claire's factual statement. "I guess you're too stuck-up to drink a real woman's drink."

"On the contrary. I have nothing against the Mexican spirit." Claire lifted the hundred from her purse again. "As a matter of fact, next round is on me. But only if that man licks all your wrists." She slapped the money on the bar and set a hard stare on Danny.

Oh. Was she challenging him like he deserved? Ian got excited.

When Danny refused to look her way, she waved the hundred in his direction, batting her eyes.

A different thought hit Ian. Maybe flirting was what she thought would get his attention, thinking he liked that in a woman. *Dammit, Danny.*

"You want my money or not?" Claire called.

Danny took in a breath and slowly turned his head, looking her in the eye for the first time. Walking toward her, he placed his palms flat on the bar and spoke low. "What are you doing?"

Lifting her nose in the air, she said, "I'm buying drinks for my new friends." She reached out and touched his arm.

He brushed off her hand. "Put your money away."

The other women snickered and Claire's face twisted. She slapped another bill down and raised her voice. "Two hundred if he takes off his shirt."

"Claire."

"What?" She cocked her head to the side. "Isn't that what's going on here, *Daniel*?"

The women cheered and shrieked, chanting, "Take it off. Take it off."

Their voices brought Emelie and Fin rushing over. Ian was frantic, scrambling to find a way to stop this spiraling insanity.

Danny shoved the money back into Claire's purse. "Shirt stays on, ladies." He turned away from her to smile at them and poured another round.

Claire deflated. Watching the women who had all his attention, she looked back at herself with a self-conscious touch to her hair.

"Oh, bachelorette party?" Emelie caught Ian's panicked look and ducked under the bar. Fin took the squealing women's sudden interest in him as his cue to leave as fast as possible.

"What are we having, girls? Tequila? Ni-ice." Emelie set the citrus wedges next to the glasses. "What the hell is going on?" she whispered to Ian out of the side of her mouth.

"He's lost his mind. Claire just called him out on flirting."

"He's flirting in front of her?"

"Well, more like he's not stopping them from flirting with him."

"Bastard. What's wrong with him?"

"My guess is he thinks this is how to keep himself from getting hurt again." He held out his watch and showed her the date.

It took her a few blinks to understand. "Maybe he should have thought of that before living with her for two weeks. He can't railroad her now because of Jessica being a bitch a month ago."

"Actually, I think it's because of these past two weeks that he's doing this. She got through." He tapped over his heart. "But he's trying to push her out again."

"That's not how she's going to take any of this, Ian."

"That's not how she *is* taking any it. Rejection is all over her face."

Emelie churned the bitter taste in her mouth and walked over, plastering a smile, and refilled Claire's wine. "Hey, you. Are you hungry?"

"No, thank you, I—"

Emelie followed her gaping expression as another woman touched Danny, running her fingers up and down his arm. His hands balled into fists, but he didn't pull back.

That same woman tugged on his black t-shirt and beckoned him closer. "I want to tell you something." He stupidly leaned in.

Ian, Emelie, and Claire froze as she went straight for his mouth.

Ten, thirteen, sixteen, eighteen, twenty-one, and twenty-five. These were the ages Ian clearly remembered Danny stepping in between him and a terrible mistake. Sometimes physically holding him back. There were more incidents, but these stood out the most because these mistakes would've ruined his life, permanently.

That's what crossed Ian's mind when full lips collided with Danny's. "*Hey.*" He dive-bombed them, shoving his hands in between, parting their faces like the Red Sea.

"Maybe it's time for some darts," Ian said, hand still covering Danny's face.

Danny's panting breath heated Ian's palm, and he hoped to *God* he understood the weight of what had just happened.

Emelie took over, saying magic words that convinced the

women that darts was the funnest game ever and led them there. Probably needed space from Danny so she didn't kill him.

Danny's breath stilled in Ian's hand before he suddenly jerked his head toward Claire. She sat rigid, saucer-eyed, bottom lip vibrating out of control as a giant tear spilled over the brim.

Danny had tested her for no reason and failed the test himself.

"Claire," he croaked and rushed toward her.

She recoiled from his outstretched hand and unloaded every hundred-dollar bill from her bag at a frantic pace. "This isn't nearly enough. I-I'll send more when—" Her voice broke and she jumped off the stool without finishing, walk-running to the stairs.

"Wait." Danny tried to get past Ian, but Ian snatched his shirt collar, calling to Fin to take over the bar. He shoved Danny into his office and slammed the door.

"*No,*" he shouted in his face. "You do *not* get to say anything to her. You don't get to chase after her and beg her to stay. Not until you admit what an ass you are."

"I didn't know . . . I mean, I didn't think that would happen."

"You knew they were itching for it. They were tipsy and using you like some damn male stripper for hire, and you did nothing to stop it. You let another woman touch you in front of Claire because you're too scared to man up and admit you have feelings for her. Listen to how stupid that sounds. I've never been more ashamed of you in my *life.*"

"I didn't want her to." Danny jammed shaking fingers into his hair and tore out the band. "I didn't want any of them to touch me."

"Why did you let them then? It's not that difficult. You do what I do—you *move away.*"

"It was the only way to keep her out."

"You thought that display out there was the best way to keep Claire out of here?" Ian backhanded his chest. "That's not how the heart works, Danny. You'll keep her out alright, but only out of Solsken. And when she leaves, that place you were trying to protect? Regret will root so deep you'll never crawl your ass out of it because it's your fault she left in the first place."

Danny held back his hair, cursing. "She was going to leave anyway." The torment on his face didn't match his nonchalant statement.

"For shit's sake." Ian poked him, hard. "Not once did she ever hint that she wanted to leave. But I'm sure she will now. Hell, she should leave because of you. And why? Because you're letting what happened to you over a month ago poison your view of her now."

"So, you know what day it is?" Danny ripped out his phone and shoved it in his face.

Ian read, **2nd month anniversary dinner reservation. 7 p.m.**

"This was my reminder that I can't give her that inch."

Ian towered over him. "That's no excuse for what you just did." He stepped even closer and shoved him. "I said it before and I'm going to say it again, *loudly*, until it gets through your thick, damn skull. Claire is not Jessica."

Danny slammed Ian back into the wall, arm jammed over his chest. "I had to stop it. Don't you understand? I had to stop what was happening to me before it's too late."

"No, you didn't. This was all your choice, Danny. And I hope you're happy with it."

Danny slammed him again and drew back a fist.

"You wanna hit me for that? Do it." His voice lowered. "You wouldn't be the first man to take his shit out on me."

A spark of recognition lit Danny's eye when Ian referenced his father, and regret flooded his face. "I-I'm sorry, Ian." He immediately released him and covered his face with his hands. "Oh God. What have I done?"

"You hurt her, Danny. Those women mocked and made fun of her clothes, and you said nothing. Did you see the way she looked at herself afterward? She was ashamed."

"Ashamed?" He dropped his hands. "How could she be ashamed? They're not even in the same league as her. None of them—not to me."

"So that's why you only looked at them and let *them* touch you? Meanwhile, you swipe off her hand. See this from her point of view, Danny."

"I stopped her because I didn't want her acting like them. She didn't need to. I didn't think . . . *shit*."

"You know the worst of it? I can't even say that you would've stopped that kiss had I not stepped in."

"I would have." He looked directly into his eyes. "I wouldn't have let her keep kissing me." He gripped his hair again. "Oh God, the look on Claire's face. What's happened to me? I don't even recognize myself anymore. I can't fix this."

"Danny," Ian said quieter. "Look who you're talking to. If a screw-up like me can make something out of his shitty life, you can absolutely fix this."

"But she's going to leave now because I'm an asshole."

"Glad we agree on the asshole bit, but listen to me. The only thing you have to resolve in order to begin to fix this, is are you willing to let her leave in order to save yourself from the possibility of getting hurt again? Or will you give her that inch?"

Danny's eyes snapped up as the weight of the situation fully sank in. His voice cracked. "If she leaves, she won't come back."

"You haven't given her a reason to want to."

Danny tore out of the office.

27

Wounded Hearts

"CLAIRE?" THE BEDROOM DOOR slammed the moment Danny hit the top stair. He knocked. "Let me in, please." He heard clear noises of a suitcase being dragged to the bed and opened. "*Please*?" He knocked again.

They never made promises to each other, yet he knew. His insides twisted and wrenched, telling him he broke them anyway.

He jiggled the knob and found it locked. "Claire, I shouldn't have let it go that far, but I promise you, I didn't know she'd kiss me."

The room went quiet, and he pressed his ear against the door. On the other side, she stifled a loud sob, and he squeezed his eyes shut. "Claire, *please* let me in. Let me see you."

"You could have told me." There was a distinct quake in her voice. "You could have told me you were tired of me, Daniel. You promised me you'd tell me if I bothered you."

"I'm not tired of you." He pressed his forehead against the door and rubbed his palms up and down it. "I could never tire of you."

"I don't know what I did wrong. Could you tell me that, please?"

"Nothing. You didn't do anything wrong. This was all me, Claire. It had nothing to do with you."

"*Lies.*" She swung open the door, and he stumbled back. Mascara smudged and dripped down her cheeks, and her lipstick was smeared off. "I don't want to hear it's not you, it's me. I had that line for fifteen years. Fifteen years of, 'Not tonight, Claire, I'm too tired.' And 'I gave you a child, why can't that be enough?'" She hugged herself. "Do you know how many, 'You were so lucky to have him,' comments I got at Brandon's funeral? Yeah, I was lucky. Lucky enough to marry a man that loved my family name more than he wanted to touch me." She hiccuped a cry and covered her mouth.

All the air emptied from his lungs at once. "Your husband didn't touch you? How is that possible? Was he gay?"

She yelled out and slammed the door, forgetting to lock it. He cursed himself and slowly turned the knob, walking in on the mess he created. "I'm sorry. I had no right to ask that."

"Get out." She smeared fingers under her eyes.

"I didn't want those women to touch me, Claire. Or kiss me."

She let out a harsh laugh. "Please, I saw everything. You couldn't keep your eyes off them."

"You misread that."

"Just admit it. The kick to the face, remember? Kick my face, don't stab me in the back."

"Claire." He took a cautious step forward. "I'm not saying you misread it because it didn't happen. I'm saying that my reason for it wasn't what you think. I only wanted to look at you." He took another step.

"Don't say that to me." She threw her hands out. "And don't come any closer. I-I need to think."

He stopped and let his arms fall to his sides, squeezing and releasing his fingers to keep from reaching for her.

She hugged her cloak tight around her. "Can you answer me one question? Just one and don't give me lies."

He risked another step. "Anything."

"Is it my clothes? I-I know they're different. Or maybe it's my hair." She touched it. "I mean, I know I have those weird tics while I'm writing."

"What are you talking about?"

"Is that why you preferred those women over me?"

The vulnerability on her face broke him, driving him forward. "*No*, Claire. I didn't—I don't prefer them over you. Tonight was an act. A stupid, careless act that I never once thought about how it'd make you feel." He gripped his hair again to keep from touching her. "You were and are the best-looking woman that has ever stepped foot in my bar. And your writing habits are my favorite pastime to watch. Especially when you chew your pencil. I would choose you over them every time."

"Then why didn't you?" Her bottom lip rebelled out of control again. "Why could they touch you and not me?"

He forgot all about not getting too close and stumbled forward, stopping directly in front of her. "That wasn't an act? You really wanted to touch me?"

"Is that so hard to believe?"

"Yes. Yes, it is. You could be with anyone, Claire. You can literally travel the world and have any man you want. Why would you want me?"

She reared back and a deep crease knitted her brow. "Have I ever given you a reason to think I wanted to be with someone else?"

He had nothing to say to that because he knew she didn't—this was *all* him.

"Haven't I told you, you're generous and kind and thoughtful? No one, not even my own family, ever believed in me the way you do. Or helped and encouraged me to be myself. Trust me, Daniel, you can't find that just anywhere. And my goodness." She dropped her eyes over him. "Have you ever seen yourself? Or seen how silly you make me with that . . . " She reached toward the head of his tattooed dragon and stopped, pulling back.

His stomach dropped, and he inched closer, hoping she'd reach out again. "I had no idea."

"How many men do you think I've agreed to live with? Besides my husband, that would be zero. Don't you think, if I really wanted to, I could have left a while ago, no matter what you said?"

"I wondered why you didn't."

"I stayed because I wanted to. Because a hurting man on a plane took the time to listen to me and look me in the eye like I was important. You don't know how special that is unless you've never had it."

"Is there anyone in your life, past or present, that I shouldn't hate right now?"

She let out a long sigh. "I don't hate them. Good or bad, they made me who I am."

Just when he started to hope that they were getting somewhere, she turned and started putting more things into her suitcase.

"I don't deserve to ask you to stay, but I'm going to anyway."

"I don't want to anymore."

"Claire, I swear to you, I'm not normally like what you saw down there. What I did shocked even Ian."

"That's not why."

He wasn't certain if she purposefully tortured him, taking her time packing every piece of lace underwear. But it worked. Unfolding and refolding — *dear God, thongs*?

His shaking hands went back to his hair. "Why then?"

"I know we've never put into words what we are to each other, but I thought what we had was special. The cooking lessons and that time you held me when I spilled pasta water. I thought that meant something."

He opened his mouth to tell her that it absolutely did, but she kept speaking. "All those hours of sharing your music with me and answering my questions. I don't know." She rubbed her arms. "I thought it meant more than that.

"I don't even talk to myself anymore. Not since being here with you. Of course, that means nothing to you, but it means *everything* to me." She inhaled a deep breath and calmed her voice again. Returning to packing, her back faced him as she slapped every item into her suitcase with each word. "Last night I was so stupid. I thought you wanted to kiss me."

His hands sprang out and stopped, vibrating on either side of her.

"To think I'd pretend to fall asleep sometimes, just so I could get you to hold me when you carried me to bed." She dropped the clothes and hugged herself, turning to face him. "No, I can't stay, Daniel, because I want something you don't. I want to lose sleep because I can't tear away from the sound of your voice. I want to find it hard to breathe because you're close to me. I-I want," she sucked in a harsh breath, "I want you, Daniel, more than a friendship. But I see now how foolish . . . how stupid I am. You don't want me. I—"

He collided with her mouth and she gasped, stumbling back. "I want you—*God* I want you." Snatching both sides of her face, he held her still, crushing her lips with his.

His kiss invaded—desperate, unhinged—the force of it knocking her back. She clutched his arms to stay upright, but then her knees wobbled, separating their lower halves.

Not one inch. He didn't want one inch between them. Gripping her hips, he hauled her against him. Feeling her. Tasting her.

Inhaling through his nose, he whispered onto her mouth, "Forgive me." He slowed the kiss, taking her face more gently in his hands. "I didn't know."

He swept his lips across hers once, twice, the third time dragging his mouth so slowly she whimpered, melting into him.

Catching her bottom lip, he sucked it in his mouth, tugging. "I want it all." He took her top lip. "All of what we have. Everything. Every day. *God*, this mouth." He lunged again, this time slipping the tip of his tongue out and found hers waiting.

He went still, savoring the feel of a tentative flick before she glided it across the rim of his bottom lip. A deep-throated growl rumbled out of him as he opened, curled his tongue around hers, and drew it in.

Stroke. Glide. She matched his urgency, and they found a rhythm. Kept pace with each other. The feel and taste of her pulling him steadily off the edge of reason.

She whimpered again, and he opened his eyes to tears streaming down her face. "Claire?" He pulled back, breathing heavily, and thumbed across her cheeks. "What's wrong?"

She didn't answer. Breaths matching his, she lifted to her toes, eyes glued to his mouth. Inch by inch, she came closer until her lips — soft, cautious — melted against his again.

It was such a slow, utterly sensuous invasion of his mouth, he didn't dare move. Breathe. Only let his eyes slide closed.

Never had he been kissed like this. Slender fingers unfurled around the back of his neck, gently kneading and tugging. Her slow movements suddenly morphed into something more. Something desperate, hungry. Tear-stained lips, tasting of wine, beckoned, coaxed, nipped. Begging him to keep his mouth on hers using quickening short, firm kisses.

He answered.

Burying his fingers inside her hair, he bumped hairpins. One by one, he removed them, dropping them to the floor and tossed her hat onto the bed. Golden-brown locks tumbled over her shoulders. His fingers raked through them, fisting soft waves as he tugged her in, tipped her head back, and dove deep into her mouth.

God, the sounds she made.

The pads of his fingers stroked down the side of her neck and snagged on the collar of her cloak. He tucked one in, keeping the feel of her soft skin on the top of his finger as he looped around the collar and stopped on a large, black button at her throat. He thumbed it through until it popped. The second button popped — the third, fourth — each time he went faster, frantic even, needing to get this damn thing off so she wouldn't leave.

He flicked his wrist, sending the cloak flapping through the air, and the bottom of his shirt suddenly pulled away from his torso.

Claire's fingers clenched around the hem of his shirt as her light-brown eyes met his questioning ones.

"Please?" she whispered with another tug, and he was undone.

He snatched her begging mouth, hooked the back of his collar, and yanked his shirt over his head.

Her breath caught as she drank in the ridges and cuts of his muscular form, pausing and zeroing in on his arms. "It's so beautiful."

Gentle fingers touched the head of his dragon and trailed up his flexed arm to his rounded shoulder.

He kept still, eyes closed, taking heavy breaths as she walked around the back of him, fingers tracing over his skin as she went.

"I've wanted to touch this since I first saw it." She moved over the body of the dragon — over the taut muscles between his shoulder blades — and spread her hand, spanning the width of his tattoo.

He softly moaned and rolled his neck, following her hand as she trailed across to his left side, circled his inked shoulder, and glided down to where the tail coiled around his arm.

"Beautiful," she said. Her heated eyes lifted and settled on his.

He rushed to her mouth again, all tentativeness gone. Hungry fingers skimmed down the ripples of his abs, back up to his chest, and spread out. Gliding, gripping, she caressed and kneaded. It was everything. Her touch was everything.

He skimmed along the hem of her blouse and caught a sliver of soft skin. She arched into him, whispering his name, and he hummed, slipping his fingers underneath. Taking his time, he palmed up her sides, her silk blouse sliding up under his hands, until his thumbs bumped lace-covered underwire.

She sucked in through her nose and he paused, waiting for permission. Hoping for permission. Having had the feel of them in his hands before, this wasn't enough — could never be enough — but he would wait. He'd only go as far as she wanted him to.

With a gentle push of her chest, she urged him on.

"Yes," he whispered and added pressure, sliding up soft lace, he circled his thumbs. At the first hint of firmness, he dropped down and took one into his mouth.

"Daniel." She gripped the back of his head, and he went to the other side. A gentle nip. A small pinch. Giving the same attention before returning to the first. It didn't matter that they stayed under lace, he savored the feel of them, their shape, her sounds guiding his every move.

Her body suddenly thrust forward, looking for his, and he rushed back up to her mouth and took it.

Soft, firm, soft, firm—his kiss asked and gave as he surged forward and she backward. His body begged to feel more of hers.

They reached the bed and tumbled down together. Dropping an arm, he broke their fall, keeping her attached with the other. The weeks of physical restraint broke away in the form of more tongue strokes and fondling fingers.

This was going too fast, he knew that, but he couldn't stop. All their emotions, the feel of her, everything compounded. He lowered firmly against her, and she arched up, sliding against his body. *That was perfect.* She was perfect.

His hands were on buttons again. This time her blouse. *This is going too fast.* But her mouth—her beautiful, begging mouth.

Her palms trailed up and down his rib cage as he popped the first button with one hand, then the next. Her body rose to meet him, and he stopped unbuttoning, scooping down on the arch of her throat and lost himself again, savoring the taste of her skin—her panting breaths.

He resumed unbuttoning, stopping on the fourth when her shirt opened to reveal a beautiful heart shape above black lace. And there were freckles. Dear God, three irresistible freckles dotting the top of her left breast. Every last argument he had vaporized. He wasn't going to stop, he decided. So long as she kept asking, he was going to answer. Each freckle received its own kiss.

Long fingers slid up his arms, spreading over his biceps, and squeezed. But when her touch reached the head and tail of his dragon, a thought shuddered through him.

This is it. If he went all the way with her, there would be no more after this. Couldn't be any more after this. Hers would be the last hands he'd ever let touch him.

And she was going to break him.

He inhaled sharply and disconnected their mouths, panting.

"What wrong?"

"Nothing." He dipped down and kissed her.

This time she pulled back, brows pinched together. "Is this too much?"

"No." Again he went for her mouth.

She placed a hand on his chest, easing him back. "You're having second thoughts about being with me."

"Never."

She went rigid, not believing him, and her touch dropped away.

"Keep them, *please*." He snatched her hands and placed them back against his chest. "It's not you, I promise. It's just . . . " Not even for a moment did he want her thinking that any of this meant he didn't want to touch her. So, he trailed two fingers along the opened gap of her shirt, over freckles, while gathering his words.

"Why?" She studied him hard. "Why did you pull away?"

"Why were you crying?"

She shook her head and closed her eyes.

"Claire, look at me." He hooked a finger under her chin. "You can tell me."

"I'm afraid to ask."

"Ask me anyway."

She swallowed, and a tear rolled out the side of her eye. "You're kissing me now but wouldn't even look at me a half hour ago. I-I don't know which to believe."

Regret twisted deep in his chest. He wanted to scream. Imploring her eyes, he cupped her face in both hands. "What you see here, right now. What I'm doing with you is where I want to be and what I want to be doing. None of what you saw in me downstairs was what I really wanted."

"How can I believe that?"

"Ah, Claire." He dropped down and pressed a kiss to the shell of her ear, whispering, "You can. I'm not lying to you."

Her body loosened, melting into the kisses he walked down her neck, but then she froze, stiffening again.

Blaring alarms went off in his head. If he couldn't convince her of the truth, he'd lose her before he ever had her. "I'm not lying." He kissed the words into her ear again, but she remained stiff.

"Claire, please listen to me." Cupping her cheeks, he ran his thumbs along her jawline. "Everything you thought was more these past couple of weeks was very, very real. You didn't imagine it or last night. I did almost kiss you. And I held you the day you made your first meal because I wanted to hold you, and I didn't want to let go." He traced her mouth with the pad of his finger. "The morning after you came here? You didn't dream I touched you. I did touch you — kissed you right here." His lips skimmed her neck.

"That was real?"

He nodded. "I wasn't fully awake and stopped when I was, but I didn't want to." He held her eyes. "If you only knew how much I didn't want to."

She went quiet and as time stretched, everything in him screamed that she'd never believe him. He recaptured her face in both hands. "I carried you to bed all those nights because I wanted to have you close to me. And every night I left you on this bed, I only wanted to lie with you like I am now."

He remembered something else. "You said you pretended to sleep. You must have felt all the times I touched your face before leaving. And what about the time I let myself touch your mouth? Do you remember that? I traced it with my finger because all I wanted was to kiss you — it's all I still want to do. That's the truth, Claire."

"Then why?" she finally said, and he breathed. "Why did you ignore me tonight?"

"That answer is going to sound like an excuse, but it's the truth."

"Kick, Daniel. Don't stab."

"Stop saying that. I can't handle that picture in my head." He caressed her cheek. "I don't want to kick or stab, I want to . . . "

He nipped her mouth, but she placed a finger in between.

"Tell me."

He lowered his forehead against hers and let out a sigh. "Today, one month ago, I signed divorce papers."

"Oh, Daniel." She grabbed his face. "I'm sorry."

"Don't be." He turned and kissed the inside of each palm. "I'm not sorry to be separated from her. But the things she said . . . I can't shake them. I hear them all the time." He fidgeted with a button on her blouse, and she slipped her hand over his.

"What I did downstairs? When you thought I was ignoring you?" He met her eyes again. "I did that because I thought if I distanced myself, I could stop what I was feeling for you. Not because I thought those women were better or prettier. Far from it."

He stroked the back of his fingers along her cheek. "God, Claire, I'm such an idiot. I couldn't possibly stop how I feel about you. But . . . "

She hung on every word, waiting for him to finish. After a few moments of watching him struggle to speak, she whispered, "You're afraid."

"Yes."

"You're afraid of me?"

"No." He took her hand, still touching his cheek, and lowered it to where his chest pounded. "I'm afraid of what you could do — *here*."

"Oh, Daniel." She pulled him down on top of her and rolled them to their sides, holding his head against her chest. He let out another breath when her long legs wrapped around his waist to his back and squeezed him.

They both went quiet. Bodies entwined. He soaked in the sound of her heartbeat, trying to calm his own.

She stirred and began lightly rubbing his back over the scaly body of the dragon and whispered, "We'll take it as slow as you need. I don't have any expectations or demands. I just want to be with you."

He sank into her warmth and closed his eyes, letting her words penetrate.

"It'd be foolish of me to promise that I'll never do anything that might hurt you," she continued. "But I can promise I'd never hurt you on purpose." Her fingers wandered up the back of his neck and stroked through the buzz of his hair to the longer strands. "I could never willfully hurt you."

He kissed the forearm that brushed against his face while she played with his hair. "Me either, but I did, didn't I. I hurt you so much."

She squeezed him again. "I'm alright now."

"Did I ruin your trust completely because I acted like an ass?"

Her chest lifted into his cheek and fell. "I only need this. You telling me the truth, good or bad, so I can think it through properly." She continued fondling his hair. "But I'm going to let you know something about me that I've never told anyone."

He went completely still.

"I developed some bad habits as a little girl because I spent too much time alone with my thoughts. I didn't have anyone to tell me if I wasn't seeing a situation correctly." She took another deep breath. "It was your silence that hurt the most, not your actions. I wasn't able to make sense of it, and I quickly fell back into the bad habit of hating myself."

His head jerked up, eyes wide and darting all over her face. "I made you hate yourself?"

"Shh." She pulled him back down again. "I didn't say that to upset or scare you. I'm better than I used to be, and I never act violently on those thoughts. I just disappear inside myself."

He squeezed her. Sliding his hand up her back, his fingers began massaging her nape. "That's why you had your cape on indoors again?"

"I hide best in that cape."

"I might have to burn it."

She smiled with a quiet laugh, and he kissed her chest where his cheek had been nuzzling. "I can't promise that I won't ever do anything stupid ever again, Claire, but I can promise to talk to you instead of shutting you out. I don't want to ever make you feel that way again."

"Licking other women's wrists better not be part of that stupid."

He chuckled and felt her silently join him. "*That* I can promise will never happen. God, that was . . . " He shuddered, and her silent laugh became vocal. "I meant stupid like Ian and I getting drunk and chasing small kids around the island, making them pee themselves."

Her restrained laughter broke, and he joined in, letting out more emotions. They finished together on a long sigh.

"Claire?" He tightened his hold. "Are you still leaving?"

"That depends."

"O-On what?"

She kissed the top of his head and whispered, "On whether my Viking is ready to accept a witchy partner for future Viking scares."

His smile spread and he flipped her to her back, burrowing his face inside the gap of her shirt. She squealed, and he growled, shaking his head back and forth, rubbing his beard against her skin until she couldn't breathe from laughter.

A knock on the door startled them. "Danny?" Ian called with a smile in his voice. "Officer Murphy is here to see you both."

"Give us a minute," Danny said.

They scrambled to right themselves, chuckles between stolen kisses before they swung open the door.

Ian stepped back, taking in the sight of two beaming faces below piles of disheveled hair. "Well, I can see you two were having a miserable time in there."

They laughed and looked at each other with rosy cheeks.

"She's staying," Danny said, unable to deflate his grin.

Ian pretended to be shocked, loud gasp and all, and held out his arms to her. She entered his deep hug as he said, "Does this mean there will be a handsome, wannabe priest in your next novel?"

"One who dispels evil through holy whisky?"

"Oh, my dear M.C.C., you are a woman of great taste."

She snickered, and Ian glanced at Danny, who let out a deep breath while watching her. He caught Ian's eye and mouthed, "Thank you."

"Anytime, *bràthair*." He released her back to him and led them to the stairs. "Wait 'til you hear the good news. They got him."

They both lurched to a stop. "Got him?"

"Yep. Kenneth Greene was just arrested on charges of harassment and stalking. You're free now, Claire."

Bittersweet Graces

KENNETH GREENE CONFESSED TO everything. In the days that followed his arrest, Claire learned that, although Officer Murphy hadn't thought him capable of organizing it, the details he gave were so precise and specific there was no doubt he was responsible.

"But how did he know so much about Brandon? The things he said to me."

"He's a stalker, Ms. Cooke. From the looks of it, he's been doing this for a long time. But," Tom removed his peaked cap, scratching his head, "there are signs he may not be mentally stable. So, he'll be undergoing a full psychiatric evaluation."

"What about how he spoke to her?" Danny asked. "Did you figure that out?"

"Sound laser." Officer Murphy pulled out a photograph of the device and set it on the kitchen table. "Directs the sound to a specific target while the user can stay hidden." Claire picked up the picture, studying it closely. "They're easily bought online, but I've never seen one like this. Most direct sounds to a receiver, but this one can mimic a human voice directly to a person. There's no serial number or manufacturer's name on it. Probably because—"

"It's a prototype," she answered.

"Yes, have you seen it before?"

She blinked a few times and shook her head. "No, not this specifically. But it reminds me of some of the devices Jacob Matthews creates. I only know because my son took an interest in his work."

He wrote a note. "Well, that's a good place to start."

After Officer Murphy left, Claire sank into a chair. Kenneth had stalked her. Used wind machines that he stored in an old storm cellar off the property. Had pictures of her, microphones, listening devices, and voice distorters. All inside his "taxi."

The same taxi she'd stupidly ridden in the back of.

"Stop." Danny took her face in his hands. "Whatever you're thinking right now, stop. Anyone could have made the same mistake."

He had to give her the same gentle reminder a few more times. But as the hours stretched into days and days into weeks, her anxiety over it began to fade. He'd been caught. The "whys" didn't matter anymore.

Instead, she let her days fill with Danny. Living side by side, they continued all their cherished couple habits. Only now with hand holding and long embraces, light touches, and careful kisses.

Every night he carried her to bed with her wide awake.

"You know I can walk."

Danny smirked. "How else am I gonna sneak a leg-feel and keep this relationship moving slowly?" He squeezed under her thigh, and she laughed.

The hardest part was not reliving their heavy first kiss. Especially when he'd walk out of his room shirtless and glistening after his morning workout routine, mindlessly torturing her. Or when she'd overheard him in the bathroom after she'd showered, cursing.

"You're killing me, Claire, I can smell you in here." And she'd slid down the outside of the door, face on fire.

They worked hard to keep the kisses chaste, sweet, innocent, but the moment their lips would touch, the match would ignite. And before she knew it, Danny would have her up against a wall, panting.

And so, for the first time in her life, with a wide smile on her face and a pout on his, Claire became the woman who put a stop to a kiss.

ON THE SATURDAY CLAIRE'S son was to arrive, Danny called a staff meeting before Flygande opened. He kept Claire close. His entire left side, from shoulder to foot, attached to her right side. Reaching out, he hooked his pinky with hers, inhaling a deep breath.

"Are you sure?" she whispered.

"Positive." He cleared his throat and addressed the small group. "I know you've all been speculating behind our backs, so Claire and I decided to let you know that yes, we are together, but we're taking things slow."

Ian and Emelie whistled and cheered, and Danny wasn't sure, but he thought he saw a quick exchange of money. If he had to guess, they'd taken bets on that announcement. Emelie came out the winner.

Danny, feeling that was all he needed to say on the matter, went over the list of things needing to be done before Greyson arrived while Claire excused herself to head up to the apartment.

"Wait." Danny followed her to the stairs and drew her into his arms, kissing her forehead. He couldn't believe he got to do that whenever he wanted now.

"That went well," she said.

He touched her cheek, looking over her face. Since this morning, when he'd asked if she was excited to see her son, she'd gone quiet. Her brow constantly pinched. There was something she wasn't telling him, but he wasn't sure if he should push.

"I'll see you soon," he said before letting her go with one last small kiss.

"We were betting on when they'd get more serious, not when they'd have sex." Emelie's rising voice echoed in the dining area. "Is everything about sex with you?"

Danny wasn't sure if he wanted to know who she was talking to, but peeked around the corner just as Fin answered, "It can be."

Danny groaned, whispering, "Not helping yourself, kid."

"I'll be back before opening, Ian." Emelie snatched her purse, tearing her glare from Fin. "Pappa's wanting me to try and talk to our long-term-er and get him to open up more space."

Danny snickered when Ian smacked the back of Fin's head, saying, "Sometimes, I think you're the biggest ass in the family."

"What did I do?"

Danny started making his way to the office as Ian answered, "For one, stop acting like Mattie and Dean. They're both single for a reason. Second, is being a vomit mouth really the way you plan to ask her out? You like her right?"

"For a little while."

"How long?"

Fin cleared his throat. "Since ninth grade."

Ninth grade? Danny pivoted. Maybe he'd stick around for this conversation after all.

Ian swiped a hand down his face. "Try a little romance, Finlay. Or at least, in your case, learn how to talk to a woman without turning her off faster than a light switch."

"This coming from the guy who couldn't even keep his woman."

Danny winced, and Ian's fingers curled in. His knuckles white. "I didn't lose, Molly," he said in a low voice. He leaned in close, and Fin swallowed, eyes wide as he eased back.

Danny moved quickly. "Start with cleaning the table legs." He threw a rag at Fin's face.

Ian's phone rang, probably saving Fin's life. All the color drained from Ian's face, and it wasn't until he answered that Danny understood.

"Molly?" His voice shook. "Hey, what's going on? You okay?"

He stormed out the front door, and Danny let out a long sigh, turning to Fin. "If you want to live until your twenty-first birthday, I suggest you never say that shit to him again."

Twenty minutes later Ian came back in, strides long and fast. He went immediately behind the bar and poured a pint before slapping the door into the kitchen with a crack.

Danny huffed a deep breath and poured another pint. Gathering himself with another inhale, he eased the kitchen door open.

Ian stared into a pit of golden, aerating bubbles around frozen breaded sticks of cheese, gulping his pint. The last time he ate Molly's favorite food was right after she moved from the island.

Danny crossed his arms, waiting.

Ian didn't speak but shook the fryer basket unnecessarily and hissed when hot oil popped onto his skin.

Danny sighed and replaced Ian's empty glass with the full one. "What's wrong with Molly?"

"She's peachy." Ian finished half the second pint. "She's getting married to *Jack*."

Danny took a step closer. "You alright?"

He took another huge gulp of ale. "I knew it would happen eventually."

"Doesn't make it easier."

"Nope." Ian popped the "p" and a cheese stick burst in the hot oil. "Dammit." He hooked the fry basket to the back of the fryer with a long sigh.

Danny studied the face he knew so well, gauging whether this would require more than ale.

Molly had been Ian's world, but when they'd realized their lives were going in different directions, they'd separated. That didn't mean Danny didn't have to pick his best friend up off the literal floor several times.

That memory tightened his chest, deepening his voice. "Are you having second thoughts?"

Ian's red eyes slowly met his before he shook his head. "It was the right thing to do. She deserved the chance to settle down and raise that family she wanted. I couldn't keep her here just to be my friend, right?" He didn't wait for an answer and dumped the pile of ruined cheese into a towel-filled basket.

"It's hard right now because you're still in between," Danny said. "Once you're ordained, everything will settle."

"What if it doesn't?" Ian swiped a hand across his leaking eyes and whispered, "What if she forgets about me?"

Like his mom did. Danny's insides squeezed. In front of him wasn't the grown man Ian had become, but the torn-up young boy who'd waited by the bridge every day for the mother who'd never return.

Danny swallowed hard. "Look, I know you don't like to talk about this, but I'm going to say it anyway. So, don't punch me."

Ian slowly faced him, lifting one brow.

"Your mom walked out on you, and you blamed yourself just like your dad blamed you. Molly isn't walking out on you."

Ian quickly dropped his head, rubbing his eyes, and Danny knew his words hit home. "She's still the same Molly who's always been in your corner," he continued. "Her getting married doesn't change anything." He eyed him before repeating quietly, "She's not walking out on you."

Ian slumped back against the table beside Danny. It was a long moment before he finally nodded. Shoulder to shoulder, they stared at the white wall across from them.

"I miss her," Ian said.

"Even when she yelled at you in Spanish?" Danny's stomach unclenched when Ian slowly smiled.

"Especially that. Still hear her in my head when I want to do something stupid."

Danny laughed, and Ian cleared the remaining evidence of his tears. "She said Jack wants to meet me."

"Molly doesn't realize he wants to meet his competition, does she?"

"My little grace has no clue." They bumped shoulders, shaking in silent laughter.

"Chicken." Claire burst through the kitchen door.

Ian wobble-balanced the basket of mozzarella sticks to keep them from falling.

"We're having chicken tonight," she said.

"Yes?" Danny said.

"We can't have chicken. Greyson is vegetarian. My son is a vegetarian, and I almost served him chicken." She gripped his forearm. "How could I forget he was a vegetarian?"

"Claire." He smiled and took her gently by the arms. "It's an honest mistake. You've had a lot on your mind."

She rubbed the healing scar on her forehead. "Yes, but I'm his mother. I should've remembered."

"You're being too hard on yourself. Look, let me think for a minute." He snapped his fingers. "Gene carries some vegetarian stuff. What does he like?"

"When he was little, he loved french fries." She stared down at her feet as they aligned together. "A couple of years ago, it was veggie burgers." She half-smiled and then it faltered. "I-I don't know what he eats now."

Danny went quiet, tipping his head to the side. He wanted to ask how she didn't know what he ate, but she turned jittery and started pacing, chewing on the side of her thumbnail. Touching her arm, he pulled her to stand still. "It's an easy fix. We'll give him lots of choices. I can make potato leek soup, or we can pick up some eggplant Parmesan from De Luca's."

Ian coughed "bastards" into his hand, and Danny flipped him off behind his back.

"I also know a few Indian recipes," Danny said. "Or Gene keeps tofu stocked and I can make a stir-fry."

"Daniel, that's too much for you to do."

"Nah." Ian munched on the busted cheese stick. "He'd love a chance to show off. The man can cook almost anything."

"It's true." Danny smiled, hoping to put one on her face.

She didn't smile but relaxed a little and took his hand up to her mouth and kissed it. "You're amazing, do you know that?"

"I don't know about amazing, but feel free to keep telling me that."

She laughed—then gasped. "Wait."

Ian jumped again. Danny didn't know how much more of Outburst Claire his mozzarella sticks could take.

"I don't know what he drinks. He's too young for alcohol, too old for juice." She held her face in both hands.

Danny let out a full laugh. "Claire, calm down. You said he's sixteen, right? We'll just serve him soda. I've got all the flavors."

"Right." She dropped her head with a deep breath. "That's what he'll probably want because he's definitely not getting any at—" She stopped and looked between them, forcing a smile. "Never mind." She placed a soft kiss on Danny's cheek and spun on her heel, pulling out her phone. "If he'd just answer my texts, none of this would be an issue." She shoved out the swinging door.

"Is she okay?" Ian said slowly. "I've never seen her that undone before."

Danny rubbed the back of his neck, shaking his head. "I haven't asked, but I think their relationship is strained."

"That poor woman is stressing and possibly losing whole fingernails over what a sixteen-year-old boy wants to eat and drink. Meanwhile, I guarantee you he doesn't give two shits about it."

"I was thinking the same thing." Danny stood in silent thought, watching the door slow down its swing.

"Besides Greyson, how are things with you two?"

Danny's mouth slowly curled. "They're good. Still taking it slow—*painfully slow*." He scrubbed his face. "She suggested we probably shouldn't kiss too much if we're going to keep it that way."

Ian fought back a smile. "How's that workin' for you?"

"My God." Danny groaned. "I think it might actually kill me, but she's right. I have zero self-control when I start." Ian barked a laugh, and Danny smirked. "Other than *that*, it's nice," he said. "She even seems happy with island life." *Unlike Jessica*, he didn't add.

"That's because we islanders are slowly corrupting her mainlander ways," Ian said. "Before you know it, she'll be normal, just like us."

Danny tried to force a smile, but it wouldn't come.

"Hey." Ian nudged him with his shoulder. "I know you meant it that you can't give her an inch without giving her all. So, it's okay to give yourself this time to get this settled." He tapped

Danny's head.

"What if it never does? What if my stupid freak-outs keep happening, and I wait too long? She might give up on me by then."

"First of all, this is Claire." Ian crossed his arms. "Second, this is Claire."

Danny rolled his eyes, but got the point.

"Just keep things open. Do that thing you hate doing." Ian leaned into him. "Share your fee-elings."

Danny shoved him, and he grinned.

Sobering, Ian said, "Trust takes time, Danny. So, give it time."

"When did you get so wise?"

"'Bout five seconds ago." Ian picked up his basket of cheese and sang, "Danny and Claire sittin' in a tree, k-i-s-s—" Danny knocked his head to the side, and Ian kicked him back with a loud laugh.

29

Wayward Son

"CLAIRE, YOU READY?" DANNY gently knocked on her door.

"No. Yes. Maybe."

He smiled and wiggled the knob. "Everything's ready. Flygande cleared out fast when I promised half-priced first drinks on Monday because we closed early. Merv had to keep George from dancing on the tables." He hoped to hear her laugh, but she didn't.

"Greyson hasn't texted. What if he isn't coming?"

"Don't do this to yourself. He's sixteen and isn't thinking about how his silence is affecting you. It takes us boys a good many years before our reasoning kicks in." Again, he failed to make her laugh and instead heard her sigh.

The sound of heels clicking across the wood floor came closer. He cleared his throat and stepped back, adjusting the collar of his navy, button-down dress shirt. Which suddenly felt too tight around his throat even though the top button was undone.

Would she be wearing his favorite wool dress with those sexy stockings? Or maybe she'd be in a new vintage year, blowing his mind even more. If that was possible.

"Come in, I'm almost done."

The door swung open, and he wasn't prepared. It didn't matter that it wasn't vintage. The modern, long-sleeved, navy shimmering cocktail dress that stopped mid-thigh was the best thing he'd ever seen. And the endless sculpted legs below it were even better.

"I raised him better than this." Claire pushed a clasp onto a long, dangling diamond-studded earring with her back facing him. She didn't notice Danny's reaction, or rather lack of reaction. He was statuesque.

She remained unaware as his thick gaze wandered from the same pair of stilettos she wore at The Pit to the cut calves they created.

"Sixteen or not, I really wish he'd let me know when he's coming."

His heavy eyes continued up from the dress that hugged her lithe form to her hair that was tied to the side in a low knot, opening a clear view to a deep scoop in the back of her dress. Almost as low as the cream-colored gown picture he'd zoomed in on.

He thought he was still breathing, but he wasn't sure.

"You all went through so much trouble for him tonight, and I don't care what excuse he may give, it's rude. Of course, I have no control over that now."

Her last comment missed his ears, and he still couldn't speak. His feet started forward, hand lifting slowly, itching to touch her.

"Do you think this dress is too much for dinner? It's the only one that would match you, but I don't know what is appropriate for Solsken. I tried to pick casual for what I'd normally wear to a dinner, but not too casual." She placed the clasp on her second earring. "I'm so grateful for everything you did. Cooking for hours. Goodness, Daniel, I don't know how you did it."

She didn't seem to realize he never answered her and had a complete one-sided conversation with herself.

His eyes continued taking their time over the contours of her hips, back down to sculpted thighs and calves—slowly trailing up again until they reached her bare back.

"I will, however, insist on paying you back for whatever food you b—" She sucked in when his fingers touched her back. Her skin pebbled as he moved them up her spine.

"My God, woman, this dress."

He stepped closer, watching her chest rise and fall in faster breaths as he ran the tip of his nose along her shoulder and up the side of her neck. Savoring the ease of her responses to him. He pressed his lips into her nape, smiling when she stuttered out, "Is-is that a yes for the dress, or a no?"

He laughed, deep and raspy, in her ear as he nuzzled his nose against it. "I believe it's a threat that I'll fight you if you change." He placed another kiss right below her ear.

She smiled and reached behind her, touching the side of his face. "I don't know how to thank you for what you did today. I hope Greyson realizes all the work you put into this."

"Whether he thanks me or not doesn't matter. I did it for you." He sank a firm kiss into the side of her neck, clamping down, and she took a sharp breath.

"Mmm . . ." He rubbed a finger over the fading mark he made, looking up to her flushed cheeks in the mirror and winked.

"Look at you," she said. Her eyes trailed over his reflection. "I like blue on you."

A shy, half-smile curved up his cheek, and he shrugged. Curling a finger under her chin, he tipped her face up and back. "Good, no lipstick yet."

"Why is that important?"

"Because." He drifted in and brushed his lips against hers. A sweet, delicate kiss that she returned with a heavy, open mouth. Danny froze for half a beat before he caved like the kiss-drunk man that he was.

Rubbing a thumb over her bottom lip, he opened it more and dove inside. Happy to find her welcoming him with a throaty hum. His hands slipped around her waist to her stomach, pressing her back against him. She clasped and intertwined their fingers.

Something in her grip and the eagerness of her kiss told him she needed this connection to calm the anxiety from Greyson. Hell, he needed it too.

She squeezed his hand, lowering it to her leg, and he forgot all about that thought. Forgot everything except how soft her skin felt as he traced the inner line of her thigh.

Arching her neck, she nipped his bottom lip, dragging a ragged breath out of him. His fingers dug into her thigh. Hand still attached, she moved his palm further up her leg and he slipped under the hem of her dress.

"Claire," he whispered and fell heavier on her mouth.

Lips scooped and tongues entwined. All thoughts of taking it slow, gone. All he knew was her scent—her taste.

Anticipation pulsed in his ears as the skin under his hand grew softer—*so soft*. He reached the top inner curve of her left thigh and paused, circling. Long fingers gently squeezed his, and he swept right, brushing against soft lace.

"Claire? Greyson is here." Emelie's voice was a bucket of ice over Danny's senses, and he peeled back, gasping for a breath.

"Shit," he whispered. "Alright, coming," he called, before Emelie got the idea to come looking for them. He groaned, lowered Claire's dress, and placed his forehead against hers with one last squeeze to her thigh.

"Sorry." She panted.

"That wasn't me asking for an apology."

"I don't want to make things hard for you. It's just . . ."

He took her face in his hands. "The only hard thing about this is that you're incredibly irresistible."

She smiled. Her cheeks tinted as he kissed each one, then her nose, her forehead—back to her cheeks. Anywhere but her mouth to keep from reattaching to it.

"I want you to know it's not just about the physical for me," she said.

"Whatever it's about, I'm here for it."

"These, right here?" She took his hands. "They make me feel things I've never felt before. I-I feel safe. Special." Her eyes peered up under her eyelashes. "Wanted."

"Yes." He stared at her mouth. "You are."

She kissed each of his palms before lowering them and interlacing their fingers. "But what's more important to me is how what I do makes you feel. I don't want you to be afraid of any of this."

Her thoughtfulness and consideration overwhelmed him again, seeping into all the cracks and holes. Lifting their joined hands, he kissed her knuckles, his voice thick. "I want *you* to know that the more I'm with you, the less afraid I am." Ducking a couple inches, he aligned their view. "And you aren't making me do anything I don't want to do." He slowly smiled. "*Really* want to do. Now come. Let's go see your son before I attack you again."

"Wait." She stopped short in the hallway. "I need to check something." She rushed back to the mirror, touching and primping flawless hair. Picking up a hairpin, she shoved it where there wasn't a single hair out of place.

"Claire?"

"Hmm?" She grabbed another hairpin.

"What aren't you telling me?"

She looked up into the reflection, into his eyes, a hairpin halfway to her head.

"You didn't know what Greyson eats or drinks and have been anxiously waiting for him to get here all day. Now he's downstairs and you're stalling. Why don't you want to see your son?"

The hairpin fell from her fingers, rattling against the wood floor. She braced against the dresser. "That's the problem, Daniel. He isn't my son anymore."

"What do you mean, he isn't your son?"

"I should have told you sooner." She gnawed on the side of her thumb. "It's just hard for me to admit."

He gently turned her and removed her finger from her teeth. "You can talk to me."

She steeled herself with a deep breath. "Brandon and I got Greyson a driver, well, more like a bodyguard, when he started school. After Brandon died," she stared down at the floor, "that driver assumed things about me and he . . . " Her eyes flicked to his and he went still.

"He what?"

She shook her head like she was trying to clear it, started to speak, stopped, then carefully chose her words. "He stepped out of line, and I sent him away."

He spoke slowly. "Stepped out of line how?"

She waved a hand, saying that wasn't what was important. "When he left, Greyson had a complete meltdown. After losing his father, I think losing someone else close to him was too much. Even when I told him he'd have full control over who was chosen next, it wasn't enough." Her eyes drifted over his shoulder and sad memories shifted across her expression. "He stopped speaking to me after that and locked himself in his room. At first, I thought, if I gave him time, he'd calm down and we could talk it out. But then the meals stopped disappearing at his door. I panicked and forced one of my security to open his door and . . ."

Danny removed her thumb from her teeth again, jolting her out of the memory.

Emotions swelled in her eyes, and she rushed out the words, "He'd crawled out the window, went to my parents' home, told them he didn't want to live with me anymore, and without talking to me, my parents had their *very* good lawyers deem me unfit and took custody of him."

"They did what?"

"He hasn't been mine for over a year." Her voice broke, and she fanned her eyes. Danny wrapped himself around her. Frustration so keen because his body, his arms, couldn't shelter her from this. "I should've fought for custody," she whispered into his chest. "But knowing he didn't want me anymore . . . I had nothing left in me to fight with."

His arms tightened, and he kissed the top of her head. "Sweetheart, you were both grieving. What he did was rash, but it doesn't mean he doesn't want you. Every child needs their mom, no matter how old they get."

"Claire? Danny?" Ian interrupted, yelling up the stairs. "You guys coming?"

"Yes," she called and dabbed under her eyes. "This is the first time he's asked to come see me without having my parents there to scrutinize and prove they were right in taking him. I-I don't know what this means."

Danny ran a finger down the worry lines of her mouth. "Maybe he wants to mend things."

"If that's the case, why didn't he answer any of my texts?"

"Hey, you guys?" Fin yelled up. "Dinner's getting cold."

Danny cursed under his breath and removed her thumb from her teeth yet again. "Whatever it means, you're not facing it alone, okay? I'll be with you." He took her hand.

After a slow, steady descent, they reached the tavern. She halted, gripping her chest. "Oh Daniel, the atmosphere. It's so beautiful."

Rows of Edison bulbs hung in swooping strands from the beams, illuminating white linen-covered tables pushed together in one long row. Interspersed down the center were mason jars filled with fairy-lights and vases of evergreens.

"How did you do all this?"

"He had help." Emelie came from the kitchen and gasped, looking her over. "That dress is gorgeous."

"You can have it if you want."

Danny shot a glare at Emelie and shook his head.

She snickered. "Maybe I'll just borrow it."

"Where is he?" Claire craned her neck, looking over the friendly faces waiting in the dining room. She smiled and waved to them.

Gerty waved back with Gunner lying at her feet, and Ylva held up a basket of baked goods, smiling. Gene, Annie, and Clark greeted her with held up bottles of wine, and Merv waved several bottles of home-brew. George grunted but nodded in greeting.

"He's at your table," Emelie said.

Danny kept her shaking hand in his as they walked to the fireplace. She stopped short when they came upon a lean, young man slouching in a chair, loafers stretched toward the fire. His profile and light-brown hair were all Claire. But unlike her warmth, he was stiff, glaring at the fire as if the flame forced him to sit there. Definitely not the look Danny hoped to see on him.

Claire stepped forward. "Greyson?"

He turned, and his view dropped to their joined hands, back up to Danny, and darkened.

"Hi, baby." She held out her arms, and he looked back into the fire, pretending not to notice her non-verbal request for a hug. She awkwardly dropped her arms and rubbed her hands together, forcing a smile. "I'd like you to meet Daniel Larsson."

Danny held out a hand. Greyson looked at it, and without a word, stood and switched his attention back to her. "Hi, Madelynn."

"Madel—" She took a step back. "You can still call me Mom." When he didn't answer, she swallowed and forced a smile again, opening her arms. "Can I please get a hug?"

"My back hurts."

And that's why he slouched in a chair? Danny's eye twitched.

"What's the matter?" Claire instinctively reached for him, but he twisted away.

Danny's frown deepened. Like hell his back hurt.

"Lacrosse injury," Greyson said.

"And no one told me?"

"Mother and the doctors said I should be fine."

Claire went rigid. "Grandmother. She's your grandmother, Greyson."

Shrugging, he stepped around them, eyeing Flygande with a wrinkled nose. "What's in there?" He nodded to an open door.

"My office," Danny said.

Greyson poked his head in, eyes darting around.

"Don't be rude." Claire pulled on his arm.

"I don't mind." Danny pushed the door open wider, motioning inside.

"No thanks." Greyson continued wandering Flygande, and his hand landed on the back of a wobbling chair. "Needs some updating, doesn't it?"

"Greyson." Claire tossed a silent apology to Danny, who gave her a small smile, unfazed.

"It's over a century old," he said. "I'd be worried if it didn't."

Greyson sniffed, and Danny smirked. If this kid was hoping

to get a rise out of him, he'd have to try harder than that.

Greyson continued to scour the place with a critical eye. "How much debt you in?"

Danny stopped short. "Excuse me?"

"That bad, huh? I thought so."

"Greyson Conner Johnson," Claire snapped. "That's enough."

"Not nearly enough, *Madelynn*."

Danny placed a touch to her back, helping her take a breath. With a grateful, whispered second apology to him, she silently followed her son until he stopped near the front door. His attention drew to a nearly invisible brown box hanging on the wall, and he stiffened.

"It's a Jake Matthews' System," Claire said.

"Ah, that reminds me." Danny pulled out his phone. "The lock is on a timer, and I need to switch it off so everyone's not locked in here."

He leaned against the wall, body blocking the view as he punched in a code he read from his phone. Turning, he smiled at Greyson. These systems weren't cheap. Maybe that would shut him up.

"Do you remember when we met Jacob?" Claire asked Greyson. "You were so excited about his equipment. You followed him around the house asking a million questions." She turned to Danny. "After graduation he's going to school for computer engineering and —"

"I dropped out," he said casually, studying the carved words over the bar.

"What do you mean, you dropped out?"

"Welcome, Family," he scoffed. "How quaint."

"Answer me, Greyson."

Danny inwardly smiled. Not even Greyson was immune to a motherly tone. He sank a little, shoving his hands in his pockets. Danny watched him push it back down. Like Claire, only not for propriety but pride, and he straightened his spine, cocky smile returning.

"I was bored, and Mother said I didn't need to go back if I didn't want to," he said. "I have a position ready for me at Cooke's Holdings if I want it."

Claire's fingers squeezed together. "You never expressed a desire to work there."

"Things change." He glanced between her and Danny. "Besides, I know more than most of those kids anyway."

"Then work ahead and graduate early. You don't drop out."

He bent his head until they were eye level. Danny started forward and stopped, holding himself back from stepping in between. This was her son. It wasn't his place.

"Well, it's a good thing it's not up to you anymore, isn't it, *Madelynn*."

Claire jerked back, touching her cheek like he'd slapped her, and for the briefest moment, Greyson's coldness vanished. Like he felt how deep his words cut and regretted it. Maybe good sense was finally kicking in? But when Danny couldn't resist the stricken expression on her face and let his hand graze her arm with the briefest touch, Greyson's coldness slid back into place.

"Quick to replace Dad with the Viking, huh?"

Claire went utterly still. "What'd you just say?" she whispered. "Excuse me?"

"You used his words." She stepped closer, her body vibrating. "You would've overheard your father and I. You dropped out of school. You know about electronic equipment. You have means." She took another step. "God, Greyson. Tell me you're not so angry at me that you would haunt me."

Danny's eyes bounced back and forth between them. Why did she ask him that when Kenneth admitted to it?

Greyson took a step back. "Are you drunk?"

"Why did you call Daniel that? The Viking."

His eyes sprang wide and he cleared his throat. "Uh . . . " Danny watched him shift from one foot to the other. He was missing something.

Greyson smoothed his hair and expression back to nonchalance.

"Have you looked at this thrift store décor? Obviously, he's pretending to be a Viking."

"Are you serious?" George bellowed from the other side of the room and Merv gripped his arm, yanking him back behind the tables. Everyone who'd been pretending not to eavesdrop, quickly turned and actively tried to start conversations with each other.

"He's Swedish, Greyson," Claire said. "He's not pretending to be. And if you took the time to actually look, you'd see these are authentic antiques, not knock-offs. Even if they were from a thrift store, what right do you have to speak to him this way?"

"Can't you see what he's doing?"

"Yes, he's being a completely hospitable host to you."

Greyson leaned in and whispered, "That's because he's hoping to snag the rich girl."

"That's enough."

"Tell me you aren't this naïve, Madelynn."

"Stop. Calling. Me. That."

"Who's hungry?" Ian said as he, Emelie, and Fin emerged from the kitchen with nine different food dishes between them. They froze. The entire room was in eerie silence.

"Yes, time to eat," Danny said, and the group on the left side that had definitely *not* been eavesdropping came alive, thanking him for the dinner invitation. He acknowledged them, but kept his eyes on Claire and Greyson. Something was definitely off with that kid.

Claire schooled away all her frustrations and tapped a knife against a glass to get everyone's attention. "I'd like you all to meet my son, Greyson Johnson. Greyson, these are my friends." She introduced them by name, and he nodded to each one in response.

Danny held out a chair for her and Greyson rolled his eyes. Danny's jaw ticked, but he said nothing, taking the seat across from Claire.

"Would you like some *limpa* bread?" Ylva smiled at Greyson, passing down a basket.

"Eggs or butter in it?"

"Yes, there's butter."

He pushed the basket back. "I'm vegan."

"Since when?" Claire asked as she took the basket and removed two steaming slices. "This looks delicious, Ylva, thank you."

"If you paid attention, you'd know it's been a while."

The table went quiet except for an indignant, "what that kid needs is a drill sergeant in his face," from George, quickly followed by a "hush," from Merv.

"I can leave."

"No." Claire caught Greyson's arm. "Please stay. We'll figure out something for you to eat." She sent a desperate look to Danny.

"I have vegan." He went to the other end of the table and brought back three dishes.

Greyson sniffed at the stir-fry. "Hate broccoli."

The more he pushed, Danny decided, the more placid he'd become. Steeling his features, he removed the stir-fry and shoved two other dishes in front of him, smiling.

Greyson hmphed. "Surprised to find authentic Indian food on this island."

Claire opened to tell him Danny made them, but he tapped her foot under the table with a small shake of his head. Greyson would eat it so long as he didn't know who made it.

"Is this your first time to our island?" Annie, who sat next to Claire, attempted to bring Greyson into conversation.

"Yes," is all he answered without looking at her, and shoveled a large bite of cauliflower curry.

"Greyson," Claire said.

"I'm not bothered one bit," Annie whispered. "I've fostered many boys like him. He's angry, but he'll be alright." She squeezed Claire's forearm and directed conversations away from them, saving Claire from more humiliation.

Danny gave her a grateful nod as Claire spooned chana masala onto her plate, cautiously eyeing her son. "How have you been?"

He raised his head, looking her in the eye. "Been the best year of my life."

One punch. Just one punch in his stupid mouth should do it. Danny squeezed that thought into his tightening fists and tapped her shoe with his, catching her eye. *Breathe for me.* He ran the tip of his boot up and down her calf, holding her gaze. Slowly, air eased out of her lungs and then her foot hooked the back of his leg in a silent hug.

"Claire?" Gerty called down the table. "Have you been out to your cottage lately?"

"I haven't had a chance."

Gerty's brow furrowed. "There were fresh prints out back when I took Gunner for a walk there this morning. Aren't the contractors finished?"

Greyson choked and coughed.

"Are you okay?" Claire patted his back. "That was my understanding," she said to Gerty.

Greyson shrugged off her patting and met Danny's raised brow with another glare.

"It's Thanksgiving break," Annie said. "Probably some bored teens."

"Maybe." Gerty nodded. "Wait 'til you see how it's come back to life again. Even new flower boxes were installed."

"My flower boxes." Claire smiled and turned to Greyson. "The cottage I rented here turned out to be a rip-off. I got them, though. Low-balled them for the inconvenience, and now it's mine. Want to see it?"

"You bought a house here? Why would you do that?"

Claire glanced at Danny. "If things work out, I-I think I'd like to stay."

Greyson threw down his napkin. "For *him*?"

"Well, I—"

"It's highly sought-after real estate," Ian said, as he, Emelie, and Fin joined everyone at the table. His firm squeeze to Danny's shoulder reminded him he absolutely couldn't hit this kid. "Lots of people want to move here and can't."

"Well, isn't she lucky." Greyson's watch beeped, and he shoved back his chair, standing.

"Where are you going?" Claire stood.

"To the car," he wiped his mouth, "that's getting me off this damn island."

"Language." She paused. "I mean, please stay so we can talk this out."

"You've forgotten my father. I have nothing more to say to you."

"I could never forget him." She lowered her voice and caught his arm, steering him from the table, but he wouldn't budge. "My relationship with Daniel may seem fast to you, but it's not. We're taking it slow. And there's so much more I should've told you sooner. I see that now. Things between your father and I weren't good for many years because he wasn't well," she tapped her head, "up here. I never told you because I wanted you to have a normal childhood without our drama."

"Are you seriously trying to claim my father, *the* Brandon Johnson, famous psychiatrist, was crazy?"

"I never said he was crazy. He got into psychiatry to help people like himself because he struggled with childhood traumas. The same traumas that made him incapable of showing me affection."

"That's the story you're going with so you can justify being with this sponger?"

"Don't speak about Daniel that way."

He puffed a laugh. "You know, I've known you were many things, Madelynn, but desperate for a fuck wasn't one of them."

Ian's arm shot out across Danny's chest right before Claire's hand cracked across Greyson's face. Horror filled her gaping eyes as she watched a handprint bloom on her son's cheek.

"I-I'm sorry Greyson." Her voice wavered. "But you . . . that was . . . take it back."

"No." He started for the door.

Claire followed. "Why are you behaving this way? Is this all really because of *him*?"

Greyson's teeth clenched. "He has a name."

"A name I won't say after what he did to—" She darted a look at Danny and he stopped mid-step toward her. Was this the driver she mentioned earlier? "There's something I need to tell you about him," she said. "Will you listen?"

"Why should I?" He bumped hard into Danny on his way to the door, stumbling. Danny caught him, and Greyson shoved him off.

"Greyson, wait." Claire chased him.

"Enjoy your new *family,* because I'm blocking your number."

"You're my family. I can't lose you again."

The last line was said in a whisper, but Danny felt the roar of it inside him. He was desperate. Needed to stop the blow Greyson's darkening expression promised. His body moved closer to her.

"You never had me back, Madelynn." Greyson yanked open the door.

She drove into it, making it slam. "*Please.*" She pressed shaking fingers over her mouth.

"Move."

"Don't leave like this, baby. Look at me. I love you." She touched a small curl of hair over his ear. "I know I should have fought harder for you."

He snapped his head away from her touch. "Not caring about me is the best thing you could've done."

"I do care. You mean everything to me."

Danny's hand instinctively reached for her when Greyson's head slowly turned. "Well, *Madelynn,* you mean nothing to me." He yanked open the door, making her stumble back, and with one more hard look at Danny, tore outside.

A deafening hush fell over the table, and all eyes turned toward Claire. Gerty held back a growling Gunner, while Merv and Gene joined George's quiet curses. Ylva grabbed Annie's hand, who sent up silent prayers while clinging to Clark's tense arm. Ian stood beside Danny, fists opening and closing, while Fin's eyes tracked Emelie's fingers swiping under her eyes.

"Claire?" Danny whispered.

Her posture went rigid. Madelynn taking a protective front and center as she turned to face them. "I-I'm sorry for my son's behavior." Her mouth wobbled, and she squeezed her hands together in front of her. "He's been through a lot with his father's death, and I failed him when he needed me the most. I . . . I'm grateful you all came to—it means so much that—" Her voice broke. "Please, excuse me."

Danny chased after her, up the stairs and into his room. Inside the door, she stumbled, voice cracking on a whispered, "Greyson." Her knees buckled, and he caught her mid-fall.

"Claire?" All the color drained from her face and her eyes rolled back. "*Claire.*" He swept under her legs and rushed her to the bed. "Open your eyes, sweetheart, please." He held her and rocked her on his lap, brushing damp hair away from her face. He should have stepped in sooner. Should have stopped it. "Please, wake up."

Her face grew paler.

"Shit." Easing her from his shaking arms, he rushed for the door, yelling, "*Doc Clark.*"

30

Shadowed Past

CLAIRE CHASED HIM. HIS body no longer tall and lean, but small, chubby. His steps unsteady. He was running for a cliff. He was going to fall over the cliff. "Greyson!"

She caught his shirt sleeve, but when he turned, he wasn't her baby anymore. His teenaged face twisted, teeth bared. "You mean *nothing* to me."

. . . nothing to me . . . nothing to me . . .

She lost her grip on him and he fell. "*No.*" She dove for him.

Claire.

She now stood on a stone walkway. Dim voices filtered over intricate topiaries and grand marble statues where a large group of people gathered around elaborate tables of food after Brandon's funeral.

Not here. She couldn't be here again.

"How lucky you were to have him as your husband," a faceless woman said.

She stumbled backward, her back colliding against a stone wall, hand pressed to her chest. The pressure was building. She couldn't breathe.

Claire!

She ran. Her room suddenly in front of her. She gasped for air, the walls expanded and shrank.

Something caught in her periphery and her head slowly turned. Not this. Not again.

The bathroom door was wide open with a clear view of the tub. A sob choked in her throat. Brandon floated in cold water. His large blue eyes, dimmed gray, gaped at her from the rim of the claw-foot tub. *It's my fault. It's my fault.*

She rushed forward with a cry and slammed the bathroom door closed.

That smell. Stale with heavy cologne. It filled her nose right before her bedroom door opened and a large, broad-shouldered giant of a man stepped in.

She should run. Something in her gut said she needed to run, but nothing worked. Her limbs hung heavy, moving like molasses.

"How are you, Madelynn?" Her son's driver said, rubbing a hand over his thick, square jaw.

"I'm . . . I'm fine. Thank you." Her eyes darted around the room. It was her room, yet something else. Wooden panels blended with murals of Tuscany.

"You don't look fine." He stepped forward. There was a vibration in his hands. An unsteadiness in his footfall . . . unease grew in the pit of her stomach. For months now, he'd been getting too attentive. Too familiar with her through light touches and lingering eyes.

The concerned tilt of his head didn't match the dullness of his eyes. She clutched over her tightening stomach. "Really, I'm alright. Maybe you should find Greyson."

His thick fingers curled into fists, taking another step, making her press back against the bathroom door for space. "Come now, Madelynn Claire, let's not pretend you weren't just begging me with your eyes to follow you here."

Phantom pain in her wrist sprang and she rubbed and rubbed over it.

"The way you've been begging me for years to take care of you like he didn't," he continued, gleaming gaze traveling to the door behind her like he could see Brandon through it. The black endless pits of his eyes returned to hers and inched down her body. "I will take such good care of you, Madelynn."

Her. Limbs. Wouldn't. Move. Heightened pain shot through her wrist. She glanced down to a scar, red and swollen, blood pulsing beneath her skin. *Please,* she begged her body to move. "I-I don't want this from you."

He smiled like she hadn't spoken, and his rough fingers slid along her jaw.

"Don't touch me!"

One large hand slapped over her scream and the other snatched both her useless wrists in a bruising grip. "You think I waited ten years for you to be free from him only to tell me I can't touch you?" His voice was a manic whisper.

Dead, gray eyes . . . Greyson . . . *you mean nothing to me . . .* Flashes of faces and words. All of it blurred together with his tightening grip.

Violently shaking, she tried to scream again. A hand swallowed it. Another hand twisted her around, slamming her into the bathroom door so hard it burst open, knocking the air out of her lungs.

Breathe, Claire.

She wriggled and convulsed. Her lungs ached for oxygen. The man's grip tightened, and the stench of his cigarette breath fanned the side of her face.

"It didn't have to be this way." The weight of his body pressed heavier, forcing her head to the side.

Her leaking eyes fell on the tub. Brandon was alive. Sitting on the edge with their son next to him. Both shaking their heads in disappointment. She gasped against the ache squeezing her chest.

"Help me," she rasped, but they looked away. No one would help her. She had failed them both.

Open your eyes, Claire.

Cold metal pressed against her cheek, and she froze at the glint of a blade in the corner of her eye. "Let me make something very, very clear. Behave or," Greyson's driver ran the blade along her jaw, "this won't be as fun for you." The knife slithered down the side of her neck, down her collarbone, and stopped on her chest.

Rage boiled from her clenched stomach, and she became suddenly aware that this was not how it ended.

She would not. *He* would not.

Claire thrust her head back into his nose and dove for the knife. He was faster. The sharp sting of a razor's edge met flesh, and she cried out. The scar was open. Blood swelled and ran down her wrist. She released a guttural scream and tore around, clawing the flesh under his eyes.

"Madelynn Claire," his voice rumbled, blood dripping over his chin. "You'll regret that."

"Claire, *wake up.*"

She gasped, eyes springing open.

"You're safe." Her body was enveloped in warmth, and her racing eyes caught worried cyan-colored ones. "You're safe," Danny repeated, brushing hair from her eyes, rocking her.

Other hands touched her, and she jolted, gaze snagging on Doc Clark and Annie.

Annie gently smiled. "Gave us a little scare, love, but you're alright."

Claire gasped again, her chest heaving.

"Annabelle said you didn't eat much at dinner," Doc said, closing a leather bag. "When's the last time you ate?"

"I-I don't remember."

"We'll make sure you get something," he said. Then turned to Danny. "Keep her resting. We'll be back to check on her."

Claire still panted, heart racing as she scanned over the wood-paneled walls. "Where am I?"

"Your room at Flygande."

"Flygande," she repeated. Her vibrating hand went to her forehead, rubbing. She felt so weak.

Danny pulled her closer, continuing to rock her, his warm palm against her cheek. "It was just a bad dream," he whispered.

But it wasn't. It was her living nightmare. The one she'd locked deep in her mind and had only relived in short bursts until now. Her tight chest ached as she tried to fill her lungs. More memories flashed through her mind, and she remembered why her caged nightmare broke wide open. "Greyson."

He'd left. Even now, he chose his driver over her. Despair crushed her insides. She'd lost her son all over again.

"Breathe, Claire." Danny's hand grasped hers over her chest. "It'll be alright." His other hand rubbed her back, helping air into her lungs. "What were you dreaming?" he whispered.

She gulped another breath and shook her head. She couldn't say it. "W-What happened?"

"You passed out." Danny brushed more hair from her face as her eyes ran over the walls again. The mural of her old bedroom was gone. She blinked and blinked again to be sure. Still caught in the between. Dream. Memory. Danny's present touch moving on her back.

"I passed out?"

"At first, but then you got stuck in a nightmare again," Danny said. "You were screaming, and I couldn't wake you."

Again? He was still there. The phantom scratch of his jaw against her cheek. His stale breath breathing in her ear. She swallowed hard, still gasping for full breaths. She shivered, and Danny tightened his hold.

"I'm going to find out when the food is coming." He reached inside his pocket. "Where's my phone?" There was a single knock on the door, and it opened before Danny answered. Emelie, Fin, and Ian walked in. One with a tray sampling everything Danny had made, one with tea, the third a bottle of McClellan whisky.

"Are you okay?" they all said in unison, a little too loudly.

Tears welled in her eyes. The way they looked at her, not an ounce of disappointment. Claire forced a wobbling smile and tried to say she was okay. That everything was fine, but nothing came out of her mouth.

She wasn't fine.

"She's in need of this, and this." Danny balanced the tray in one hand and grabbed the teapot. "But sorry, she doesn't like whisky."

"This is for us." Ian yanked the cork and took a long swig.

They came further into the room, and to Claire's great relief, Danny stepped in front of them. "She may need a minute."

Emelie peered around him at her. Her eyes soft like her smile. "Just call us if you need anything else. We'll be in the living room."

"Have you seen my phone?" Danny said. "Maybe I left it on the table downstairs."

"I'll check," Fin said.

"Claire?" Ian held the bottle out toward her in a shaking hand, pointing. His eyes so piercing she held her breath. "You didn't fail your son." He pointed again, like his finger could push the words into her. "Trust me, I would know." His voice cracked on the last word, and he took another fortifying drink. "You're amazing, and we love you."

The tears fell. "Thank you," she whispered.

Danny pushed the door shut with the heel of his boot, studying her. "Let me help you sit up." He wiped her damp cheeks before steadying a bowl of creamy potato leek soup in her hands. She felt his heavy attention on her as she lifted shaking bites of soup.

"Do you want to talk about it?"

She closed her eyes on a heavy exhale. The pain in her wrist was fading back into memory again. She shook her head.

"You know I'm not with you for the money, right?"

"Of course, I know." She rubbed her forehead with a small groan. "Greyson said such awful things. I'm so sorry."

"I'm not asking you for an apology." He shoved buttered bread between her teeth. "I just needed to make sure that was clear."

She caught a waver in his voice and gave him a thorough lookover. "What's this for?" She touched a crease between his eyes.

He avoided her gaze, trading her empty bowl with stir-fry. "I need to ask you something."

Dread stilled her hand, fork halfway to her mouth. "What is it?"

"I don't want to be the cause of tension between you and

your son."

Her fork, suddenly heavy, sank back to her plate. "This is the mess I warned you about," she whispered, her food blurring in her eyes. "But I under . . . I understand."

With a sharp tug, he tipped up her chin, eyes darting over her face. "What do you understand?"

"That you're finished with this. With me."

His face went slack, jaw dropping open. "You think . . . " He snapped his mouth closed and pushed the fork back into her hand, lifting it to her lips. "You've got to stop putting words in my mouth, Claire. I don't throw people away like old shoes. Eat."

"What is it then?" She spoke around the food, froze, then realized how little she cared about etiquette right now.

"I was going to ask if you needed me to, um . . . " He rubbed the back of his neck. "To give you space to fix things with your son."

The panic she'd woken with melted into something else. Something hot and liquid in the pit of her stomach. "You're asking if *I* want space from *you*, and what? My son will come running back into my arms again? Sure, Daniel." She buttered more bread so hard it tore. "Because you being with me is the reason he ran away from me to begin with."

"Claire."

"*No.*" He blinked at her sharp response. "No, I don't want space from you to fix things. Because you aren't the reason he's angry. You're just another excuse to justify his rash decision to leave me to begin with." She went still. Her own words smacking her in the face.

Danny leaned in, a small smile curving up his left cheek. "Exactly," he whispered, kissing her forehead. "Like I said earlier, him leaving wasn't your fault."

He removed the empty plates and poured two cups of tea, settling in next to her.

She let out a long sigh and melted into his warmth, head on his shoulder. Her nightmare of a past continued to fade into faint sensations.

"Can I ask you something else?" he said.

She brought the mug to her lips, nodding.

"Why did you stay with him?"

She stopped mid-sip, not needing to ask who he meant. "I'd thought of leaving Brandon many times, but in the beginning, I stayed to give Greyson a more normal childhood than I had."

"And in the end?" he asked quietly.

"In the end, I planned to leave him anyway and told him that the night he . . . " His empty, gray eyes filled her mind.

"Shit." Danny gathered her in his arms and pressed a kiss into her temple. "I'm so sorry, sweetheart." He stiffened, tilting his ear toward the window.

"What is it?"

He rose and pushed back the curtains, squinting. "It's Greyson." He held up a hand before she could stand, face twisting into confusion for a moment, but then said, "He's leaving now with his driver . . . Claire?"

Her eyes snapped up to his, but he was staring at her hand. The one she didn't realize was rubbing her wrist. He took a step closer, and she pushed down her sleeve. The darkness in his expression told her he was making connections she'd kept secret from him. "Daniel."

He snatched her sleeve, yanking it up. His trembling finger ran over a fading pink scar. "I said 'driver' and you touched this." His voice was low, dark. "Why?"

"I'm okay, Daniel."

"He did this." It wasn't a question but she slowly nodded. "He's your nightmare. Why you keep yelling at someone not to not touch you. Did he . . . " His teeth clenched tight.

"No." She brushed a soft touch over his pulsing jaw. "I fought him. That's how I got the scar."

Green took over the blue in his darkened gaze. "What's his name?"

"It's not important."

"It is to me."

She closed her eyes and laid the back of her head against the headboard. She didn't want the taste of his name in her mouth. "Henderson. Donald Henderson. But he's gone, Daniel. I sent him out of the country on an early retirement."

"He should be in jail, or *dead*. Not retired."

"My son had just lost his father," she whispered. "I couldn't do that to him."

He took her face firmly in both hands. "This has to stop, Claire. You, thinking of everyone else's well-being without a thought to your own. It stops now. Do you understand?"

He wavered in her vision. For the first time, she saw the utter truth of his words. How right he was. In sacrificing herself to spare her son, she lost him anyway.

Danny held her gaze until she nodded. "And you're sure he's out of the country?"

Her phone buzzed once and when she lifted it, she showed him her daily security notification, confirming his absence. "Even without this notice. My phone will buzz three times continuously if something goes wrong. Then a location of where I'll be safe will pop up. Jake Matthews is worth every penny he sucks away from me."

She looked closely at this man in front of her. The one who fed her and held her. Who could make her laugh and snort in her tea. She really looked at him and made a decision. She wouldn't let these precious moments break against the rocks of her past anymore. She'd let her past wash away instead and hold on to this peace, this joy.

Pulling Danny in, she lost herself. Erasing her dark with his light, she kissed away every worry line on his face.

Icy Waters

THE COMMITTEE IN CHARGE of the Nordic Dive were monsters. You couldn't convince Ian otherwise. He shuffled from the living room to the kitchen and blinked bleary-eyed at Danny. "How are you awake before me?"

Danny stared without blinking at the dripping coffeepot. "Define awake."

"I can't define anything." Ian stumbled to the pot and inhaled a deep whiff, hoping the swirling fumes would start soaking the caffeine into his body through his nose. "Why do they insist that this dive start at sunrise?"

"Tradition."

"I'd like to tell them where to stick their tradition."

"Our tradition. Your great-grandfather's and mine, remember?"

"Stupid, competitive, early rising bastards."

Danny snickered and shoved a steaming mug into Ian's hand before picking up his tea. "Kilt today?"

Ian adjusted the tartan over his swim trunks. "Yeah, tradition and all that bullshit."

"Forgot about your sailor's mouth when you're grumpy."

Ian plopped into a kitchen chair. "Yeah, well, staying up 'til three seemed like a good idea at the time."

What he didn't say was how he couldn't have gone to bed sooner even if he'd tried. Watching Claire struggling, fighting for her son. The old, wrenching grief from his own mother leaving him without a goodbye — without so much as a note for the past twenty years — had nearly swallowed him whole.

Danny and Claire had later joined the group in the living room. Where after drinks, many hugs and laughter, his grief was numbed again. He even managed to make Claire laugh so hard, wine came out her nose.

"How's Claire?" Ian asked.

Danny's yawn nearly swallowed his head. "She finally fell into a deep sleep about an hour ago."

"You gonna wake her?"

"Nah, I'll let her rest."

"But she'll miss your dive."

He waved it off, but Ian saw the disappointment. Sure, it was a silly competition, but it brought out the entire town, including tourists if the snow hadn't arrived. Braving the cold, they'd cheer for their favorite diver and end up at Flygande for celebratory potluck and fellowship. Danny had looked forward to sharing it all with Claire.

"Fin's first time, isn't it?" Danny opened the oven and pulled out some of Ylva's re-heated bread, placing it next to a spread of strawberry jam, soft-boiled eggs, thinly sliced cucumber, and cheese.

"Yeah, it is." Ian did a double take of the table. "How long have you been up?"

Danny shrugged and slathered butter on the steaming slice before layering cheese and dipping it in an egg.

A thump and a low curse came from the living room. A few more bumps and a few more curses later, a ragged-haired Fin staggered into the kitchen with his shirt inside out. "Wait. Emelie is still sleeping? Forget it, I'm not going."

Ian caught him by said shirt and pointed to the tag. "Can't just dive for the ladies, Finlay."

"Sure I can."

But he didn't have to. A loud bang from a door opening down the hall was followed by sloppy, stumbling feet. Fin scrambled to fix his shirt before an every-hair-out-of-place, raccoon-eyed Emelie barreled into the kitchen and gripped the wall. "Did I miss it?" She panted.

They all grinned.

"Coffee." Danny handed her a full mug. "We leave in an hour, but the dive isn't for another two hours."

"Where's Claire?" They all pointed to the room, and she gasped. "No, she has to get up."

Danny caught her arm. "Let her sleep. It was a rough night."

"You don't understand. She and I . . . I mean, she worked so hard . . . I mean . . . she has to get up, okay?"

She tore out of his grip, and Danny cast a confused glance at Ian. "Hell, if I know."

Danny had just finished filling another mug with tea when two very disheveled women appeared in the kitchen to the joy of two men. You could read it on Danny and Fin's face that the sight of messy hair, pillow-wrinkled faces and half-opened, puffy eyes were the highlight of their morning.

"I was going to let you sleep." Danny held out a steaming cup for Claire.

She stumbled past it and planted her lips on his. Fin snickered and Ian quickly caught the cup before it spilled, while his best friend received a wake-up call better than caffeine.

Either Claire wasn't awake enough to notice she had an audience, or their renewed promises not to allow Greyson to tear apart the good they had pushed her over the line of not caring.

"Damn." Fin shook his head and Ian silently agreed.

The woman could kiss. No wonder Danny was tipsy for it. They both gawked for a few more seconds until her tongue slipped into his mouth. Ian coughed up coffee while Fin tossed puppy eyes at an oblivious Emelie.

Claire tore away and left Danny without a breath to breathe. "Just wanted to thank you again for helping me last night." She reached around him for her mug like she didn't just send him into another dimension.

Fin and Ian elbowed each other when he didn't move.

"You ready, Claire?" Emelie, now freshly caffeinated, retied her ponytail. "Almost out of time."

"Coming."

This woke Danny from his stupor. "Where are you going? What about breakfast?"

"It's a surprise, and I'll get food." She smiled. "Don't worry, I'll be there in time to see you dive." She touched his lips with her fingers and then dove in for one more heavy kiss before tearing away and following Emelie down the stairs.

"Where are they going?" Danny asked again, clearly disappointed at how abruptly that last kiss ended. "She's been heading out with Em several times a week, but they never tell me what they're doing." He rubbed the back of his neck and groaned. "What the hell can be so important this early in the morning?"

"Don't know." Ian slurped down the rest of his coffee and stuffed one more of Ylva's bread slices in his mouth. "Come on, both of you. None of us are backing out now."

Danny glanced around the apartment. "Fin, you sure you didn't see my phone on the table last night?"

"Nope. Even checked under it."

"I swear I had it in my pocket."

"It'll show up," Ian said. "Come on, I'm already exhausted, and we haven't even started yet." Ian dragged them out the door, each holding heavy wool blankets in their arms.

THE SOUND OF VOICES rose on the wind as they neared the stony beach. Fishing boats floated in a half-circle with battery-operated lanterns creating the dive borders. The early sun barely kissed the horizon.

"It all began with Torbjörn Larsson and Farlan McClellan," Merv recited the history of the Nordic Dive through a megaphone. Having heard the same story of the men settling a fight by racing in ice-cold water every year since his childhood, Danny let his mind and eyes wander over his shoulder, searching for honey hair. Unease still lingered from the night before. Why did he have to lose his phone?

"Divers, line up," Merv announced, and all the men huddled near the edge of the water.

Annie, the on-call medic for the dive, was dressed in a cold-water suit. She kissed a speedo-clad Clark before climbing into a motorboat with a few young medic trainees.

"You all know the drill," Merv said. "Up to Ted's boat, touch, and back again."

"Isn't that out an extra hundred yards this year?" Ian called out.

George, one of shameless streakers, who was also forced to the front to hide his wrinkled ass, scoffed. "'Tis the same as it is every year, McClellan. But feel free to wimp out now." He flexed his skinny arms.

Ian grinned.

"Time's up, lads," Merv said. "For those that aren't already, it's down to your trunks or skivvies."

Again, Danny glanced over his shoulder. He thought of Claire trapped in her nightmare by a man he couldn't put a face to. He thought of the details he'd withheld from her about what he saw outside his window afterward. Greyson arguing with his driver in the shadows, arm swiping over his face before handing him something and leaving.

"She'll come." Ian's voice snapped him back. "'Course, at this rate, I'm hoping she misses it, so you'll be distracted and I'll out swim ya."

"Wanna place a bet on that?" Danny peeled off his sweater, slapping his arms to warm his muscles. "Bottle of single malt."

"That's sacred ground you're trod'n there, Danny Boy. Dammit, I'm already cold." Ian removed his kilt and sweater, hopping up and down. "It's a deal with the devil, to be sure, but a deal nonetheless — oh, *hell* no. Cover that ass, Finlay. You're not going to win Emelie over with that blinding light."

Danny snickered, and Fin grumbled but secured his swim

trunks back around his waist.

"Tell me again why I agreed to do this?" Danny slipped off his sweatpants, crouched into a few squats, and smacked heat into his thighs.

"Because you've been undefeated for the past four years, and you have to maintain your Viking reputation."

Danny smiled, dipped a hand into the water, and splashed it onto his skin, acclimating to the temperature. "I think it's colder."

"You say that every year."

"Psst," Fin said.

Danny's eyes tracked over his shoulder and fell on a bundle entombed in a down-filled coat with an edible face peeking out, waddling next to Emelie. His face split apart.

Emelie waved to them and broke from Claire to join a few other friends. Fin's arm froze mid-wave and floated down.

"Bit of advice." Danny stepped next to him. "Stop expecting things from her. Too many people do that already. Just let her see that you're there."

"Fin." Mattie and Dean beckoned to him. "We saved you a spot."

"Remember what I told you," Ian said from the other side of him, then mouthed, "Romance."

Fin side-glanced him, then Danny. "Maybe next year," he called.

"Afraid we'll kick your ass?"

Fin flipped them off, and they laughed while Danny jogged to meet Claire.

"Sorry I'm late." She panted and eyed up his swim trunks. "I see you're not a purist."

"That depends." He thumbed inside and ran along the waistband.

Her eyes followed. "O-on what?"

"On whether or not you say please."

A small peep squeaked out of her, and he barked a laugh. Snapping the band back into place, he kissed the point of her nose.

She puffed a white cloud through her scarf. "You're mean."

"Tell you what, M.C.C." He dipped toward her ear and lifted the end of her fluffy, pink earmuff. "When the time comes, this?" He swept his hand up and down over himself. "Will only be for you to see."

Her hand clutched her throat. "Did you say when and not if?"

A crooked smirk slipped up the side of his mouth. "You heard me."

"You're not afraid anymore?"

His breath warmed her ear again as he gently kissed it. "I'm not afraid anymore."

It didn't matter that her scarf covered the bottom half of her face, and her hat nearly covered the other half. Her smile seeped through it all. "Better not freeze out there then, Viking."

"Ten-nine-eight . . . "

Danny grinned and ran with the rest of the men toward the water. The sun made its red orb appearance over the choppy surface as his feet neared the water's edge. He turned one last time to wave, but it wasn't Claire he saw. It was a man in an ivy cap and wool coat with an upturned collar standing twenty feet behind her. A stoney smile wormed its way up a jagged-scarred cheek.

The whistle blew and the sound of bodies splashing into the sea barely registered. Danny had never missed being the first in the water. And when he looked back over his shoulder, the man was gone.

"Danny, come on," Ian's watery voice yelled.

He turned and dove in. The icy liquid sent a bolt of shock to his heated core, threatening to shut down his brain. Adrenaline kicked in. His mind and body warred against the icy water and the thought of that chilling smile.

Who was he? And why the hell was he looking at him like that?

He swam faster, hoping to clear his head.

Ian reached the boat first. Damn, it was cold. At least the cold made Danny want to keep moving to stay warm — or at the very least sane. He started to close in behind Ian, but his mind wasn't in it. Probably just exhaustion, but he couldn't shake the look on that man's face.

Cheers from the crowd faded in and out as his ears bobbed in and out of the water. For the first time since he started diving at age fourteen, the cold penetrated to the bone. A painful cramp seized his thighs, and his joints locked.

"Ian." His voice gurgled as his mouth filled with salt water.

"Danny?"

His head dropped beneath the waves.

Annie was first in the water, but Ian was closer and wrapped his arm around and under his chin, lifting his face out of the water. He spit out air.

"Is this how you plan to win?" Ian panted, and Danny groaned as he was dragged toward Annie.

"I can finish."

"Get in the boat, Danny."

"No, I'm good. Cramping stopped. Promise. Thanks, Annie." He shoved Ian off and picked up speed again.

"Cheater."

Danny forced a laugh. His legs still ached. Clark made it back first with a caveman-like holler while he and Ian remained neck and neck. Danny could feel Ian's eyes on him, and in an effort to show him he was fine, he ignored the burn of his thighs and pulled ahead, making them come in fourth and fifth place.

Drag-crawling out of water, they were met by volunteers who cheered and covered them in warm blankets.

"You okay?" Ian asked, shaking out his hair.

Danny rubbed the blanket over his head and stretched out his aching legs, looking over the crowd. "Not enough sleep."

"How . . . did you," Fin panted, "old men make it back before me." He wheezed and crawled out of the water.

"Old?" Ian threw a blanket at his head and turned to Danny. "You sure you're alright?"

"Yeah." Danny sighed. "There was just some guy glaring at me right before the dive and I got distracted."

"Lots of guys glare at you. Usually because their women are staring at you."

Danny rolled his eyes, but then caught a group of mainlander women doing just that. He cleared his throat and shifted further under the blanket.

"Any idea who the guy was?"

Danny was about to answer, but stopped when he saw Ian rubbing his stomach. A sign that his sixth sense for trouble was kicking in. "Why, you feeling something?"

"Pretty sure this is because I saw your head go under."

"I was only soaking in the moment."

Ian sucker-punched his arm.

Claire waddle-rushed up to them and threw an extra blanket around Danny. "Did I see that right? Did you go under?"

"He was looking for attention."

Danny shoved Ian away and opened his blankets wide. "Come here, my little burrito." He surrounded Claire's poof-covered body and shook his wet head all over her. She screeched.

"We have to get you dry." She pulled him toward the hill. "Are you sure you're okay?"

"I cramped a little, but I think it's a lack of sleep." He stopped her and patted her down. "Are you even inside this thing? What's this." He cupped her butt and squeezed.

She laughed and swiped off his hands. He reeled her back in and planted a wet kiss over her scarf. "That won't do."

"It's going to have to, Mister Larsson. Dry first. Kiss later."

"How about kiss now and later." His free hand started lowering her coat zipper.

"*Daniel*," she squeaked, and he grinned, sliding a wet hand under her sweater.

He tugged on one of her underlayers. "How's a man supposed to get a feel in?"

Wriggling and laughing, she pulled his hand out and led him

further up the hill. Her phone buzzed, and she glanced down at it. All her joy vanished. "He did it. Greyson really blocked my number."

Danny sighed and pulled her closer. "I'm sorry. I know we never talked it out last night, but do you know what you're going to do about him?"

"Probably what I should have done a year ago." His brow furrowed, and she said, "Get some *very* good lawyers of my own and fight for him."

"That's my Claire." He tugged down her scarf, eyes dropping to her lips. "That mouth."

"Dry," kiss, "first," another kiss, "kiss," a deeper one, "later." She grinned when he grunted and restored her scarf.

"Fine." He turned her around and moved her in front of him. "But first . . . " He swept the blanket around her front and shoved the corners of it into her hands. Again he slipped under her sweater and jerked yet another layer up. She laughed, shoving it down. He playfully slapped her hands away and dug underneath again. "You lead us. I have a Claire to find."

She kept losing hold of the blankets, laughing harder when he continued to find more layers.

"Claire." He groaned. "This is torture."

"We're almost there too. You're running out of time."

"Screw it." Dropping both hands to her pants, he thumbed open the button.

"*Daniel.*"

His deep laugh rumbled over her muffed ear as he dipped inside and ripped up all her layers at once. "There you are." His fingers glided over a warm, soft belly and pulled her to a stop. "Look up."

A fluffy, white flake landed on her nose, and she gasped. "It's snowing?"

He slowly turned her, and the blanket dropped and draped over his shoulders.

"You'll get cold." She reached to cover him, but he peeled

down her scarf.

"It's good luck to kiss on the first snow in Solsken."

"You just made that up."

"Doesn't mean it's not true." He feathered his mouth across hers.

Claire's smile faded, and she closed her eyes. Her body softening against his. His eyes never closed but soaked up details. The way her expression shifted through emotions with every touch of his lips.

This kiss. This gentle, savoring kiss was different from all the rest, and the words formed. Right on the tip of his tongue gliding against hers — they were there.

But could he say it?

Thick flakes clung to his lashes as his warm hands cupped her cool cheeks. He sank into her mouth again, slowly. So slowly her knees wobbled. He hummed, enjoying yet another reason to pull her in tighter, closer.

He was going to say it. Danny pulled back, dragging her lips with him, and her lids fluttered open.

Inch by slow inch, her eyes tracked up from the bobbing of his throat to the ice crystals forming on his trimmed beard. They wandered higher to his mouth and nose, before stopping at his eyes.

Her breath caught, and a flicker of emotion flitted across her expression. Did she know? Could she see the words in his eyes? His thumbs brushed wet snow from her cheeks.

"My sweet Claire," he whispered.

God, the way her eyes drifted closed when he said that. Her lips parting. He wanted to live here. Right here in this moment and never leave.

He took her mouth again.

"Daniel?"

He hummed, but didn't pull back.

"Did you mean it when you said you weren't afraid anymore?"

He moved up and down on her lips.

"When did that change?"

"Last night." He kept his mouth on hers. "When you murdered

that bread after I asked if you wanted space from me." She laughed and he smiled, swallowing the sound of it.

"But how?" she whispered.

He pulled back, just enough to look into her eyes. "I don't know how. All I know is it settled something in me."

"What did it settle?"

He took in every inch of her face. "It made me realize something I couldn't see before."

She rubbed up and down his arms like she could keep off the cold, but she didn't know he was already blazing. "Tell me."

"It showed me that I—"

"Oi, Danny, Claire," Ian called from the gate, officially becoming the best friend with the worst timing. "Plenty of time for smooching. Get your asses in here and dry off."

"What were you going to say?"

Danny slowly smiled. "I'll tell you later."

Her bottom lip jutted out, and he stole it one last time. He ended it quick because Ian still obnoxiously waved them in.

"Don't go into the kitchen," she told him when they stepped inside. "Just change first, and I'll meet you up there."

"Does this have anything to do with why you've been sneaking off with Em?"

She pinched her mouth closed and locked it with an imaginary key. "Get," she ordered, and he grinned, hopping up the stairs two at a time.

With his dresser still occupying Claire's room, he slipped inside and closed the door, humming to himself.

He peeled off his swim trunks and pulled out a pair of boxer briefs when his door opened. "Whoa, hey." He laughed. "I'm not ready yet, woman."

"My God, I forgot how sexy you are, Danny."

He whipped around, shoving the boxers over himself and stumbled backward, stuttering, "J-Jessica?"

32

When the Devil Comes Knocking

HE HAD TO BE hallucinating. The woman of his recent hellish life laid back against his door in her signature short skirt and tight, nearly see-through, button-down blouse gaping at the fasteners. She smiled with half-lidded eyes.

"Hello, Danny." She peeled off the door and slinked toward him.

He stumbled further back. Definitely not hallucinating.

"I've missed you."

This can't be happening.

"Aren't you going to say something?"

"What the hell are you doing here?"

She threw a hip to the side and had the gall to look shocked. "Isn't it obvious?"

"Obvious?" His mind fumbled and crashed, raced and jammed up again. "*W-what*? How . . . no, just get out."

He meant to yell the last part, but it came out hardly above a whisper.

"Aww. Is that how we're going to play this?"

"I'm not playing, Jess."

She giggled and swayed, her eyes settling over where he covered himself. "Isn't anything I haven't seen before, baby."

"Don't call me that." He clung to his front and backed up again, crashing into the dresser. "An-and I said get out." Why did his voice have to sound so pathetic? Weak.

"Remember when we talked about coming here for the holidays?" Her arms swung out wide, straining her shirt. "It's early, but here I am."

No, *he* talked about coming. She was very clear about not coming. Swore she'd never set foot on his "Godforsaken, frozen island from hell" ever again.

Why is she here?

She pitched forward into a staggering sashay, and he noticed it then. Her pupils fully dilated, and she was thinner than he remembered. A lot thinner. Her skin more ashen. Her auburn curls muted and tangled.

When they'd first met, she'd been on one of her many, "I'm getting my life back together" inspirations. Over the year they dated, she'd had exactly four more inspirations followed by more relapses. But this? He'd never seen her this disarranged. This—

"I miss *us*, Danny."

His stomach bottomed out. Ears hearing, eyes seeing what they couldn't before. Standing with her hip out, shoulders back, bringing attention to her full chest. It was the sultry and sweet of her voice. Full lips pouting.

This was what she'd always done when she wanted something from him. And maybe because of being around unassuming Claire, he could finally see the manipulation in it.

His skin crawled. She was here to seduce him back.

But why?

Her wiry hands sprang out, and he ducked away, making her crash into the side of the dresser. She hiccuped a laugh while his fingers scraped along his clothes drawer, snagging a knob, and yanked. She plastered her body against it, slamming it shut, and wagged a finger.

"Get out, Jess." Risking one hand, he pointed to the door.

The door.

The same door that at any moment, Claire would come through and find him—find her.

Jessica followed his gaping expression and smiled, fingers

drifting to her shirt buttons. "She's an interesting replacement for me." She popped the first one.

His head snapped to her. "She isn't a replacement."

"That's right because Madelynn Cooke-Johnson is way out of your league."

"How . . . how'd you know about her?"

She smiled again but didn't answer. "Honestly, do you really think a woman like her will stay interested in a man like you for long? She was married to *the* Brandon Johnson. You know who that was right? The man was gorgeous *and* smart."

Everything inside him choked and shriveled. He didn't measure up. Again, she was telling him he wasn't enough.

"Aww, don't look like that. It's why I'm here, baby." Somehow, another button was unfastened.

"Stop it." Why couldn't he make his voice stop shaking?

"You know you're just her plaything, right? A shiny new object." Her voice snaked around his mind. Withering all that was budding and healing. "You'll see. She'll get bored of you soon."

"Like you did?" He winced. He hadn't meant to say that. Damn his shaky voice.

"You're the one that left, Danny." She opened another button.

God, how she twisted the truth. "Keep your damn shirt closed. I don't know what you're high on right now, but I'm telling you to stop. I don't want this."

She laughed. "Of course you do." The next button popped, and the familiar sight of her full cleavage burst from her shirt.

He jerked his head away. "*Stop it*, Jess." The corners of his eyes pricked. His heart pounded. Damn his shivering body.

He never should've looked away.

Nails scraped above his hands and yanked the boxers out of his grip. Snatching her wrist he hissed, "*Jess*."

"Daniel?" A gentle knock came at the door. "Are you decent?"

He was going to throw up.

"She's knocking?" Jessica giggled. "You mean you two haven't . . . "

"Be quiet." He spotted the wool blanket he'd dropped before Jess came in, lying between her feet. If he could just—

She kicked it out of his reach right as her voice sang out, "Come in."

The door swung open, and Danny's last hope of fixing this insanity crumbled with it. There, in the doorway, stood his entire world. Tea-colored eyes darted from him cupping himself to Jessica. Who'd somehow managed to open the rest of her shirt and was swinging his boxers from one finger.

"This isn't what it looks like."

When have those words ever helped anyone? Damn those words. Damn this moment. Damn Jessica's finger swinging his boxers.

A breadbasket slipped from Claire's trembling hands and crashed to the floor. Delicious-smelling *kanelbullar* bounced and rolled out of the room.

That was the big secret? All those long hours she'd learned to make his favorite food?

"Hello," Jessica purred. "Danny and I were just getting reacquainted."

"No, we weren't. Claire, I—"

"You're Jessica."

She wasn't looking at him. Why wouldn't she look at him?

"I am."

"How did you get into our home?"

Our home. Danny let out a small breath.

"I have keys."

"Locks will be changed."

Jessica scoffed. "You can't keep me from my husband."

"I'm *not* your husband."

Claire's eyes stayed on Jessica as she slowly moved into the room, hands curling into fists. "You need to leave."

"How 'bout, no." Jessica tipped her head back and laughed.

Claire was suddenly there, body shoved between him and his cackling tormentor, towering a few inches above her. Dear God, was she trying to protect him? Danny barely held on to the hope that this meant she believed him.

"Move." Jessica shoved a palm into Claire's chest, but she was a pillar of unmovable stone. "Bitch, I don't care who you are, you better get out of my face."

"Claire," Danny whispered, placing the tips of his fingers against her back. She was vibrating.

He'd seen Ian angry many times. Knew exactly what to do and when to step in to defuse a situation. But this? Claire was so still, so quiet. Like the moment before a storm breaks, when the air becomes thick and charged and eerily calm.

Problem was, he didn't know which direction she'd release her storm.

She took one step forward, and Jessica was smart enough to step back.

With the dresser now cleared, Danny scrambled to snatch some clothes and covered himself with the blanket. "Claire, come." He tugged on the back of her shirt.

"Where do you think you're going?" Jessica moved to push past Claire.

Claire slammed into Jessica, hands on her shoulders, driving her back until she crashed into the wall.

Jessica yelled, "Who the hell do you think you are?"

"I'm Madelynn Claire Cooke." Her voice went low, each word razor sharp. "And I will rip your damn hand off if you touch him."

Well, shit.

Jessica literally growled, then lunged. Danny wrapped an arm around Claire's waist and twisted her away, feeling nails claw down his back as he dragged Claire toward the door.

"You see this right?" Jessica yelled after them, gesturing to herself. "You won't keep him, *Madelynn Claire Cooke*."

"Shut up." Danny finally found the volume he wanted, and while gripping his clothes and blanket in one hand, he half-carried, half-walked a still-flailing-to-get-Jessica Claire out of the room, slamming the door.

Blood pounded his ears, and his eyes flooded. She didn't

question him. Not once did she question him in that damning situation, but fought. Claire actually fought for him.

He let her go and took one heavy step, tangling his fingers in her hair. "Do you have any idea?" His forehead pressed against hers, body so close her heaving shoulders brushed against his chest. "What you did. How you —" He swept down on her mouth on a deep inhale. Lips and teeth and skin.

She held on to him, fingers squeezing his shoulders. This kiss. All heavy breaths, heat, and fire. He wanted to lose himself. Give her everything right here, right now.

"Daniel," she whispered between kisses. "I need to know."

Oh, God. He'd been wrong. She'd demand answers, and what could he say? That he'd cowered? That Jessica's voice had paralyzed him?

He broke the kiss, panting, head still pressed against hers. He didn't want to open his eyes. Didn't want to see the accusation in hers. "Please. I'm so sorry about her."

"Sorry?" Her sharp tone snapped his eyes open, and what he saw wasn't an accusation. It was rage so wild he didn't dare move. "You don't apologize for her. Don't ever apologize for her. *She* is not your responsibility anymore. Do you hear me?"

Air eased out of his lungs as he slowly nodded. Shoulders still heaving, she took his face firmly in both hands. "What I need to know is, did she hurt you?"

He shook his head.

"No?"

"No." He let his head drop to her neck on a heavy exhale. His free arm wrapped around her waist, drawing her in. He needed her closer. Wanted to stay here and never move, calming himself in the realness of her skin, her delicious citrus flowers. "I was so scared you wouldn't believe me."

She lifted his head until their eyes met. "I saw the look on your face, Daniel, and I knew."

Jessica's fist vibrated the door, and they jumped apart. "You can't lock me in here."

"She does realize she's on the inside."

Danny rolled his eyes as he crouched. "She's too high to know the difference." He began carefully picking up every roll off the floor. "I can't believe you made these for me."

"Seems silly now."

Rising slowly, he said, "Are you kidding? This is the nicest thing anyone has ever done for me." He stepped into her space again, lowering his mouth to her ear, and whispered, "And when this is over, I plan to thank you properly."

The bedroom knob jiggled. "Hurry to the guest room," Claire said. "I'll take care of her."

"No." He tucked the breadbasket under his arm and snatched her hand, tugging her down the hall to the room, locking the door behind them.

She spun toward him, hugging herself. "You don't think I can help you with her?"

"It's not that." He uncurled her arms, squeezing her hands. "She's an addict, Claire. And one of her addictions includes recreational drugs. But by the looks of her, she's turned to the hard stuff."

"So, you're wanting me to be more understanding." It wasn't a question.

"No." The back of his fingers brushed her cheek. "I brought you in here because when she's like this and doesn't get her way, she can become unhinged. I don't want to see you in the crossfire."

Loud bangs came from the kitchen, followed by Jessica yelling, "He won't be happy, Danny. I was your last chance."

"What is she talking about?"

He shook his head. "She always talks shit when she's high. Do you have your phone? Send a text for backup while I get dressed."

DOWNSTAIRS, IAN AND EMELIE slammed shoulders, trying to squeeze out of the kitchen at the same time. "Does Claire mean

Jessica, Jessica?" Emelie shrieked.

"Do you know of any other Jessica that would make the nicest person we know say she wants to kill her?" Ian said.

They stumble-ran up the stairs and fell over each other when they reached the top. All of Danny's kitchen chairs lay on their sides around broken mug shards.

Both of their phones buzzed. DANIEL ALSO SAID TO TELL YOU SHE'S HIGH ON SOMETHING STRONG.

"Shit," Emelie said, while Ian said nothing. His hand gripped the back of his neck as he remembered another time Jessica was high.

He'd never told Danny that two weeks before they'd eloped, she cornered him and began removing her clothes, telling him he was the cuter one. When he'd torn away from her without so much as a glance, she threatened to tell Danny that he touched her if he dared tell him what happened. Normally that wouldn't have worked, but she'd gotten so deep inside Danny's head, it could've been the one thing that broke their friendship.

"Da-anny," Jessica sang from the living room.

"I don't want to see that woman," Ian said.

"You don't have to. Go find Danny." Emelie pressed on her fists, popping her knuckles.

Down the hallway, Ian slowed, listening to their carrying voices.

"I can't believe I'm looking at your damn face right now," Emelie said.

"Feeling's mutual. Oops." There was a thump, followed by Jessica giggling. "Wow, when he delivers, he delivers."

Ian cursed. Why the hell was she here?

"I won't say it twice." Emelie's voice tightened. "Get out or I'll throw you out."

Ian gently knocked on the guest door. An adorable, glaring Claire peeked out and immediately softened.

"Is she gone?" she whispered.

"Emelie's working on it." His eyes met a haggard Danny over her shoulder. "You alright?"

"Not really."

"Come, I'll sneak you guys past the living room."

"I swear to God." Emelie's voice boomed. "If you don't crawl your ass back into whatever hole you came from—"

There was an "oof" followed by another thump and Emelie yelling, "Bitch, did you just try to kick me?"

They all froze in the hallway when Jessica stumbled into it. Danny gripped Claire, easing her back while Ian put himself between them and her.

"McClellan." She staggered a step. "If you think you can—"

"Jess," Danny said in a low, firm voice. "Leave. Now."

Her dark glare moved to Claire. "You'll be sorry you stole him from me."

"*Stole?* That's it." Emelie snatched Jessica by her haphazardly buttoned shirt.

"He's co-oming," Jessica sang.

"Shut. *Up.*" Emelie shoved her toward the stairs, following behind her.

Not until her steps faded did Danny and Claire let out a long breath. He wrapped an arm around her, drawing her in tight.

"Get off him," Emelie yelled in the stairwell.

Feet sprinted up the stairs before Fin appeared, red faced and wheezing. "That woman's crazy."

"Jessica has that effect on people." Ian reached out and fixed his haphazard collar.

"I found it." Fin made his way to Danny. "At least what's left of it." He held out a decimated phone.

Danny lifted it between two fingers. "Was it used for target practice?"

"A grenade maybe."

"Where'd you find it?"

"On the road near Sven's lane."

"I don't remember taking it outside."

Fin shrugged. "Also, you've got a group of angry people downstairs. Hey, is that Ms. Cooke's *kanelbullar?*"

"Who's angry?" Danny stuffed a cinnamon roll into his mouth and moaned, kissing Claire's cheek. "So good."

He offered the basket to Fin.

"Everyone who didn't know that you and she were officially a thing."

Danny lifted a brow. "And how did they hear about it now?"

Fin sheepishly grinned and bumped Ian's arm with the basket. "Want one?"

Ian startled, and the hand rubbing over his stomach froze. "No, thanks." He snatched Danny's phone, looking it over.

"But you never turn down food."

"You feeling okay?" Danny's eyes dropped to the hand on his stomach.

Ian forced a half-smile and took a roll anyway. "Yeah."

His sixth sense was only off because of the insanity with Jessica and lack of sleep. His nerves would calm down. He was sure of it.

It was fine.

Everything was fine.

33

Yea Though I Walk
Through Death's Valley

IAN WOKE WITH A start. His chest tight, heart pounding. He blinked hard around the dark space and made out the silhouette of shelves and old books. Danny's living room came into focus. He didn't know what woke him, but he was afraid — no, not afraid — he was terrified.

The last time he'd felt his sixth sense this keenly was the first anniversary after his mam left. The night his father stumbled into his room and beat him nearly to death.

Ian threw back the covers and rushed to Danny's guestroom. The door lay wide open, and the light was on, but he wasn't there. He called Danny's name and grated a palm over his face, trying to force his mind to think. To see if the dread in the pit of his stomach would fade.

Claire's door stood ajar, and he ran inside to an empty room. He checked the clock. Two a.m. Where the hell were they?

Under normal circumstances, he'd assume they were making out somewhere and mind his own business. But something hovered in the silence. A quiet so loud it screamed at him.

He took three deep breaths. The last thing he remembered was Claire saying she had to call her attorney, and Danny saying he'd catch up on paperwork while she did it.

Ian scratched through his thick, dark waves and heard the creak of the front gate. A loud cry followed, and he rushed to the window and tore back the curtains. Claire tripped and ran up the road toward Sven's lane.

He cranked open the casement window and yelled for her, but she didn't stop. Her fading sobs dampened inside the heavy snow.

"Danny?" He tore out of the room and down the stairs to Flygande. Dim lights illuminated the spotless pub, but—

He went still. A sound coming from Danny's office punched the wind out of him. A woman laughed, followed by a recognizable, deep, male voice. Ian's vision tunneled, and against his own will, his body drove him toward it. He had to be wrong. Those sounds weren't what he thought they were.

He threw open the door.

Behind Danny's desk in his chair was a wig-wearing Jessica, dressed in Claire's clothes. She straddled Danny's lap, topless, and he gripped her ass with his face buried deep into her chest.

"Oh, look." Jessica smiled over her shoulder. "We have another visitor."

"Claire?" Danny mumbled, without looking up.

"Not this time," she sang out.

"Claire," he said again.

Ian rushed forward and slammed a fist onto his desk. "Danny, look at me."

Jessica squeaked, but Danny didn't move.

"Face me right now and tell me what the hell you're doing."

Danny's head rolled back, and his eyes lolled open. "Wh-wha . . ." His face flopped back into her chest, and she laughed.

Realization slowly dawned and Ian gripped his hair. That wasn't his best friend. "What did you do to him?"

"Only what I had to." She ran her hands through Danny's hair. "He was very specific."

"Who was specific?"

Danny groaned, gripping her tighter. His lips smacked against her skin, and she threw her head back in hysterical laughter.

Ian twisted away to avoid seeing the front of her and spotted Danny's tea mug nearly empty on the desk. He snatched it and sniffed. A strange smell mixed with the milk. "Did you drug this?"

Jessica pinched her lips closed and slowly smiled.

"Tell me." His heart thundered in his ears. "Was it one of your mushrooms? Or something stronger?"

She giggled, shaking her head, and his hands automatically sprang toward her throat. He stopped short, curling them into fists.

"Just tell me what you gave him. How much did you give him?"

She lifted Danny's head and his eyes rolled side to side, drool dribbling down his beard. "What he needed. Isn't that right, Danny?" His eyes rolled back into his skull.

The lights flickered, but it wasn't the lights. Ian's vision blurred and sparked around the edges. He became acutely aware of every thump of his heart, every muscle curling his fingers tight into his palms. Telling him what he couldn't accept. Wouldn't accept.

Danny had overdosed.

Danny was going to die.

"Get *off* him." He tore Jessica away, and she fell with cackling laughter.

Taking Danny by the shoulders, he quickly looked him over. Eyes were bloodshot. T-shirt torn, showing nail marks running down his skin.

"Shit." Ian darted a quick glance to Danny's zipper and sighed. It thankfully was closed.

Danny blubbered something incoherent, and Ian took him by the face. "Hey, hey. Look at me, *bràthair*." He tapped his cheek. "Come on, open your eyes, Danny."

"He was so smug throwing me out." Jessica laughed from the floor. "Not so tough now, are ya, baby?"

Ian closed his eyes, inhaling through his nose. Think. He had to ignore her and think.

"Auntie." He tripped on his way to the phone and looked down at the shirt tangled in his feet. Jessica laughed again, and he threw it at her. "Get dressed, witch."

Under the phone, a notepad in Danny's writing caught his eye.
My Claire,

I love you. That's what I wanted to say before Ian interrupted us outside. I LOVE YOU. There's so much more I want to say, which is why I'm writing this out like an ass, because I lose words when I'm around you. And I don't want to miss telling you everything.

I was drowning before I met you, and now I can't imagine breathing without you. I want to taste tea lips every morning for the rest of my life, if you'll have me . . . The last word had a long line squiggling from it. Ian swallowed. That must've been when the drugs kicked in.

"Oh God, Claire." Ian pressed a fist against his mouth, remembering how she'd left. She must've seen them but didn't understand what was happening. How the hell was he going to fix this?

"The look on her face." Jessica cackled.

Ian bit hard on his tongue. "Ignore her, help Danny, then find Claire. Ignore her, help Danny, then find Claire."

Danny's head lolled forward with a moan, and his eyes drifted open with a slow blink. "F-Fin?"

"No, it's Ian."

He squinted. "Are you sure?"

Ian spun toward Jessica. "Did you use a hallucinogenic?"

She grinned and pretended to zip her lips.

"Danny, listen to me, you've been drugged." He took him by the face again. "I gotta get you up to Doc Clark."

He slowly smiled. "Doc? I'm not s-sick. I just feel a little f-fu-uny." His head dropped forward.

Ian gripped it. "No, stay with me." He picked up the handset and quickly dialed the number. A groggy voice answered. "Auntie?" His voice cracked. "I need to bring Danny in."

"Ian? Clark's asleep. He stayed up drinking with Gene last night. What's wrong?"

"Danny accidentally drank some sort of drug." He glanced

at Jessica, hoping for an answer, but she was slumped against the wall, eyes closed but smiling. "I-I'm not sure what it was, but—" Danny's head slammed down on the desk. "*Danny*. Auntie, oh my God, I think he's overdosed."

"Jesus and Mary. Of all the nights for Clark to . . . never you mind, bring him in. I know what to do."

"Thank—"

The line went dead, and he looked down. Jessica held up a torn phone cord. "Oops."

"You little—"

Danny groaned, snapping Ian out of that violent thought. Body shaking, he secured Danny's arm over his shoulder and heaved him up with a grunt.

"Come on, *bràthair*."

Danny's eyes fluttered open, and his brow furrowed. "Where's Claire?"

Ian strained to walk him forward, tuning out a hysterically laughing Jessica. "She's not here."

"Of course she is." He smiled and his head flopped to Ian's shoulder. "She was just kissing me."

"That wasn't Claire, Danny." He refused to think about that future conversation. The one that might permanently break his best friend if Claire decided to leave him without getting an explanation.

Only one hope kept him focused. Snow. If this storm was as big as they predicted, it would close the bridge and keep her here, for now. That's what he would focus on. Not the ball of razor wire cutting up his insides.

He hefted his barely conscious friend out the office door. Danny was going to be okay. He just needed to keep him talking, and he'd be okay. "It's going to be cold out, but you won't mind, will you, *bràthair*?"

"Nah, I'm the Viking." Danny's smile avalanched off his face, and his feet followed.

"No, Danny, wake up." Ian groaned under his weight and

squeezed his side. "Stay with me."

Danny fully lost consciousness, and the weight of him took them both down hard.

Ian scrambled to his feet, pulling on both his arms. Danny's limp, heavy body wouldn't budge. He tried again. "Wake. Up."

Danny slipped through his hands, landing with a thud.

"*No.*" Ian dropped and checked Danny's racing pulse before ripping out his phone and dialing Fin. "Pick up, pick up." It went directly to voicemail. He dialed again and the call dropped. The dreaded "no signal" popped up in the upper corner of his phone. "No, no, no, come on." He dropped the phone and gripped Danny's arm, hefting him over his shoulder.

Groaning, Ian put all Danny's weight into his aching thighs and started to stand. His knees buckled, and he yelled out. Two nights of no sleep and that damn dive.

He grabbed Danny's shoulders and shook him. "Wake up. Come on, wake up"

It rose in the pit of his stomach, and he clutched over it. Dread, oily and thick, swelled and seeped into every muscle and nerve, shutting down his mind.

He'd told Danny about his graces—those people and things that came into his life at the right moment—but he never told Danny he was the biggest grace of all. His constant. The rock under his feet in the upheaval of his life. His *bràthair*. The one he could count on when he lost his way.

He never told him, all those nights as a kid, how much it meant to him that he would look for his sign in the window. The one only Danny knew that told him Ian's old man wasn't sober.

All those nights when Danny climbed up to his room to check on him. And on the bad days, carried him all the way to his aunt and Clark for help.

Ian never told him because he was ashamed of all the trouble he'd caused without wanting to. Ashamed that he always seemed to drag Danny down with him.

Danny didn't know. "My God, he'll never know."

Danny gurgled, and Ian looked at his face. It wasn't the right color. "No!" Ian slapped him hard. "Wake *up*. Don't do this to me." His eyes shot toward the ceiling. "Don't you dare take him. You hear me? This should be me, not him. Me." Spit flew from his mouth, and he smacked his chest. "I'm the one you should've let overdose all those years ago."

He violently shook Danny. "*Wake up*. You have a whole life to live. Claire to love. Babies to make." Tears streamed down his face, and he choked on them. "Please." He yanked on his arms, yelling all his strength into pulling him up and his legs gave out, slamming him down onto his best friend's chest.

"Don't leave me." A sob tore free, and the broken boy inside him escaped. He grabbed Danny's face. "You promised me. Remember? We were twelve, in my room, and you promised you'd never leave me without a goodbye like Mam did." He had no more voice. "Danny, please. You *promised* me. You—"

Danny convulsed, and Ian swiped an arm across his eyes, looking him over. Another convulsion and Ian quickly rolled him to his side, so he didn't choke on his vomit.

The front door swung open and two snow-covered bodies stumbled in, laughing. "I'll be fine walking home by myself. I just want to grab my purse from Danny's kitchen—" Emelie spotted Ian.

"Help," he croaked.

"Danny?" She ran to him and dropped down, pulling his head from the mess onto her lap. "What happened? What's wrong with him?"

Ian had no strength to tell her, but his eyes fell on a tall, young man with a familiar face. "Finlay, h-he needs Auntie."

"Shit, Ian. Of course." He dropped down and took one of Danny's arms, easing him up to sit. "Get his other side." Ian's foggy mind latched onto Fin's instructions and together they started lifting him.

"Please tell me what happened." Emelie lifted from the back.

"Drugged . . . Jessica," was all Ian managed to get out.

"She did what?" she yelled. "But how? I watched her leave

in a black town car."

"Well, she's in there and won't tell me anything." He nodded toward Danny's office. "And, Em? She may have successfully and permanently destroyed his relationship with Claire."

"Get him to Annie." Emelie faced the office, and Ian had never heard her voice go so low. "Leave her to me."

EMELIE STOOD IN THE doorway to Danny's office, arms crossed, inhaling deep breaths. For the first time since it had happened, she understood how Danny had almost killed Seth.

She had always believed that even if she disliked a woman, there was a fundamental level of camaraderie that all women bonded over.

Complete and utter bullshit.

Time ceased as she remained in the doorway, talking herself down from everything she wanted to do to the wretch crawling across the floor of the office. She watched as Jessica pulled herself up by Danny's desk and read something below the phone before cursing and flopping back into Danny's chair.

For him. Emelie told herself. For Danny's sake, she'd keep her feet planted in the doorway and not kill Jessica.

Her phone buzzed in her pocket, and she ripped it out, gusting a relieved breath. Service had momentarily come back, and a text came through from Fin. WHO'D HAVE THOUGHT THAT THROWING UP COULD BE A GOOD THING? HE'S WEAK, BUT AUNTIE SAYS DANNY'S GOING TO BE OKAY. THOUGHT YOU'D WANT TO KNOW.

"What are you doing here?" Jessica's voice snapped her back.

Emelie shoved the phone into her pocket. "I was debating whether I should kill you or beat you first."

"You can't—" Jessica's butt slid from the chair and hit the floor. "Unless you want to end up in jail with Danny."

Emelie flexed her hands and stepped in slowly. "The only one going to jail is you."

"Rape." Jessica smiled before her face contorted into fake

trauma. "He tried to rape me, officer." She finished in a fit of hysterical giggles. "Who will they believe, Emelie?"

"That'll never work, you piece of shit."

"Wanna bet?"

Emelie took a heavy step forward and stopped, eyes darting up to the corner of the room. She eased back and rolled her shoulders. "He was drugged. It'll take one simple test to prove that."

Jessica pulled herself up by Danny's desk again, wobbled, then steadied herself. "Yes, but those same drugs can be found in my system. Who's to say he didn't force them on me before he took them himself and attacked me." She smirked.

"You have this all planned out, huh?"

She giggled and swayed. "It wasn't all my idea. But yeah, it's a good plan."

"You mean the plan where you drug Danny and dress up like Claire to destroy their relationship?"

"Yes, and it worked just like he said it would."

"Who's he?"

"Shh." Jessica lifted a forefinger, missed her lips, and bumped her nose. "I'm talking."

Emelie rolled her eyes.

"He contacted me a few weeks ago and told me he'd give me the good stuff if I seduced Danny away from that stuck-up, entitled bitch. Drugging Danny was my idea, though."

"Yeah, because you couldn't seduce shit."

Jessica sniffed and rubbed her nose, and Emelie didn't have to guess what the good stuff was. "Well, he said my idea was genius."

"Always in need of attention, aren't you?"

Jessica waved her off. "Why don't you go call your handsome cop friend so I can tell him what Danny did to me?" She fake pouted.

Emelie slowly lifted a finger and pointed to the corner above her head. Then she traced an invisible line to the next corner and the next, circling around back to Jessica. "It's hard to see them. But Jake Matthews is thorough, if nothing else."

"Did you snort something?"

"Cameras, Jessie-pooh. They've been there recording everything you confessed and everything you," she slowly smiled, "did."

Jessica's eyes darted to every corner. "You're lying."

"Am I?"

She collided with the desk, straining until she saw them camouflaged with the wood. Her mouth dropped open. "That's why he suggested I be in Danny's office. That bastard *knew* they were here."

"Who's the genius now?" Emelie grinned and leaned a hip against the desk. "Just think, soon you'll be in prison with no men to manipulate or seduce. All without your happy pills."

Jessica snapped toward her and slipped a shaking hand inside her bag. "I won't go to jail."

"Yeah, you will."

Jessica ripped out an unmarked bottle and emptied the contents down her throat.

Emelie collided with her, toppling her to the ground. Straddling her writhing body, Emelie pried opened Jessica's mouth and shoved two fingers down her throat. "You won't do this to him. You don't get to kill yourself and make Danny live with the guilt."

Jessica gagged and Emelie thrust her face to the side as she emptied the contents of her stomach onto the floor. Emelie wiped her fingers on her leg, took her by the arms, and dragged her to her feet.

"Where are you taking me?" Jessica coughed and wiped her mouth.

Emelie pulled her without answering into the storage room, glared at the wide-open back door with Jessica's keys still in the lock, and snatched a container of zip ties on her way back to the office. She plopped Jessica into Danny's chair.

"What are you doing?"

"Keeping you still until the cops pick you up." Emelie tightened a tie around each wrist and secured her ankles.

"Wait. You don't understand, it was his idea. He planned all of this."

"For the love of God." Emelie stood and rubbed out a kink in her lower back. "Who the hell is 'he?'"

"If I tell you everything, you have to promise me leniency."

"I don't have to promise you shit." Emelie pointed to the cameras.

Jessica sat back with a huff. "I'm not going to jail for him."

"Jess, I swear to God, if you don't say —"

"Donald Henderson."

Emelie went still. When Danny wasn't able to fully calm after Greyson left, he'd confided in her and Ian about a man named Henderson. "I thought he was out of the country."

Jessica snorted. "No, honey. Jake Matthews may be thorough, but I think he'll be out of business once it comes out that he failed to protect his biggest client." She laughed. "He couldn't even keep her son from helping him, scouting Flygande . . . " She paused glaring at the cameras. "Probably how Henderson knew about those." She sniffed again. "He even pulled a bump-swipe with Danny. Stole his phone right out of his pocket for some security code."

Emily cursed. "That's why the alarm didn't go off when you snuck in. Why the hell would Greyson help that man?"

Jessica leaned forward again. "Between you and me, I think ol' Henderson became a daddy replacement."

"The dinner was a setup."

"All part of the plan." Jessica awkwardly winked. "Henderson thinks he's some super smarty, but he can't play me. I'm letting it all spill out." She spread her fingers in dramatic emphasis. "Like how he convinced his own brother to go to jail for stalking."

"Wait. Kenneth Greene? He's Henderson's brother?"

"Half brother, but he looked up to his big bro enough to help out. Starting with a taxicab at the airport, and a text with Madelynn's location when she arrived."

"That's how he knew where to stalk her." Emelie plopped in a different chair with a heavy sigh. "But why would Kenneth go to jail for him?"

Jessica rubbed two fingers together. "Money. A lot, actually. The same amount he'd offered me, but I knew better than to take cash. I told him upfront that he had to provide half the goods before I did anything, but Kenny . . . " She stopped talking and stared at her hand like she forgot it was tied.

"Kenneth?" Emelie urged.

"He wasn't smart enough to realize he'd never see a dime."

"But if he's in jail, that means Henderson could still be here on Solsken."

"Look who's catching on." Jessica slowly smiled, stage whispering, "And with you all preoccupied with me, who's left to keep him from dear, precious Madelynn Claire Cooke?"

A blaring alarm went off, and Emelie threw her hands over her ears.

"I didn't do it," Jessica shrieked.

Emelie ran to the front door of Flygande, using her shoulder and one hand to block her ears. Her free hand froze on the alarm. It was no longer camouflaged but lit up in flashing colors. "I didn't know it could do that."

The words: *Enter Code,* flashed along the screen.

"Why are you asking me for a code? The door is unlocked. No one set you."

Enter Code . . . Enter Code . . . Enter Code . . .

She quickly entered the security code, but it beeped. *Invalid . . . Enter Code.*

A chill streaked down her spine when she remembered something Danny had once told her. Some of Jake Matthews' systems had a built-in fail-safe. A way he could communicate with the customer when all other communication systems failed. Danny had paid for the extra service because of the spotty cell service during winter.

She ran up the stairs to Danny's apartment for her purse.

Praying she kept the scrap of paper he'd written the code on. Snatching her purse, she dug deep. "Oh, crap." She pulled out a crumpled piece of paper that she'd stupidly wrapped around gum. Carefully peeling it back, she rushed down to the still blaring alarm and squinted, putting in a series of complicated numbers, letters, and symbols.

The silence was deafening, though the box still flashed in colors. It beeped again, followed by a scrolling message:

EMERGENCY … THIS IS JAKE MATTHEWS … MADELYNN COOKE-JOHNSON'S LOCATION NOT FOUND … REPORT IF KNOWN … EMERGENCY …

The haunting gong of Old Governor reverberated in the air outside. "Oh, my God." Emelie sprinted out the front door, not hearing Jessica's fading demands for an ear doctor.

Lost Promises

WET SNOW CLUNG TO Claire's boots as she skid-clomped aimlessly through the heavy snow. All she could see were Danny's hands touching Jessica. All she could hear were his soft moans mixing with her gleeful laughter.

At first, she thought she'd walked in on two strangers and went to excuse herself. But then the fire-breathing face of his dragon peeked out at her, and Jessica looked over her shoulder and laughed. "Told you you wouldn't keep him."

Claire collided with a tree, gasping for breath.

He hadn't even had the decency to look at her when she yelled for him — begged him. Only mocked her name while he devoured another woman.

Her throat swelled, and she choked on a sob. They'd been together in her room, naked, and she never asked — never even questioned. *Stupid, naïve, Claire.* How could she believe he'd done nothing with her? Even drugged, Jessica was all sensuous curves and beauty.

The bridge. She'd leave and walk over it if she had to. Smearing an icy glove under her nose, she forced herself forward on wobbling legs down a quickly fading shoveled pathway.

She'd never seen snow like this. Thick, heavy flakes so dense she couldn't see through it. Even dressed warmly, the relentless wind found any exposed skin. *Don't fight the wind, Claire. Embrace it.*

"Daniel." She covered her mouth to keep his name in. He'd

taught her that on their last outing, arms out like he was hugging the wind, a wide smile on his face.

She lost her footing, sliding into a drift with a loud cry. Something hard thumped against her thigh as her hands sank deep, struggling to stand. Reaching inside her coat pocket, her fingers brushed against cold metal. She'd almost done it. Pictured it so clearly.

The crack-bang, the gentle recoil. She envisioned the back of a caramel-colored wig bursting into a sea of red. She was headed straight for his moaning voice and her laughter. But outside the office, she stopped when a different vision took over. A vision where the bullet missed and pierced through him instead. That's when she tore out of Flygande.

She struggled forward again, unaware she left one glove buried in the snow.

Foolish Claire. Ian, Emelie, the entire town . . . were they part of it too? Some grand scheme to dupe her? Fooling her into false friendships—*family.* All while laughing behind her back at her stupidity?

A hidden rock tripped her unsteady feet, and her body collided with a boulder. This time, she didn't move. Cold stone numbed her cheek as she let hot tears slide down unhindered.

It had been real this time. The kisses, the promises. The unspoken meanings in the changing color of Danny's eyes. She'd been so sure of it.

Staggering to a wobbly stand, she shook her head. How could she reconcile the Danny she'd known these past two months with the man she just saw?

Through blurry vision, she spotted not the bridge, but the silhouette of her cottage. Fresh white plaster and a bright-red roof and a red door. Exactly the way she'd wanted it.

"My flower boxes," she whispered, devastation collapsing in. She'd never get to live in the home where her independence was born.

Clamoring up to the now-solid front porch, she sank to her knees when she saw a padlock on the door. Why did the contractors add a padlock without her permission? Furious, she yanked on it and yelled.

A noise brought her ear to the door. "H-Hello? Is someone in there?"

Bright light beamed down on her, and she screamed. The silhouette of a tall, broad figure stood to the left of the porch, completely shadowed behind the flashlight.

"Madelynn Claire." Even with the howling wind, a deep voice came through clearly.

She lifted a hand to shade her eyes. "Do I know you?"

He took a slow step onto the porch.

Skittering to her feet, she kept a hand shading her eyes, but the light kept her blind to him. "Who are you?"

He took another step.

She stumbled backward, hit the edge of the porch, and tripped. Her leg swallowed inside a snowdrift.

"My, my, what happened to the perfect, put-together Madelynn Claire? Let me guess, your life fell apart?"

Humiliation stained her cheeks, and she grunted, trying to free her leg. "I said, who are you?"

His responding laughter was deep and raspy. Just like . . . just like . . .

Her phone vibrated. Not once. Not twice. Three short bursts that sent terror clawing over her skin, seizing her joints.

Jake Matthew's emergency signal. *She wasn't safe . . . she wasn't safe . . .* Her body violently shook as her fingers curled over the phone. It should have a safe house listed. But if this was — "Show your face."

"You mean this face?" The man flicked the beam of light directly under his chin, shooting distorted shadows over a thick square jaw and a crooked smile. A jagged scar lay directly under his left eye.

He wore a flat cap. A coat with an upturned collar.

It was him. The man who stared at her outside the tavern was *him*. Vinegar seeped into the walls of her stomach and blood rushed to her head in a flash of vivid memories.

His body pressed against her . . . The stench of his breath . . . Pain in her wrist . . .

Her phone vibrated three times again, snapping her back.

"What's the matter, M. C. C.? Speechless?" He lifted a voice distorter to his mouth, and the rumbling ghost voice hit her. "Boo."

She spun and ran.

"Where you gonna go?" He called after her, laughter caked in his voice. "The bridge is closed, and your Viking is busy."

That reminder tore a cry from her throat, and she veered left off the path that led back to Danny. The same path Henderson must have shoveled for her to get here.

"I'm a good writer, too, don't you think? Tsk-tsk, you should have looked . . . "

She tripped.

" . . . behind the curtain on a hook."

Crawling, dragging, sobbing, she shoved her way up again. The wind whipped snow in her eyes, slowing her frantic pace.

"The water's turned cold, my actions now bold . . . "

She threw her hands over her earmuffs. Sobbing. Wheezing. Wind burned her cheeks. The moisture in her eyes froze crusty crystals over her lashes.

" . . . to get you to see. You'll never be rid of me."

Her legs sank thigh-deep into another drift. *No.* Whipping around, she squinted and strained, but couldn't see him. Panting. Gasping for air, she fumbled her phone out and was met with a blank screen.

"Oh, God." Panting breaths clouded in front of her. The drama of the night before. The crazy day that followed.

She'd forgotten to charge her phone.

"Madelynn Cla-aire . . . " His voice took on the familiar ghost-like echo. "I thought you, of all people, would appreciate my little ode to *Phantom Love.*" He laughed again.

She bit hard on her tongue. He'd haunted her using a twisted interpretation of her most popular and beloved novel. She felt sick.

"I'll admit, I made a mistake when I drove you straight into the Viking's arms. But the frightened look on his face when he tried to protect you after the Viking scare?" He laughed again. "Now that was worth it. And to think his bravado was for nothing. Where is he now, by the way? Oh, that's right, balls deep in his 'ex.'" He tsked. "Tell me, Madelynn Claire, how does it feel to be passed over so easily for a drug addict?"

A bruise formed on her lips from the fist she pressed to her mouth, trying to keep the sob in. Saliva grew thick in her throat, and she choked on it.

"Aw, there, there now, Madelynn. It's alright. I'll tell you what." His voice had a smile in it. "How 'bout I give you some money and ship you out of the country? That'll make everything better, right?"

That sound in his voice. The same maniacal tone he had right before he attacked her in her bedroom. Her shaking hands dropped her useless phone, and she scraped and clawed her way out of the snow drift.

"Now, I must admit," his voice followed her, "when you first sent me away, I was devastated. I mean, ten years, Madelynn. Ten years I waited patiently for you, only to have you scar my face and force me out of my own country. What right . . . " His control slipped, and he yelled, "What right did you have to do that?" He took a deep breath. "Well, I just couldn't sit south of the border while you went on living carefree now, could I?"

He was to her left, she was sure of it.

"So, I took it all away. One by one, I broke your life into pieces and took everything away from you. The way you took *everything* from me."

He was to her right.

"I took your Viking, your son, even—"

Everything inside her went still. There wasn't a thought she remembered thinking. No movement she remembered making. Only that her numb fingers had wrapped around the gun in her coat. That she'd stepped out from the safety of the boulder and now stood directly in front of him. Gun raised. "Where. Is. My. Son."

His hands slowly raised.

"I said, where is he?"

"A bit tied up." His crooked smile lifted, and he nodded toward the gun. "What are you going to do with that? You're not a killer. You have to plan these kinds of things. Make it look like an accident." He took a slow step forward. "Like I did for Brandon."

"Brandon?" The gun rattled in her hands.

"Tell me, how do you think your meticulous husband took more than his regular dose of anti-anxiety pills?" He took another careful step. "Ten years of building his trust. I convinced him, Madelynn Claire. I overheard your argument about leaving him and convinced the Great Brandon Johnson that he needed a night to relax. And he did. Fell right to sleep. Do you know how easy it is to hold a man underwater when he's asleep?"

But Brandon's eyes had been open. Oh, God, he'd woken up while drowning. She was so fixated on that thought, she didn't see Henderson's next step.

"And Grey? He's the reason I knew you'd be here." His smile didn't reach his dead eyes. "But then that little prick thought he could stop me when he realized what I had planned. I couldn't allow that, now could I?"

Pudgy baby fingers. Greyson's precious baby pudgy fingers reaching for her from his crib, his toothless smile pushing up the apples of his cheeks. The smile he only gave to her.

"You should have seen Greyson beg—"

She forgot to take a breath first. Forgot to relax her shoulders back and aim for the broadest part of his body. His yell was drowned from her own screaming as her fingers pulled nonstop on the trigger.

But he didn't fall. Hand holding his arm, blood dripped through his fingers. The demon remained standing with only a graze when no more bullets came from her gun.

"That was a mistake." His voice went low and quiet. "That was a big, big mistake." He lunged forward. The force of him knocked the gun from her hand, and she sprawled backward in the snow. He snatched the gun and whipped the butt of it across her face. Starbursts of pain shot through her mouth. "You think you can just shoot me?"

Tears streamed down the sides of her eyes as blood filled her mouth and she gurgled, "Where's my baby?"

His fingers clamped around her throat, yanking her up. She gripped his hand with both of hers, gasping for a breath as he pressed his face into hers and said, "In hell."

A raw sound strangled from her throat, and she pounded his chest. He kept her by the throat, shoving her backward. "Let's go for a walk, shall we?"

Her sobs were cut off, airways blocked. She yanked on his viselike grip as he kept pushing her backward.

"I have dreamed of this moment." His dark eyes cut to her. "All those hours and days in that sweltering heat, using all your goddamn money to plan out every perfect detail just so I could see this pathetic, hopeless look on your face." He suddenly stopped, hand still wrapped around her throat as he whispered, "Such a waste of a pretty face."

His mouth slammed over hers. She wrenched her body, clawed, and slapped, nails making useless scrapes down his coat. Tearing his mouth away, blood from her bleeding mouth dripped from his. He laughed, giving her another hard shove, and let go.

Snow fell away from beneath her feet, and she flailed to catch her balance. The edge. He'd pushed her to the edge of the cliff.

"Goodbye, Madelynn Claire."

"Wait—" One final push and she careened in the wrong direction, her stomach plummeting as her body went into a free fall. Arms and legs swam in the open air as his scarred face faded from view.

She had heard when you're about to die your life flashed before your eyes. But Claire didn't see her life. She saw Brandon's ashen face and Greyson's baby hands. And she saw eyes, cyan eyes, twinkling with a smile.

35

Sometimes it Takes an Entire Town

IAN'S HAND AGITATED THROUGH his hair, knee vibrating up and down. A rosary sat unmoving between his fingertips. No more prayers left his lips as he stared at the slow rise and fall of Danny's chest.

He'd almost lost him.

"*Claire.*" Danny shot up in bed.

"Hey." Ian eased him back. "It's okay. You're alright."

Danny's eyes darted around the room, and he groaned, holding his stomach. "Where am I?"

"You're at the medical center, Danny." He coughed, trying to clear the emotions out of his throat. "But you're okay."

"My God, my head. What happened to me?"

"Sip this." Ian handed him a glass of water before hesitating. "Do you remember anything?"

"Yeah. No . . . maybe?" He blinked hard and held his head. "I remember writing out a note before . . . I don't know, did I fall asleep?"

Ian slowly blinked. "No," he whispered.

Danny didn't hear him and now held both his head and stomach with another groan. "What the hell is going on? I keep having these weird flashes in my head."

"Like dreams?"

"Maybe?" Danny rubbed his temples. "Wait. Why am I here?" He patted himself down. "Did something happen to me? Or Claire?

Is Claire hurt?"

"She's okay." At least Ian hoped she was hunkered down in her cottage. "Tell me about your dream flashes."

"Why do you want to know?"

"Just humor me."

"I'm not telling you my damn dreams, Ian."

Ian scuffed his snow boots along the pale-yellow linoleum. He'd hoped that the most he'd have to do when Danny woke was keep him calm and work through what happened. But this? How the hell was he supposed to broach this subject if he didn't remember anything? He took a deep breath. Maybe if he started with something, Danny could fill in the blanks.

"Did you dream you were making love to Claire?"

Danny froze. "Why would you ask me that?"

Ian lowered his head. "I wouldn't ask if there wasn't a good reason."

"Yeah? And what reason is that?"

He slowly met his eyes. "I'm not judging you, Danny." His phone buzzed with a text from Fin. Now the damn thing decided to work?

SHE ISN'T AT HER COTTAGE. IS THERE ANYWHERE ELSE SHE MIGHT BE?

He'd sent him out to find Claire. With an explanation, maybe she'd be here to patch things up so he could stop asking his best friend super awkward and uncomfortable questions. He sent a desperate text back. PLEASE KEEP LOOKING. TALK TO GERTY, THEY HANG OUT SOMETIMES.

"You look pale," Danny said. "Did you get another message from Molly?"

"No." Ian pulled both hands down his face. He didn't want to have this conversation. He'd even give up his precious Scottish heritage to avoid having this conversation. But if they didn't find Claire, and Danny found out why she ran away *and* that he'd kept it from him? It'd break every friend trust they had.

"You weren't dreaming," he blurted.

Danny blinked fast. "Come again?"

"Don't make me repeat it."

"You're gonna have to."

Ian sighed. "If you dreamed what I think you did, well, it wasn't a dream." Danny's face twisted, and Ian scuffed his boot along the floor again. "You were drugged, Danny. What happened wasn't your fault."

"Drugged? How? Wait, you're saying I didn't dream that Claire and I —" Ian watched in dreaded silence as Danny's foggy mind began to clear. "It was real?"

Ian lowered his head again and nodded.

"I still don't understand. Who drugged me?"

Ian swallowed hard, staring down at the floor. His knee vibrated up and down.

"Answer me."

He slowly looked up and a knot formed in his throat. The answer was already sitting in Danny's eyes. Teetering between horror and hope, he silently begged Ian to tell him it wasn't true.

"I only know one person who keeps a stash of drugs." Danny's voice was just above a whisper. "But even she wouldn't go this far. She wouldn't . . . she wouldn't drug me."

"And yet she did."

"Why would she —"

Ian saw the moment it all crashed in on his best friend. The whoosh of air emptying from his lungs. The color draining from his face.

"Danny? Danny, look at me."

Danny's heavy breathing increased.

"It wasn't your fault. Do you hear me? You were out of your mind, and she was dressed like Claire."

Danny went completely still. "It wasn't Claire?"

Ian realized he hadn't put that particular piece together yet and wanted to swallow his own tongue. "No," he sucked in a deep breath, "it was *her*."

"No," Danny said slowly.

"Don't worry, I got there before she forced you to—"

"No," he said again. "It wasn't . . . I wouldn't . . ." His teeth clamped together so hard Ian winced. Danny tore off his covers and ripped out his IV.

"Stop." Ian grappled with him. "It's okay, you didn't go through with it."

"It's not okay." He twisted out of his grip and stood on unsteady legs. "I touched her, Ian. Oh, my God," he dry-heaved and covered his mouth, "I touched her and . . . and God, Claire. Where is she? I have to see her. I have to talk to her." His eyes stalled on the closed door of his room. He swayed and latched onto the bedrail. "Ian," he whispered. "Tell me the other memory I'm having right now was a dream. Tell me," his eyes squeezed shut, "Claire didn't walk in on me when I was . . ." He couldn't say it, dry-heaving again, and Ian couldn't answer.

"Please, sit down, *bràthair*."

Danny shoved him away.

"Dammit, Danny, you're bleeding." He snatched some gauze out of a cabinet and blotted where he'd torn out the IV. "Listen to me. I know what you're thinking. But you didn't cheat on Claire. You're a victim."

Danny's bloodshot eyes met Ian's, and his voice cracked. "Does she know that? Does the woman I promised I'd never hurt—who trusted me without question—does *she* know that?"

"What's with all the yelling in here?" Annie walked in and gasped. "Daniel Larsson, get back in that bed. Do you know how close you came to dying?"

Old Governor's loud gong clanged outside, and Annie closed her eyes with a slow, deep inhale. "I'm going to kill Clark." The gonging continued as she gathered medical supplies and an emergency kit. Rushing out of the room, she yelled, "Ian, get him in that bed."

He didn't hear her over Danny's slew of bellowing curses. "It's just a coincidence, *bràthair*. Look at me, Claire's fine. The bell has nothing to do with her."

Emelie burst through the door, heaving for air. "Danny, you're awake, thank God."

"Who rang the bell?" Ian said.

"Fin. Officer Murphy is already with him, and Danny? Jake Matthews sent an emergency message for Claire because," she swallowed and moved to his side, licking her chapped lips, "Henderson is here."

"Here?" he and Ian said together.

She touched his arm, and her bottom lip began to vibrate. "There were gunshots, Danny. Fin heard gunshots near Claire's cottage, but he can't find her."

DANNY BARELY HEARD EMELIE and Ian calling for him to wait as he stagger-clomped down the hall in untied boots. His face lost all feeling. His heart slammed in erratic beats.

Gunshots. There were gunshots.

"She's going to be okay." Ian caught up to him, handing him a coat.

"She has to be." Emelie pressed a hat into his hands.

Gunshots.

Annie came through the front door in a gust of wind, stopping when she saw Danny. "Guess there's no talking you out of going is there?" She sighed and patted his arm. "Merv's got the emergency kit, and I helped George get Gus hooked up to the medical sleigh. It'll be ready to go in a few. And, Danny?" He paused with his hand on the front door but didn't turn. "I'll be praying."

He nodded once and shoved out the door. Gripping the frozen rail, he slipped and swayed down the steps to the organized chaos of Solsken during an emergency. Voices dampened by the snow called out orders. While groups of volunteers gathered around Officer Murphy as he and other officers handed out flashlights, flares, and radios.

These people and friends Danny had known his whole life became a blur behind actual memories, not dreams, flashing in his mind. Her frightened voice. Claire had yelled his name, and he'd answered her with reassuring kisses. But the skin he'd felt on his mouth, the warm body in his hands—not Claire. His stomach convulsed, and he gripped over it. It was never Claire.

"Danny, where are you going?" Ian's voice came over the rush of wind, but he didn't stop. His heavy, unsteady steps headed right for Fin's running snowmobile parked near Old Governor. He threw a leg over.

"Wait for the sleigh," Ian yelled. "You're in no condition to drive."

Danny squeezed the throttle, leaving him behind. Leaving everyone behind. At full speed, he let the icy snow numb his face, his body. But he couldn't numb the new memory now seated in his mind. The one of Claire begging him to stop, to look at her, followed by a heart-shattering sob.

CURSING THE ENTIRE WAY back to the sleigh, Ian slowed when he saw Fin puffing toward him. He took a moment to look over his shivering form, his wind burned cheeks. "Finlay, maybe you should stay here and warm up."

Fin's eyes shot up, and the redness around his irises made the green pierce through. "I'm going." Without another word, he swung his long legs into the back of the sleigh and slid in tight against Emelie, making room for Ian.

"Follow my snowmobile," Fin said.

Ian studied his cousin's stony face as George took the reins with a snap. "Thank you."

He grunted. "What for?"

"You've been out here for nearly two hours looking for her."

"But I missed it, didn't I?" His jaw pulsed. "Somehow, I missed seeing some psycho stalker that might've killed her." He held up both hands when Ian opened to respond. "I screwed up just like everything else in my life. And you know what? If we find her and she . . . " He fisted both hands. "And she's not okay. I'm leaving this damn island."

The sleigh slowed down in front of Claire's cottage, and Fin squeezed past a wide-eyed Emelie and jumped down. Hunching toward the wind, he stalked toward Danny, who was frantically yanking on a padlock.

"Footprints on the east side." George pointed.

"You can see that?"

"Merv, I told you, I don't need no damn new glasses."

Ian whistled, signaling to Fin and Danny, and the group fanned out in a line. Close enough to see each other, but enough of a distance to cover an area without missing anything. The way the harsh island winters had taught them to do.

"Found a phone." Merv pulled it out of the snow.

"That's hers." Danny snatched it and brushed wet crystals from a black screen. It wouldn't turn on. "Did she try to call—" He smacked the screen, yelling, "Claire."

"More prints over here." George pointed out two separate prints. One large set, straight and steady, another smaller set, sporadic and disjointed. Danny shouted her name again and stumble-ran toward them.

Ian followed close behind him, wincing when Danny fell face first and staggered to a stand. The man wasn't just born on this island. His usual ease with the elements was the island itself weaved into his very makeup. But when Ian got closer and saw him shivering, wheezing for each breath, he wasn't sure if it was because of his recent brush with death, or the dying he was doing on the inside.

Coming up beside him, Ian took his arm, steadying him. "I'm here," is all he said. All he could give.

The first tear he'd ever seen from his best friend rolled down his cheek, quickly followed by another. Not when he broke his arm as a kid, not even with everything Jessica had done, did Danny cry. But these tears, like tiny fissures against the pressure of a dam, broke him wide open.

"Please," he yelled on a loud sob, eyes darting all over the snow. "Please, I'll do anything, *anything*."

Ian tightened his grip and rubbed the tightness in his chest. That sound Danny made matched an echo in his memory. The sound of a little boy after his mother left, pleading with the father who raised a hand to him.

A long howl followed by yipping barks broke Ian's dark thoughts. Gunner hopped over snow drifts in front of Gerty, who waved at them with her shotgun. Without stopping to greet any of them, Gunner bounded past straight for the cliff's edge.

"No, no, no." Danny took off after the animal.

"Spread out," George bellowed. "Don't lose sight of him."

Gunner stopped to sniff some snow. Letting out a long howl, he yipped once before jumping clear off the cliff's edge.

"Claire!" Danny lunged forward.

Ian caught him, yanking back. "No, Danny."

"She's down there."

"And we need a plan to get her, not go over blind. You know this."

Danny's middle trembled beneath his arms. "The last thing she saw, Ian . . . was me . . . with *her*."

Ian got in his face. "Don't do this, Danny. Don't you dare do this to yourself."

"I love her." His voice cracked. "God, I love her, and she doesn't know. I didn't say it."

"I know." Ian pulled him in. "I know, *bràthair*."

Emelie screamed, and they all whipped around to see her pointing to the snow where Gunner had sniffed, hand cupped over her mouth. Ian got there first, and when he saw a bright-red circle with a long trail leading directly to the cliff, he whirled, hands bulldozing into Danny's chest.

"*Don't*." But it was too late.

A cry roared out of him before Danny's eyes rolled back into his head. He crashed down, the weight of him swallowing him inside the snow.

Merv and George rushed to help Ian lift his face out of the

snow, turning him to his back.

"Danny," Emelie cried as she sank into the snow, bringing his head to her lap. "I'm so sorry, so sorry." She brushed snow off his cheeks.

"Claire," he groaned, eyes fluttering.

Ian slowly kneeled, helping Danny sit up, his watering eyes locked on the blood trail. *She can't be gone.*

"What's wrong with everybody?" Fin said. "We don't know shit yet."

Ian swiped an arm over his eyes to see his cousin coming back from the sleigh with a rope. "What are you doing?"

"What's it look like?" He wrapped and looped the rope around his legs as a harness.

"It looks like you think you can go down these cliffs."

He yanked hard on a knot. "I've rappelled down them before."

"Not here, you haven't. Only Clark is experienced enough to go down the steepest point of the island."

"Clark isn't here," he yelled. "And we don't know if she . . . we can't just . . . we *can't*, Ian." He took a deep breath. "Look, if Gunner can go down, there's a way down." He cinched the final knot and looked around at everyone. "Well? Is someone going to help me, or do I have to do this myself?"

Ian stared. Shock slowly melting away to pride. His young cousin finally stepping up like the man he always knew he could be. Drying his eyes, Ian pulled Fin in for a quick, firm hug.

"How are we getting him down safely?" Ian double checked the knots on his harness.

"This rock will make a great anchor." George began wrapping the end around it.

"Hang in there, Danny," Emelie whispered, hugging him. "They're going to get her."

"Has anyone seen Gerty?" Merv asked.

"Over here," she called from a few yards away, peering carefully over the edge. "I've got my eye on Gunner. He'll signal if he finds something." As if he heard her say it, a long, screeching howl drifted up from below. "Over there." She pointed to her right.

"Ian, help me hold the rope," George said. "Fin, get ready to go over."

"Wait." Flashing lights from a snowmobile reflected off the snow, soon followed by a tall man in uniform. "McClellan?"

"Which one?" Ian called.

"Whichever one of you sanctioned a search without a radio."

Ian had no idea who was to blame for that but raised his arm, showing Officer Murphy where they were located. "We may have found her. Fin's heading down."

Tom trudged forward and attached a radio to Fin's belt. "How the hell were you going to communicate with anyone up here?"

"A few tugs on the rope?"

Tom sighed and helped steady him as Fin prepared to rappel backward.

"Finney?" Emelie's voice shook. Fin met and held her eyes. "Be careful."

With a quick nod, he began his descent.

"I want every detail you've all kept from me, right now." Tom moved next to Danny, helping him stand.

One by one they filled him in, starting with Emelie mentioning Jessica being tied up in Danny's office. Before he could follow up with questions, Fin's voice scratched over the radio.

"I need more slack. There's a flat ledge down here and I think . . ." They quickly gave it to him. "Yes, I see her."

As if the next thing out of Fin's mouth would shatter the universe, Danny went still, covering his mouth.

"There's a pulse. Quick, send down the stretcher."

Danny let out a loud cry, and Emelie pulled him into her arms, weeping. Tom disappeared and returned carrying a stretcher with attached ropes.

"Ian, go help them." Emelie dried her face and took his place with George on Fin's rope. Merv, Ian, Tom, and Danny began lowering the stretcher.

"She's secure," Fin said. "Bring her up."

"Come on, Gunner." Gerty gave a series of loud whistles and wiped her eyes. "You did it, boy. Come on up. I got a nice steak waitin' for you at home." She whistled again.

Hand over hand, the four men drew on the ropes while George and Emelie worked to bring in the slack of Fin's rope.

"Is it supposed to be this loose?" Emelie asked when they picked up speed to keep up with the increased slack.

"Maybe he's faster coming up than going down?"

Claire's stretched-out body appeared over the edge and a mix between a yell and a cry burst from Danny. He dropped beside her.

"My God, her face." His shaking hands gingerly lowered her scarf and brushed her bloodied, split lip and bruised jaw.

"Give me a little space, Danny. I need to check her." Merv moved in with the medical kit while Tom held up a flashlight, and Ian held up a blanket, blocking the wind. "Pulse is slow but steady. Abrasions look superficial," Merv said. "Ankle may be broken, though, but there are no gunshot wounds. The blood wasn't hers." There was a collective sigh of relief. "We need to get her out of the cold and back to the medical center as soon as possible, especially for this." He lifted her gloveless hand.

"Shit." Danny took it carefully between both of his and blew heat on it. "This is her writing hand."

Ian noticed Emelie slowly reaching down to touch a familiar looking harness secured around Claire. He cursed, handing off his blanket to George just as she whispered, "Finney?"

They both rushed to the cliff's edge shouting for him.

"I don't see him," Emelie shrieked.

Tom lifted his radio. "You still with us, McClellan?" He was answered by static. "Fin, do you copy?" More static.

"Finlay," Ian and Emelie yelled together.

"You know, it's a bit hard to answer a radio when you've got no free hands." Fin grunted as he clung to the top of the edge. "Gunner made this look so easy."

"Damn, Finlay." Ian laughed as he and Tom took him by the

arms and lifted him.

"Why would you do that?" Emelie smacked his chest, and he stumbled back. "Why the hell would you do that, Fin? You could've fallen."

"I was afraid the stretcher might catch on something, and she'd tip over." He caught her hands mid-slap. "Wait, did you just call me Fin?" She went still. "Were you worried about me or something?"

"No." She wrapped her arms tight around her middle and twisted away from him, stomping back toward Claire.

"I don't understand," he said to Ian. "Did that mean something?"

"It sure as hell didn't mean nothing." Ian gave his shoulder a small squeeze.

"Ian, Fin," Merv called. "Help us carry her to the sleigh."

With Claire bundled and secured, George got Gus going again with a crack of the reins. Ian's hand idly rubbed over his stomach as the runners cut through the thick snow. The quiet was only broken by Danny's whispers. He hovered over Claire, eyelashes damp, warming her hand with his repeated words, "Forgive me, love. God, I'm so sorry. Please forgive me."

THE SKIN OF HER hand was clammy. His breath insufficient. Danny's eyes squeezed shut. *How long? How long?* It felt like hours, years before the sleigh glided up to the Medical Center. Annie was already outside with a shell-shocked Clark holding a steaming mug in his hand.

"Take her into room three," she said. "Danny, I want you back in your room to rest."

"No." He kept Claire's hand as they carried her in.

"Daniel Larsson—"

"Annabelle." Clark touched her cheek. "It's alright. We may need him." He followed the men carrying Claire, directing. "Heating pads and electric blankets are through that door there. Annabelle, buckets of warm water for her hand."

"Will she lose her fingers?" Danny's voice was barely above a whisper.

"Too early to tell." Clark took a deep breath. "I'm so sorry, Danny. Gene and I were celebrating my dive win and—"

"Just help her, please."

With a nod, Clark switched to what he did best. "We need to get her temperature up as quick as possible. Danny, body heat will help."

His shirt was halfway up when Claire moaned, "Greyson."

"Hey, love." Danny cupped carefully over her bruised jaw. "Don't worry, I'll call him."

She sucked in a breath, eyes blinking open. He saw the moment she remembered. The tremor of realization iced over her body, cinching her muscles into cold rigidity.

"Claire," his voice shook, "it's alright."

"Get away from me."

"Sweetheart, you nearly froze to death. I need to help warm you."

"I said, get away from me. Greyson?"

"Keep her still," Clark ordered, cutting the boot from her swollen ankle.

Danny took hold of her shoulders with firm but gentle hands.

"Don't *touch* me." She thrashed and he recoiled.

Those words. The same ones she used for Henderson paralyzed him.

"Merv, take over," Clark said. "Danny, maybe step out until we calm her."

A phone on the wall rang, startling Danny into forward motion. He tripped over a chair, and sprawled to the floor. His eyes locked onto Claire's swimming gaze.

"Go. Away."

His wet boots squeaked as he rushed out, hands fisting his hair.

"Hey, hey. She's just upset." Ian came up beside him. "Give it some time, alright? Then try to talk to her."

Danny pressed two fingers into his eyes, shaking his head. If he answered, he'd lose the last of his control.

"Ian, Danny?" Annie called from Claire's door. "Do either of you know a Jake Matthews? He keeps calling and insisting on talking to Claire. I didn't tell him anything, but—"

"I'll talk to him," Danny said.

"Line two." She pointed to a phone in the hallway and gently patted his back.

Danny jammed a finger on line two and said, "If she loses her hand, I'll kill you."

"Uh, hello? Who's this?"

"Why the hell aren't you here? Huh? Sitting there in your fancy home with your goddamn billions, and you can't keep one man, *one man*, from shoving her off a cliff?"

Ian tore the phone out of his hand, covering the mouthpiece with a quick shake of his head.

"Give it back."

"Take a walk."

He shoved fingers back into his hair with a growl and paced. Ian took a deep breath, knowing that's as good of a walk as he was going to get and pressed the speaker button. "Jake Matthews, this is Ian McClellan, Danny Larsson's manager at Flygande."

"Ah, so that lovely gentleman ripping me a new asshole must've been Danny then."

"He's a bit upset, as we all are. And frankly, I'd like some answers to his questions too."

"Is Madelynn alright?"

Danny took one heavy step, but Ian eased him back, answering, "She's alive. But it's too soon to know how bad her injuries are. Now, how about you answer our questions? Starting with, how did this happen?"

Jake let out a long breath. "A few hours ago, my head of security caught a glitch in our system. A message sent to replay every day to Madelynn's phone."

"You mean the daily safety message she depended on, you

useless prick?"

"Danny," Ian warned.

"Unfortunately, *Mr. Larsson,* finding who was behind this wasn't as easy as you think. Nor is messing with my security program."

The same security program he advertised as unhackable? Danny's hands fisted.

"But that's beside the point," Jake continued. "By the time we did find out," he sighed, "well, you know the rest. The bastard also stole prototypes of mine and gave them to Henderson. Apparently, it doesn't matter how well you pay someone, everyone has their price. And my guy's price was a hefty gambling debt that Henderson took care of. I assure you, all my available resources are working nonstop to fix this, and my entire compromised, international security team has been," there was a slam followed by Jake hissing a curse before he spoke in a barely controlled voice, "handled." After a long beat of silence, he continued, "None of that is why I called, though. I needed to know she's okay. You mentioned her hand?"

Danny's jaw welded shut, so Ian answered. "Her right hand was exposed. We're not sure how bad the frostbite is yet."

"Dammit, she needs that hand. Did you know she hand writes all her novels?"

Danny's molars ground together over his familiarity with her. Because, unlike Claire when they first met, he knew all about Jake Matthews. Mr. Playboy with his perfectly chiseled face plastered over every business and social magazine. It's hard to forget the youngest man to become a billionaire. The boy genius, who made his fortune overnight when he sold his online security software, had also grown up to repeatedly hit number one on every Sexiest Man Alive chart.

Ian's calming squeeze on his shoulder eased Danny back down.

"How's her son holding up?" Jake asked.

"Her son?" Ian said. "Wouldn't know. He isn't here."

"Hang on." Papers rustled in the background. "The reports I printed out said Greyson's phone tracker was located at the northeastern most point of the island only an hour ago."

"Northeastern." Ian and Danny both looked at each other.

"Officer Murphy?" Danny yelled, running down the hall.

"Wait." Ian caught his arm. "You need to rest. I'll go."

"I can't just stand here," his eyes darted toward Claire's door, "and do nothing."

Tom poked his head out of Claire's room. "You called me, Larsson?"

Danny glanced at Ian's grip.

"Okay," Ian said, releasing him.

"Tom, I need you to find a pair of bolt cutters and meet me at Claire's cottage." Danny paused outside Claire's door and laid a hand against it.

"Go on," Ian said. "I'll stay with her."

"GREYSON?" DANNY POUNDED ON Claire's cottage door as Tom grunted and squeezed the cutters into the lock. "It's Danny Larsson and Officer Murphy. Are you in there?" A distant thump came from inside, followed by another. "I hear something."

The lock snapped and Danny threw open the door. "Greyson?"

Another bump came, followed this time by muffled screaming from Claire's bathroom.

"Greys—" Inside he froze. Claire's duplicated tea-colored eyes looked up at him, red-rimmed below an oozing gash on his forehead. Hands and feet bound, mouth gagged between blue lips, Greyson shivered in a tub full of water.

"Holy shit." Danny rushed to him, heaving him out, and they both collapsed, bodies and soaked clothes slapping against the floor. "Tom, find blankets. Hey, shh, you're okay. I got you." He carefully untied his bonds, and removed the gag, wincing at the blooming blisters and the raw rope marks on his skin. "Let me look at you."

"No." Greyson pulled away, coughed, and sputtered as his body violently shook to stay warm. "I need to find m-m-my mom."

"She's being taken care of at the medical center."

His blue lips vibrated. "She's alive? B-but I heard a gun."

Danny let out a deep breath. "I think she might've shot the bastard."

The boy covered his face, and a low cry strangled out of him.

"Hey, hey." Danny clasped both sides of his head. "No, it's okay. Greyson, look at me."

"It's not okay. I t-told her she meant nothing. I'm so stupid. I believed every damn thing Henderson told me, that she didn't want me. And — And I wanted to hurt her for it. But not like . . . not like . . . " His shoulders shook. "God, sh-she'll never forgive me."

"Listen to me, even with everything you said to her," Danny wrapped an arm over his shoulders and pulled him in, rubbing warmth into his clammy skin, "your mother loves you. Hell, before I came here, she was asking for you."

He slowly straightened. "For me?"

"Yes." Danny wrapped the blankets Tom brought around the boy and continued to rub his arms. "And as soon as we get you out of these wet clothes, I'll take you to her."

"Bu-but I stole your phone and . . . " He blinked, shaking his head hard. "Why are you being nice to me?"

"A phone I can replace, and I've been called worse insults than 'sponger.'" Danny slowly smiled. "Besides, if my mom started dating some wannabe Viking with thrift store decor, I'd give him hell too."

"MOM?" GREYSON CALLED AS Danny and Tom walked him into the medical center. "*Mom.*"

"Greyson?" Claire's voice came from her room.

He stumbled forward. "*Mom.*"

"My baby. Let me go. I need to see him." Her voice reached

shrieking levels.

Danny and Tom rushed Greyson forward. "Where's Ian?" Danny spotted the empty chair outside Claire's room. "He wouldn't have just left."

"Finlay McClellan?" Tom spoke into his radio. "Do you have a location on Ian?"

"Hey," Fin drew out the word. "Yeah, so um, Emelie's dad reported water running in the pipes at Solsken Inn when all the guests are supposed to be checked-out. Ian thinks it might be Henderson. We're looking into it."

Tom closed his eyes with a quiet curse. "I have officers in that area searching for him. I'll send them and be on my way. If he's there, whatever you do, do not engage him."

"Uh . . ."

"I hear something." Ian's voice came from a distance.

"Finlay? You tell Ian to wait for me or one of my officers to arrive. Do you copy?" He was met with empty buzzing. "Finlay McClellan, do you copy?"

"I got him." Danny hefted Greyson further down the hall, calling over his shoulder, "You and I both know that if it's Henderson, Ian will engage the hell out of him. And if not? You better hide that bastard far away from me, because I fucking will."

Tom pivoted on his heel, feet pounding down the hall as he barked orders into his radio.

Reaching Claire's door, Danny took a fortifying breath before he opened it.

"You have to stay still, or you'll make your injuries worse." Annie, Merv, and Doc Clark fought a flailing Claire.

"Mom?"

Claire went still, eyes frantically scanning her son before she erupted into a sob, arms reaching out. Danny walked him over, letting him go, and he curled into a ball in her arms, crying. "Mom, I'm so sorry."

"Greyson, . . ." she whispered, curling him tighter. "It's alright, baby. It's alright."

"No, it's not." He lifted his face and touched hers. "What did he do to you? I didn't know he'd . . . I-I didn't mean what I said . . . you mean everything, *everything*. Oh, your face."

"Shh . . . " She kissed his fingers and brought him back to her side. "I'll heal. Don't you worry."

She checked and rechecked him like she was afraid he'd disappear.

"Mom." Greyson carefully wrapped an arm around her. "I don't want to live with them anymore. Please? Don't send me back to them."

Despite the pain that still made her tremble, Claire adjusted her body to fit him closer. "Shh, now." She smoothed back his tangled hair with her good hand. "Don't you worry, my lawyers are already working on custody."

Relief shook his shoulders, and when she tucked him closer, her eyes met Danny's.

For one glorious moment, he'd forgotten he wasn't part of her family, that she didn't want him near her anymore. Unable to catch a breath, Danny dropped his gaze and slowly backed out of the room before he, too, fell at her side and begged to be held.

Penances

A DIM LIGHT SPILLED out from under a solid oak door that Ian had his ear pressed against. "I don't hear anything anymore."

"I can't believe Henderson has been the long-termer all this time," Emelie whispered, arms curling around her stomach.

"Are we sure it's him?" Fin asked.

"It has to be," she said. "He can't leave since the bridge is closed, and with all the surveillance equipment we found in the other two rooms attached to this one?" She pressed the heel of her palm to her forehead. "I can't believe I've been feeding Claire's stalker all this time."

"Don't." Fin's fingers skimmed her arm, and when she zeroed in on them, he quickly dropped them away. "None of us knew, Emelie."

"And you've never seen him in person?" Ian asked.

She shook her head. "Even when I spoke to him, we spoke through the door. And this is one of the original rooms before the build-ons. It has its own private back entrance, so he never came down through the lobby."

Ian's head snapped to her. "Back entrance?"

"Shit, shit, shit."

Ian rushed toward the emergency stairwell.

"Wait for Officer Murphy," Emelie called.

Ian gripped the metal railing and swung over, landing hard on the next level. His legs swept out from under him, and the edge of a stair bit into the center of his back. The pain didn't register.

Nothing registered. Not Fin yelling behind him. Not the alarm blaring when he burst out of the emergency exit and slipped in the snow. Not even the cold that penetrated his now sopping pants. Only the sight of staggering footprints with a small trail of blood, and a man making his way toward a motorboat.

It didn't matter that crossing the ocean pass to the mainland this time of year was as good as committing suicide. There was a small chance he'd make it.

And an even greater chance he'd come back.

Every muscle in his body contracted. Every nerve ending sparked as Ian's vision tunneled to a sharp point on the broad frame dragging giant duffel bags through the snow.

"Ian . . . stop . . . might . . . gun . . . "

Fin's shout muddled in his ears. Distant. Disconnected. Ian didn't feel. Didn't hear. Lost all sense of the world around him.

Only once had Ian detached from himself like this and ended up in juvenile detention for nearly killing a kid. A hulk of a bully that had set his sights on the new girl in town named Molly. But unlike then, he didn't have his best friend beside him.

There would be no Danny to step in between this time. No holding back. No, Henderson would meet the real Ian McClellan.

The broken boy who became a broken man.

Sprinting, every detail from the unending nightmare of a night replayed in his mind . . . Jessica's laughter while holding up Danny's drooling face. Danny convulsing on the floor. Claire's body being dragged over the cliff's edge.

He slammed full force into the wall of a man. The impact sent them both over the peak of a small hill and down, tumbling over rocks and snow-covered grass. At the bottom, Ian's fingers wrapped around a thick neck, and a roar tore from his throat.

Nails clawed at him as he drove fist after heavy fist into a hard face. Strangled yells and bloodied curses sputtered out of Henderson as Ian lost control—lost himself. Blood soaked his knuckles as he gripped Henderson's throat again, fingers squeezing, cutting off his airway. He slammed Henderson's head into the frozen ground, brought it up to another heavy fist, and slammed it again.

It took a long moment to realize he was screaming, "Die!" And an even longer moment to feel cold metal pressed into the side of his head.

"You die first," Henderson said.

Ian twisted away as a shot rang out. Fire blazed through his shoulder. Another shot and the rock beside him splintered. Shards showered his coat before a heavy body crashed into him. Henderson straddled his chest, pinning his arms under his knees, gun pressed into Ian's forehead.

"Don't you fucking move." Blood dripped from Henderson's mouth, and he coughed, wheezing on an inhale. The gun slid an inch, and he coughed again, realigning it. His free hand tucked inside his coat and gripped his side. He was shaking, his breathing erratic.

Ian cursed and struggled. Waves slapped against the stones on the beach behind them with the faint hum of the boat motor. Henderson blinked hard and swayed a little, eyes unfocused. "Stupid wannabe Scot—" His words cut off with a wet cough, and his hand shook as he repositioned the gun. It slipped again and Ian wrenched and squirmed, but the man was a mountain of cinder blocks on his arms.

"Full-blooded Scot, thank you." It didn't matter. But it absolutely mattered.

"I don't give a shit." Henderson hacked another cough, and Ian realized that the blood coming from his mouth wasn't just from his fists.

"Broken ribs suck, don't they?" He wrenched hard again, hoping to aggravate the injury.

"I said don't move." The gun stabilized on his forehead and pressed in. Capillaries split and broke under his skin, and Ian wrestled again, grunting under the weight of the man crushing his arms. Henderson chambered a round and he went still.

Dear God.

He wouldn't get to say goodbye.

The tears he'd held onto released and rolled down the sides of his eyes. Danny, Claire, Emelie, Finlay, Solsken's residents that had become his family and . . . "Mam," he whispered.

He focused on a single snowflake breaking free from the swirling wind and drifted toward his face. With a shaking breath, he released the broken boy inside — his constant companion — and abandoned his need for revenge.

Looking up beyond his island, beyond the cloud-filled sky, he embraced this final penance for every mistake, every wrong. "Save a dram of your finest for me, my friend."

Fin's voice tore through the quiet. "*Ian.*"

Three shots rang out and Ian's world went black.

Wake Up and Smell the Coffee

DANNY STARED AT THE ticking clock over Claire's door, holding his head in one hand, a mug of bone broth Annie had insisted upon in the other. He hadn't moved from that spot since Greyson had been taken to an adjoining room for a closer checkup. His last words to Danny still echoed in his ears.

I'm sorry. She still won't see you.

"I'm going to be a priest." The front doors blew open, and Danny fumbled with his mug before rushing to Ian being hauled inside by Fin.

"What happened to him?"

"He had a God moment." Fin rolled his eyes with a small smile. "This big idiot went after Henderson alone and nearly had his brains blown out. Would have too if Officer Murphy hadn't gotten there in time."

"He's dead then?"

"Aye." Ian smirked through a busted lip and clapped the side of Danny's neck. "He died and crushed me. Thought I'd died and ended up in the wrong place for moment, but it would seem my friend upstairs has work for me here." He smiled wider. "I'm going to be a priest."

"Yeah, we knew that already." Fin dragged him to the chair Danny vacated, and they both eased him down.

"But I didn't." His smile slowly faded. "I'm a screw-up, Finlay. I don't understand why he called me."

Fin bent forward, coming eye to eye with him. "I'm beginning to think the screw-ups are his favorite."

"Sweet Jesus, Ian. What did you do this time?" Annie came down the hall with a tray in her hands.

"Did I ever tell you you're my favorite aunt?"

"Finlay, put him in room four." She looked pointedly at Ian. "I'll be in soon to deal with *you*."

Ian grinned a bloody-toothed smile.

"Here, I brought some tea for Claire. She needs hot beverages." Annie shoved the tray into Danny's hands.

"But she doesn't want to see me."

"Danny Boy, are you really going to give up so easily?"

"I—"

She patted his cheek. "There's an extra mug for you too."

"But I can't drink it." He swallowed hard. "I can't drink tea anymore."

CLAIRE HEARD THE CLICK of the door. She didn't have to turn to know he was there. His quiet presence filled the space like oxygen filled a needy lung. But she didn't need him anymore—no, that wasn't true. He was the sun in her darkness. The rain on her desiccated heart.

She braced against the tide of him. The pull his mere presence asked of her, demanded of her. All she had to do was speak one word, and his all-encompassing warmth would replace the insignificant heating pads around her.

Her uninjured fingers curled into the underside of the blanket. She couldn't ask. He wasn't hers anymore.

How did one learn to live with only a fraction of themselves?

His footsteps neared, and she kept her eyes closed, listening to his weighted sigh as he set a tray down near her bed. The back of warm fingers brushed against the side of her face, checking the temperature of her skin. Heavy blankets drew up higher and the underside of her eyelids pooled when the tips of his fingers gently tucked the blankets securely around her.

"Ah, Claire," he whispered, his hand coming back to her face. This time it ran along her cheek as he moved her hair away, then traced her bruised jaw. "How am I going to fix this?"

He went quiet again, and she wondered if he was thinking of how to lie to her. To manipulate her into staying with him.

She clamped down hard on her lip and heart, speaking through clenched teeth. "You can't."

The hand on her cheek stilled but didn't lift. "Are you warm enough?"

Slowly, she turned, brows drawn together. "Did you hear me?"

"I heard you. Careful, love, you can't get up." He eased her back as his bloodshot eyes roamed her face.

"I want to check on Greyson."

"Sweetheart, not yet. I'll make sure they—"

"Stop calling me those names."

"What names?" He looked genuinely confused.

"Sweetheart, love . . . just call me Madelynn."

His jaw pulsed. "I'm not calling you that." He reached down and the top of her bed slowly lifted. "Annie made you tea."

"I don't want tea."

"You need hot liquids. When Annie finishes fixing Ian up, I'll make sure she updates you on Greyson."

"What's the matter with Ian?"

"He pulled a McClellan on Henderson and nearly lost." Her brows slowly lifted and he half-smiled. "It means he almost died when his fists couldn't compete with Henderson's gun. If it hadn't been for Officer Murphy's good aim, he'd be singing with the angels right now."

She gripped the blanket over her chest. "And Henderson?"

His darkened gaze didn't waver. "He's gone, Claire. He can't hurt you anymore."

She sank back with a heavy breath, and he repositioned her pillows, propping her up. He held out a mug. Her eyes froze on the vibration in his hand, then slowly traveled up the stretch of his sweater sleeve along his corded forearm and over his thick bicep.

Those arms had held her, carried her. Longing pulled taut in her belly, and she blinked it away before giving in to the need to touch him.

"Claire," he whispered. "Please, don't look away from me."

She dropped her head and took the mug, careful not to touch his fingers. "I have my tea. You can go."

A chair scraped and plunked down close to her, and Danny dropped into it, taking his own mug. His heavy stare burned into the side of her face as the silence stretched. "Why haven't you asked me?"

"I have nothing to ask you."

"Yes, you do, lov—Claire, so ask me."

The question swelled and caught in her throat. She shook her head.

He leaned forward, whispering, "Kick my face, Claire."

Her eyes cut to him. "So you can lie to me?"

"When have I ever lied to you?"

"All of it, *us*, was a lie."

"That's what you think?"

He hissed as black liquid splashed from the rim of his cup onto his hand.

"Coffee?"

"Yes." He held her eyes as he snatched napkins. "Coffee."

But he hated coffee.

"Ask. Me," he said between clenched teeth, and she closed her eyes.

"Just leave, Daniel."

"No." His voice was suddenly closer, a gentle wisp near her ear. "I don't want to lose you."

She jerked away. "Perhaps you should have thought of that before you dressed your *wife* up like me to screw her in your office."

"You think I…I didn't. *Wouldn't.*" His voice deepened, fingers curling into fists on his thighs. "And don't bullshit this conversation by giving her that title. She isn't my wife anymore. She never really was. Nothing with her was real. Claire, look at me."

She shook her head.

"Please, swe—Claire."

She kept still, swallowing all her words.

"If you won't ask then I'll say it. I didn't cheat on you. I would never do that to you."

Fire blazed from her belly. "I *saw* you."

"What did you see?"

"Is this a joke?"

"No." He jammed a shaking hand into his hair. "Far from it."

"Then why would you ask me to relive it?"

"I'm asking because . . ." He reached out, but she pulled back. "Claire, I'm asking because I don't remember much."

"You don't remember that you . . ." She scraped away traitorous tears. "That you . . . you said my name while you, you . . ." A sob gushed out.

He sprang up and took her face in his hands. "I said your name because it *was* you, Claire. In my mind, I was with you."

"What kind of sick game are you—"

"I thought I over brewed it." His voice cracked. "But the bitterness in my tea wasn't because the leaves were too strong. There was something in it. Something I had no idea would make me do what I did. I didn't know—*God*, Claire, I didn't think Jess would go so far as to drug me and dress up like you to get me to touch her."

She winced at the word "touch" and tried to turn away. He kept her face in his hands and gently thumbed under her eyes. "I didn't want to touch her, Claire. In my messed-up state, I thought I was touching you."

"That's quite the story, Daniel."

"It's the truth, I swear it." He pressed his forehead against hers and whispered, "I love *you*, Claire."

Her bottom lip shook, and she clamped down hard on it. "I

don't want to hear that from you." Not now.

"Please, let me say it. I love you. *Only* you." He removed her lip from her teeth and stroked a delicate caress along it. "I've loved you from the moment you took the time to apologize to this bitter, hurting man at a bar for the shit his wife did to him. And I would —" His voice broke. "I would do anything to go back and not drink that tea. To take what you saw out of your mind and put what was in my mind, what I saw, what I thought I was doing, so you'd know I'm telling you the truth."

"I-I can't do this."

Tears fell unchecked as he dropped beside her on the bed. "Tell me you don't love me then. Say it to my face."

She shook her head.

"Say it, Claire. Or better yet, tell me you think I'm the kind of man that would cheat on you — *in front of you.*"

"Just stop." She closed her eyes. She couldn't get a clear thought.

"Claire, I know this is a shitty mess, but give me a chance to show you the truth. Please." He bent lower and the tip of his nose stroked along her cheek.

She squeezed her eyes so tight they ached. "I need you to leave."

"Love, please."

"Leave," she whimpered.

"Claire —"

"*Leave me.*"

He swung off the bed, and his heavy, unsteady feet staggered to the door.

She expected a door slam. A loud curse. But instead, it was a silent retreat. A door closing with a quiet click.

A sob tore free.

She gripped the blankets he'd tucked around her and sank into the pillows he'd anchored.

She'd made a mistake — no, she hadn't. She'd seen them. But his story. Drugged? But he . . . her mind misfired. Every thought and feeling, thick. Dark. Clarity just out of reach. She couldn't . . .

couldn't . . . everything—all of it too much to sift through. Flashes of thought moved in a tangled web, running the gauntlet of her emotions.

I'm asking because I don't remember.

His arms wrapped around Jessica.

In my mind, I was with you.

His lips on her body.

I love you. Only you.

Her name on his mouth . . . *her* name, not Jessica's.

I would do anything to go back and not drink that tea.

The smell of coffee wedged into her thoughts, and she followed the scent to Danny's abandoned mug. Her racing mind suddenly cleared of every thought but one.

Why coffee?

Tingles burst and scattered across her skin, raising the tiny hairs. "Oh, Daniel." She knew. Of course she knew.

But she'd let him go.

No, oh God, she pushed him away.

A thump vibrated her door, and she startled, cocking an ear to listen. Another noise came, followed by another, and it drew her to the edge of the bed. It was muffled and distorted, but there was something within the sound. Something so raw her heart raced. "Who's out there?"

The bump crashed again, and the door broke open. There, on the floor, was a large, crumpled body. Knees up, hands yanking on blond hair, Danny's shoulders curled into themselves. His body twitched in uncontrolled jerks.

Then it came. The sound of him sliced through the opening straight into her center. It was a cry so fractured she splintered with it, and his words after their first kiss rushed in. *I'm afraid of what you could do to me — here.*

She broke him. Without realizing, she did exactly what she promised him she'd never do.

"Daniel."

Her body forgot its brokenness and lunged forward, twisting

her wrapped ankle. She cried out, catching the rail in her good hand, and swung halfway off the bed.

The door slammed into the wall, and a moment later, warmth wrapped underneath her, scooping her up. After all she'd said — all she did — he was here, face blotchy and wrung, watery eyes darting all over, checking for fresh injuries.

"Oh, Daniel, I'm so sorry." She reached for him and missed.

His face didn't register hearing her as he eased her down onto the bed with a gentleness that defied the strength of him. He avoided her eyes before turning to leave.

"Wait." She caught his forearm, and he went still. "Darling, I-I believe you."

Air choked up in his throat, but he didn't move, didn't look her way.

"Please forgive me."

"Don't."

"I should have believed you, Daniel. I'm so —"

"Do *not*," he whipped around, grabbing her face, "apologize to me again."

He was so angry. His face twisted in . . . disgust? She shriveled, sinking backward.

"No." He kept her face in his hands, not letting her slip through.

"I understand why you're angry at me."

"I'm not angry at you." His bloodshot eyes bounced back and forth between hers. "No more assuming things by my face anymore, okay? Just ask me. And with what you'd seen with me and . . . I don't . . . why, Claire? Why do you believe me?"

"You hate coffee," she whispered. "But you gave up drinking tea because of her."

"No, not her, you." The last word hitched. "Claire, you almost died because I had to have one more cup of tea."

"Daniel, it wasn't your fault." She was touching him. When had she started touching him? Drinking in the dampness on his face through her fingers. "I broke my promise to you."

"No, Claire. This shitty mess of mine —"

"Ours." She swiped under his eyes and then curled her fingers around one of the hands still cradling her face. "Our mess, not yours. And listen to me." She pulled on the back of his neck, closing the chasm between them, until his forehead anchored hers. "If I had to be in a mess with someone, to drive straight into a great big pile of shit with anyone, I'd want it to be you." More tears rolled over her uneven smile. "Because wherever you are, my love, it is so, so beautiful."

His hands tightened on her face, eyes blinking fast, voice tight like he strained to keep control. "Say that again, Claire."

"You and me. Together. Driving through shit. Making our messes beautiful."

A laugh gusted out of him and ended in a choked sob.

"No, no, Daniel. Oh, come here." Curling her good arm around his neck, her fingers tucked into his hair and brought his head down to her shoulder. She stroked through his thick, tangled strands. "I do love you. I love you so much I can hardly breathe sometimes."

His face turned, burying in her neck, and with a gentle brush of his mouth on her skin, he whispered, "I haven't taken a full breath since I met you."

She squeezed him, and his arms slid around her, finding the exposed skin where her hospital gown tied shut and slipped inside. They lost themselves in each other's arms, each other's warmth, breathing together until their heartbeats slowed and their minds accepted this moment as real.

"Will you do me a favor?" she whispered.

"Anything."

"Would you get under these covers and kiss me?"

His lips slowly pulled up at the corners. "God, yes."

She chuckled, and he said, "I love that sound."

His mouth lightly skimmed hers. Pulling back an inch, he drank in her features before quickly returning, his kiss hungry but careful over her cut lip as she opened for him. They took their time re-exploring, tasting, savoring.

"Claire, my Claire." He moved from her mouth to cover every cut, every bruise on her face. "I love you so much."

Slipping off his boots and shirt, he carefully scooted her over and crawled in, surrounding her with himself. When the heat of him consumed all of her, they exhaled together.

"Only you," he whispered, walking delicate kisses down her neck.

"Only ever you," she answered.

38

All Things Have Become New

DANNY CURLED HIS HANDS around two brass knobs on a set of double oak doors and looked up past the chipped white paint to a small steeple.

"You ready?" Ian asked behind him.

"I think I'm gonna pass out."

"Deep breaths. Can't have you falling on me and wrinkling my freshly pressed kilt."

Danny chuckled. "I'm serious. What if I say the wrong thing?"

"Listen, it's simple. Repeat after me, I Danny, take you, Claire, to be my wife. Now let's get the hell out of here and consummate this thang."

Danny's head fell against the door on a deep laugh. "I'll give you all of Flygande, if you promise never to say that again."

Ian grinned. "What would great-granddaddy Torbjörn say if he knew you offered a McClellan that?"

"He'd tear the weapons off the walls and slaughter my ass."

"As fun as that would be to watch, I may have a better gift." Ian lifted out a long velvet box with a red ribbon from his tuxedo jacket.

"Sorry, man. I'm already promised to Claire."

Ian smacked his arm and shoved the box in his face. Grinning, Danny slid off the ribbon and when he opened it, his smile slipped.

"What's this?" He lifted a long gold chain with a circlet around three crowns. "The *Tre Kronor*?"

"I replaced the chain to match your wedding rings."

"But I thought you got rid of this."

"It was your great-grandmother's necklace, Danny. It belongs to your wife."

"My wife," he whispered and then looked up at him through pooling eyes. "She's going to be my wife, Ian."

"Aye. But not if you don't show up."

"Shit." Danny pressed fingers into his eyes before throwing a firm hug around him. "Thank you."

"Anytime, *bràthair*." He straightened Danny's tie. "Everything's ready too. So, when you're . . . " He cleared his throat with a wink. "*Done*, give me a call so I can get everyone situated."

Danny slowly smiled and waggled his brow. "You all may freeze to death before I'm *done*."

Ian barked a laugh and shoved him forward. "Git in there."

Standing at the front with his best friend at his side, Danny looked over the sea of faces. His jaw ached. He couldn't stop smiling. It didn't matter that only those within the town could attend due to Solsken putting down record-breaking snowfall, keeping the bridge closed. He was the happiest he'd ever been.

His sweeping gaze stopped on the tablet held in Emelie's hands. His parents' and sister's faces smiled through a live feed and waved at him. "*Älskar dig, Mamma*." He blew his teary-eyed mom a kiss.

The music started, and his stomach dropped to his feet. At the back of the small chapel stood Claire in a mermaid-shaped gown of vintage ivory lace with a matching hat cocked to the side and netting covering only her right eye. The tears he thought he'd reeled in began rolling as she took her first step forward. There was still a small limp to her gait, but with her hand tucked tightly into her smiling son's arm, he led her carefully down the aisle.

It'd been two months since her accident, and recovery had been so tedious and painful, he hardly dared touch her. Even when she begged for more than a kiss, he was afraid he'd hurt her. But when they got the all-clear from Doc, he'd forgotten his grand romantic plans for a proposal and fell on one knee in the middle of the office. Kissing the healing skin of her frostbitten hand, he'd asked the four words he never thought he'd get a chance to say. Before he could get the last word out, she'd burst a loud "Yes," to the squeal of Annie in the doorway.

Neither of them wanted to wait until spring, so the entire town went into a frenzy of excitement in order to give them a wedding within a week. Even her dress had been a gift from Annie.

As if she shared his same memories, Claire's shimmering eyes caught his. Smiling, her hips swayed with each step between pale-pink ribbons and evergreens billowing off the pews. "Only you," she mouthed, and Danny's smile grew.

He wiped his eyes. "Only ever you," he mouthed back and didn't exhale until her hand slid into his.

Vows and rings were exchanged before the officiant spoke the final words, "I now pronounce you husband and wife." The chapel erupted with whistles and hollers as Danny dipped his bride backward in a deep kiss.

Swinging her back up, his mouth red from her lips, he grinned and faced the guests. "Everyone is invited to Flygande for the reception." He side-glanced Claire, and her cheeks burst with color. "My wife and I will be joining you later."

A shrill catcall vibrated the windows, and a sound very much like an old Scottish battle cry came from the back of the room as Danny swept Claire up into his arms.

"Em?" Claire's only bridesmaid rushed over with a large fur-lined blanket, laying it over Claire with a kiss to the cheek.

Danny carried her through showers of rice to a sleigh decorated in boughs and ribbon. As the cheers grew distant, Danny slid her closer and nuzzled her cheek. "You ready, Mrs. Larsson?"

"I'm so ready, Mr. Larsson."

He laughed and slapped the reins, bringing Gus into a trot down to what the town voted to rename Larsson's Lane. The sleigh cut through the snow toward Claire's cottage—their new home.

In each window, electric candles glowed. The red roof and door stood out in bright cheerfulness as they slowed to a stop in front of it. Claire released a satisfied sigh. "Look at her."

"I am looking at her."

"Not me." She laughed as Danny's hands slid under her legs, lifting her into his arms. An inviting glow of firelight spilled out from inside when he carried her across the threshold.

"You know, the ligaments in my ankle are almost fully healed now."

"And your point is?"

She giggled and kissed his cheek, pointing her foot toward the bedroom. "You should put me down in there."

"Oh, I'll put you down." She laughed louder and planted small pecks all over his face until he stumbled from laughter. When he laid her on top of the warm quilt, she popped back up, standing. "Get back on that bed."

She grinned and placed her palm against his chest, pushing him to sit. "Promise me you'll stay here and not move until I call you."

"Woman, I just married you. I'm not letting you out of my sight."

"But you may enjoy the sight if you do."

Shit. He cleared his throat and loosened his tie, making her smile again. She planted a kiss far too light for his taste and wiggled her fingers as she limped out and closed the door.

He groaned and plopped back. A loud clang came from the kitchen. "Everything alright out there?"

"Everything's fine," she sang out.

He chuckled and took in the space that would be their bedroom. The remodeling was beautiful. Claire had spared no expense on the details. Finding and refurbishing items from Gene's antique section of the general store, she'd matched the cottage style. Danny's family crest hung on the wall next to the Swedish landscape painting she'd admired at Ylva's Café, which Ylva insisted she have.

Next to their bed sat a picture from their engagement party. He stood behind a smiling, teary-eyed Claire, arms wrapped around her waist, kissing her cheek. He picked up the frame and ran a finger over her image. He still got shaky sometimes when he thought of how close he came to losing her. Even this morning, he'd woken in a sweat, haunted by the image of the pool of blood and her body half frozen in the snow.

He took a deep breath, easing the tension out of his muscles, and untied his shoes. When he removed his jacket, the sound of the Beatles' "The Long and Winding Road" echoed through the house. He slowly smiled.

"Mr. Larsson," she called. "I'm ready whenever you are."

He sprang up, suddenly out of breath, shook out his arms, and stretched his neck. "Coming, Mrs. Larsson."

He followed the music, shaking the last bit of jitters out of his hands as he came around the corner to the living room.

Lit candles cast a soft glow in every corner, and the fireplace flames cracked and popped—but he saw and heard none of it.

His wife stood in front of the fireplace in a sheer, cream-colored robe over a lace corset with a garter belt and leggings attached. Her hair, which had been pinned up for the wedding, now cascaded over her shoulders in waves, and she held a tray propped in her left hand.

If you asked him, he never saw the tray either.

"My God, woman."

"I wanted heels for this, but my stupid ankle."

He smirked. "They wouldn't be staying on long anyway."

She fought back a smile and motioned to a wood-framed, vintage chaise lounge. "Please, have a seat."

He took a slow step forward instead, eyes scorching down over curves and smooth skin. "What if I don't want to sit?"

"Trust me, you do."

He raised an eyebrow, and she pointed to the couch again. Without taking his eyes off her, he sidestepped and lowered down.

With a slight limp, one foot in front of the other, her hips swung wide, and he leaned back, letting out a slow breath. He had to admit she was right. This was a hell of a view.

She held his gaze as she bent forward, setting the tray on the coffee table and let the front of her robe gape. Staying in that position, she watched him watching her as she picked up a ceramic cup and placed it in his hand. He didn't even question what she gave him.

"Sip," she said, stepping around the table.

As he brought the edge of the cup to his mouth, she dropped her robe. Sweetness touched his lips as sweetness stepped in front of him and slowly turned, bending to pick up her own cup. On a slow exhale, his hand reached out, cupping the full curve of her backside. Skin gave way to lace under his palm as he moved, voice dropping low. "Come here."

She slid onto his lap, straddling his legs, and caught his hand before he set down his mug. "Not yet."

"Are you kidding me?"

Every soft part of her touched every hard part of him as she leaned forward, whispering in his ear, "Trust me."

At this point, it wasn't about trust but self-control.

Sitting up, she lifted his free hand to her throat while she drank and let the feel of her swallowing flow under his palm before guiding it down to the top curve of her breast. If there was ever a time he wanted both hands involved in something, it was now.

She set down her cup.

"Wait, you can put yours down, but I can't?"

"Uh-huh." She smiled.

All arguments he prepared to give vanished when she pushed him back into the couch and began unbuttoning his shirt. Her half-lidded eyes stayed on his as she stroked up the ridges of his abs, over his heaving chest and slipped the shirt over his shoulders. Anticipation thrummed in his ears as she eased toward him, eyes dropping to his mouth. Every thought wiped from his mind the moment her lips touched his in a slow, sensuous kiss.

Nope. He still wasn't allowed to put down his mug. Even

when she split his lips with her tongue and slid inside.

"What are you thinking about right now?"

"Are you serious?" He nipped her bottom lip. "I'm thinking about how much I want to throw this mug and strip you."

She smiled again. "Haven't you figured it out yet?"

"I'm afraid my brain isn't what's working right now."

"Take another sip and tell me what comes to your mind."

As hard as it was, he enjoyed this little game. Especially when soft lips descended his throat to his chest. He groaned and closed his eyes, drinking like she asked. Warm, sweet liquid trickled down his throat, and when he opened his eyes to make note of it, he swallowed the words at the sight of her kissing him.

How did he get here? This beautiful woman, his wife, savoring him like this. He curled his fingers into her hair, bringing her face up close to his. "I love you, Madelynn Claire Larsson."

"I love *you*, Daniel—" She sucked in a sharp breath.

"Mikael."

"How am I just learning this now?"

He grinned. "We've been a little busy."

Mortification shrouded her features, and he quickly kissed her. "Nope. Stop it."

He kissed her again, slower this time, his free hand sliding up her thigh. She melted into his kiss, and his hand curved around her bottom and squeezed.

"Claire?" he whispered. His touch traveled up her back and hooked the top of her corset with a tug. "I need to see you."

Biting the edge of her lip, her fingers drifted to his belt, his zipper. "I'm afraid there's nothing I can do about that." She held up her frostbitten hand, the skin still sensitive. "Emelie had to help me into this thing."

"I see." He kissed each healed finger, then her palm. "So, it's all up to me, is it?"

"Afraid so."

He peered up at her through thick blond lashes, holding the mug, begging.

"Sorry, no."

"You're killing me." He slipped a hand between her thighs, and her smile disappeared.

"Daniel." She braced against his shoulders.

It wasn't enough. He wanted to feel all of her—needed to feel all of her. "I'm going to break this damn mug."

"Not yet." Her eyes slammed closed, like his touch was too much for her to stay controlled. "I want you to forget."

"I could never forget this—" It hit him then. The taste lingering on his tongue was so familiar he'd missed it. "Tea." He breathed out into a full smile and looked down into his mug. "You made our tea?"

"Yes, my love." She opened her eyes, baring the depths of herself to him. "You told me every time you see our tea, you think about how I almost died. I wanted to change that. To give you a different memory to attach to it." Her fingers ran through his hair and gently removed the band in it, freeing his wild strands. "I don't want you to live with what-ifs, Daniel. I want you to live with what is, right now."

Holding her gaze, he drank every last drop before letting the cup tumble and roll away. He gripped her hips, pulling her against him, and took her mouth. The taste of tea mixed with the taste of her was a heady combination, and both hands worked on their own, sliding up her thighs to unhook her leggings. Rough palms moved against soft skin as he slid them off and then returned to her hips, curling around with a squeeze.

"You're incredible, you know that?" He lifted her, stealing her breath, and steadied her on her feet. "Turn around."

She did so, slowly, and his head tilted to the side as he drank her in before his fingers went to work. Each hook of the corset gave way beneath his fingers, his lips trailing down the opening at her back, and her eyes closed again.

"I love you," he whispered as her top fell to the floor. The warmth of his hands slipped along the coolness of her skin and cupped her before sliding down below her stomach, catching on the last barrier between them — a bit of thin white lace — and lowered it. He paused, soaking in the view before he squeezed her hips, slowly turning her to face him.

All the air emptied from his lungs.

"My God, you're so beautiful." Taking his time, he let his eyes roam and savor every dip and soft curve before he brought his mouth to her, following the same discovery trail.

Tears slid down her face as she held onto him. "This is real," she whispered, like she had to remind herself out loud.

"Look at me," he said, wiping her damp cheeks. "Keep your eyes on me." He guided her back down and onto himself.

With her small gasp and his deep groan, they connected beyond body to the soul.

"This is very, very real," he said. "And I'm gonna make sure you never doubt that again." Keeping them joined, he twisted to lay her back against the lounge, hovering above her.

And he began to move — showing her exactly that.

THE SLEIGH SIFTED THROUGH the snow as Claire snuggled into the warmth of Danny's side. The world was brighter somehow. Details of the glistening snow against the green of spruces, sharper, more crisp.

Her eyes slid up to her husband's profile. *Husband.* She smiled. He was really and truly hers.

A smile spread across his face. "Do you need a *third* reality check?"

She laughed, nuzzling deeper into his side. Relishing the memory, the lingering feel of his hands, his mouth, over every inch of her skin.

Her head popped up as they glided past Flygande Norseman. "Isn't the reception that way?"

He only smiled and pulled out a handkerchief. "Put this over your eyes — don't argue with me, woman."

She laughed again and did as he said. Warm lips touched hers and she hummed. "Is that the surprise?"

"No, that's just because."

The sound of murmuring voices surrounded them as the sleigh slowed to a stop. "Where are we?"

His arms answered her, lifting her down to stand. "Open your eyes," he said near her ear, untying the hankie.

"Surprise!" The entire town stood before her with wide smiles and glasses of champagne.

She covered her mouth with both hands. "What is this?"

The crowd split to reveal Ian and Fin gripping ropes on either side of an attached tarp hovering over the doorway of a gray stone building. Together they yanked, and the tarp fluttered down, revealing a wooden sign that said, MADDY'S CORNER BOOKSHOP.

"I don't understand." Her vibrating fingers clutched the three crowns necklace Danny had given her.

"It's yours, sweetheart." Danny slipped a key into her hand.

"Mine?" She scanned around her. Familiar faces smiled back while nodding.

"Consider it our way of guaranteeing all your future novels will be written here, with me as your beta reader." Ian grinned.

Emelie shoved him. "*Us* as your beta readers."

A throat cleared. "I-I'd like to read them too."

"You, Finney?" Emelie asked.

He leaned in close, and Claire bit back a smile when he whispered, "There's a lot about me worth getting know, *Emmy*."

"What do you think?" Danny squeezed her hand.

"But how?" Claire asked. "Don't I have to be voted in to own a business here?"

"It was unanimous." Ian handed her a rolled-up paper and kissed her cheek. "Never in the history of Solsken has any resident been unanimously voted in by the entire town. Even George here, and he never votes yes."

She turned to the elderly man, who held his hat in his hand. His cheeks tinted, and he lightly bowed his head.

"I don't . . . how can . . . "

"Open it, love." Danny pointed to the door and steadied her by the elbow. With shivering fingers, she unlocked the door, and Danny flipped the switch. "There's even room in the back if you want to expand beyond children's books."

Soft lights blinked on, revealing colorful shelves filled with books. At the head of each shelf was a different blown-up sketch of Maddy with one of her encouraging quotes.

Claire's eyes swam as she scanned over walls, painted so children could draw on them. Multicolored, padded carpet covered the floors where bright bean bags and little stools sat around tables filled with art supplies.

Her fingers slipped over her mouth. "What did you do?"

"Rejected or not, I wanted Maddy and children like her to have a place." Danny held up a wrapped gift to her.

Tears leaked over the brim as she slowly unraveled the paper to see a leather-bound copy of the first story she'd let him read. The outside cover simply said, MADDY.

"I know you wanted to edit it more, but I liked this one the way it was."

"Daniel." She hugged the book against her chest. "I don't know what to say."

"Say you'll get a different agent, or publish her on your own. Say you'll let your inner child run free, Claire."

She released a small cry and threw her arms around him. She only had a moment to relish his warmth before friends and loved ones surrounded her, wanting to hug and congratulate.

George received an extra kiss from her, and she smiled when he touched his cheek, open-mouthed.

She felt the constant warmth of Danny's attention as she mingled. And every time she glanced his way, his eyes were on her. A smile on his face.

It wasn't until she felt the heat of his hand sliding around her waist, and his voice in her ear saying, "why don't you sit for a minute," did she realize the ache in her still healing ankle.

Danny led her to a seat in the set beneath a picture of Maddy splashing in a mud puddle and propped her foot on his knee, rubbing out the small swell in it.

"Are you happy, Mrs. Larsson?"

Her wide smile and glistening eyes met his. "I am, Mr. Larsson. Are you?"

"I have everything I've ever wanted."

"Everything?" She glanced up to where his eyes settled on Mud-Puddle Maddy. "What about children?"

He lowered his gaze, swallowing. "With everything going on with your recovery, we never really talked about it. Either way, I'd still have married you."

She reached for him, pulling him to sit next to her. "I've always wanted a big family."

Glassy pools formed over his eyes. "Do you mean that?"

"Yes." She touched her forehead to his. "I want nothing more than to have as many little Vikings and writers as we can handle on this beautiful island of yours."

"Ours. This beautiful island of ours." Salt mixed with sweet as their lips touched, and the book he gave her fell from her lap with a thump.

They broke apart and looked down to see the little girl who'd had nothing for so long, smiling up at the man and woman who gained more than they'd ever dreamed.

Acknowledgements

TO MY POPS. I wish I'd gotten to tell you how much your random phone calls of encouragement meant to me while I navigated this unpredictable and difficult writing/publishing journey. You weren't able to stay long enough to see your prayers for this book to be published come to pass, but I think it wouldn't surprise you that I decided to take matters into my own hands. You raised an independent daughter, after all, and I hope I've made you proud. My heart will never be whole again without you, I miss you so much!

To my husband and constant. You transitioned into my new writing habits with the ease of a saint and kept me going despite all the fears and doubts and closed doors. Thank you for being my sounding board, and the one to ask the hard questions. For telling me I could when I absolutely could not. Thank you doesn't seem enough, but I am so deeply grateful for your faith in me and for not letting me quit. You have the whole of my heart, always. I love you!

To my four boys, my biggest fans. Thank you for your never-ending, enthusiastic love and encouragement. Being your mom, is my favorite thing. I love you!

To my "Fan" club, Rachel and Hannah. Your exuberant and ardent love of this story, especially in its earlier stages, pushed me to not give up on it even when it seemed I would fail. I kept on because I wanted to make this story worthy of all the praise and love you gave it. I hope I succeeded. Thank you for trusting me even when I deleted some of your favorite lines, knowing I'd make you fall in love with new ones. Thank you for always being willing, even when I asked last minute, to help me. You're both what every writer wants and needs. I'm truly blessed to call you my friends!

To my editor and dear friend, Elle. If it wasn't for your initial feedback, this story would've been all wrong. You were the first person to say it didn't work, and though I initially balked at the idea, you were right. So, so right. Thank you for always being honest with me and for loving my story, seeing my vision for it, and helping me get it where it needed to be. You're amazing, and I will sing your praises to everyone I meet!

To all my beta readers, my CP, and local writing group, Writer's Block. Thank you for giving me all the support, encouragement, and perfectly timed input and feedback. This story is what it is because of you!

To Editions. Dawn, I'll never forget the first time I saw your sign lighting the road, having no idea it would become a second home to me. Thank you for opening up a place for writers like me to come and build our dreams. You're vital to the book community both locally and beyond. Thank you for all that you do! And a big thank you to your dedicated staff for the innumerable Americanos they've provided, keeping me both sane and focused. Jenn, thank you for your brilliant idea to start a writer's group where I've met some of my forever friends. You're a beautiful soul! And to Scott, you will always be my favorite antagonist.

To Jordon, you were my first writing friend and the first to show me I could do this writing/publishing thing. Thank you for your gentle encouragement from the beginning and for patiently walking me through all the scary parts of publishing. You are an incredible person and cherished friend.

To my online writing community. Thank you for coming along with me on this chaotic and beautiful mess of a writing journey! I hope this book has been worth the wait. And although I cannot name you all, there are a couple of you that I must: Mary, you have been a constant support and encouragement to me, and I love how we've grown together as both writers and friends. Thank you! Dianna, my sweet Canadian friend, you've been with me from the beginning and were one of my first beta readers. I hope this latest version touches your heart as much as the first one did. Thank you both for always checking in on me and lifting me up when I needed it the most.

And to you, my dear readers, for taking a chance on me and my work. I hope it gives you the escape you desire and fills your story-loving heart with all the feels you want and need to feel. Thank you!

About
B. K. Clark

Growing up in rural Pennsylvania, B.K. Clark spent most of her time outdoors spinning grand stories of people and faraway places. It would take years before she'd think to put those stories to paper — and then a writer was born.

From contemporary romance and suspense, to fantasy and science fiction, and more, B.K. doesn't limit what world her stories are born in. Only hopes that they pull you in and make you fall in love.

She now resides in North Carolina with her husband and four children and can almost always be found with a cup of black, absolutely no sugar, coffee in her hands.

Visit B. K. Clark online at
www.bkclarkauthor.com

www.ingramcontent.com/pod-product-compliance
Lightning Source LLC
Chambersburg PA
CBHW031840310726
48972CB00005B/1351